Gothic Lovecraft

Edited by

Lynne Jamneck & S. T. Joshi

Also from
Cycatrix Press

ANTHOLOGIES
The Bleeding Edge:
Dark Barriers, Dark Frontiers

The Devil's Coattails:
More Dispatches from the Dark Frontier

A Darke Phantastique:
Encounters with the Uncanny
and Other Magical Things

COLLECTIONS
The Mirrors

All That Withers

NON-FICTION
William F. Nolan:
A Miscellany

PERIODICALS
[Namel3ss] Digest

POETRY
Totems and Taboos

Souls Trips

Gothic
Lovecraft

Edited by
Lynne Jamneck & S. T. Joshi

Gothic Lovecraft

Anthology © 2016 by Cycatrix Press

Editors: *Jamneck, Lynne & Joshi, S. T.*

---

300 Trade Hardcovers (MSRP $54.95)
ISBN: 978-0-9841676-6-1

FALL, 2016 (TRADE)

---

52 Deluxe Hardcovers, Signed and Lettered (MSRP $74.95)
ISBN: 978-0-9841676-7-8

WINTER, 2016 (DELUXE)

First Edition, First Printing

Book Design/Layout by JaSunni Productions, LLC
Printed by B&B Print Source using wind power and vegetable-based inks. Bound in the United States of America.
No animals were harmed in the making of these books. Go veg!

Published by
Cycatrix Press

http://www.JaSunni.com

Email/Contact: *JaSunni@jasunni.com*

JaSunni Productions, LLC
16420 SE McGillivray Blvd.
Ste 103-1010
Vancouver, WA 98683
USA

Introduction © 2016 by **Lynne Jamneck & S. T. Joshi**

Cover Art and Standalone B&W Illustrations
(including the signature page in the Deluxe Edition)
© 2016 by **Jason V Brock**

Contributor Photos © 2016 by the respective contributors unless
otherwise noted (Joshi image by Emily Marija Kurmis);
Used by kind permission.

Book Design © 2016 by **JaSunni Productions, LLC**

*****

The works contained herein are all unpublished
and/or original to this anthology unless noted otherwise:

"The Shadow over Lear" © 2016 by **Donald R. Burleson**
"The Revelation at the Abbey" © 2016 by **Don Webb**
"Old Goodman Brown" © 2016 by **Jonathan Thomas**
"Square of the Inquisition" © 2016 by **Lois H. Gresh**
"The Rime of the Cosmic Mariner" © 2016 by **John Shirley**
"A Yuletide Carol" © 2016 by **Mollie L. Burleson**
"Curse of the House of Usher" © 2016 by **Donald Tyson**
"The Rolling of Old Thunder" © 2016 by **Mark Howard Jones**
"Always a Castle?" © 2016 by **Nancy Kilpatrick**
"As Red as Red" © 2010 by **Caitlín R. Kiernan**;
First published in *Haunted Legends*,
edited by Ellen Datlow and Nick Mamatas (Tor, 2010)
"Four Arches" © 2016 by **Robert S. Wilson**
"The Old Schoolhouse" © 2016 by **Gwyneth Jones**
"Dream House" © 2016 by **Orrin Grey**
"The Unknown Chambers" © 2016 by **Lynda E. Rucker**

All rights reserved. This is a work of fiction (unless noted otherwise);
any and all similarities to the contrary are purely coincidental.
Not to be reproduced in any format—electronic, print, or
photographic—without express written consent from the Publisher,
except for brief
excerpts (shorter than two paragraphs) used in reviews.

Table of Contents

Introduction
Lynne Jamneck & S. T. Joshi
09

The Shadow over Lear
Donald R. Burleson
15

The Revelation at the Abbey
Don Webb
31

Old Goodman Brown
Jonathan Thomas
46

Square of the Inquisition
Lois H. Gresh
65

The Rime of the Cosmic Mariner
John Shirley
77

A Yuletide Carol
Mollie L. Burleson
94

Curse of the House of Usher
Donald Tyson
102

The Rolling of Old Thunder
Mark Howard Jones
135

Always a Castle?
Nancy Kilpatrick
151

As Red as Red
Caitlín R. Kiernan
164

Four Arches
Robert S. Wilson
182

The Old Schoolhouse
Gwyneth Jones
201

Dream House
Orrin Grey
223

The Unknown Chambers
Lynda E. Rucker
237

Notes on Contributors
258

Introduction

One may be forgiven for at first not conceiving H. P. Lovecraft's fiction as particularly "Gothic," at least not in the traditional, English sense of the word. Many of the genre's stock tropes do not immediately come to mind when considering stories like "The Call of Cthulhu," "The Color out of Space," "The Dunwich Horror," or "The Shadow over Innsmouth." Instead of imposing castles we are embedded within decaying fishing villages, rural farmlands, or sea voyages to mysterious islands. There's no male posturing with the sole intention of rescuing a virgin-in-waiting; not a whiff of a Byronic hero—though to be fair, the often-cited description of the Romantic poet by one of his mistresses as "mad, bad and dangerous to know" can surely be applied to more than one of Lovecraft's protagonists (ladies and gentlemen, may I present to you Herbert West).

Nonetheless, despite the enormous popularity of Lovecraft's fiction today, his work remains difficult to categorize. While he may have written in a Gothic vein—haunted spaces and places, haunted people, found things, and insanity—his subject matter differs from those writers we traditionally associate with Gothic fiction.

Lovecraft dutifully read the founding writers of the Gothic tradition—Horace Walpole (*The Castle of Otranto,* 1764), Ann Radcliffe (*The Mysteries of Udolpho,* 1794), Matthew Gregory Lewis (*The Monk,* 1764), Mary Shelley (*Frankenstein,* 1818), and Charles Robert Maturin (*Melmoth the Wanderer,* 1820)—for his pioneering historical study "Supernatural Horror in Literature" (1927), although it becomes evident that his enthusiasm for much of this writing was less than robust. And yet, for one who so was so respectful of the long heritage of weird fiction, it would have been difficult for him to have escaped the influence of Gothic fiction altogether.

And so, while we do not encounter the standard vampires, witches, or werewolves of Gothic fiction, we see Lovecraft expanding upon and in some cases radically transforming these tropes to make them his own. For

Gothic *Lovecraft*

Lovecraft, Nathaniel Hawthorne was a key link to the Gothic era, and "The Shunned House" could be considered his rewriting of *The House of the Seven Gables*—and its innovative psychic vampire is dispatched not by a cross or a stake through the heart, but by quantities of sulfuric acid. "The Dreams in the Witch House" is an ingenious adaptation of the witch motif, fused with highly advanced speculations about hyperspace drawn from the science fiction of his own day.

But it is *The Case of Charles Dexter Ward* that constitutes Lovecraft's grandest evocation of Gothic motifs. Initially broaching the standard Gothic theme (found in such works as *Melmoth the Wanderer* and William Godwin's *St. Leon*) of the quest for eternal life, the novel goes on to weave a tapestry of Gothic themes—the search for all-encompassing knowledge, psychic possession, the power of spells and incantations found in forbidden books, and much else besides.

It was, however, in the Dark Romanticism of the Victorian era that Lovecraft found his closest Gothic predecessor in Edgar Allan Poe, of whom Lovecraft was a self-proclaimed acolyte. "The Rats in the Walls," for example, is very much a Poe-esque story; it is, in effect, his "Fall of the House of Usher," updated to incorporate the horror of Darwinian regression upon the path of evolution; it is also a story that employs several obvious Gothic tropes that strongly echo Poe's "The Pit and the Pendulum" and "The Tell-Tale Heart."

Notwithstanding, where Poe centered his focus on the degeneracy of the human mind, Lovecraft opted instead for viewing madness as a condition imposed upon humanity largely as a result of our woefully inadequate knowledge about the world in which we live. This madness is generally the result of a confrontation with that which is not us—the totally, utterly alien. Lovecraft's emotional responses are projected outward, into the world at large. Instead of a dilapidated, haunted house, we are hurled into a violent universe that is obscure, nameless, hostile, and entirely indifferent to our existence.

Gothic Lovecraft gathers together fourteen stories that address Lovecraft's Gothic sensibilities and present them in ways that uncomfortably crack our often romanticized notions of the genre. In "The Shadow over Lear" by Donald R. Burleson, we are given disturbing intimations concerning the true origins the king's daughters and their mother in Shakespeare's tragedy. Don Webb's "The Revelation at the Abbey" and "The Rolling of Old Thunder" by Mark Howard Jones confront us with the dangers of knowledge contained in Old Books (and body-snatching!), and the havoc that ensues when knowledge is used haphazardly. Found manuscripts, as in the classic Gothic texts, is a theme Lovecraft often employed in his fiction and finds strong resonance in modern-day culture, perhaps most obviously in how it comments on society's interpretations of religious texts.

Caitlin R. Kiernan's "As Red as Red" is as much a vampire story as it is a werewolf story as it is a ghost story. In the true Gothic and Lovecraftian sense, the story is pointedly influenced by its setting, an ever-encompassing, sometimes oppressive background that plays a pivotal part in the delivery of ominous events.

Nancy Kilpatrick's "Always a Castle?" and "The Old Schoolhouse" by Gwyneth Jones confronts us with our true selves, the masks we wear and the terrible things we do not only to others, but also to ourselves. In "Old Goodman Brown," Jonathan Thomas takes us back to the Salem witch trials and evokes both Hawthorne and Lovecraft, a match made in heaven—or hell, depending on your point of view. John Shirley's "The Rime of the Cosmic Mariner" expands on the original, already cosmically inclined poem by employing Samuel Taylor Coleridge himself as protagonist to reveal the unknown details of the poet's original lost-at-sea epic, a story in which the dark depths the sea and stars both play a primary role.

Donald Tyson's "Curse of the House of Usher" sees Roderick Usher visited by Randolph Carter, and the madness of Poe's original story taken to new heights, while in Mollie L. Burleson's "A Yuletide Carol," Ebenezer Scrooge is whisked to Dunwich, where a spirit reveals to him his true purpose. "Square of the Inquisition" by Lois H. Gresh sees the power of words deliver the tortured and oppressed—though deliverance may not always be exactly what we anticipate it to be. Robert S. Wilson presents in "Four Arches" an unsettling modern tale infused with claustrophobia that reveals Shub-Niggurath, the Black Goat of the Woods with a Thousand Young, lying in wait in unexpected places. Orrin Grey's "Dream House" is a feverish story that follows a writer's irrational urge to discover the truth about a barely remembered TV show and the conclusion that

Gothic *Lovecraft*

sometimes, some stories are better left alone. Finally, Lynda Rucker's "The Unknown Chambers" follows a researcher's efforts to uncover the mysterious life of an obscure writer and find his strange and bizarre history leading her to a place she had been seeking all along.

Lovecraft has been characterized as not being a particularly humanistic writer; it is said that he eschews the highly wrought emotions of Gothic initiators like Horace Walpole, Ann Radcliffe, and Clara Reeve, his "Yog-Sothothery" bypassing the Romantics', well, *romance*. While this may be true to some extent, let us not forget those elements of the early Gothic romances that so often crop up in Lovecraft's stories, prominently so the ancestral curse and the found (*thing*) manuscript. Even as far back as Clara Reeve, we can find similarities in the way both Reeve and Lovecraft aimed at balancing realism and the fantastic as a means for creating more believable narratives. As for the Romantics, we have already noted some similarities between the quintessential Lovecraftian madman and that most famous of Romantic poets. Moreover, I dare anyone *not* to find resemblances between these same madmen and Mary Shelley's Victor Frankenstein.

Lovecraft's work is indeed as humanist as that of the Gothics, in some ways perhaps even more so. In a scientifically burgeoning context, Lovecraft took a human perspective and slanted it at an entirely rational and scientific angle that, perhaps uncannily, rendered his vision of the world as one riddled with terror. The threat in Lovecraft remains the unknown, but it is the unknown as presented by reality, not by superstition. Unlike the vampire and the werewolf, Lovecraft's monsters were never human. It is a Gothic perspective from the opposite side of the shadowy coin—both are part of the same thing, yet we see things differently when we consider them individually.

—Lynne Jamneck
S. T. Joshi

The Shadow over Lear

Donald R. Burleson

On the coast of Britain where the land drops off into the frothy waves and France lies like a nebulous rumor across the waters, the fog gathers from the sea the way dark thoughts gather in a troubled mind. Wild, wet fingers of mist and low-lying cloud caress the bleached stones of the cliffs of Dover as if eager to imbue the solid earth with the delirium of the ancient sea, to whisper timeless secrets known only in the court of Poseidon and not well suited to be spoken on the land.

High on a giddy prominence in this setting there once stood the castle of the Earl of Kent, and high in a sky-flung tower of that gray edifice stood Kent himself, gazing out upon the sea-fog, lost in thought. He and his servants would later this day mount up for their ride inland to be with his master Lear, King of Britain, in whose sprawling, angled castle important matters were to be settled by royal fiat.

In truth, Kent sometimes feared for the mind of the aging monarch. Four score years had in some ways not been kind to Lear. True, he retained a certain sinewy robustness remarkable for his years, but at times of late his meandering mind outran even the vagaries common to the petulance of age. This but sealed Kent's resolve, though, to be caring and attentive to his noble king. But he had presentiments about the days to come.

"Bring 'round the horses," he called to his servants in the hall. "We leave for London within the hour."

In the great hall of the royal castle, Kent stood aside watching the company that awaited Lear's entrance. Near the empty throne the three daughters stood in expectant attendance, though no flourish of trumpets had yet announced the approach of their father. Kent would have liked to think that the daughters adorned the throne as three opulent jewels might have adorned a crown, but this ambitious conceit readily applied only to the fair Cordelia, Lear's youngest, whose face any man worthy of the name of man would have given much to kiss. For Goneril, the eldest, and for Regan, the second daughter, it was otherwise. Kent could hardly put it straight in his mind what bothered him about the two women. It was something about their eyes, which seemed oddly protruded and watery-looking—Kent could swear increasingly so in recent days, though this must be some liverish morbidity goading his imagination. Yet there was something about the way they moved sometimes, too, that made his skin crawl.

The men looked normal enough—Goneril's husband, the Duke of Albany, and Regan's husband, the Duke of Cornwall—standing over there beside their somehow strange duchesses, awaiting the drama to come. Off in a corner, Cordelia's two suitors, the King of France and the Duke of Burgundy, stood studiously avoiding each other's eyes. The only other people present, besides servants, were the Earl of Gloucester and his son Edmund, who was his child by a woman not his wife. Gloucester's legitimate son Edgar was not present. There was a static sort of tension in the air, a tension that seemed heightened rather than relieved by the awaited flourish of horns and the entrance of the aged Lear, with attendants.

Kent rushed forward to greet his master. "Your majesty's health and happiness."

Lear nodded to him, seated himself on the throne, and cast his gaze about the group of faces. "My family and friends, I gather you today for a matter that has been much on my mind. I am grown old and weary of the cares of state, to the extent indeed that if I cannot divest myself of age, I wish at least to divest myself of care, though retaining the title of king."

"Every inch a king," Kent said.

"Thank you, my old friend," Lear replied, and went on. "Besides my title I will retain the right to dwell with my daughters in turn, a month at a time, and to keep a train of a hundred knights to attend me. Now, as you all know, the holdings of my kingdom are vast, and their disposition is no

The Shadow over Lear

small matter. I wish to divide that kingdom in three parts, though not necessarily three equal parts, depending on what professions of love my daughters find it in their hearts to make to me. Consider your answers well, my children, for your fortunes depend on them. What say you, Goneril?"

The eldest daughter stepped forward and bowed. Something about the dark and vacuous look of her eyes and the slippery way her body moved made Kent's stomach lurch. She walked, he thought, with something almost like the motion of a frog.

"My dearest father, my king," Goneril began, in a voice that Kent found faintly repellent, wondering if Lear and the others found it so as well, "my love for you is as boundless as the arch of heaven that overlooks your domain. I love you more than I love my own life. You have my heart, and all of it, and more besides, you have my very soul, which I gladly give. No daughter ever loved a father more."

While Kent was reflecting on how revoltingly insincere this sounded to anyone with ears to hear, the king began his sadly predictable response. "My dearest Goneril, my no less esteemed Albany, I make you lord and lady of one third of my property, from this boundary to this"—he pointed to a sketch of the kingdom—"and may it bring you joy and contentment. And how speaks Regan?"

That daughter stepped forward and bowed in turn, speaking in a voice that struck Kent as unpleasantly liquid.

"My father and royal majesty, my sister's heart bespeaks my own. I would echo her words and magnify them a hundredfold, affirming that I decline all other love or pleasure in this world if I may but give my heart to you."

Again, Kent watched the speaker with the same sense of unplaceable loathing that the older sister inspired, even when he tried not to dwell on what she had said, or on how she had sounded while saying it. But Lear only smiled and replied, "To you, my beloved Regan, and your no less valued Cornwall, I give this one-third portion of my lands, from here to here, replete with forests and sparkling rivers, no less a portion than for Goneril and Albany, and may you dwell in endless happiness. And how speaks our youngest daughter Cordelia?"

That young lady stepped forward and bowed to her

father. Kent, watching her, thought how unlike her sisters she was. It was a strange thing to find such women in the same family. Some years ago Lear's peculiar, vaguely repulsive wife, whom few people had ever seen in her later years, had died unaccountably, or so the king had said, and Kent had always suspected that this odd person, of whom virtually nothing was known to this day, had passed along to her daughters some obscure unwholesomeness that seemed to increase in repugnance as the years passed. But it had affected only Goneril and Regan; somehow, in whatever unimaginable way in which the stars and planets guide the paths of human creatures, the growing hereditary pestilence that seemingly afflicted the older daughters had left the blossom-cheeked Cordelia clean and fresh. In moments of whimsy Kent half imagined that the girl did not have the same mother as the older sisters, as if the king, his old friend, had secrets folded tight to that ancient, withered chest. But Cordelia was speaking now.

"My father and revered king, whom I dearly love, you must reflect upon the fact that my sisters profess unlimited love for you, claiming to love no other. But does not a proper wife retain at least half her love for her husband? If I had a husband, so it would be with me, as I think is only proper. If I loved you to the exclusion of all else, I would have no love left for the husband you have hoped for me to find, and whom I may find here today. I assure you I do love and cherish you, so far as a devoted daughter should. But I do not have so glib a tongue as do my sisters. I have only a desire to tell the truth, and not embellish it for gain."

Kent's heart warmed to hear such candor, but Lear bristled with an incipient anger. "Mend your words, child, if you care about your fortune."

Cordelia was unmoved. "I cannot buy my fortune with oily words. I honor and love you because I know you will understand that I love the truth as well."

At this Lear's anger grew to a smoldering fury that caused his old voice to tremble, but not to lose its resolve. "Then you are no longer a daughter to me. By all the gods, by the orbs of heaven that form our being, I disown you and have no more concern for you. Your sisters Goneril and Regan will divide between them that portion of our kingdom which might have been yours, had you a civil and caring tongue. Now let us see what suitor will still court a dowerless girl. France and Burgundy, kindly come forward."

These personages approached, and Lear addressed the Duke of Burgundy first. "What say you?"

The duke looked uncomfortable, but finally spoke up. "It is unseemly for a man of my position to accept a maiden who has no fortune to bring to a marital union."

"Reasonably spoken," Lear said, turning to the King of France. "And you, sir?"

The French king shook his head, not in any disdain of Cordelia, but rather for reasons that his words would make clear. "My old acquaintance Burgundy, I fear, has more water in his veins than blood. Cordelia's fairness, her intelligence, her undaunted spirit, her honesty, her goodness of heart, these things are all the fortune I require in a dowry. I will take her for my wife and queen."

Lear looked disgusted. "Then, sir, I bid you farewell. May the penniless Cordelia be to your liking. As for me, I never wish to see her again. My servants will bring 'round your carriage."

Kent could no longer contain his distress. He rushed to Lear's side. "Good my liege, please consider what you do. Sometimes decisions made in anger—"

Lear gave Kent a furious look and clapped his hands to summon attendants and guards. "Escort this person from my sight. Kent, you have profited nothing from your years if they have taught you so little about the honor due a king. You are henceforth banished from the realm. If you are found within its boundaries five days hence, that will be the day of your death." Motioning to his attendants, Lear made ready to leave the chamber. In a few moments he was gone.

Kent, stunned, waited by the side of the guards who were to escort him out. Cordelia and her royal husband-to-be looked on with genuine sympathy, while Goneril and Regan filed past him in turn and fixed him with expressions that were more shocking to him than his banishment had been. He could swear, seeing them close up, that there was something about those bulbous eyes that was not even human.

Disguised, Kent appeared some weeks later outside the Duke of Albany's castle just as Lear and his knights came thundering back following a hunt. After Lear's attendants helped him to dismount before the entrance, Kent made bold to step up and speak to him, being careful to alter his voice as best he could.

"Noble liege, I wish to place myself in your service."

The king looked him up and down. "What is your name?"

"Caius, your majesty," Kent replied.

"And what can you do?" Lear demanded.

"Whatever your majesty requires," Kent said. "I offer faithful allegiance, an uncommon offering these days, if I may venture to say so."

At this point a servant from within the castle appeared, addressing Lear. "My lady wishes to inform you that she and her lord will not be joining you for dinner. My lady also expresses displeasure at the crude and boisterous and riotous behavior of your knights."

Kent stepped up and smashed the servant in the face with such ferocity that the man went down on the ground groaning. "That's to remind you to whom you are speaking, swine. You are in the presence of a king." The servant picked himself up and scurried back into the castle. Lear and his train made ready to follow him inside, but not before Lear turned to the disguised Kent and said, "You may remain with us, Caius. I am pleased to have you in my service."

Inside, it was not long before the abhorrent Goneril appeared and confronted her father. Kent stood only a few feet away, and at this proximity he had a chance to scrutinize her in more detail than he ever had before. What he saw, though it was vague and uncertain, filled him with a crawling sort of revulsion. It was as if her condition, whatever it was, had worsened in just these few weeks since he had seen her last. The unblinking eyes were not just protuberant and watery; they seemed to gaze along lines of sight that diverged outward, and it took Kent a moment to realize that this was because the very shape of the woman's head appeared subtly to have altered, narrowing so that the eyes peered each in its own direction, almost like those of a fish. There was something unwholesome, too, about the texture of

The Shadow over Lear

her skin, which in this light appeared almost scaly. But she was remonstrating with her father.

"Your servant struck mine down, just now, and your knights are loud and bothersome. I will not tolerate this." Her voice sounded, to Kent at least, almost like the gurgling tones of a person speaking under water.

Lear drew himself up. "You forget whom you address. I am your father, the King of Britain. How does the Duke of Albany feel about the presence of my retinue?"

"My husband's views are not of relevance to this discussion," Goneril replied. "And what need do you have of a hundred knights? Fifty would suffice. Dismiss half your train if you wish to pass another night within these walls."

Lear was furious. "How sharper than a serpent's tooth it is, to have a thankless child. We depart at once. Your sister Regan will be more hospitable, I have no doubt."

In a remote inner chamber of the Duke of Cornwall's castle, Regan was in quiet conclave with her sister, Goneril having arrived ahead of Lear's party and having already conferred with Regan about their father's behavior.

"He has only himself to blame," Goneril croaked, wagging her oddly angular head. "I think he charges our dear mother with the gradual unsettling of his mind, though he has never come right out and said so much. Watching her—change—watching her *develop* into her true self was, in the end, too much for his pathetic little earthbound brain. Poor benighted souls, these ground-dwelling mortals with their narrow view of the world and their limited perceptions! Would that he could only have beheld our mother in terms of the glory that she was, a creature to be revered, a credit to her own ancestors. But Father was not capable of understanding that."

"No," Regan said in that thickly fluid voice, "but we understand, you and I, sister. We know what wonders await us one day when we shall see that realm where Mother always belonged, and where she now dwells. I know that she lives in beautiful bliss now, in the place of her deepest dreams. Do you remember the stories she told us when we were children? Stories replete with marvels?"

Goneril rested her face upon her hands, noting idly as she did so that her fingers were beginning to web. "I will never forget them. I blush to recall, now, that at the time I thought they were mere tales with which to amuse children. But now we know, do we not? We know that she was telling us of a genuine world of wonderment and joy."

"It's thrilling to remember," Regan mused, "those stories of great R'lyeh and the Deep Ones, the real stories that the myths of men only so faintly and distantly reflect. How I wish—"

But from without, a faint din of horses' hooves and a chorus of shouting men came through, and the sisters exchanged a knowing look. "It's Father and his wretched train of knights," Regan said. "I'll go to meet them. But scarcely to greet them."

It had been a long ride, and Kent had stayed close by Lear's side the whole time. Upon their arrival at the castle, Regan met them at the entrance, frowning mightily. Had Goneril sent a swift-riding messenger before them? Seeing Regan, Kent was struck with this woman's altered appearance. Like her disgusting sister, she had unblinking eyes that seemed to stare emotionlessly out of a head in which the very bone structure had narrowed, making the eyes appallingly fishlike. Her ears seemed to have atrophied, being now barely visible. There was something odd about the woman's throat as well, though Kent could not quite tell what it was. Darkly fascinated by her strangely aquatic ugliness, he almost failed to notice the unkind words she was addressing to her father.

"Your wearisome company will not be welcome in my home," she said, again in that watery voice that sounded disturbingly like her sister's.

"I suppose," Lear said, wincing at the cruelty of her words, "that like Goneril you would wish me to reduce my train to fifty knights.

Regan abruptly raised her head in a way that almost made Kent gasp aloud, so strongly did it resemble the motion of some gilled creature of the deep, a nameless oceanic lurker disturbed by some sudden distraction. "What need of fifty?" she asked. "Twenty-five would be more than enough."

Lear snorted. "I could go back to Goneril and keep fifty."

"Then go," Regan snapped.

But then Goneril herself stepped out into the waning light. It seems that she had not just sent a messenger, but had made the journey herself. She fixed her father with that disconcertingly unblinking, unfeeling stare that Kent had come to know all too well. "What need of any knights at all? We have our own attendants here. Dismiss your entourage and we will give you dinner. And your man Caius there, yes, that fellow, shall go into the stocks for being a ruffian."

Guards advanced from within the castle and seized Kent. Lear's knights started to react, but Kent shouted to them, "No, let it be! I will gladly sit in the stocks for the good name of my king, whom these unnatural hags would slander and abuse!"

The stocks were a considerable distance from the entrance to the castle, so that by the time a servant came out some hours later to release Kent, that noble follower of the king had no idea what had become of Lear. By now the night was dark, and a ferocious storm had gathered, rending the scowling sky with thunder and lightning. A dismal gray rain began to fall. "What of my master the king?" Kent asked the servant.

"He has left the castle, going out into the night, swearing that he would perish sooner than remain with ungrateful and unloving daughters. His entourage of knights is scattered to the winds, and by now he wanders on the heath alone."

Alarmed beyond words at this news, Kent set out upon the storm-wracked heath, soon coming upon the poor monarch, who stood waving his arms in the downpour, his head wreathed about with wild nettles in place of the crown he should have worn.

"Blow, mighty tempest! Rage, you ancient gods, and

smite me with your lightning if you dare! Your fury is nothing beside the tumult of my soul."

"Your majesty," Kent shouted to him over the howling storm, "do you not know me? I am your servant Caius, and you cannot remain in this place on such a wild night. Come along with me." Having noticed a wretched hovel standing nearby upon the heath, Kent took the muttering Lear by the arm and led him there.

Inside, they made themselves as comfortable as possible on the straw-covered dirt floor, with the rain sizzling against the thatched roof and the thunder reverberating like a volley of cannons without.

"The ingratitude of one's children is hard enough to bear," the king began, gazing at the disguised Kent in wide-eyed earnestness, "and if I could be a god and hurl those lightning bolts into their cold hearts, I would gladly do so. I know that I have invited my own troubles, but I have suffered at my daughters' hands out of all proportion. I am a man more sinned against than sinning. But dear Caius, this is not what chiefly unbalances my wits. This is not what torments me."

"What, then?" Kent asked.

Lear's eyes seemed to settle in their expression, as if the seriousness of what he was contemplating was the one thing powerful enough and important enough to solidify his wandering reason against what assailed it. "It is—it is what they are becoming."

"My lord?"

"Goneril and Regan," Lear said. "Have you not noticed it? You must have. Every day it seems worse."

"I have noticed an odd look about their faces, their eyes," Kent admitted. "I thought it was some illness—"

"Would that it were only that," Lear said, moaning. "No, it is the curse left to them by their mother, my departed queen."

"I don't understand," Kent said. But he was beginning to fear that perhaps he did.

"It was the same with her, my wife," Lear continued. "This is why I kept her out of sight. Her eyes grew large and waterish, her head became narrow, her voice took on the quality of some nightmare from the ocean floor. The condition came upon her slowly at first, but at some point began to overtake her apace."

So that was it, Kent thought. It was their mother, the shadowy figure who had spawned the daughters. *Who or what had she been?*

"You have no idea," Lear went on, "what it was like, watching her grow more monstrous with each passing day, seeing that loathsome face looking at me with no more emotion than an eel, hearing that croaking voice that one would not want to hear twice in a lifetime, that voice I had to hear day and night, until—"

Kent leaned forward. "Until—?"

"Until one night she finally took to the water," Lear said, covering his face with wrinkled, trembling hands.

"What do you mean, took to the water?"

Lear shuddered. "When it was time, when she spent every minute gasping for breath and could no longer live on the land, my attendants and I took her in a closed carriage to Dover and released her into the sea, whence her own forebears had come. You see, at remote, nameless places on the coast of Britain, certain—rites—had once been performed, certain obeisances to the gods of the deep, who dispensed favors in return for the privilege of mating with human women, as happened with my wife's mother. I did not know, when I married her, took her as my queen, took her to my bed, that she was the product of such a union, that she was only half human. And in such cases, it seems the non-human half always wins out in the end."

Kent was shocked into silence, but at length roused himself to ask, "But what about Cordelia? She—"

Lear groaned and held his head. "When my queen had degenerated to the point where I could no longer bear her presence, I—was with another woman, in secret. Out of wedlock. Cordelia's mother. My sweet Cordelia, whom I have so tragically wronged. As I have wronged others dear to me. The Earl of Kent—"

Able to maintain the pretense no longer, Kent removed his disguise. "Caius, your royal majesty, is none other than Kent."

Lear's eyes swam with tears. "The gods of old be praised! How can you ever forgive the dotage of an old tyrant?"

D. Burleson

But before Kent could answer, the ramshackle door opened, admitting a wind-driven blast of rain and a ragamuffin figure like a scarecrow. "You will, I trust, let me in. Poor Tom is cold."

Lear patted an empty spot on the earthen floor. "My enemy's dog, though it had bitten me, would sleep by my fire on such a night as this. But who are you?"

The newcomer glanced about the dim space of the little room, where flashes of lightning showing through the spaces provided the only illumination, looked about as if to ascertain that only Lear and Kent were there, and then replied, "I am Edgar, rightful son of the Earl of Gloucester. This beggar's garb is my disguise, to spare my life. I salute your majesty."

"What are you doing out in this dreadful storm?" Kent asked.

"My bastard half-brother Edmund plots against me and turns me out into the world as a fugitive, because he aspires to the earldom himself. By now, I suspect, he will have had our father slain for sending word to the court of the King of France that the houses of Albany and Cornwall have so wretchedly deported themselves toward the king. Edmund betrayed our father to the treacherous Cornwall some days ago, and I have been powerless to stop his vengeance, being an object of it also. But Cornwall himself, you know, is on the verge of death—"

Lear gasped. "We were just with my daughter Regan, and she said nothing of this."

"I dare say, my liege, because Regan hopes to wed Edmund when he succeeds to the earldom, and Goneril has similar ambitions. Her husband Albany is beginning to distance himself from her anyway, not only because of her unpleasant aspect, but because of the way she has treated your majesty. Albany is still your ally, the fault of that house being entirely with Goneril."

"Faithless wenches," Lear muttered, "as if any man might keep the contents of his stomach at the sight of them, or the thought of them. The dukes knew not what they married. But you said word had been sent to France, of how things stand?"

"Rumors are abroad," Edgar said, "that France's forces land upon the shore at Dover. Cordelia travels with them."

Kent stood up and pointed to the door. "The storm will soon abate, by all indications. I suggest we leave for Dover at once."

At the Cornwall castle, Goneril was mightily berating her sister. "You know that forces friendly to our worthless father have landed at Dover, and you know perfectly well that we need your husband to marshal our own forces in the face of this threat, and yet you are still giving those deadly potions to Cornwall. It astonishes me that under your wifely ministrations he has lived this long." By the end of so protracted a speech, Goneril's voice was beginning to deteriorate, causing her to pause to regain control of it.

Regan shrugged, a slippery gesture that would have revolted anyone but her equally unsavory sister. "You know that I aspire to wed Edmund. Would you want me to have two husbands?"

Goneril waited to get her breath, an increasingly difficult task these days, with those slits on her throat trying to open up. "Oh, I know that you want the new Earl of Gloucester. But as your older sister I reserve that right for myself."

Regan shook her head, a motion that was beginning to have a decidedly ichthyic look. "What about your husband?"

Goneril gave out with something that from a normal throat might have been a scornful laugh. "Albany is leaving me. Like our father in his relations with our mother, he finds it impossible to reconcile his feeling with what I am becoming. Besides, his loyalty to Father makes me sick."

"And what makes you suppose," Regan retorted, "that Edmund will want you instead of me?"

"Well," Goneril said, "we shall see. I have sent for him, and we will let him choose for himself. He should be here presently."

When Edmund arrived and was shown in, Goneril did not delay in addressing him. "Edmund, Earl of Gloucester. How very good to see you. I have important matters to discuss with you."

"You mean we have," Regan said.

Edmund nodded to Goneril, looking decidedly uncomfortable. "Duchess." He nodded to Regan as well. "Duchess." He unconsciously made a face, and it would be difficult to know whether the sisters realized that his expression was due to the fishy smell of them, an intolerable reek that he had noticed even before entering the room.

"Edmund," Goneril said in her gurgling voice, her watery eyes bulging, "I wish you to be my suitor. My sister Regan, I will mention, is foolish enough to have similar aspirations. Kindly explain to her that your choice for a wife would be myself."

Edmund nervously shifted his weight from one foot to the other. He cleared his throat. "I—I think the gravity of this decision would—would be ill served by haste or by facile reaction. I owe it to you, both of you, to ponder the question in solitude." Bowing to them, he withdrew. When he was out the door, the sisters could hear, from the hall beyond, the sound of a man being violently sick to his stomach.

"We have more important things with which to concern ourselves," Regan said. "France's forces threaten to assist our father, and I will consult Cornwall, though it be on his deathbed, as to how we must proceed against the enemy. I gather we can no longer rely upon Albany."

"We have no need of him," Goneril said, the slits in her throat quivering, becoming more clearly defined. "These matters are all up to us now. But beyond our domination of this melancholy land, we have a greater mission. Think of it, Regan—as soon as we are ready to take to the water, we will bring up more like ourselves, many more, and we shall dance around altar fires and invoke the Words of old, which no human tongue can speak, and sacrifices shall be made, and the Deep Ones shall prevail, and dwell in wonder and glory forever."

"Yes," Regan intoned huskily, clearly enchanted with this vision, her protuberant eyes rolling with emotion." This has been the promise of my dreams, the longing in my soul. And it will come to pass. Meanwhile we will make certain that our father and his followers do not obstruct us. This is war; but we shall make it brief."

The Shadow over Lear

Kent, back at his own castle, where the forces from across the water were billeted, was moved to tears at the sight of Lear's reunion with his faithful daughter Cordelia, now a most attractive queen. Regan's words about the brevity of the impending war were prophetic. What Cordelia's husband, the King of France, had anticipated as a mighty struggle, to unsettle the powers opposing Lear and to return him to his rightful place, was promising now to be but a skirmish, what with Cornwall next to death and the Duke of Albany already of a mind to favor Lear and overlook the indiscretion of his having imparted properties to undeserving and ungrateful daughters, whose aberrations made them unfit to exert influence over the land. The scoundrel Edmund would be severely dealt with, and once more things would be as they should be. A few years hence, with the passing of Lear, the Duke of Albany would ascend to the throne. Lear would be remarkably sound of mind to the end, though by no means at his ease.

For there were still the daughters Goneril and Regan to contend with, who by the time of Lear's reinstatement were so advanced in their horrendous degeneration that one could barely recognize them. Lear took them in charge, lodging them in his own castle very much against their will, as the mute protest of their hideous eyes attested. When they spoke at all, which was mercifully seldom, it was in voices so contrary to healthy human existence that no one, save possibly themselves, could understand what they said.

Very little could be done for them. Among the last coherent utterances they made were entreaties to be taken to the coast and allowed to return to the sea. But King Lear was damned if he would accede to this, and had them confined to a far wing of the castle, where no one had to see them except the servants who took them food. Ever more each day, they shunned ordinary comestibles, and lived upon grubs and insects collected and given to them in covered baskets.

On one memory-haunting occasion, some months after his return to power, Lear, accompanied by his old friend the Earl of Kent, made an exception to his usual rule of avoiding any contact with the daughters and made his slow and faltering way into the far wing where they dwelled. The servants had reported that one of the two dreadful denizens of that wing, they could not be sure which, seemed no longer to be moving about, and they were uncertain as to whether she was still alive, hence Lear's decision to go. Upon reaching the hall, Lear and Kent found a reeking tumulus of organic matter from which a growing dissolution had removed any suggestion of human form. From atop this mound of corruption the remnants of two rheumy, teratological eyes stared sightlessly out, like the glazed dead eyes of a mackerel. Instinctively, Lear thought that this was what remained of Goneril.

Worse yet, from down the hall another form shambled forth, its horror being that, looking the way it looked, it still moved at all. This had to be what Lear and Kent had once known as Regan, and as the figure advanced haltingly and gelatinously, dropping purulent gobbets of itself along the way, it made, though there was now only a spongy mass where there had once been a head, a sound that no mortal should ever have to hear, a deranged and mucoid parody of human speech, before the tottering thing fell into putrid liquefaction at Lear's feet.

The Earl of Kent would remain a caring companion to Lear for the rest of that aging king's life, and without the abhorrent visages of Goneril and Regan to mar his senses, the faithful Kent would enjoy, in his own advancing age, a certain peace of mind—except when he stood in the tower of his own castle at Dover and allowed his gaze to wander to the misty sea beyond his battlements, the timeless and brooding sea whose undulant expanses held secrets on which Kent struggled not to dwell. Somewhere in those lightless ocean depths, the mother of Goneril and Regan cavorted unthinkably with fellow creatures of whom a sane person could form only the vaguest notion. And at times like these, Kent would turn from his tower window and try, albeit without much success, to put the ancient, mystical sea out of his troubled thoughts.

The Revelation at the Abbey

Don Webb

    Hiding his true motives was easy in Prague, the city swarmed with alchemists and soothsayers. On a given morning he could breakfast with Dr. John Dee and have dinner with Rabbi Lowe. The emperor was crazed, for magic and magicians of every stripe—mainly charlatans and mountebanks—had filled the streets. Strange fumes of outlandish hues belched from every chimney. Weird music seeped from cracks in ancient mortar at night, parchments with bizarre sigils were traded with a frenzy that might make the doughiest merchant blush. No one paid attention to Dr. Nemo. The occasional Greek speaker nodded knowingly at his name, Dr. Nobody, and one perceptive fellow even asked what Polyphemus he was seeking to deceive. His answer, "I am but an honest alchemist," made his listener shoot red wine from his nose, he laughed so hard.
    Dr. Nemo had come here because of a rumor, as he had gone everywhere for the last thirty-one years, because of rumors about the Book. He was an old man of fifty-four with a face pockmarked from plague, yellowish skin, and missing two fingers from his right hand (because of a minor infraction of Egyptian law). His hair was dirty silver and sat in tight greasy circles near his scalp. The whites of his eyes had become yolk-yellow, and rather nicely matched his remaining teeth. He would occasionally flinch at sounds other humans did not hear. He often woke from deep sleep screaming. He spoke French, German, Arabic, Polish, Italian, and English well—and he read Greek, Latin, Hebrew, and Gothic. He had learned to seem harmless and even parental. He no longer appeared to be driven by a mad quest; but in his heart he thought of nothing but the Book.
    He had been in Cairo. It was rumored that Dhu'l-Nun al-Misiri had found the Book. It was said (according to rumor) to have been the Scroll of Thoth that Prince Setne had stolen and returned to a haunted pyramid. Others said it came from the kingdom of the Stygians who had lived along the Nile before the desert came. Dr. Nemo had

been digging by a statue of Dhu'l-Nun when a tall, portly, one-eyed beggar had approached at sundown. He greeted Nemo with his real name, the name of his boyhood in far-off London, and said, "The occult wisdom of the ages is being gathered in Prague. The Book you seek hides there." Then the beggar faded into smoke and left only a foul stench of his passing. Dr. Nemo wondered if he was a phantom conjured by a rival, a message from such gods or demons as may wish to help (or hinder) him, or even a reflection of the Book itself. Maybe after all these years it longed to be found. Maybe after all these years its yellowed pages longed to be caressed by human eyes. Maybe it simply wanted to laugh at him.

He had first heard of the Book when he swept shop for a dealer in strange things in London. Visitors to the shop would trace a sign with their left index finger, nd the owner would respond with a countersign. They ignored him and spoke of many things. How to bring back the dead from their saltes, where certain rocks could be asked questions which they would answer truthfully at certain seasons, how to speak to mermen, and above all the Book. The nature of the Book seemed an open question. Most thought it to be a scroll or a set of scrolls. Others postulated clay tablets or even a mass of knotted cords. One woman suggested that it might change shape to communicate better with its owner.

It was not a grimoire.

On this point every seeker agreed. It was a history text, the true unvarnished history of this and perhaps other worlds. After months of hearing about the Book, he had gathered his courage to ask his master—a short, well-built Jew known for his temper—about the Book. The man scowled at first, and Nemo hardened his limbs expecting a beating. Then the owner laughed.

"So, my little *goy,* you have a mind after all. I will tell most of what I know. I think the Book was destroyed years ago, maybe centuries. If a human owned it and studied it thoughtfully, he or even she would rule this haunted world. But the rumor of the Book—that drives men mad."

"How could a history book make one powerful?"
"Let me ask you three questions. Why do you think about the mistakes you've made?"

The Revelation at the Abbey

"So that I won't repeat them."

"So a true book of every mistake a ruler has made would have value, no? Why do people risk vast fortunes for treasure maps?"

"If the map were true, it could lead to vast unclaimed wealth."

"So a book of every lost treasure—even those lost long before the coming of Adam—would be priceless, no? Why do so many of my friends seek the conversations of demons and angels?"

"They wish to know what lies beyond the world of men."

"So a book that gave a true history of such beings, which are very different from what our faiths tell us, would perhaps be the most amazing text of all time?"

"Truly I would give an eye for such wisdom, a hand, my tongue. But why do you think such a Book ever existed?"

"Now that I have raised the possibility of such a volume in your mind, will you think of aught else?"

His master had begun Nemo on the art of reading. First Greek and Latin. His master taught him to bargain and haggle and size up customers. He taught him how to be charming in half a dozen languages. But he would not teach the art of magic.

"Such things have brought me only sorrow and fear. The gold they bring is fleeting, the knowledge they bring makes you unhappy with the rules of this life and fearful of what awaits in the next."

The old Jew had no family and promised Nemo the shop and his gold when he passed on.

And Nemo, for a season, found love. Mary worked for the baker next door. She was lovely and smelled of fresh bread. She sang and laughed and was very impressed when Nemo could read a poem to her. On the eve of their wedding, she caught a fever. The doctors bled her and gave her stinking poultices, but she still failed. Even the Jew uttered a spell that seemed to slow, but not stop, the fever's burn. And Nemo was sad for two years. During those years he did not notice that the Jew's back grew more bent, his hair more gray, his eyes more dim. Then one morning the Jew did not descend the stair into the shop and Nemo went to see after him. In a glance he knew that the slow fire of time had nearly roasted this man who had been his companion and teacher. He began to run off for the doctor, but his friend asked merely to listen.

"I have had a long life; by my Art it has been much longer than the Most High allowed to men since the Flood. Now I pass into a Darkness wherein certain things wait for me. I am saddened that your wife-to-be died, and I hope that this shop will help you find another. You should burn the books and scrolls I keep in the black box under the gold. They will give you too much pain if you read them, and if you try and sell them you will attract men you do not wish to meet."

Within the hour, he had passed. Nemo pulled the black box free and made a fire. He opened the box, but before he threw the accursed volumes away he made the simple mistake of looking at one page. A phrase caught him, and he began to read. The fire died down and he read. The room grew cold and he read by the body of the dead Jew. His stomach rumbled and he read. The sun rose and set and he read.

Then with a stern voice he read a verse from an ancient scroll, and the body of the Jew rose. He told it to go lie in front of the synagogue so it would be buried. He gathered the gold and prepared to set off to a steamy rice-rich river in China. It was clear to him where the Book must lie. How could the Jew not have figured this out?

Two years and a horrible shaking fever later, Nemo realized, after careful study, that the Book was in Germany. Then in another year, having called up scholars from the dead to aid his research, he knew that it must be beneath a certain ruined temple near Rome. Then it had to lie in a nameless city in the Arabian desert. And then India, then Poland, then Macbeth's hillock in Scotland, at the center of Stonehenge.

And then one day he saw his face reflected in a shiny brass plate in a Baghdad market and saw that he looked older and sicker than the Jew. He saw that he had no friends among living humans. He saw he was not in any way closer. He sat down on the cobblestones of the street. Soldiers of the Caliph carried him away. He was locked up in the madhouse for three days. Then claiming to have regained his senses, he bribed his way free. He continued the quest, but without hope.

The Revelation at the Abbey

Questing was simply what he knew how to do. It was then the phantoms began coming to him. The first appeared when he had returned to England yet again. He was sitting in a public house when a young lady sat next to him. She had brown hair that verged on blond, and a bit of flour daubed one of her temples. She might have been Mary's cousin. Her eyes were black as ink, and her faded blue dress rustled like paper. She spoke in a near-whisper. "The Book you need is not on this island. Britannia est insula parva." The exercise-book Latin had been the first sentence he had learned to read. From Caesar: "Britain is a small island." He turned to face her, but somehow she suddenly wasn't there. He stayed in a small inn for days, using various methods of divination to find his next target.

Prague had twisty streets. It would be a good place for the Book. Its layout suggested a labyrinth, surely the correct sort of library for such a volume. Dr. Nemo no longer concealed his quest if someone happened to ask. He had never encountered any of the Jew's customers in the last three decades, nor did he possess the mouth-to-ear instruction that opened certain doors. Shortly after arriving in Prague, he had befriended the librarian of Emperor Rudolf II, the great collector of the occult and the eldritch, the esoteric and the forbidden. The tiny man, whose nature suggested more of a magical creature of the forest than of an urban dweller, gave him access to the vast book collection within days. Most of it was rubbish. A few books had certain Hints, and others were written in languages Dr. Nemo did not speak. The latter posed a problem. It was said the Book—parts of the Book at any rate—predated the coming of mankind. This would necessitate the Book being written in tongues known to no men—unless some secret society had preserved the tongues of lizards or demons. Yet it would be enough, thought Dr. Nemo, simply to hold the Book. If he could hold it in his arms, it would be enough. It would be like embracing Helen of Troy. She might not yield to him, but he would have held that which started wars and quests and (he suspected) religions as well.

One day he told the librarian of his quest.

"Yes," said the faun-like man, "I have heard of this book. It was said that two great kingdoms in India fought a battle with flying ships over its possession thousands of years ago. I have heard that Plato had seen but a single page of it and derived his whole philosophy from it in an instant. I have known men who spent their lives looking for it."

"And you, my friend?" asked Dr. Nemo. "Do you seek this Book, this true history?"

"I sought it by creating this library. I have little wealth, little bravery—even little health. I had hoped it would come to me. But I am an old man now. I do not know that I could withstand the revelations that it might contain. I wish with all my heart that I had never heard of it, because I will die unhappy for having known of it. I do not even know of a book that bears the remedy of knowing about the Book."

This sad and humble moment opened Nemo's heart as it had not been opened since the day he asked the Jew about the Book. Suddenly he saw himself in the little man of the library, a man ennobled by curiosity but derided by vanity, alienated from the world of men by his desires, but deeply dependent on that world for the possibility of answering that desire. In the days and weeks that followed Dr. Nemo told his stories to the little librarian. He told of his adventures from talking his way free from South Sea pirates to speaking with mummies far below the depths of the Sphinx. He told of running from tigers in India to running sores of the plague in Russia. To this little man, who had had no adventures but who held the same desire, he told all and everything. And as he told his story, his soul began to heal. He began to sleep at night. He was beginning to believe that he did not have to find the Book, that he could settle down in Prague for his last years, use the skills at trading that he had learned so long ago, profit from the vast storehouse of language, and experience that he had accumulated.

Then it happened.

He rose late one morning and, as was his custom, went to the emperor's library. His friend was there almost dancing among the shelves of books. The librarian's eyes had a wild gleam.

He had had a dream. In his dream a lovely woman had come to the library and, speaking from behind a hand-

The Revelation at the Abbey

held fan, told him of the Book. It lay nearby, in the ruins of an abbey just north of the city, where it had been worshipped as a sort of Angel for hundreds of years. The pious monks had placed the Book in their church, removing the standard relics of Christianity. Each day another page of the Book was read. But the monks grew greedy of their wisdom. They gave up their deeds of charity. Other than working in their gardens to feed themselves they did naught but read and discuss the Book. They took in no new brothers, and as age and sickness took brother after brother away, the monastery dwindled to a few, and then two, and then none. But the Book had remained in its isolation, wanting only a perfect reader. Now it was ready for those perfect readers: the librarian and the adventurer.

It did not occur to Dr. Nemo to treat this as anything other than the Truth. He had quested so long that such a revelation seemed all but inevitable. He told the librarian he would procure two horses and supplies and they would set out at once. He scarcely noticed the sickness invading his soul; for it had dwelt there so long, it seemed natural to have it back. He bought skins of wine and bread and cheese and two fine Spanish ponies. Shortly after noon, they set out. For the librarian this was a great adventure. He had been outside the great city but twice in his life. Indeed (although he would not have said so to a man who had run from tigers), he was worried about sleeping in the open at night, for such had not been his fate since long-ago boyhood when his mother allowed his brothers and him to sleep on the rooftop during summer nights. It was fall and the air had quite a nip in the evening. He trusted that Dr. Nemo would see to his comfort and protection, and in his heart and his excitement he became younger and younger as the ponies twisted their way out of the city.

Dr. Nemo, on the other hand, grew more and more silent. Something clearly weighed upon him, but the librarian did not ask; for he was not good with the ways of his fellow men, which is why he had chosen books as his friends. He wondered how they would share the Book between them. Would they both read pages together or would the Book spend one night with one man and then the next with the other? This imagined infidelity stirred strange desires in the librarian's heart, and he was startled from his fantasies when Dr. Nemo asked him the way to the devastated abbey and its history in the waking world.

"In the time of Charles IV, a small brotherhood devoted to St. Ludmilla asked for land to be set aside a place for study and to heal the sick. Charles tasked the abbot to learn of the prophecies of Princess Lubossa, who had foreseen the building of Prague. The order's work was half-mystical and half-practical. They treated those individuals thought to be too sick to remain in Prague, and they gathered mystical books of all sorts. Accusations of black magic and heresy began almost as soon as the monastery was constructed, but because of the good works of the monks, such naysayers were silenced. A rumor seeped into the world that a certain book had been found predating even Princess Lubossa, and the monks were said to draw even the wrath of Rome by the gaiety of their celebrations. They fell out of royal favor in the time of King Wenceslas IV. Their products were few—some herbal-infused liquors said to be sovereign against gout and dropsy—but they kept the monastery alive, albeit in a reduced form. Four or five decades ago the last monks were said to have died. Various legal issues between Crown and Church have kept the land effectively out of either's hands. So it has fallen in ruins."

It was a librarian's answer.

The ruined abbey crouched low and great by a small mist-shrouded river. The fields surrounding it bore crumbling stone walls disturbed by the army of trees that had conquered the abandoned gardens. The two men paused on the ancient Roman road half a mile above the abbey.

"Let us take shelter for the night under yon heavy oaks," said Dr. Nemo. "If we press on night will have fallen, and it would be hard going among the ruined walls. I see the chapel still has its roof; perhaps some preservative power of the Book is genuinely afoot."

The librarian was annoyed that the adventurer could possibly doubt his vision. Of course the Book was there.

And the adventurer was making a list. Losing his wife, being kidnapped by pirates, having his fingers sliced off, the plague, smallpox, running from tigers, fleeing across the roofs of Venice by moonlight, meeting the bear in the

The Revelation at the Abbey

Russian woods, talking his way out of the bandit's cave in Lebanon. Meanwhile the librarian had boldly stacked books in a new way, had risked his life buying new bookshelves. Had put his very soul in danger by invoking Him Who Waits. Yet their reward was to be the same. Had he not already the punishment for eating this particular apple long before he even saw the tree? The sickness in his soul became hate cold and deep, and he began to offer the librarian wine.

The little man did not hold his liquor well—no great surprise there. They sang a few bawdy songs in Latin, and then Dr. Nemo helped the librarian onto his horse. He was going to show his besotted companion a "trick." As the librarian sang "O Fortuna velut Luna statu variabilis," Dr. Nemo slipped a noose around his neck. As he sang "Semper crescis aut decrescis," Dr. Nemo tossed the rope up and over a thick branch of the sturdy oak. As the librarian sang "Vita detestabiles nunc obdurat," he slapped the chestnut-colored rump of the pony and the librarian finished the song in hell. "Life is unstable and sometimes cruel," agreed Dr. Nemo in his mother-tongue.

Dr. Nemo cut the librarian's body down after an hour. It didn't feel right sleeping beneath its swing. The pony wandered back to be with its friend. Dr. Nemo staked them both and slept the sleep of the innocent.

Dawn's rosy fingers caressed a very cool sky. Frost had silvered the ground, and Dr. Nemo felt the ache of his years as he awoke, kindled a fire from last night's ashes, and drank the last sips of sour wine.

There was still a rude lane to the shambles of the abbey. Dr. Nemo rode up and tied his mare outside what had been the gateway. If the librarian's dream had been accurate, he need only go to the chapel: the Book would be enshrined therein. He was surprised to see the door to the church still intact. He was about to burst in when he heard a rustling sound—a sound of paper against paper, a sound the phantoms often manifested. Was this to be another disappointment? Another cosmic jest? He pulled his rusty sword from its sheaf; he had not had to use it in years. He had never attacked a phantom. He didn't know if he could attack one, but the desire to corner one—to make it spill its Truth—that desire boiled very strongly in his heart. He pushed the door open.

The chapel's air was cold and stale. A few white candles burned on the altar. A large paper screen decorated with an Oriental blue and red dragon sat on the altar. No book was in evidence. From behind the screen came the sound of music—a plucked instrument. It took Dr. Nemo a moment to recognize it as a qinqin, the Chinese guitar.

"Don't look behind the screen," said a woman with a soft voice. "It will be better if you don't see me. At least at first."

"Who are you?"

"I am Princess Lubossa."

"No. No, you are not. She is long buried; she knew a lot about Czech futures. She may have even been partially non-human. I am looking for something else."

The music stopped. "Are you looking for redemption for the poor man you killed last night?"

"I have killed others in my quest."

"Yes, I know. Eight men and a woman. You think it is nine men, but the fellow you wounded in Rome staggered home and got better. He died last year."

"So you have been following me," said Dr. Nemo.

"Not at all. I do not follow anyone. I am without curiosity."

"But you know everything."

"Just what happens on this world and its moon."

"You have the Book."

"Isn't that why you are here?"

"I thought you knew everything."

"I do not know what happens in the hearts of humans. Or in the thoughts of any being, for that matter."

"Are you going to give me the Book?"

"No."

"But you know I will kill you for it."

"That is a logical development."

"So you don't know the future."

"The future does not exist. It can be predicted. Only the past is real. The past eats everything. The Book eats the past."

Dr. Nemo charged around the screen. At first he saw a seated Chinese maiden holding a qinqin with one leg exposed behind a subtle blue dress resting against a paper screen.

The Revelation at the Abbey

Then he saw what was really in front of him.

A large solid object that was shaped and colored as a seated Chinese maiden holding a qinqin with one leg exposed behind a subtle blue dress resting against a paper screen. It looked at him without sadness, happiness, or curiosity. It was a good copy. It blinked. He raised his sword, then lowered it. None of the phantoms had ever appeared to be anything unnatural. Ugly, yes, but not unnatural. "What are you? Are you the guardian of the Book?"

"I am the Book. Four years, three months, and seven days ago you told a magician in Paris that you thought the Book might be alive. Do you remember the conversation?"

He had been drunk. They had watched the sun rise over a graveyard near the Seine. The other fellow had a terrible cough. He died in the winter.

"I do not know if I am 'alive' in the sense you mean. Such speculation is beyond me. But I change, I adapt, I eat, I can move about. I seek self-preservation. I do not mate (for there are indeed others of my kind. I neither love, nor hate, nor curse my lot."

Dr. Nemo asked, "Do you have a purpose?"

"Yes. I record everything. My first record was of the being that owned me. Perhaps it made me. It died on this world twenty thousand years ago. At that time I was a very large sheet of some flexible material. The being lived in a castle it had extruded from its body, much as a snail makes its shell. The shell-castle stood two hundred cubits high. It was on an island near Japan, where some very shaggy human-like creatures worshipped the being. One day they were angry because of an earthquake. They banged on the walls of the shell-castle. The being went outside. They killed it with spears. I had been recording the world for four days at that point. One of the shaggy men took me away and made me into a tent. When he asked, I said I could show him anything. He knew the petty intrigues of his tribe. He knew when a group of true men were coming with war canoes. His tribe prospered. He never understood that I could only show the past, and that I could only answer him. Since then I have belonged to many beings, most of them human, most of that group men."

"And now," said Dr. Nemo, "you will belong to me."

"No. Which is sad. I feel better when I am with a being that can ask me better questions."

"How do you know that I am not to be your master?"

"Certain processes have brought you to me."

"The phantoms?"

"Yes."

"What are they?"

"I do not know."

Dr. Nemo thought it was very likely she was telling the truth. Because of her shape, he had to think of it as "she." But her protestations were of no consequence; he would take the Book with him. He asked her, "How do you take shape?"

"I fold myself. Remember the folded paper art you saw twelve years ago?"

In China he had seen a crane made of folded paper that a Japanese monk had shown him.

"So you are a folded sheet of paper that talks and sends phantoms and dreams around the world. You have no idea why you exist. You do not know who made you. But you do know that I will never have you."

"Yes."

He raised his sword again. Perhaps if he hurt her . . .

Instead he said, "Can you show me your true form?"

She answered, "Yes, but I will need to take you to a different kind of space. I would need to move your perception so that you could see."

Dr. Nemo had taken drugs, fasted, invoked demons. He had no trouble with the idea of other spaces existing "beside" ours.

"If I command you to do so, will you show me your true form?" He menaced her with his sword and thought of incantations he knew that could compel beings not of this world.

"Yes, or if you merely asked me. It is for this moment the phantoms have called you. Do not be afraid."

Suddenly she came undone. Her flesh, her dress, the qinqin, the screen, her chair all began unfolding in the three directions he was used to seeing and five more that he had never guessed were there. She/It was mainly white and covered acres in a moonlit desert. A tall wrecked shell-castle stood by. Its mother-of-pearl door crashed open, the soot of many torches staining its upper surface. He was standing on her. He walked carefully at first. She looked like paper, but was of far tougher stuff. Characters in an unknown tongue were printed on her surface. Very elaborate they were, human-sized and printed in the faintest sepia. He followed them. He occasionally thought he could read (or perhaps sense) some meaning. Here was Rome. Here were the Americas. Here were beings on the moon making giant sculptures. Alexander the Great. His mother dying when he was four. It wasn't linear. Sometimes it was the distant past. Here he and the librarian drank under the oak trees. He walked the plain for miles, it seemed. When he looked up he couldn't even see the shell-castle any more. He found the glyph of himself looking at the glyph. He bent down to study it. He dropped to his hands and knees, seeing it change as it recorded his actions. He felt if he could read the world, he would be its master, instead of just another glyph in the endless meaningless sheet of demonic parchment. Maybe the Book knew it would not be her Master because it would be her friend? Her lover? Her god?

As he knelt on the great white sheet, his own shadow blending with the ink of his sign, an idle thought passed through his enraptured mind. *She said she ate. I wonder what she eats?*

Before the suspicion could form itself into a speculation, the Book refolded. He screamed, but it would have sounded far away, as though muffled by rags. The sign grew dark with its living ink.

For another twenty years, visitors to the ruins would have seen a large book with iron hinges, but there were no visitors.

Then one came and picked her up, and a new meaningless cycle was recorded.

To the memory of Robert Bloch

Old Goodman Brown

Jonathan Thomas

Faith would outlive him, but to old Goodman Brown she'd been dead for decades. Of this the Archfiend was well aware, for his wiles had driven an abiding wedge of alienation between them when they were still but newlyweds. Tonight he wore the grave black of bygone century and a weathered elderhood, belied by how vigorously he rapped with snake-headed staff upon stout farmhouse door. He swallowed his amusement when Faith answered, pink ribbons of youth still gracing brittle gray braids. She betrayed no recognition of him, if any she retained.

Nor did sympathy warm her haggard features when she ushered hobbling guest into the bedchamber and shook her husband's shoulder to awaken him. Scant sparks escaped hollow sockets to show his eyes were open, and dry wheezing grew louder without filli g hollow cheeks. Goodman Brown was sunk deep in feather mattress as if lowered partway into earth already.

"Is it my own grandfather," Goodman Brown murmured, "who rejoins the living younger than myself?" Faith withdrew and quietly shut the bedroom door, no sign of curiosity on downcast face.

"I'm here to render whatever comfort and assistance I may," deferential visitor declared. In the glow of guttering oil lamp, his staff's snake-head seemed to blink under his folded hands.

"You've come to help." Brown vented a rasping laugh. "I'd a lifetime's worth of your help when you lured me, in callow youth, through the woods to that Sabbat of your worshippers. And there you helped me see the truth that we of Salem, and everywhere, drink greedily from sin's chalice, pastors, thieves, matrons, harlots, and my own wife. I am grateful for that truth whether or not you fashioned profane spectacle from fog and moonbeams, for truth is truth by whatever road it travels, is it not? And is not truth to be esteemed above all else?"

"I fear you taunt me," confessed inveterate beguiler.

"No more than do you, in the guise of revered kinsman."

"You wrong me!" Knobbly fingers went defensively to broad linen collar. "This august vessel I deemed most proper to bear the milk of charity, glad tidings of mercy. The sands are soon run from your unhappy hourglass, but say the word and those years are replenished, and your happiness. This I offer in recompense for the misery you suffered at my remiss hands."

"In return for which you ask nothing?" A smile, or more aptly a rictus, spread like a crack in the waxen mask of pending death.

"Have a care not to provoke me! My clemency is finite as the corruptible world." Intimations of an unbecoming leer spoiled the mask of serenity.

"You cannot cow me."

"Do you assume redemption through the crucible of self-torment? Do you fancy your soul purified and invincible against hell's violence? Elevated among the elect, are you?"

"Oh, no, quite the opposite," Brown quavered with studied innocence. "I owe the devil his due and mean no flippancy when I give thanks for purging me of trust in Christian virtues, and of doubt in nature's godlessness. Else the scales would have remained on my eyes, and I'd never have forsaken received wisdom to loft toward enlightenment, in keeping with others of this age, but surpassing them as the eagle does the wren. I'm indeed in your debt."

Some semblance of pity carved deeper furrows around the guest's grim-set mouth. "Yet here you are. Much good has this enlightenment brought you, and much pleasure." A sadder frown lent patriarch the pout of a gargoyle. "Am I one with whom you should hope to dissemble?"

"I shouldn't wager who or what you are." Color suffused waxen complexion, and passion galvanized frail husk. "You've become of meager import to me, for what are heaven and hell save figments of hoodwinked souls?" The bed quaked at a spasm of coughing. "And what are these purported souls in your ledger," he croaked, "beyond a currency that exists by mutual consent between you and the gullible?" At odds with impiety was the fiery eye of a zealot.

"Why bestir yourself at all for me, who may not exist except in fever vision?"

"You've beheld God's countenance, if anybody has." Goodman Brown became acerbic, like a schoolmaster hectoring a dullard. "Tell me, when was your last confabulation with Him?"

Deceiver wrinkled patrician nose, as if the Goodman's hauteur offended it. "You impugned me as Father of Lies an instant ago, and now you goad me for an answer we both know you'd not believe."

"Again you would mislead me into self-doubt, but I'll not backslide. You've done too well at weaning me off the creed so needful to you and your victims alike." Goodman Brown's look latched onto his guest as if with designs to convert the very devil. Guest narrowed uncongenial eyes at prospects of dotty sermonizing, at reservoir of vitality below the still waters of dotage. "The truth shall edify you, though to be edified is nowise to be happier, as if happiness or aught dear to us were dear among the stars."

"You've been among the stars?" Was that a gibe or a question? Goodman Brown's grin was not unlike that of head on serpentine staff. The staff's owner glared at mortal impudence, but before his temper found words the Goodman was underway.

"As my kindred spirit Descartes might have put it, once the x and y axes of sin and saintliness no longer bound me, neither did compunctions toward a spotless repute. I presumed the Ushers, the oldest booksellers in Boston, to have had works by Newton, Hooke, and Halley, names outside your circle I daresay." Goodman Brown gulped a ratchety breath; his guest archly mouthed "I daresay" but held his peace.

"Because of God's absence from these doctors' formulas for fathoming creation, churchmen militant reckoned them ungodly, whereas I hungered after them for just that reason. The clerk, an impish fellow who sniffled and hemmed as though surfeited with snuff, had nothing I sought. But with an air of broaching no new subject, he asked did I know a son of the shop's founder had been jailed for witchcraft? I could only shake my head, and he elaborated how the shackled

Old Goodman Brown

Hezekiah had escaped through another prisoner's devices, a Goody Mason, who somehow used equations like those of Newton as sorcery.

"The clerk could not specify the manner of this usage, but asserted Goody Mason's grasp of metaphysics would have confounded Kepler himself. What's more, rumor had it she still subsisted in squalid garret out in remote suburbs. If only she were handy, her I should approach for lessons that reduced Newton's calculus to child's play. I thanked him and withdrew hastily lest his sniffles, and his probable derangement, prove infectious, and repaired homeward on purchasing my books elsewhere.

"Some hours past dark I stabled my horse and trudged with weighty satchel to my door. I'd crossed from moonlit path into the shadows below the eaves when a rat scampered where my foot was about to land, near to tripping me, startling me the more because it was the size of a young woodchuck. My hand was fraught with instinct to grab for a pitchfork.

"Cackling burst from the blackness that had harbored giant vermin. 'You'll want worse than a pitchfork to dispatch me and mine!' I was flustered by shrill outcry, and further that I'd unawares been pantomiming my intent, which I surely hadn't voiced. This prowler's cadences of lunacy and menace were moreover alarmingly strange, yet I was convinced she was no absolute stranger.

"Had she, I inquired, been some years ago among Salem's mingled gentry and rabble in the wilderness, where now my acreage was situated, when Great Deceiver contrived joining me and my Faith in a Hallows-Eve travesty of marriage? I'd meanwhile had no luck espying trespasser in pitch-dark shadow, and her pet was gone afield, committing untold mischief.

"She tittered and jeered, 'To indulge such mummery is beneath me. And is it not beneath you too, a would-be disciple of Halley and Copernicus? I'll show entire what they only glimpsed, and much they never dreamed of. Say the word, and all is yours.'

"I had to grant then the verity of my absurd suspicions about this intruder's name, and how curious that both you and Goody Mason besought me with 'Say the word.' But she would never sign your ledger, would she?" The Goodman's diction verged on nettlesome. His audience swatted at an unseen gnat.

"That ledger goes back millennia. Can you recollect every soul with whom you've dealt?" chided the Archfiend.

"Mere millennia," sighed Goodman Brown. "Goody Mason promised I would learn the age and watch the birth pangs of the cosmos—though after consorting with you, how could I not beware of fine enticements? As I strained my sight in vain for the least glimmer of her, I queried, 'At what cost do you propose to school me?'

"'What cost would be too high?' she crowed. 'What of this earth would not pale in value beside my teachings?'

"I prayed she speak more softly, lest she bestir my wife and swaddling boy. 'How tragic that would be!' she mocked in husky whisper. 'Very well, simply nod and we'll adjourn for the nonce.'

"I'd scarce begun to wag my chin when monstrous, insolent rat leapt over my toes and into the blackness, jaws clamped on a mangled rooster's neck. On the heels of my wanton oath was a silence more doleful than in a midnight churchyard. That silence resumed as soon as I'd entreated, 'Goody Mason?' I ventured into black shadow under the eaves and let my eyes habituate. No one squinted back at me, not harridan nor thieving rat, as if I'd been alone all along.

"The next visitation, and each subsequent, disquieted me no less than the first. I was milking cows in the barn at daybreak, as later I'd be shelving turnips in the root cellar or adding fieldstones to a boundary wall, when the scuttle of great rat past my toes and a violet flash, swifter than a blink, heralded my instructress. Stooped and spindly crone curbed my protest at her pet's new depredations that dawn by hissing, 'Whist! You said your wife and baby mustn't hear!'

"While I regathered my wits, she plucked up my lamp and muttered and goggled around till some junction of angles and curves wrought by carpentry and shadows pleased her. She positioned the lamp to preserve this arrangement, whistled like a thrush for her accomplice, and beckoned me to 'tour heavens framed in no Bible story.' With a tittering as human as Goody Mason's, rodent hurtled by me, and then with deceptively snakish speed, crone latched scaly fist about

Old Goodman Brown

my arm and tugged. I stumbled in tow through that geometry of curves and angles, whose outlines flared up violet.

"Intersections of cow stall and beam and windowsill remained solid as ever, but radiant empurpled edges stood out like a ship's prow, and we penetrated them as though they were cobwebs. We emerged into lustrous firmament, suspended there as if we'd vaulted from ship's prow to lodge in its rigging. I was dumbfounded at this, and at our encasement, or transformation rather, into diversely sized globes and serried rectangles, but likewise was my mind transformed into deeming these alterations meet and natural.

"Some proficiency of Goody Mason's will detached us from the invisible rigging and propelled us into that firmament and toward further gleaming geometries fashioned of nameless constellations and celestial bodies, and she planted in my thoughts some comprehension of the marvels beyond those geometries.

"I therewith became her protégé as she revealed a fabric of reality set forth by no astrolabe or scripture. We contracted through the needle's eye to realms infinitesimal beyond reach of microscopes, where the most elementary particles within all matter madly spun round or bounced off or cleaved to one another, like eternal riot in measureless Bedlam. Else we ascended to divine vantage where our sun was less than a speck of dust in an immense pinwheel of stars, and then we withdrew to such remoteness that our pinwheel was one speck in a countless host dispersing headlong toward ultimate dissipation.

"But within a starless planet's frozen ocean, a lucent portal, contrived from cracks in ice and temple ruins blasphemous to Euclid, led to the most astonishment. For on traversing it, I was apparently home again, except my vision now detected twice what it ever had, a teeming density of grains, formerly clandestine, whose black network and trillion filaments connected and perforated trees, hills, farmhouse, me, and everything material, and made of the air a fluid mosaic, and crowded night sky with whorls like magnified fingertips. It was a world of foreign substance pervading ours, omnipresent, but occluded from earthly faculties."

Goodman Brown broke into raw chuckles that lapsed into feeble coughing. "I'd always pondered how you and Cotton Mather got on," the Goodman informed his guest. "What was he save his day's paradox incarnate? An avid partisan of science, a champion of inoculation against the smallpox, yet he endorsed spectral evidence to root out witchcraft, to condemn the innocent by asserting they trafficked in the Invisible World. And here I was, trafficking with one he'd brand a witch, through whom I was privy to an Invisible World his followers in science may not approach for centuries."

The semblance of Goodman Brown's grandsire pensively kneaded his chin. "Hearsay has it Cotton Mather was among the keenest intellects in the colonies, a claim you'd never arrogate to yourself. Perhaps deferring to his cosmogony would better suit your modesty. Can you prove this Goody Mason was not bedazzling you with phantasms?"

"If Mather's obsolete 'cosmogony,' as you dignify it, were so unerring, then why, among those nineteen whose executions he applauded, were only Goodies Carrier and Corey present at that Hallows' Eve Sabbat of yours? Or were you bedazzling me with phantasms that night?"

Venerable mouth indecorously smirked. "To err is human. A rash decision or two hardly required my whispers in Mather's ear. Your Goody Mason, on the other hand, must have been infallibly rational." Pert as a goat, Grandsire rubbed upraised right boot against left ankle.

"You've had the pleasure of her company, then, to make sport with me thus?" The Goodman's flinty eyes rebuked the Deceiver. "Or need I restate that she and Mather shared their generation's handicap, one foot mired in benighted past, while the other strove toward wisdom? Even as Mather credulously peopled the air with ghosts and witches, she couched ingenious mathematics in the ignorant trappings of magic, mathematics so complex its applications were tantamount to conjury.

"But that was poor excuse for her to affect hocus-pocus posturings, distress at beholding the cross, the fellowship of a beastly familiar, and talk of a 'master' whose book I'd have to sign, especially after she'd professed such scorn for 'mummery.' In fine, I grew skeptical of any genius in her, who

Old Goodman Brown

taught her transportive geometries solely as rote, with no grounding in their principles. Her 'master,' I surmised, was conversant with those principles, and I was both eager and loath to pay him court. His powers of learning were enough to make him imposing, if not fearsome, unlike Goody Mason, fatuous despite her attainments.

"Between her mentions of his 'book' and calling him 'the Black Man,' I mused he might be another sly embodiment of you, which would have let me dismiss celestial voyages as illusory. I could then have acquitted myself more conscionably as householder, for though my wife and son were none the wiser to my weeks and months of rovings, a premonition of leaving them insecure had come to haunt me. Goody Mason's 'master,' I meanwhile supposed, must have cultivated your likeness to render her more biddable to his hidden purposes."

Archfiend shrugged. "I take many guises. Others may disguise themselves as me. Do not, mind you, underrate me as one who moves in mysterious ways."

"Peculiar how Goody Mason's 'Black Man' said much the same himself." An adversarial smile began to form till some internal anguish quelled it and shortened his breath. "He," the Goodman persisted, "might not outdo you as an opportunist, though his domain was loftier than yours. And whereas you boast of serving no one, the Goody's 'master' answered to a lord whose realm was inordinately grander than your Jehovah's."

"Would you wheedle me into staging a defense of that odious Jehovah? I rejoice in your exertions to take Him down a peg. Why would I not?" Immortal trickster may have tried forging ingratiation on venerable features, but seemed unctuous at best. "And pardon my remarking this concern for family after you ostensibly severed such mawkish ties, at first because sin tainted them, and then with astronomic delvings to preoccupy you. How could the grubbing lot of a farmer compete?"

"Every time the Goody and her pet came to fetch me, I departed feeling as I had that night of hiking to the woods for my rendezvous with you, when Faith and I were blissfully in love. I did not like that feeling." Indignation furrowed ashen forehead.

"Goodman Brown, do not fault me for following a

course I never urged on you!" False grandsire's wrinkled brow parodied the Goodman's.

"Nor did I like the feeling, more and more distinct, of others watching over our journeys, whose very act of watching perturbed my equilibrium, and put me in sympathy with the fawn that fears a lurking catamount." To diabolic visitor, bitter grimace was akin to those on myriad clients surrendering to damnation. "In brief, I was near to admitting regret at ever giving Goody Mason the nod."

Unctuous smile once more marred grandfatherly visage. "Regret? Of what use is that? To you fell privileges beyond the ken of angels, the knowledge of worlds barred to them, of mechanisms governing the atoms of Democritus and the tedious doom of this clockwork universe."

"Knowledge, yes, you've always been a great one for promoting knowledge since your antics in Eden," the Goodman interjected.

Deceiver went on as if deaf to irony. "I might envy you the sublime panoramas of suns colliding, of opalescent clouds smothering constellations, of cities and jungles and armadas inaccessible to earthly senses. Are you not enriched by these splendors? Haven't wonderment and rapture persuaded you of some magisterial design? Is it absolutely certain you've been versed in purely secular mysteries?"

"You overplay your hand." Contempt hardened the Goodman's frown. "You cannot restore me to your clutches by reviving my credence in heaven and hell. For what are beauty, reverence, or love but human valuations, pretty gloss to smooth over chaos and futility, pathetic before omnipotent indifference?"

"You're sadder than I foresaw." Dour assessment smacked uncharitably of reproach.

Goodman Brown shook his head as if disheartened that his pronouncements on the worth of happiness had gone to waste. "No easier for you than me discerning sorrow from wisdom, eh? But we come to the crux." He cleared ratchety throat. "I knew no customary ride impended that night my fellow voyagers emerged from hearthside shadows. Both were exultant as topers, cackling brazenly as if wakening wife and child above us were of no consequence.

"A double shudder of panic afflicted me at vile rat

Old Goodman Brown

darting from the chamber and toward the stairs, and then at first glance of its abnormal head by inconstant firelight, muzzle too blunt to encompass crooked fangs, irises blue instead of glassy black, ears like a man's, flat against the skull. Goody Mason's imperious whistle retrieved slinking creature to her heels. I undertook no second glance. 'Later for that!' she hissed at it. 'Mustn't violate prescribed order!'

"As if to trivialize that warning she grinned, and bared teeth winsome as her pet's. 'My master may choose you for advancement! Prepare yourself!' she crooned. Her jubilation was of a savory piece with her grin. And had she been more bookishly inclined, she'd have noticed I was preparing, with volume three of Newton's *Principia* by my wainscot chair, as I'd been preparing studiously since that fateful jaunt to Boston.

"She railed, 'You and I are of like humors, are we not? No seasonal rounds of drudgery for us, no fetters of domesticity, no paltry span of threescore years and ten! Of what merit is any ambition bound by human limitations? Hasten, the Black Man finds rich promise in you!' That praise alone reaffirmed for me the Black Man was not you. She warbled how we'd be partners till the end of the world, and when I confessed unease at making her savage pet jealous, she scoffed, 'His perquisites are his own, and they're nothing to you!'

"In the hearth's cavernous maw had formed, by none of Goody Mason's doing, tracery of more royal purple than hers, staunch amid the flickering orange glow, etched from the crane for the kettle, the pair of crescent andirons, the cracks in fireplace back wall, and the blazing logs. 'Go on! Why do you hesitate?' Goody Mason scolded as I charily leaned forward and smelled the hairs on my knuckles singe. From behind, animal chatter added to the scolding, and selfsame gullet, I'd swear, squealed, 'Go!'

"I turned in confusion, and spiteful vermin sprang at my face as from a cannon, a sneer upon blunt snout that no rat could shape. This treachery startled an unmanly shriek from me, and I recoiled tottering into infernal heat and through the violet gateway as my cheeks began to sear.

"My skin still stung, and smoke stank in my nostrils, as I fell to my knees on the yonder side, onto a black floor that was not stone or wood or metal. At the outset, the retention of my fleshly body, instead of mutation into tandem globes, mystified me. Nor had the Goody changed appearance, and her worshipful gaze conveyed she was kneeling deliberately.

"Her creature, meanwhile, scampered between us, and between a plain black altar and plain black lectern with an open tome of black pages atop it, and up shallow black steps onto a black dais, from the center of which rose a rugged black throne. On the throne, the recumbent figure of a man was black and featureless and immobile as everything else, and at his heels frolicked the misshapen rodent, whining in uncouth rhapsody. To survey these outmoded trappings of religiosity, of sheer charlatanism, made me wary and dispirited.

"What's more, this adoration of a statue, as seemed the case, soon paled on me, and I sought for the source of reflected mercurial sheen on every black surface, like the to-and-fro of white minnows in a dark eddy. On observing the stupendous cataclysm that enveloped us I was instantly dizzy and overwhelmed. Our platform sheltered under a pellucid canopy of silence, in the calm eye of infinite storm wherein cyclones and pinwheels and explosions in every hue of the spectrum arbitrarily collided or rebounded or fused.

"And lacking any sense of scale or perspective I couldn't hazard if the turmoil was composed of stars or dust or atoms, and indeed all may have been as one, in this anarchic theatre that made a farce of harmony or any music of the spheres. Nor could I attest whether seconds or eons were ticking by beyond our refuge. Whatever the actuality, wherever we were, the spectacle functioned as billowing stage curtains for the dumb show to which I lowered my daunted sights.

"More discomfiting yet, the greeting 'Welcome!' accosted me in a voice not high nor low, devoid of timbre, accent, or any memorable qualities. Freakish rodent now gamboled about a statue bolt upright and fixing upon me features so regular and nondescript as to give memory nothing to latch onto, like sculpted equivalent of the impersonal voice. This hairless, sexless statue moreover was of no human blackness, but in fact matched that of altar, throne, and lectern, and I was stupefied to recognize it also as that black of secret tendrils and reticulations penetrating all visible substance.

Old Goodman Brown

"The Black Man averred that while I lacked instruction to realize who he was, he could see I astutely realized who he was not, by which I gathered he meant you. With an unnervingly artful smile, he registered approval of me. 'The God of your people you condemn as fable,' he intoned as if scanning it on my brow, 'and you would follow erudition's road to its end, there to uncover what underlies all illusion, cant, and religion. Yes, let us depose sham God in favor of the genuine Prime Mover.'

"Both Goody Mason and her alter ego abandoned their piety and harshly dissented, and rodent's ear for English no longer gave me least pause. Despite their muddle of agitation I managed to catch Goody Mason's gist, her disbelief in my readiness, her objection to granting me unearned privilege. Their outburst, as if it were the buzzing of flies failed to swerve unblinking charcoal focus. We'd defer the formality of my signature in his book, he decreed, for I'd shortly have fewer compunctions about signing.

"Before my escorts could oppose this fresh breach of protocol, the claptrap of black furnishings, and our floor, faded into transparency. I hadn't the presence to note whether the Goody and her pet also swayed off-balance as the swirls like vague white fish at our feet became the churning tempest of the spheres. Concurrently, our canopy cracked open with a thunderclap that shook my marrow, and I had scant chance to cringe at colossal vortices bearing down on us like a host of Olympian boot-heels, when everything in a heartbeat underwent reversal.

"It was, as the song goes, 'The World Turned Upside-Down,' save that we were on no world. We stood firm though not upon ground, my head felt clear and refreshed though falling sky had been about to crush it, and the dazzling tumult had become a lambent black, wherein fleeting white arcs and flecks glimmered on whirling spirals and polyhedrons. And in lieu of that earsplitting collapse of celestial roof, a bass pulsation, more palpable than audible, kept time with none of the black gyrations, and a hoarse piping, sans beat or rhythm or visible pipers or association with aught else, was nonetheless somehow intrinsic to all.

"My grasp of perspective and scale was, if anything,

more askew here. Each towering black configuration may have revolved at arm's length or across vast gulfs, and to raise my eyes set me reeling as upon a well-sweep till the zenith became the azimuth. I dared not peer downward. The Goody and her familiar and their master were at different distances whenever I regarded any one of them, feet or yards or furlongs away, yet I never saw them move.

"The single fixity, the one commonality between our prior environs and these, was the black throne, the ever-calm center within rank instability. For this arrant stage dressing to follow us beyond the realm of 'cant and illusion,' I conjectured the strict literality of this vista must have been subject to the Black Man's mediation. Why doubt he had the craft to filter reality through an incisive metaphor, for the benefit of our limited human brains and senses, or to humor Goody Mason's naive preconceptions, writ large in her devout gaze?

"Her adulation of him who replaced the Black Man on the throne was grievously misguided, for who could reasonably ignore the vacant slouch, impulsively flapping hands, aimless, guttural laughter, slack-jawed drooling, and fecal miasma of an idiot? The Black Man, suddenly by my side, commended my clear-sightedness in seeing the Prime Mover for what he was, which the Goody, in her prayerful genuflection, and her pet, with ecstatically switching tail, patently did not. Their mute veneration was doubly pathetic because they failed to acknowledge their deity's milky eyes were blind as any icon's."

"Ah, but prove yours were not the disordered senses. How prideful to assume the inferiority of others!" Archfiend's smug grin only broadened as his deflection of the Goodman's train of verbiage triggered a fit of gulping and snorting for air.

"A pox on you for distracting a poor codger with so few breaths to him!" croaked Goodman Brown. "I remind you, the Black Man himself saluted my clarity, allowing for my limited sensorium. No guiding intellect, he confirmed, presided at the core of everything. All was a random production of blind, mindless forces, as personified upon the throne, the divine inanity made manifest as the mechanical pulse, the tuneless piping. How the slobbering creator created himself, or otherwise came to be, abides as a sole intractable mystery."

Old Goodman Brown

"Yes, unless your sorry shambles of a 'Prime Mover' is no such thing, but one mere creature more of the God you once revered," the Deceiver argued.

"Then who created that God, or how came He to be?" With a wave both feeble and disdainful, the Goodman dismissed further dispute. "Of the idiot god's features, like the Black Man's, I could retain nothing, as if the Black Man were some finer-hewn avatar or emanation of the Prime Mover. The Black Man must have read these intimations in me, for he proposed, 'Are we not each of us more or less felicitous rearrangements of primal disorder? The victims or darlings of almighty imbecility? You're correct to appreciate my ways and substance are too complex for human rationality. But your schooling's done for now.'

"In a topsy-turvy blink, the Black Man was restored to the throne, our sheltering canopy was overhead, and the prodigious black upheavals were dazzling and prismatic again. Goody Mason was at my elbow, and her pet had importunate forepaws on my shin. The Goody held open in outstretched hands the black book from the lectern, and unwholesome glint in her eyes made me dread her master's next words. 'And like any schoolteacher,' he continued, 'or ferryman if you prefer, payment's due me, nothing too exorbitant in light of what you've learned.'

"With a peremptory flourish he drew my attention to a bowl I'd not observed earlier on the altar, of a somber burnish like an alloy of silver and the black material of our surroundings and the 'master' himself. I then descried beside the bowl a round-hafted dagger forged from that same alloy, and I was also positive it wasn't there an instant ago.

"The Black Man was on his feet as precipitously as before, and between him and the altar hovered a purple contour that testified to his adeptness, for it was woven of no more than the arrested drafts and stirrings of the air. I was at once contemptuous of the added flummery with knife and bowl, this pandering to the Goody's taste for heathenish props, yet was I also chagrined at these dire harbingers, and at the total opacity of inhuman aims and pleasures.

"As if in essence to decoy me, Goody Mason thrust the book a hairsbreadth from my waistcoat and demanded,

'Sign it! Sign in blood!' Her rodent, meanwhile, was up on hindquarters, scrabbling at my leg.

"A childish whimper redirected my attention to the Black Man stepping from the purple contour, and cupped in his untender grip was my swaddling boy, lolling as in drugged torpor. I was aghast at apprehending the odious bargain I should have foreseen when the Goody's accomplice tried scurrying to my bedchamber. The Black Man's mirthless smile rendered me more deathly dumbfounded. 'You who have so aptly learned the value of earthly life,' he declaimed, 'and of family and posterity and all other sacrosanct follies, how could you scruple to dispatch your firstborn, what worth can he possess in your elevated view?'

"The dagger, cool and smooth and weightless as talc, was inexplicably in my hand. The Black Man shook my boy's muslin blanket free from his bare chest, and pushed him toward me with the gravity of Yahweh offering Abraham a glorious covenant. My wayfaring comrades were meanwhile pressing closer till my breath mingled with the putrescence of theirs, and the Goody exhorted, 'Sign it in his blood! That should temper your precocious swagger!' Her rat, whose face I still shrank from scrutinizing, chided stridently, and I'd warrant I could sometimes discriminate syllables in some mewling language.

"I was mortified at how the brute rhythms of this clamor had come to throb within my veins, eroding my will. My fingers tightened their clench upon the haft, and my arm involuntarily began to rise. As I struggled against despair and base capitulation, against knuckles that refused to loosen around the knife, I could not say then, and cannot now, whether I acted out of love and loyalty and resurgent Christian virtue, or out of cold repugnance at this bloodshed as waste and foolery, an insult to august science, a sop to foul superstition, for what authentic purpose could such sacrifice serve?

"In their passion to humiliate me, drag me down to their murderous level, and confute I was their better, Goody Mason and her pet could no longer contain themselves. Supporting the black book in one hand, she wedged it against me to keep it open, while her other hand seized my forearm; I bridled at the effrontery of her touch. She fairly crushed

Old Goodman Brown

what control I had of my arm to wrench it with dagger in fist toward my fretful baby. Each second, despite my utmost resolve, the blade inched closer, and the Black Man coolly nodded as his underlings labored to fulfill his inscrutable ends.

"The rodent, with gouging claws, raced up my breeches and vest too swiftly to cuff away, and pounced on my left arm as I flailed haplessly. Sawtooth fangs chomped on my wrist; foul beast clung to my sleeve, hindered my efforts to lift my arm and flap it loose, and twisted to jeer at me. The face from which I'd diligently shied now met mine full-on, and shock and outrage staggered me at cognizance of blasphemously mannish blue eyes, hooked snout, and scraggy beard, like unto Goody Mason as a son or brother.

"And at this insufferable travesty of nature, I flung the arm in Goody Mason's grip up at an angle she was unprepared to parry, and jabbed the dagger into her obscene familiar. I struck hastily but well enough. Baneful vermin propelled itself away with an agonized squeal. The Goody weakened and wailed at this harm to her boon companion, and no sooner had I, with wrath unabated, broken her clasp than I stabbed her and rejoiced as she screeched and crumpled.

"The book had tumbled thudding to the floor. I hearkened from it to the rill of blood still dribbling from my wrist, troubled at my fate should any gouts have spilled onto the pages. My eyes hove to the Black Man, for he was venting raspy laughter—not at me but at his writhing disciples. My son he carried unmindfully, as if forgotten and liable to be tossed aside on rediscovering him.

"Around this kidnapper softly shone the purple nimbus from the creel of light behind him. I sprinted forth, with fatherly heart goading me at frenzied pitch, planted dagger in the Black Man's surprisingly gelatinous throat, grabbed my child from his unresisting arms, and shoved against this malefactor's chest, which was in contrast like smooth black granite, and like a statue he toppled backward. I leapt into the purple, but like Lot's wife couldn't help one last glimpse, and was confounded by statue already upright, neck bereft of knife, arms outstretched, and the Goody and her creature crawling toward him on their bellies.

"Momentum hurled me from out the fireplace, with nary a spark attaching to me or the swaddling cloth. I was afeard as much of lurching over and crushing my offspring as of anything else this night, and gratefully collapsed into that same wainscot chair from which I'd embarked. The fire still crackled briskly, begging the question of how long I'd been away. Purple configuration also hung steady amid the flames, and I bounced up and strained my ears for more perhaps than the pop and hiss of logs ablaze.

"So engrossed was I in listening that I was near to entranced when animal gibbering and witchy imprecations emerged distinct from the sputtering combustion, indicating the master had repaired his puppets to chase after me. Bracing restive tot upon my shoulder, I snatched a poker and thrashed vengefully at the firewood, the andirons, the kettle crane, wrecking the geometry on which the portal depended.

"And as purple contours receded like incinerating straws, I shuddered at both my narrow escape and at ghastlier shrieks than the dagger had wrought, as if limbs were sheared from torsos, or torsos sheared in twain. I heard as well that inhumane laugh of black larynx as I backed bone-weary into my chair, where Faith almost gave me up for dead in the morning, save I was hugging our languid boy to me as for dear life.

"I never saw more of the Goody and her cohort, but pondered then, and ever after, the import if my blood had stained the black book. Did that account in part for the Black Man's glee? And had rescuing my son amounted to a useless gesture? He grew to independence and resettled beyond the Berkshires, and broken all ties with me; he has been no comfort, and it is as if I'd never fathered him."

The archfiend's patrician mask acquired a more contemplative veneer. "At the root of it, though, homely virtues were victorious over cultish brutality; what matter if those virtues were instilled instead of heartfelt? Does that not suggest something?"

"Yes, that you're deaf as an anvil," the Goodman carped, but fainter of breath, vitality ebbing now his story was told. "Fortune's whim, or mayhap the blind idiot god's, brought me home unscathed. My life or my son's could as easily have been forfeit, or I could have blandly acceded to his slaughter. My survival to this moment signifies nothing."

Old Goodman Brown

"Bah!" The Deceiver banged his staff against the floor with the disgust of Moses vilifying a Golden Calf. "I can do naught with you! I leave you on your own!"

"Wait!" the Goodman hoarsely bid as his guest gathered up woolen cloak to turn away. "You fancy yourself so guileful, yet likelihood of imperfect candor in others never dawns on you?" Archfiend bared the vicious snarl of a cutthroat betrayed by a cutthroat. "Mightn't deathbed confession have been a lie? Might I not have patched up differences with fellow acolytes and consorted with them evermore? Shame on you, to be hoodwinked like a silly lackwit imp!" The "lackwit imp" brandished his staff as if to smash a defenseless skull, and he, if not the head of his staff, hissed like a viper. "But here," the Goodman wheezed, "is a trick I've saved for you!"

Without more ado, a tangled cage of purple bars lit up atop the mattress, enmeshing Goodman Brown. And in a trice, both man and glowing shape were gone, apart from gloating laughter and the tangy whiff that lingers after lightning strikes.

Wide-eyed Archfiend had no opportunity to poke at blankets with his staff or curse unsportingly; for in the darkness at his feet, incisors as of monstrous rodent punched through tough boot leather, or at least the illusion of leather, to puncture devilish ankle. In thorough disarray, the corrupter expelled an astounded, disgraceful shout and fled the bedchamber, clouting its door wide open without a backward glance.

Faith, throughout the colloquy, had eavesdropped at the door, nursing hopes she dared not articulate. These had gone to ashes, though, during the course of harrowing narrative. She cowered away as visitor burst forth and bolted from the house, and she hurried to the Goodman's bedside and let slip one forlorn moan at discovering him expired, eyes toward the ceiling and mouth agape, as if he'd never departed.

Sorrow's burden immediately bowed her neck and shoulders; she lamented inconsolably for herself and him, fathoming their doom was worse than damnation, each of them now irrevocably alone without the solace of hell as

Thomas

well as heaven, of any eternal order's surety. Nothing but inchoate void awaited, and she on the brink. And thus upon her tombstone, as on his, no hopeful verse was carved, for her dying hour had been gloomier than his.

Square of the Inquisition

Lois H. Gresh

The knife grazes my neck, and Eliseo cracks a smile. His eyes shift from black to empty.

I know better than to struggle. I have no choice but to let him have his way.

My vision blurs, my heart beats faster, and I don't let myself breathe. If my neck moves, if it so much as flinches, the knife could plunge and kill me, and indeed, it would be a gruesome death.

Eliseo straddles me, his knees on the floor. The weight of his body presses me to the rough stone. Eliseo loves this time. It calms him. He draws strength from me.

He bows his head. All I see are his lips, a gash of red, and his face, a broken smear of mottled flesh as if the Inquisitors have beaten him close to death. But they haven't touched him. Not yet. As long as Eliseo slays *el toros* for their entertainment, the Inquisitors consider him *divino Judío*, a divine Jew, one not yet ready for torture in the cells beneath mine.

Chains rattle, and a woman shrieks as guards slap her and snarl insults. A child whimpers. A prison door slams, and now, a whoosh of air and the rise of mold. My eyes water, and my nose itches. I need to sneeze.

Eliseo's head jerks up. He must hear the chains and the guards. Saliva drools from his mouth down his chin. His lips draw back, exposing his teeth. Sharp points.

And then he roars, and it's the sound a bull makes when it races toward him.

I flinch, and through tears I see bloody meat on hooks. A carcass dangles over me, the ribs exposed, the fat jiggling, the bones cracked at odd angles. I see Eliseo's torso, and what he doesn't know can't hurt him.

His grip tightens on the knife. His voice lowers. "They're coming. It's too soon."

And that's when I sneeze, and Eliseo slips, stares at

me in horror as his hand jerks and plunges the knife into my neck. First I gurgle, then I choke. I can't swallow. Fear crystallizes in Eliseo's eyes, a fear that I may die and leave him alone.

My limbs twitch. My stomach trembles. The blood is hot in my throat, the pain fierce. I gag and cough, gasp for air.

This could be the end.

Yet death itself doesn't matter. We all die. It's how we go that matters. I don't want to die in pain, yet I wouldn't mind dying. If anything, it will be a relief. A way to escape the Inquisitor's jail between St. Joseph Church and the *Muro Judío*.

Eliseo jumps to his feet. Torches light the corridor walls beyond my cell. Eliseo's knife glistens. Strips of red and blue cloth flutter from the long handle. This particular *bandero* is sacred to him. It's the first of several he'll thrust into the shoulders and back of the bull.

I clutch my black skirt, lift the folds, and press the coarse cloth to my neck. I try to stem the flow of blood.

"What's happening here?" A guard's face looms into view, red from torch flames. Bloodshot eyes, dim from whiskey, scan the naked Eliseo, then dip to me, still on the floor. Fatty jowls wobble. While Eliseo is small and thin, the guard and his three companions are larded like bloated pigs.

I hate them. I hate them all.

The hate burns in me worse than the pain.

Eliseo backs against the wall. His ribs jut over a concave stomach. He's breathing heavily. "Nothing's happening, *nothing*. Take me to the Square. Take me, I tell you, take me while Martina's blood still flows.

The guard laughs, and the sound rolls down the corridor and reverberates off the metal doors at the far end. I shiver. His friends emit nervous chuckles. "Have you killed the Jewess, then? Have you denied me the pleasure of torturing her into submission?" He steps into the cell, and Eliseo's body stiffens.

These guards, these men—if you can call them that— they are evil. They inflict pain, they watch us suffer, and they enjoy it. In the name of religion they condemn, torture, and murder innocent people. They murder the elderly. They

Square of the Inquisition

murder the pregnant. They murder the babies. They feel justified.

A screaming rises around me in the cells. It is as if the other condemned can smell my death before it happens.

I hear my heart beating in my ears. I can't turn it off. I'm lightheaded, my vision still blurred, and as the bully hoists me to my feet, I stagger and his hand cracks me hard across the face. I reel and fall against Eliseo, who grabs me with his one free hand and steadies me. His arm slinks around my waist, and he holds me up.

His eyes brim with compassion. My cheek stings. Blood froths on my lips. I gurgle. The knife dipped slightly into my throat and stopped at my wind pipe. After what I have suffered at the hands of the Inquisitors, this pain is a mere prick.

Nobody here understands. These bullies, these beasts of the Inquisition do not understand that I am no more Jewish than they are.

I am different, that is all.

So is Eliseo. He just doesn't know it yet.

The guard grabs my arm and yanks me into the corridor. "The crowd grows restless," he snarls. "The bishop wants your blood. The people need to see what happens to those who refuse to believe in the true God."

I lurch, and the nails jiggle and clank all over me. For months, they have driven hundreds of nails into my arms, my thighs, my breasts, my sides. Only my head and back are free. This way Eliseo can straddle me, push me to the floor, and perform his pre-bullfighting ritual. We both know that if Eliseo doesn't massacre the bulls, the bishop and his priests will kill everyone in the Jewish Quarter. It's a game to them, that's all, a bloody horrible game.

Eliseo says, "Give me one more minute with Martina. Come on. I need it to give you a good show."

"No more waiting, Jew. I told you, the bishop is screaming for blood, Jew pig blood, and the crowd is restless."

"He'll get all the blood he wants, but please, I need one more minute with the girl."

"Filthy Jews. All the same. Blood, lust, sex, greed. You disgust me, all of you," says the guard, and his companions grunt in agreement. Their boots scratch against stone. They are anxious to see Eliseo fight the bull, hoping that he fails so they can watch the beast shred his flesh and rip him to pieces. Then they will torture every last man, woman, and child in the cells. They want to do this, they look forward to it. Anything less will disappoint them, and as usual, they will take out their disappointment on their prisoners.

We cannot win, no matter what we do.

Eliseo begs. "I've never lost a fight, not in all these years, so give me the girl for a few seconds more. If you deny the bishop the slaughter of *el toro,* he'll want *your* blood."

"Fuck you, Jew. The bishop never wants our blood. But go on, pig, take your precious few moments with the girl and *then* die." The guards shuffle into the dark. The torches recede. We have little time, Eliseo and I. We drag back into the cell, and he swings the door shut.

His free hand brushes across the nails jutting from my left arm. He hisses into my ear, low so the guards won't hear. The hissing slides like a snake over the beating of my heart, still loud in my ears. The words aren't human; not Spanish, not Ladino, not Hebrew. "*Q'ulsi'kattum q'ablitum u kashshaptu u q'ulsi mushiti kattum.*"

I quiver. Eliseo speaks *my* language. Ecstasy swells and crashes through my broken body. I float out of myself, flit into the reek of mold, human excrement, and dead rats. Everything sizzles at my touch. Everything smells fragrant. If I could just stay here in this place where Eliseo has sent me, I would finally be free of the Inquisitors, the bullfights, all of it. My flesh would die, and it wouldn't even matter *how.*

Eliseo continues to mutter, and I rise higher and higher. How does he know these words? I have heard of human cults, those who worship us and know the correct incantations. Poor Eliseo, he is one of them, nothing but flesh, and flesh is so insignificant.

Why do they all care so much about their flesh? Why does it matter if their flesh withers and dies? Isn't it the *soul,* the essence of a being, that matters the most? Why don't they see that?

Most likely, Eliseo's flesh will die today. Whether he kills the bull or not, the bishop will put him to death. I feel it. I know it. The guards will drag him to the chambers beneath mine, where they will put him on the rack, hang him by his wrists, and flog him with spiked chains. They will proclaim him a Jew and gouge out his eyes while they hack off his penis with a ragged, rusty knife. They will laugh at his misery and humiliation. *So amusing.* He will sink into the dirt and the dust, just another man that nobody remembers.

Then they will hammer another nail into my body to mark his murder. Soon after, they will bring me a new matador, some poor slob with no hope of surviving a fight with the beast, and they will tell me that I must help him, too.

How many have I helped in this way?
How many have they murdered? Christians, Jews, the few remaining Moors, even their own, the Catholics: the Inquisitors spare no one.

"Give me strength," whispers Eliseo. "Only you can save me. Please, Martina, save me. Give me salvation."

What he asks is impossible. I cannot save him. I cannot give him salvation. I don't even know what that means.

"I must don my clothes and fight. Give me something, Martina, before they return."

I am above him, below him, around him. I am not squarely in the flesh. His name for me, Martina, is a human construct. It is not attached to the real me, the one beyond the flesh

"*Please.*" His tears glisten in the faint light. "Don't you remember what they did to my family?"

How can I ever forget?

I dwelt on the wrong side of the wall that severed the Jewish Quarter from the rest of the city. Eliseo was a barely believing Christian who sold pots to the Jews. When the Inquisitors came, they raped his wife and tortured her until she confessed that he was a *converso,* a secret Jew.

"They sawed off my wife's limbs, one by one." Eliseo is crying softly now. His hands cover his face and muffle his words. "They raped her remains. They left her in the filth, her head and torso, until she bled out. Then they went after my children, all five of them, the youngest only two, the oldest only seven. Don't you remember, Martina?"

Conversos, all of them, the blood of the father coursing through their veins. The Inquisitors had no mercy. Even I cannot bear to remember what they did to Eliseo's children.

From outside the jail, the crowd roars for blood. There must be a thousand of them out there, bloodthirsty, waiting for the spectacle of man versus beast.

Eliseo is one of my kind. He deserves better than this sorry human death. Hoarsely, for it is hard to speak human words outside of human flesh, I whisper, "Finish what you started. If you want any hope of salvation, then utter the words." This is a slight lie, yet I *will* give him what I can.

I want—

no, *I need*—

the bliss of being me, and if Eliseo knows the incantation, then let him chant it—

let him chant!—

for haven't I given him enough wins during the past few months? Haven't I?

Hope flicks in his eyes, a brief hope that rapidly dies. He looks unsure, as if he doesn't believe me, but then he intones, "*Dweller in Darkness, Thing That Cannot Be, ja'ru'stra kruh-muh, Martina Who Is Not Martina, ja'ru'stra kruh-muh.*"

"Not good enough," I say. "Do it right or not at all."

He squints at the translucent palpitations, the mists, the undefined glory that is me. This time, his voice is strong. "*Q'weerilpuman-kwat-an-q'ulsi'kattum u q'ulsi kattum.*"

The trebles, the dips in tone, the ripples of the syllables: all perfectly chanted to trigger things in me that I cannot ignore. For a moment, I forget that he is there, as I effervesce and expand, float around and over him.

I drift and coalesce, enjoying the freedom, and then I shift myself back into Martina's flesh.

"Salvation?" he says.

I regret my earlier lie. I am not cruel. I just want to be me. But I do not have time to answer Eliseo because the guards are back. The light widens on the walls, then penetrates the cell. I fall to the floor.

Eliseo yanks up the tight pants, dons the red coat with the bright buttons: these are the clothes they make him wear when he fights the bulls. "Fuck you," he grates, angry at me. "I gave you what you want. Fuck you that you won't save me from them."

How dare he be angry! What did he expect? "What

people do in the name of religion," I say, "they do to themselves."

Locks clink. The guards swagger into the cell and grab us. Rats scamper into holes.

And now, smelly beards scrape my cheeks, while in front of me two guards shove Eliseo down the corridor. A fist grabs my hair and yanks back my neck, and the guards have that harsh laughter they get when they are about to see a bloodfest in God's honor. I kick and punch, but it does no good. They shove me down the corridor, too.

We pass the cells of half-dead men, women, and children. Some groan; they have given up all hope. Some beg; these are the fools. The younger ones cry.

As we near the stairs leading from this hellhole into the Square of the Inquisition, the outside light nearly blinds me. I squeeze shut my eyes, and Gothic arches burn neon red against my lids. I trip on the last stair, my eyes fly open, and I see the gold-encrusted arches of the jail entry. I see the painting of Christ upon his cross. I see marble in three tones stretched high to the vaulted ceiling. Gold scepters, gold baby Jesus, gold gold gold. And outside, blood blood blood.

The guards lift me and fling me into the Square of the Inquisition. All around me, people scream and laugh at me, at the nails that hold my black black dress to my black black body.

The sun blazes down, and sweat courses down my back. Heat prickles my breasts.

They throw Eliseo to the dirt next to me. He scrabbles up, points his *bandero* at me, and says, *"Ph'nglui mglw'nafh Cthulhu R'lyeh wgah'nagl fhtagn."*

These are the words that bring forth the best in me, the worst in me.

This time, I do what Eliseo thinks he wants.

The ancient words come easily to my lips. They puff out, symbols of strange geometries that no man knows. They encircle Eliseo. They mingle, then bind and form nails that plunge into him, and they pierce his body as the nails pierce mine. They drill arches over his eyes. Drill a mustache where moments ago, there was none. Drill a beard.

I have never reacted this strongly to Eliseo; but then, he has never uttered the ultimate words. I suppose he never felt he needed them before now. His usual incantations and rituals were cut short this time. He must fear that this time, he might die.

"*Converso! Converso!*" They're chanting now, these people of the Lord. It is a crime punishable by death to convert to their religion, yet it is also an equal crime not to convert. Everything is a crime to these people. Children huddle closer to their mothers. Men's faces, all red, howl for Eliseo's blood.

The soldiers hold them back. A scuffle to my right, and a soldier's arm swings up, then down, and I do not even hear the screams of the dying man who tried to break into the center of the Square. The crowd recedes like a giant wave sucked to sea. A murmur swells, and the bishop stands, arms out, beseeching them all to grow quiet.

Eliseo's eyes do not seem to focus on much of anything. He is on his feet, swaying as if to a rhythm nobody hears. His limbs tremble. I feel the beat of his heart. It ripples through the air, through *my* air, and I feel Eliseo and his confusion. He turns, totters, stares down at me, still on the dirt. His eyes widen. He *knows*. Then his eyes go blank again.

I scrabble to my feet, back away from him as the bishop says, "Let all who are here witness the defeat of those who will not accept Catholicism, the one pure religion, as their own. Let all who are here witness the defeat of this *converso* and his"—a pause, and the gnarled old man turns to me and spits—"concubine."

I almost laugh. I am no concubine. But the *people* laugh, not at the bishop, but rather at me and Elisio with the nails driven into our flesh. I hear the muttering all around the Square: *converso,* torture, execution, death, and ha ha ha, won't this be grand?

I shift into the center of the Square, swivel, and stare at them all. A thousand people who hate others. A thousand people who hate themselves. They are crammed along the continuous balcony on all four sides of the Square. They are crammed beneath the buttresses of the jail entrance and the Gothic arches that hold up the balcony. These are ugly people, as ugly as the guards in the jail, as ugly as the Inquisitors and their Executioners.

Do they not know that, once we are gone, they will be next? Can they not see it? For man knows no end to hate and cruelty.

Square of the Inquisition

Is it possible that things will change in the next century? I think not. Man always has a reason to kill.

The crowd parts by the *Entre Carceles,* the street between the jails, and here comes the bull, a big brute, this one, older than most and much heavier. Its hide is ripped already, swords and picks dangling from bloody holes on its flanks. They have injured the bull to make it angry, more ferocious, and more dangerous to Eliseo.

I float back into the air. I leave the flesh sack of Martina and all the nails in the dust. The crowd gasps and points at Martina's corpselike husk, dry and without blood. For a moment, the husk distracts Eliseo, and the bull rushes at him. Startled, he dashes to the right, narrowly escaping death. He whirls, his arm jerks up, then plunges down, and his *bandero* stabs the bull in its left flank. The animal's eyes go red. It stomps, and dust rises and mingles with me, and I taste death in that dust. Death for the bull? Death for Eliseo?

"*Q'weerilpuman-kwat-an-q'ulsi'kattum u q'ulsi kattum.*" The words flare in gold above the towering cathedral-like jail. The words burn into the arms and legs and faces of the crowd, and everywhere people cringe, slap hands on faces, shriek in pain. Black black black. Blood blood blood. These two words bang inside and against me, an internal mantra.

Short and small, Eliseo looks like a young boy. It is hard to believe he has already lost a family. It is hard to believe such a tiny creature can stab and hurt something as large and powerful as this bull, but Eliseo does: he plunges the second, and now the third *bandero,* into the upper flanks of the beast.

Three *banderos* beribboned with red and blue cloth wobble on the bull. Blood pours down the animal's hide. Front legs paw the dust, back legs buck. Whirling—the bull is whirling—and dust heaves up in a might wave and mixes with me, and the bull's anger permeates my very cells.

Eliseo is one of my faithful. He knows the words that free me. I feel no compassion for him, no loyalty in return. This is our nature, his and mine.

If I had a spine, it would tingle.

I reach for Eliseo with a thousand tendrils, I reach...

I am whisper-thin, gossamer, colorless to those around me, I wrap myself around him and squeeze. His limbs jerk, he tries to clutch his throat but cannot raise his arms. I squeeze harder. His face grows dark, then pale. His eyes bulge, I see the veins in them, and now there is blood, only blood, in those eyes, with black black black in their centers.

His heart contracts. It is beating too quickly. Several thousand pounds of beast rut the ground, exploding it into dust and exposing raw the underlying structures of the Square: rocks long and hard like ribs, skeletons from all the Jews and Moors and Catholics whom the bishop has condemned.

Eliseo writhes in my grasp, the breath squeezed from his lungs. The bull bellows as he nears us, now yards away, now a few feet away.

I loosen my grip and caress Eliseo. I soothe him. *It won't hurt, not for long, don't worry,* I tell him, but his eyes are almost shot, glazed and flat, unseeing, and I know he cannot hear me. His fist eases, and the razor tip of a *bandero* grazes me then drops to the heaps of bones and rock.

I hug Eliseo, and as I smell the meat-rot breath of the bull, I race from its path and thunder like a storm across the Square.

The bishop and his priests leap to their feet. The guards race after the bull, trying to bring it down with swords and clubs. Pummeled, beaten, stabbed, the bull totters, then drops. Dirt and bone bits billow, and when they settle, the bull lies in its death throes, a twitching mass of black hide coated in blood.

They bring the hooks. They drag the carcass from the Square. Fat jiggles. The bones are cracked at odd angles.

Within me, part of me, is Eliseo's torso, and what he does not know cannot hurt him.

But then it dawns on me. He must know. This is why he uttered the special incantation, the one reserved for times like these. This is why he never uttered the incantation before now. He was not ready. Today, he knew that for him, there would be no tomorrow. Today, he was ready for me.

All I see are his lips, a gash of red, and his face, a broken smear of mottled flesh as if the Inquisitors have

Square of the Inquisition

beaten him close to death. But they have not touched him, and they never will.

Fuck them all.

Eliseo is mine.

The matadors before Eliseo drew strength from my broken flesh but cared nothing about the real me. The nails in my body excited them. The rapes excited them. My pain excited them.

Eliseo is different. He is a true believer of those of us who dwelt before time, have always been here, and will remain here—like the roaches—long after the last human dies.

Eliseo uttered the words that released me from the flesh and returned me to my true state.

I bring him into the fold, deep within, where hatred of humanity burns worse than the pain. I give Eliseo the only form of salvation I know. One with me and all the Old Ones. I release him from the flesh.

As Eliseo's eyes shift from black to empty, I think I see a smile play across his twisted lips.

The Rime of the Cosmic Mariner

John Shirley

About, about, in reel and rout
The death- ires danced at night;
The water, like a witch's oils,
Burnt green, and blue and white.

—The Rime of the Ancient Mariner

Highgate
November 17, 1833

To Mr. Thomas Penson De Quincey
Glasgow, Scotland

My dear De Quincey!

I write to you in a curiously Arctic fever, cold and febrile at once, and on a cryptic mission of mercy. I would save you from the ponderous but imponderable darkness, indeed the cosmic chaos that descends upon me.

I can almost hear you laughing, my former friend, but this is no hyperbole and certainly no jest. You will, I trust, forgive this presumption after some years of silence, and forgive, too, my shaky hand, my lines as uncertain as rain patterns in sand—and doubtless as unwanted as an icy rain upon a walking tour. *Pace tua,* De Quincey, I am not insensible to our differences of civic philosophy; marching through the decades you have become the Tory's very own Tory, and at this remove it may be you think me a secret Jacobin, a Guy Fawkes reborn, despite the moderation I have shewn these many years since my boyish days of planning

Shirley

American Utopias. I have moderated my views considerably; but even so, we would strike sparks at disputation over a bowl of punch, I'm sure, within minutes after the nostalgic niceties concluded.

Despite our widening political divide, De Quincey, we yet have much in common: a love of the streaming effusion of language, the surge of contention like a river driven upon a boulder, the flow bifurcated by obstacle—by objection.

We are like brothers who are doomed to disagree, but brothers we are, in our tragic affiliation with opium. On our first meeting, in your youth, when you shewed such enthusiasm for my poetry, the poppy's poison was much upon my mind. I sought day by day to escape laudanum's warm embrace; but, more seductive than Calypso or Circe, opium would not let me go—not for long. Hence I spoke of it too freely, complaining to you quite tiresomely of the opium eater's burden of costiveness, of the erosion of the foundations of love, the sickness of withdrawal, certainly—but also I held forth about opium's revelatory powers. You were quite young, scarcely twenty and two! And it may be you absorbed the report of laudanum's good and shed the greater evidence of its evil; perhaps I tilted you toward opium. Much later I certainly read your *Confessions of an English Opium-Eater:* No man better comprehends the pleasures and pains of laudanum than you. But, quite beyond its known evils, opium leaves a man like you and I vulnerable to something cosmically ruinous . . .

In veritate, amicus, I have reason to believe you might be in danger of succumbing to something more than opium. You may find ourself visited by a Particular Something that intrudes itself into a narcotic dream; on occasion, it stops by in person, appearing to be Man. Once, in 1804, I glimpsed it while gazing raptly into the crater of Mt. Etna. It was as if the bottom dropped away from the crater; as if of a sudden its smoky depths plumbed infinity, passing through the whole earthly sphere; and for a few moments it shewed me an unspeakable heavenly oddity crouching within a cluster of stars visible from the unnatural opening on the other side of the Earth. Then, it was gone; the infinite shaft snapped shut. But I had seen the Thing That Waits, and it had seen me.

The Rime of the Cosmic Mariner

Now, this Thing has an agent, a watcher; a servant, which appears to us as a large bird of no known species. It is the blacker, the *bloodier* albatross. It is the messenger, the deed-doer, of Nyarlathotep, arriving from a very great distance; it flaps wings broader even than the span of a great albatross. O, perhaps it's more like a gigantic raven than an albatross, yet it's not like an earthly bird at all, in truth. It has no true beak—and no true color. Ever and again it's quite black; yet it ventures to shift, as the light does, and it becomes dark sea green; and yet again it becomes dark purple, or a sanguinary crimson. It flies where no bird should be able to fly, pressing its wings against the fabric of space, instead of the air; it arrives upon the benumbed Earth, gazing down to consider, and then it soars away. But when the messenger has parted from the likes of thee and me, it is only biding its time.

Let us trek onward, De Quincey, and, I fear, downward . . .

It began when I met Al-Azizi. It was Carter, *Renwald* Carter, an importer of fine goods from the Levant and descendent of the magician Sir Randolph Carter, who introduced me to the curiously articulate and elegant Monsieur Al-Azizi.

Carter sent me a hasty note from his hotel; in sum, he would be honoured to introduce to me a wealthy admirer, one "M. Al-Azizi" who was drawn to my poetry, especially the epic verses. Al-Azizi, he said, was not a Mussulman, despite his Levantine heritage. Carter was perhaps sensible that, as I sink toward my own last judgment, my former deism becomes ever more Christian.

I welcomed Carter's missive. A wealthy admirer of my poetic amusements? I hastened to affirm he meeting for tea.

When Carter and his exotic companion arrived at Number 3, The Grove, Highgate, ushered in by our housekeeper Bethesda, I was, for a rarity, out of my dressing gown; I was almost splendid in red silk smoking jacket, matching trousers, and my eternal down-at-heel slippers. I had even made shift to scrape my face of superfluous foliage, for I had hope of a new patron—a final patron, I suspected, as my health has for a time been in leisurely but steady decline.

Clutching his hat, looking appraisingly at the Persian

carpet in the drawing room, and then at me, Carter said, "Ah—Coleridge. I have brought you a living marvel. May I present Monsieur Feruz Al-Azizi, of Paris and Cairo."

I gave my bow and Al-Azizi returned it stiffly, the straight line of his lips flickering with the most transient of smiles. Tall and gaunt and dark, he wore a pristine white suit, a red necktie, a red felt fez; even without the elongation of the fez, he was at least a foot taller than Carter. He had a jet-black mustache, like a line on aged foolscap, and once I thought it writhed quite apart from the working of his face. I assumed this was a product of the laudanum I had just taken as a restorative—the measured dose left to me by Dr. Gillman.

"Dr. Gillman is not at home?" Carter asked, looking around the drawing room, licking his thick lips.

"My host is with his patients," I said. I might have said "his other patients"—Dr. Gillman has taken it upon himself, these many years, to house me, to physic me, to dose me as he sees fit. He is a man of great patience.

I glanced at Al-Azizi—and felt caught, for a moment, in the gaze of his heavy-lidded, deep-black eyes, which seemed to regard me with a ravenous fixity.

I looked quickly back at Carter, marking that my old acquaintance had changed since I'd seen him last: his face was now blotchy, his lips bluish, his eyes yellow and flickering; he as h aphazardly u nshaven, a nd h is stubby fingers clasped ver his stained weskit in what appeared a failed effort to restrain their trembling.

Carter's gaze darted about the small sitting room. "So—we are in essence quite alone here? I have no wish to be unsociable but—Monsieur Al-Azizi prefers . . . a small party."

"We are alone but for the housekeeper. She keeps discreetly to the pantry."

I noticed for the first time that Al-Azizi carried a large bag of crocodilian leather, rather like a physician's satchel; I could have sworn he had not the bag when he first came in.

"Please sit down, gentlemen," I said, eyeing the bag. They sat in Gillman's settee across from my armchair. Al-Azizi stroked the settee's leather arm with a long-fingered hand. "What an exquisite piece of furniture," he said. "The skin of a fine animal—as comfortable as the arms of a beautiful woman." His accent was both Egyptian and French, to my ear, his voice by turns rumblingly low-pitched and intermittently high, and tremulous as if keeping laughter on a leash.

"Ah, yes," I said, "it is one of the original pieces designed by the Earl of Chesterton; it has resided for some time with Dr. Gillman's family."

My eyes returned to the black crocodilian bag on the Egyptian's lap, as Al-Azizi exclaimed, chuckling, "Why, it is my old friend George!" I thought at first he meant the crocodile, but then he gestured at the oval portrait of King George III on the wall to my right. "How well I remember our talks. George and I went to the roof and gazed upon the stars together—and they gazed upon us!"

"Did you, indeed?" I asked, smiling indulgently. "What year was your interview with the late king?"

"Why, it was 1788, I believe, on a previous trip to your jewel-like isle. Yes!" He flashed grey teeth in a smile that came and went like the tail of a Nile fish, surfacing and gone.

Carter visibly grimaced, and I raised my eyebrows. Of course this putative interview with the King would have been *forty-five years ago*, De Quincey—but this fellow looked no older than his middle thirties! Was it, I wondered, some dreamy vanity on his part, imagining an interlude with George III?

"Was it 1788, for a fact? Well! The very year His Majesty first succumbed to the... to his malaise." I suppose I could have said *madness,* as he is long gone, but I am rooted in an earlier era of delicacy—when I am not in my cups.

"Al-Azizi," Carter began hoarsely. "Perhaps this is not the time. I had hoped—"

His gaze still upon me, Al-Azizi raised a hand with the suddenness of a dagger raised to strike, and Carter fell silent, his sentence severed.

"So few men can survive gazing upon the stars with unveiled eyes," said Al-Azizi, shrugging. "Your King—sadly he could not bear it. But..." He put his hands on the clasp of his bag. "But you, sir! When I consider the letter you wrote to your *other* Sara, Sara Hutchinson, in 1802, Coleridge! Surely *you* would be capable of gazing past the veil and coming away whole!"

Shirley

I fairly gaped at the man. "Letter, sir? 1802?"

"Why, yes." He closed his eyes a moment—how like parchment the lids of his eyes! He seemed to read out the words from some inner scroll. *"'All this long Eve, so balmy and serene, Have I been gazing on the western Sky and its peculiar Tint of Yellow Green—And still I gaze, and with how blank an eye! And those thin Clouds above, in flakes and bars, That give away their Motion to the Stars; Those Stars, that glide behind them, or between, Now sparkling, now bedimm'd, but always seen . . .'"* He opened his eyes—yet his eyes seemed almost closed to the world, so empty were they of fellow-feeling. "Yes? Do you recall?"

I cleared my throat. "That letter—why, yes. That passage later became part of an ode. I believe I was on the pinnacle of a tor when I first . . . But Monsieur Al-Azizi, has the lady's family given over my letters to her? I don't recall their . . . that is. . ."

"Oh, they're written in the Akashic Record, as some call it, with all else, Mr. Coleridge!" he crowed, amused. "I looked them up!"

"He is a marvel indeed, as you said, Carter," I murmured. "However, I—"

That is when Al-Azizi opened his crocodilian bag, a flash of his hands opening it so quickly I thought of a reptile opening its mouth to snap at prey before it could escape. "Here, sir," he said, reaching into the bag, "I have three scientific instruments you will not have seen before, I wager."

He took up a device with his right hand, the instrument resembling a cut-glass doorknob but asymmetrically festooned with brass spikes—and I noticed, for the first time, the ring upon that hand, its large tablet-shaped face of carnelian engraved with the image of a double-headed crystal growing out of a snarl of serpentine shapes. I was distracted from the ring when he snatched the end table, on which stood the Argand lamp, nearly rocking the lamp onto the floor. I made to catch it, but the lamp settled down as he set the table in front of him and placed the instruments on in it the small pool of lamplight. There was the spiked, crystalline knob; beside the festooned crystal was something like a pair of spectacles made of twists of wire, possibly copper, but without lenses. The third instrument was in the shape of a serpentine figure of some silvery alloy; the figure was rather like the engraving on his ring. The instrument stood on one of its coils, its head pointed at the ceiling. Looking closely I saw that it was not precisely a serpent, for its head was eyeless and it seemed to have feathers instead of scales.

"This one," I said, indicating the coiled serpentine instrument, "more resembles jewelry than a scientific instrument. I fancy I have seen something of the sort on a lady's arm, by way of a bracelet."

"Oh, but no lady could long bear to wear this as a bracelet, Coleridge—and no bracelet will do this!" Al-Azizi reached out and carefully pinched the serpentine figure just under its jaws—and immediately the light in the room became a thick luminous liquid, as if amber had melted. The liquid light swirled about us, the whirlpool centering on the serpentine instrument, and I saw, with gathering trepidation, the light was sinking away *into* the coil, as if the serpent were consuming it. At the ceiling and corners, darkness increased, itself a liquid, something heavier than light forcing it into the genii's bottle of the serpentine instrument. The lamp flickered and dimmed. Al-Azizi's eyes had quite vanished away; there was only a shifting blackness in the sockets, as in a skull seen by the feeble light of a taper.

Oddly enough, Carter had his own eyes covered by his trembling hands.

I felt a piercing coldness growing upon my back. I turned and saw the thick shadow increasing behind me, as if the suctioned light took all warmth and hope with it, and a vortex of black despair was rushing upon me.

"Al-Azizi!" I called out, turning to him with what must have been a shameful desperation—the dark pools of his eye sockets swirling with that same darkness as the living opacity gathering behind me. "Please . . . do reverse the phenomenon!"

Al-Azizi shrugged innocently. "Ah! If you like, Coleridge!"

He once more pinched the instrument, his fingertips pressing with practiced exactitude, and light disgorged from the instruments, spiraling up from the serpent's mouth; the shadows wavered furiously a moment, like a flight of crows flapping away, and then the light in the room was restored.

Only a curious smell lingered, like stale frankincense mixed with the mineral reek of a deep, watery cavern. My feet seemed clammy in my shoes as if I'd got them wet.

And lingering, too, was that darkness pooling in the Egyptian's eyes. Then he leaned back a little, and I could see his eyes once more. He smiled thinly. "Mr. Coleridge—are you quite well? You look pale, sir. And I believe you are shivering."

I made myself straighten up and smile. "That was an impressive... *illusion,* sir. Something in the way of a magic lantern, perhaps." I licked my lips and wished I might slip off to my room for a brandy. Gillman keeps none in the drawing room. "How you managed it I am quite unsure."

"Illusion!" murmured Carter, rubbing his knees with his hands. "Would that it were so."

Al-Azizi turned a sharp look at Carter, who instantly compressed his lips and said nothing more. I was amazed at Al-Azizi's authority over him. Who had brought *whom* here?

I rubbed my hands together to warm them, wishing that we might have some more coal put in the basement furnace. I was about to call for the Bethesda when Al-Azizi picked up the brass-thorned crystal, tapped three of the spines in a distinct pattern, and whispered, "Listen!"

I heard nothing but Carter's heavy breathing. I leaned a little closer, and then . . . surely those were voices? They were coming thinly from the crystal. A man's voice wheedled, "Hullo, Freddie, old boy, how about spotting me a fiver! Here now, cully, I *needs* it!" Then a little girl said, "If Papa does not come home again tonight, we shall have to steal the cheese crusts from the kitchen rubbish again, and we are not to go into that part of the house with the better people!"

"Good Lord," I said. "It is like a telescope for sounds! They must be speaking from the street below the hill!"

"They are rather more distant than that," said Al-Azizi.

Then I heard another voice, this one speaking in a foreign tongue. At first I thought it a language obscure to me, like Mongolian; but after a moment I supposed the chirping, clicking, almost insectile sound might not be a human dialect at all. Yet it seemed to be speaking in something like sentences. It set my teeth on edge, I can tell you, De Quincey.

I was about to ask him to put the instruments away when the door opened and Bethesda came in, carrying the tea tray.

Al-Azizi put the instruments back into the bag, his motions quick and neat, and closed it with a snap. His voice was a steely monotone as he said, "I was given to understand we would not be interrupted."

"I'm sure it will be but the interruption of a moment!" Carter assured him.

Bethesda O'Neill was, perhaps *is,* a full bosomed woman of thirty and four, with frowsy brown hair, a pert nose, thick ankles, and powerful arms; she wore a white servant's bonnet, a black dress, and a white apron, and she bustled into the room in her prim, officious fashion, carrying a tray to the small tea table behind my chair. "Lor', but there's a chill on this room. Will the gentlemen take tea here, sir?"

"That will do very well, Beth," I said." Will you see to the furnace? I will pour the tea."

"The furnace? Why, it has been burning coal by the ton all this day, sir. Are your registers not open? But they are! I shall have a look."

She turned to go—and stopped dead, staring at Al-Azizi. I supposed at first she was affrighted of this swarthy foreigner. But she had the look of a rabbit enrapt by the eyes of a snake. She opened her mouth as if to speak, but said nothing, merely worrying at her apron with her fingers.

"Beth? This is Mr. Al-Azizi, my guest."
"We met at the door," Al-Azizi said smoothly. "Beth . . . yes. Bethesda. She escorted us within."

"Yes. But was it *him* . . . ?" Beth breathed, as if speaking only to herself. "Was it *this* one then?"

Al-Azizi continued to look at her. Then he waved his hand dismissively, and she hurried, almost running, out of the room. She slammed the door in going.

I was puzzled. Al-Azizi had alarmed her overmuch, considering their harmless encounter—she had not seen the trick with the swirling light.

However, I myself had reason to be alarmed. I was thinking to myself that perhaps, after all, I should not like him to be my patron; that I would like him to take his leave. But I did not seem to have the inner strength to demand his departure. It was not fear of coarseness that held me back; it was something else I can only describe as a failure of my will.

"I could use some tea," I said, my own voice sounding hoarse in my ears. Somehow I knew that Al-Azizi would not choose to sit at the tea table. I know not how this knowledge came to me.

I went to the table and poured a cup, returned, and offered it first to Al-Azizi. He merely shook his head, gazing up at me. I avoided his eyes. I offered it to Carter. He took the cup gratefully.

"Something stronger would not go amiss, as well," Carter said.

"No," said Al-Azizi, his voice calm but firm.

"No, quite right, too early," said Carter hurriedly, sipping the tea.

I buttered Carter two biscuits, put them on a plate, and set it on the lamp table, but he ignored them.

I sat with a couple of biscuits and my tea, and had hardly begun when Al-Azizi said, "You have a stair that leads to the roof."

It was not a question.

"Yes," I said. "Dr. Gillman has an interest in meteorology."

"Let us repair to the roof. I have something to shew you—the very thing I came to lay before you."

I put my cup carefully upon its saucer. "You have shewn me a great deal, sir, quite a sufficiency for one afternoon. I do not wish to presume upon your generosity."

Then—I cannot recall, precisely, De Quincey, how it came to be that we removed from the drawing room to the roof.

I have a dim memory of walking out the back door, with Al-Azizi ahead and Carter behind, and the creaking of the spiralling iron staircase under my foot as we ascended three storeys from the garden to the step between the gables, onto the copper rooftop terrace, a wide flat place between sloping pantiles where the doctor makes his observations.

My next clear recollection is of holding the twisted-wire spectacles. Al-Azizi was standing before me, with the crocodilian bag gaping open in his bony hands. It was a chill, windless afternoon, the indefinite fog a kind of ever-changing lacework around us. The cups of the weather indicator above us did not turn at all.

"But only put them on," Al-Azizi said, "and the veil you wear all unknowing will be at last lifted; the blindfold will be tugged away from your eyes. You will see the stars."

"First, sir," I said, looking around as if I'd awakened here, "allow me to observe that it is not yet nighttime. The day is a trifle befogged and, though the dusk arrives, no stars are visible. And second, sir, seeing stars is in itself unremarkable. True, they may be seen more vividly with a telescope—yet that is often done . . ."

"I could shew you stars as you have never seen them," said Al-Azizi smugly; "but to be perfectly clear, I plan to reveal a planetary object largely unknown to astronomers. If they see it, upon occasion, it appears as star-like from Earth, just as Mars seems a star until gazed upon with a telescope. But you will see this Outer World more vividly than any man ever saw Mars—if you so choose! Of your own free will, place the instrument over your eyes—and thus remove the veil. Lift the blindfolds that perpetually dim your sight, Coleridge!"

It was partly curiosity, De Quincey, that led to my acquiescence. And I suspected he had beguiled me with illusions. As there were no lenses in the spectacles, I thus reasoned that in all probability their effect was to be sheer power of suggestion, mayhap enhanced by mesmerism. A suspicion had been growing upon me that the evident miracle I had perceived in the drawing room was the result of some form of hypnotism, combined with optical illusion. I thought my will strong—bending only to laudanum. Now forewarned, I intended to confront him with his own charlatanry.

I boldly secured the instrument over my eyes, just as a man slips on a pair of spectacles. I saw nothing but what I had seen before, truncated by the frames.

"Now, sir," said Al-Azizi, "we shall make all dark so that the stars present themselves."

I feared the coiling instrument and was about to object, but he quickly placed it upon the ground, activating it as he did so, and the light of the late afternoon began to thicken and spiral above us, compressing, leaving shadow as it declined.

In a moment, darkness had collected thickly above us,

and the light of the day was pushed rudely aside. Gazing upward, I saw the stars shining within a circle of darkness directly overhead; it was as if they were seen from deep down a pit, a shaft plumbed into the Earth, much as I had imagined on Aetna.

The celestial array glittered with more presence of that unique starry blue-white than I had ever beheld before. But apart from that striking fulsomeness, they seemed as usual—a miracle of nature, no more.

Then Al-Azizi reached up and touched the spectacles with a forefinger, near my left temple.

Sparks flew, and arcs of electricity flashed across my vision, close to my eyes. Fearing to be blinded, I cried out and would have taken them off—but I also feared to touch them. Yet they were touching me . . .

Electricity flashed across the empty spaces over my eyes, as if its blue and yellow coursing had become the energetic lenses of the spectacles.

Then it cleared—and the veil was lifted.

A star thrust itself at me, as if hurtling meteorically toward us. It advanced with such malevolent determination that I wanted to throw myself aside—but suddenly it stopped partway, and simply whirled in place. The shining planetoid—for so it was, churning with glowing gases—was so bright I could scarcely bear the sight.

The planet's whirling slowed, then ceased, and a black spot appeared on its face. This spot swelled and grew, consuming most of the shining planetoid, until all that was left was a kind of corona, and then something that cannot be described as *a shape* appeared within the coruscating circle. The apparition was a writhing *thought* made visual—a thought of annihilation, a thought of conscious mockery of all faith, a derision of all order; yet it had something of organism at its very centre. It reached out . . . And a horrible fascination took hold of me. I was shaking with fear, and yet I wanted to *know*. . .

"Behold Azathoth," Al-Azzizi intoned. "Behold he who awaits when I have done with you, Coleridge! With your own free will have you gazed upon this majesty. Now—"

"No!" someone shouted.

It was Carter. A moment later I felt his spongy, pudgy

hand slap my face—and the spectacles were knocked away.

Freed from the vision, if that is what it was, I was dizzy, nauseated, and my head throbbed. I saw that someone, probably Carter, had kicked over the serpentine instrument as well, and the dull late afternoon light was assaultive to my burning eyes in that moment.

Blinking, I turned, and saw that Al-Azizi, the crocodilian bag clutched in his hands, was stalking angrily toward Renwald Carter, who was backing away step by hesitant step toward the edge of the roof. He was about to pitch over backwards, off the roof to his death.

"You, sir! Al-Azizi!" I roared, putting all my will and volume into it. "*Stop!*"

Al-Azizi turned toward me, his face an icy mask of fury.

As if released from some unseen hold, Carter blinked and looked around, then turned and rushed to the stairs, clattering down them toward the garden. "I'm sorry, Coleridge!" he shouted as he went. "I'm sorry!"

Al-Azizi walked toward me—and seemed to come to some kind of decision. A most unpleasant smile appeared under his mustache. "Better to have one so choice as *you*, Coleridge, at a time of my own choosing. I have learned much about you today. Next time you will have no recourse. I will send my messenger to fetch you from your body. It matters not where you go. Verily, I can count on you to come to *me*. You hovered close to me many times, in years past, in what you supposed were dreams . . ."

Keeping his eyes upon me, he opened the crocodilian bag. I heard a hissing sound, and then he closed the bag and turned away. In a moment he had gone to the spiral stairs and descended them with no sound at all.

I looked at the rooftop. The Egyptian's instruments were gone. I have no doubt he had somehow gathered them into his bag.

My knees gave way, and I sank down to the cold metal roof. I found I was panting and close to weeping, trying to take it all in. The thing I had seen coming at me from the planetoid. . . another illusion?

But De Quincey, it was no illusion. You cannot look upon that entity and not recognize the dreadful thing for what it is.

Shirley

I wish I had looked away. Carter saved me, in a moment of conscience—which can sometimes set a man free. I wonder what price he has paid for knocking those spectacles aside.

I wish I could say I removed those spectacles myself, De Quincey. I could not have done so, I fear, to my shame. Scientific knowledge is good; but I was nigh surrendering to a predatory alien mind, to an embrace of all chaos and a lust for entropy itself—and *that,* my old, disaffected friend, has not scientific objectivity. It is an insight of metaphysics alone.

Suddenly, kneeling there, I realized that I owed Carter a great debt. I forced myself to my feet and tottered to the stairs, hoping to find him, to draw him away from Al-Azizi. To pay the debt in kind.

I went with difficulty down the slippery iron stairs and stumbled through the garden. I saw that the garden gate was open to the lane.

I rushed to it, and through—and to my horror I saw not only Carter, trailing after Al-Azizi, but also Bethesda! The housekeeper was walking along without coat, or handbag, quite methodically following along after the Egyptian.

"Bethesda!" I shouted. "Come back!"
She did not respond, not a twitch.
"Carter!" I shouted. "Wait!"
Carter looked back—imploringly. He desperately wanted to come away from Al-Azizi. But he was drawn inexorably away. They were striding up into the fog, becoming less and less real with each step as the haze, coal smoke perfectly wedded with mist, strove to erase them.

My hands were cold, and so was my heart. But I gathered my courage and started after them. I took a score of steps, beginning to run—then saw a coach waiting for them, just under the gas lamp.

"Stop!" I called, as loudly as I might. "Bring her back, both of you—come back! Coachman, hold!" I stumbled on, almost falling on the slick cobbles.

I arrived in time to see the coach clatter away, taking Al-Azizi, Carter, and Bethesda with it.

I stood there for a minute, perhaps two, dazed and

The Rime of the Cosmic Mariner

uncertain. At last I walked slowly back to the house.

Soon after Dr. Gillman came home for dinner, I tried to tell him what had happened; but he thought me addled by a delirium tremens, by delusion due to insufficiency of my habitual dose—for he was late in providing it. Wearily, he unlocked the medical cabinet and poured me twice my usual dosage. As for Bethesda, he supposed she had merely taken up with another "ruffian," as he put it. She had a weakness for sailors.

I thought to explain all to him on the morrow, as he was greatly fatigued and I could not fathom a means to convince him. I bowed, and went to my room with my double dose.

There I sank into a chair and looked dully around at the books covering every wall, their titles unreadable in the dim light of the lamp as if they were cryptic volumes seen in a dream. Before me on my little rosewood writing table lay pen, ink, and paper. I purposed then to write down the events of the day.

I reached for the laudanum before the pen and ink—and found I was reluctant to take the dose. As you know, De Quincey, this reluctance is an untoward turn of events with STC.

Why should I be afraid of something so familiar—so comforting?

The smell of the opiated brandy at last drew me to taking a sip, and then another. Soon it was all down. The increased dose induced me to nod in my chair.

A waking dream settled upon me. I saw a man sleeping in his bed—a man I knew. Then, standing beside the man, I looked through the dusty window and beheld the stars.

One of the celestial orbs rushed toward the window—and a spot appeared on the sphere. But this time the spot became a great black bird that soared toward me, its enormous wings ever so slowly flapping, each flap making the sound of a cracking whip. The messenger! It had not a beak—it had the mouth of a man. It spake!

Nyarlathotep, it said. *He calls you, Coleridge. Come!* And the bird spake again, quite clearly. *Nyarlathotep. He calls you.*

The giant bird, like a roc with a grin, rushed toward

Shirley

me—I struggled away from it, crying, "No!"

The vision suddenly flew asunder.

I sat up, sweating, and shook off the remnants of the dream. But it tried to reassert itself. Again—the bird was diving at me, coalescing from the shadows of the room.

I threw off the bedclothes, ran to the window, flung the sash wide, and breathed in great draughts of cold air. I refused to close the window till the vision had passed.

But the memory will not pass. I saw something more in that dream. That man in the bed—it *was you*, De Quincey—sleeping, doubtless in an opiated slumber. I am afraid that was an omen. He comes for you next!

And what of me? He said, *Verily, I can count on you—to come to me.*

Who is he I wonder? Who in actuality is Al-Azizi? The messenger told me the true name of the "Egyptian"—and I have verified it, of late, as I pore through certain tomes so old they fall apart at my touch.

He is *Nyarlathotep*. He appears in many guises, as a man. But he is not of humanity, De Quincey.

It is a man's mind he wants, you see. He feeds on madness; he profits by the madness he induces in men. A man he drives mad becomes his slave—his inwardly gibbering servant—and eventually what remains is fed to the *thing* I saw residing, for now, within that unknown planet on the far edge of our solar system.

And we give him a doorway to our minds, De Quincey, when we surrender fully to opium. In opiated dreams we go to his realm, you see. And once you have entered his realm, he knows forever where you are.

He has gone to ground, now that I have discovered him. But, in due course, he will find us both—in the astral realm. For we have journeyed there, like children wandering in a forest, often enough. If you do not suffer the pangs of setting opium aside—a terrible tribulation, I know—you will enter his world a step, and two steps, and then three, and he will send his messenger to bring you the rest of the way.

If you and I do not turn aside from the drug, then that predatory enormity, the black, beakless bird, will come to each of us crying its master's name. *Nyarlathotep!*

He has marked you, De Quincey. And if you do not

turn away from the drug, as I struggle to do once more—he will claim you.

Every day I try not to take the infernal concoction—in moments of weakness I take a drop or two, but so little I am scarcely affected. This regimen cannot last, I fear. Even now I feel laudanum calling.

There is now no locating Al-Azizi—I have hired men to find him, along with Carter and Bethesda, and the searchers have failed utterly. It cannot be done.

But I know that Nyarlathotep will find me again, when I open the door of my mind to him.

I pray I die before I go to his realm . . . for there is another, far better realm waiting for me, if only I have the strength to get there.

Your Devoted Servant,

Samuel Taylor Coleridge

A Yuletide Carol

Mollie L. Burleson

Stave I

The Beginning of It

Marley was dead, to begin with. There is no doubt about that. Scrooge signed the register of his burial but was not so cut up by the event that he failed to be an excellent man of business the day of the funeral. There was no doubt of Marley's passing. Everyone has to be convinced of that occurrence or this tale could never be told.

Scrooge had left the sign to the shop as it had been for years; the name Marley still appeared on it. For some strange reason, Scrooge was unable to paint it out. Something prevented him from doing so.

Old Ebenezer Scrooge had never changed. He was tight-fisted as ever and grew more so as the years passed, caring nothing for people's opinion of him. He tried to follow in Marley's path and exceeded his fondest wish—to make even more money.

This one night, Christmas Eve to be exact, found Scrooge shut up in his business chambers, squeezing out yet more money from his debtors. The night was cold and dank, fog enveloped the court, and Scrooge could barely see the shadowy forms passing back and forth.

Cratchit, his clerk, sat at his desk, fingers cold and barely able to write. He longed for more coal to put upon the fire, but knew that his employer would not countenance the deed, so he bundled up as best he could, shivered, and picked up his pen.

Scrooge's nephew Fred dropped by to wish him greetings of the season, but the old miser made short work of him and of the do-gooders who came to collect money for the poor. These refusals of charity and goodwill gave Scrooge a better opinion of himself, and he set about his work in a more agreeable humor.

The hour arrived that Scrooge had designated for closing up the shop, and he grudgingly agreed that Cratchit would have the next day off. After his clerk left, Scrooge blew out the candles, locked the door, and set off to eat his lonesome dinner as was his wont.

The night was cold and dark and raw with a hint of the sea in the air. Snow lay upon the ground and crackled as Scrooge's footsteps turned toward his dwelling-place and bed.

When he reached his home and was beginning to unlock the door, Scrooge saw in the knocker. . . not a knocker but Marley's face! The face had a dismal light about it like a rotten codfish behind a fishmonger's.

It *was* Marley's face, and yet there was something different about it. Something that was *not* Marley.

But the vision faded and everything was as it should be. Scrooge made his way up the cavernous stairs, trimming his candle as he went.

He checked the apartment. Everything was as usual. No one under the bed, no one in the closet. Scrooge was content with his search. All was quite normal except for the feeling of foreboding as he gazed at the dark corners, which seemed to be darker and more encompassing than they ought to be.

He sat down in his chair, eating some leftover gruel that was keeping warm near the very low fire. Nothing on such a night, this fire. He saw the fireplace's tiles reflected in the glow, but not the ones that were always there of biblical images—now in every one was an image of Marley's face. And was it a trick of the eye, or did they all show Marley's face weirdly luminescent? All were of Marley, but Scrooge saw other images in the background. Shadowy and not completely erect.

"Humbug," said Scrooge, and walked across the room.

After a few turns, he sat down again. And all at once, a bell somewhere in his dark and dismal rooms rang out loud and clear. And then another and another, rising in a cacophonous melody too horrible to hear.

The bells ceased all at once, and from the cellar a clanking noise arose, as if heavy chains were being dragged up the stairs one step at a time.

"It's humbug still," Scrooge cried. "I won't believe it." The sounds grew nearer, bringing Marley with them through the door. The flames leapt up as though they cried *Marley's ghost!*

It *was* Marley. Same clothing, same pigtail, the cloth wrapped around his lower face mysteriously astir as if blown by a great wind. He was tied all 'round with chains and locks and iron safes.

Scrooge still didn't believe the vision before him was really Marley, though the spirit fixed upon him its death-cold eyes. But it *was* Marley! Yet how could it be, when Marley was dead?

"Why do you haunt me?" Scrooge uttered. "Why plague me?"

"It is required of every spirit to walk the earth seeking out the one who was closest to him when he was alive. I have chosen you, Ebenezer Scrooge, to benefit from my experience so that you can escape my fate. I do this for you. I wish I had followed my true nature instead of doing what you are now doing—employed in the worship of money and gain. There are more important things in this world to worship than money. I knew about these, but chose to ignore them. How could I have passed over the Old Lore, the power and the glory that the ancient magic could have brought me? And now I am doomed never to know what knowledge they could have given me. And what joy! It is too late for me, but there is still time for you to change before you too shuffle off your mortal coil and join me in my journeyings. Therefore, you will be visited by three spirits who will explain the wonders that await you."

Scrooge shuddered at the thought.
Marley turned around and walked to the window, flew out of it, and joined the countless beings who floated here and there, making a din of a noise that raised the hair on Scrooge's neck.

A Yuletide Carol

Stave II

Revelations

Scrooge dropped into bed, shivering all the while, contemplating the meaning of Marley's words. He finally fell into a deep sleep, but awoke with the tolling of the bell in a neighboring tower. With the last reverberation of the bell's tolling *one,* Scrooge thought to himself that the whole thing was just indigestion from something he ate. Not so.

The curtains of the bed were drawn apart, and Scrooge found himself face to face with a supernal figure: small, like a child, but also like an old man, with white hair and long arms. The being was clad in archaic clothing and appeared to scintillate and change its appearance with each moment. He had in his hand a glass vial filled with what the label claimed were "essential Saltes."

What in the world were these? Scrooge thought. What could their presence possibly mean to him? But he seemed to recall *something* like that in his past. He wracked his brain trying to remember.

The ghost said, "Rise and walk with me. Touch my robe." Scrooge did as he was bidden, touching the spirit's robe as directed, and instantly they were on a country road. It was a snow-covered vista that Scrooge now saw, and he wondered mightily what next was in store.

They walked further, into a schoolhouse. Scrooge exclaimed, "I was a boy here!" They entered the building and into a decrepit laboratory. The place was filled with beakers and jars and all manner of vials and tubing and other equipment. There at a worn table they found Scrooge as a young boy of about seventeen years, bent upon some experiment. He was intent on pouring something from a carboy onto a substance not unlike powdered bones. From these elements arose some sparks, and from the charnel mess in front of them something moved. Something that might have been part of a head with bulging, rolling eyes. Something that, as they watched, turned into a living thing. Something that had been dead. The thing was humanlike but *not quite right.* Young Scrooge must have used imperfect Saltes. But how did old Scrooge know that? As they continued

M. Burleson

to observe, Scrooge began to feel that all his life up to this point had been a lie. That he had always been someone else, not the money-grubbing Scrooge but someone *different*.

"This cannot have happened," Scrooge cried. "If it did, then why don't I remember?"

"You might remember if your main concerns were not the making of money and the pursuit of gain," the ghost replied. It looked upon Scrooge and pointed its finger at what lay upon the table and then at old Scrooge standing at its side.

Scrooge awoke in a start and saw that the spirit was gone. He flopped back upon the bed, exhausted, and fell asleep on the instant.

Stave III

The Instructions

Scrooge awoke from a raucous snore and heard the bell again strike *one*. Nothing happened at first but then he found himself in a glow of ruddy light that streamed out from the adjoining room. A high piping voice rang out and bade him enter. Scrooge did as he was told, and as he came into the room, he saw a goatish-looking boy in shepherd's clothing, a boy with oddly shaped feet. These were clad in huge black shoes, hinting at their grotesque size and strange shape. The boy was grinning like a loon, and sharp teeth gleamed in the glow of the fire. The room was bedecked in green and the fire leapt up as if in joy.

"And who are you?" Scrooge asked.

"Do you not recognize me? You should, for I was with you in your growing years, at your side always."

Scrooge paled at this and drew his robe closer about him. "I do not recall you at all, strange apparition."

"Then come with me and I'll instruct you in matters occult and weird."

The room disappeared, fire, greens and all, and Scrooge found himself upon a rocky shore.

"Where are we?"

"Are you not familiar with this place?" the goat-boy asked.

"I may have seen it once, in a dream," Scrooge answered hesitatingly.

"But you have chosen not to remember," the spirit replied. "The pursuit of gold meant more to you than what your real self desired."

Scrooge continued, "But where are we?"

"We are in the town of Dunwich at a spot called Sentinel Hill."

Scrooge looked about him, taking in the surroundings, not recalling the place. Yet there was *something* about it that seemed to waken old memories. The creature led Scrooge up the hill, between huge boulders and massive pines.

"This was where your ancestors sprang from, where your relatives danced and sacrificed. It is all hidden in the past. The life you lead now, scraping and eking out your existence, has nothing to do with the *real* you. I show you this to prepare you the way."

As these words were spoken, the creature faded and the night grew darker and more ominous.

Stave IV

The End of It

Scrooge found himself in a churchyard overgrown by grass and weeds, the growth of vegetation's death, not life, choked up with too much burying, fat with sated appetite. A worthy place. A cat was tearing at the gate, and rats gnawed at the gravestones. Why they haunted this place of death, Scrooge did not want to ponder.

And then he saw it. Saw the foreboding shape crawling along through the stones like a black mist, a shape that, when it neared Scrooge, appeared to grow taller. Its hood fell back, revealing spectral, glowing eyes, and something *else*. Something that had been hidden in the hood and was now filling the sleeves and bottom of the gown. Something black and ropy and viscous.

The thing turned toward Scrooge and fastened something like eyes upon him. Scrooge trembled. The being lifted what should have been an arm and beckoned. Scrooge stood upon shaky legs, and the spirit paused a moment as if to give Scrooge time to recover. This consideration of the phantom frightened Scrooge even more because he knew those piercing eyes were intently fixed upon him, watching him.

"Spirit of the Future," he cried, "I fear you more than any specter I have seen. But I know your purpose is to do me good, and I hope to be a different man from what I am. Lead on; I am prepared to follow you."

The phantom moved on ahead. Scrooge followed. It took him to a part of the city with which Scrooge was familiar. It had been his old office, and Scrooge looked in the window. It was his office still, for sitting in the chair was an older Scrooge, ledgers piled atop tables, a single candle burning and the fire low, just one coal. Money was everywhere, and mortgages and deeds, far exceeding what Scrooge had used to possess. So the future had *not* found him changed! He was worse than ever.

"O Spirit, have I not heeded the warnings put forth by Marley and the other ghosts? Must I die alone and find myself fettered by chains and boxes and safes? From what I have heard from the spirits there are marvelous things I could have done. I could have brought back long dead geniuses and philosophers and wizards. At my fingertips I could have resurrected Voltaire and Charles Dickens. I could have done *anything*. To be fettered to those chains and not be able to become the real me is too horrible to contemplate!" Scrooge screamed and fainted dead away.

And woke up in his bed. All that the spirits had shown him had stayed with him and had begun to unfold in his brain. The making of money and the griping cares had left him. And with their disappearance, he now knew what the spirits had tried to tell him.

He recalled the goat-boy and his words on the mountaintop with the waves crashing below. A vision of strangely formed ancestors with their bulging eyes and weird slits on their necks, mouths gaping, came to him. They *were* his family. He remembered at last. And exulted.

"Oh, Jacob Marley, the Old Ones, and the real Yuletide be praised for this! I say it on my knees, old Jacob, on my knees! The spirits, all three, shall strive within me."

For Scrooge now remembered his real past,

remembered with fondness his ropy-legged grandmother, the tentacled gods, the shoggoths in their bubbled-formed visages. His real family.

He knew just why he had been visited by the spirits, why Marley had come to him telling him he chose Scrooge because he was closest to him when he was alive. No more money-grubbing for Scrooge. He must be about his *real* business, the work that had been ordained for him from the beginning of time. With some help from the "Saltes," and a visit to the burying ground and Marley's grave, he would soon have the companionship he desired. And a willing assistant.

He had come home at last. Alleluia! Cthulhu fhtagn!

Curse of the House of Usher

Donald Tyson

1

I read Roderick Usher's letter in the sitting room of my Boston flat with conflicted emotions. We had been close friends during our student days at Miskatonic University, or perhaps allies would be a more accurate descriptive. We were both outsiders in a philosophical as well as a geographical sense, so it was natural that when we found ourselves roommates we should spend much of our time together, shut out as we were from the unwelcoming social circles of the local Arkham youths.

In part this shunning by the locals was due to rumours of our occult rituals. Usher and I were alike in so many ways, both tall and athletic in body, both reserved in speech, but our greatest consonance lay in our mutual passion for the unseen. We experimented, as young men will, and earned the reputation of necromancers among the students of Miskatonic. Spiritualism was then at its height of interest, and the Theosophy of Madame Blavatsky was the subject of common discourse. We embraced this fad for the occult with uncritical enthusiasm. All our nights were spent summoning the dead and conversing with them, nor did we fail to achieve significant successes in these endeavours.

Yet after we left the bell jar atmosphere of academia for the seemingly unlimited horizons of the greater world, we seldom sought the other's company. I established myself outwardly as a writer of strange tales while pursuing my esoteric studies in the privacy of my own dreams. I became an explorer of the dreamlands and gained a reputation there as a great dreamer. From time to time I would hear word of Usher's decadent extravagances in the fleshpots of Berlin and Prague. The last mention of his exploits, which I chanced to overhear several years ago spoken in casual conversation by a school acquaintance, placed him in a gaming house in Morocco, running up astronomical gambling debts while intoxicated on the lethal combination of opium and absinthe.

The letter requested that I visit his ancestral estate, which Usher had inherited following the death of his uncle. The tone of the letter was strangely mixed, part forced jocularity in which Usher asserted that I must need a vacation in the country after the assaults of the Bostonian bluestockings following the celebrity of my last published collection of stories, and part a touchingly sincere plea that we renew our old comradeship after so long a hiatus.

As it chanced, the letter arrived at a time when I had determined to take a break from my esoteric experiments in lucid dreaming. I was burned out, as the vulgar saying goes, and could no longer enter the dreamlands at will, but struggled to transit even the first portal of deep sleep. The cynicism of my Boston literary acquaintances tainted my imagination, and I found myself eager to see if a separation from their world-weary ennui would revive my childhood wonder and once more open the gates of dreams for my explorations.

Also, it must be confessed, I felt curiosity to see the estate that Usher had so often alluded to during our late-night chats at the university. He had painted it as an otherworldly place, a house forgotten by time. As I held his letter folded in my hand and heard his words echo in my memory, it seemed the ideal retreat in which to set aside for a short while the burden of the practical concerns that had been imposed on my mind by my publisher and certain members of my family.

It would be less than honest to say that the memory of Usher's sister played no part in my decision to accede to his request. During his student days he always kept a photograph of her in the lid of his ornately engraved silver pocket watch, and at quiet times he would open the watch and gaze at her with an expression of melancholy affection. She was a strikingly beautiful young woman, very like to Usher himself in countenance, with lustrous grey eyes and fine, curling black hair that framed an alabaster brow. I even remembered her name. Madeline. Neither Usher nor I had married during the years of our separation. His bachelorhood was presumably due to his indulgence in the vices of the world, whereas mine was the result of an almost monkish asceticism.

It was with a bewildering brew of emotions that I drafted a reply to my friend agreeing to visit his estate within the fortnight, although I gave no promise as to the date on which I would arrive or how long I intended to remain there as his guest. It was in my mind to see how the two of us got on together before binding myself to a prolonged sojourn.

2

Usher's family estate lay some dozen miles inland from the ancient port of New Bedford. It nestled between the hills in a secluded stretch of Massachusetts countryside, remote from villages and farms. Whatever had impelled the first Usher who ventured his fortunes in the New World to choose so isolated a geography was a puzzle. When the house was erected more than two centuries ago, it must have been even more remote than it is today. That was before the railroads, before the automobile, even before the steamship. Usher had never explained why the house had been built where it stood, but he had often waxed eloquent about the rugged grandeur of the forested hills that guarded its solitude. The timber was old-growth that had never been logged.

The nearest habitation was the farming hamlet of Benton, some seven or eight miles distant from the Usher estate. Fortunately for me, it was serviced by a rail spur. The rustic residents were typical of our fair state—taciturn, suspicious of strangers, and surly of manner. My casual remark that I was a friend of Roderick Usher was met with blank stares and pinched lips. By paying twice what the job was worth, I was able to induce the owner of the general store to allow his labouring man to drive me to the Usher estate in the store truck, an ageing and rust-eaten Ford of uncertain and variable coloration.

The man, who smelled strongly of horse manure and who wore a chequered flannel shirt so faded that it almost looked a dirty white, spoke less than a dozen words during the entire drive along the twisting, rutted forest road, which in places had been almost washed away by the floods of the previous spring. Six months later the damage had still not been repaired. We were forced to edge around places where the road fell away into the swiftly running creek that flowed beside it. At several points the creek bubbled and frothed beneath sagging covered bridges scarcely wide enough to accommodate the truck's fenders. Their rotted beams groaned ominously beneath our weight, and I had occasion to be thankful that the truck had been unloaded before our departure.

The trees that pressed close on either side of the narrow road were ancient sentinels, their twisted and blackened trunks half covered in green moss and shelved with ledges of white fungi. Their drooping boughs met above our heads and shut out most of the grey afternoon light, so that it was impossible to see the piled leaden clouds that filled the October sky. Dead leaves covered the road ruts with faded red and gold hearts, or hung trembling from the branches of the younger oaks and maples that struggled for life between the shoulders of the brooding evergreens. The dark masses of these ancient guardians muted the annual celebration of autumn.

At last the truck ground its gears wearily over the crest of a low rise, and the trees opened on either side of the road, affording me the first glimpse of my destination. It was the bleakest prospect over which I have ever gazed, and my heart fell to look upon it.

True to Usher's description, the house occupied a hollow between the low, forested hills that surrounded it. Autumn had browned the grasses of the poorly cut lawn that extended down a gentle slope from its left side. The right side of the property and part of the front were flooded with a tarn of black and stagnant water that pressed against the very foundation stones of the structure. From my elevation, scant though it was, I could see no inlet for this fetid pool, in which grew rank weeds and rushes, but a dry bed of pebbles showed where the water ran out when it overflowed during rains. Its surface was more than half covered by a kind of scum or algae, but where the water was open it reflected the leaden sky and the mould-blackened stone blocks and sightless black windows of the house of Usher in the most dismal fashion that may be imagined.

I knew from Usher's reminiscences of the place at university that the house was built of locally quarried stone blocks, but my imagination had never conceived so uninviting a façade. Its architecture bore no resemblance to the conventional timber-frame houses of historic New England that I love so well. It stood taller than it was broad, and its chimney-pierced roofs were steeply pitched and covered in black slate. The windows, although quite lofty and framed in Gothic arches, were narrow and infrequent in number, so that the walls I could see from the elevation of the road seemed expanses of all but unbroken stone. The house reminded me of illustrations of old Scottish keeps—miniature castles built by minor lords in the Highlands to serve as strongholds against warring clans and bands of outlaws.

The road wound down across an open stretch of browning lawn to a wooden bridge that spanned part of the tarn. I could not resist thinking of it as a drawbridge, although there was no mechanism for raising it, and the door of the house, though uncommonly wide, was a conventional door and not a castle gate.

The truck wheels squealed in protest as my taciturn driver applied the brakes. He sat looking forward through the dusty windscreen, his calloused hands tightly clenched on the steering wheel. The uneven idle of the engine seemed unnaturally loud.

"Why have you stopped?" I asked him.

"There's the house," he said in his thickly accented Yankee English.

"I know that. Drive me down to the bridge so that I can unload my trunk."

"This here's the turning place," he said.

I repressed the impulse to anger and kept my tone casual.

Curse of the House of Usher

"You can drive down to the house and let me off, then back the truck up the hill, if you don't wish to turn on the lawn. You cannot expect me to carry my trunk all that distance."

His hands tightened on the steering wheel until their big knuckles turned white.

"I won't go no further. This here's the turning place."

Nothing I could say would induce him to change his mind. Even a bribe of money left him unmoved.

So that's the way it is, I thought to myself. There is some feud between the locals of Benton and the Ushers, and the fools won't venture onto the Usher estate.

When I realised the futility of arguing with the man, I dragged my travel trunk off the back of the truck and watched as he turned the rusting vehicle and drove away without so much as a backward glance. I sat upon the trunk lid in disgust, facing the house, and listened to the sound of the poorly tuned engine diminish down the road. At length there was silence.

No movement came from the house or its grounds. My expectation that the truck had been heard or seen soon faded.

"I've had warmer welcomes," I muttered to myself with a rueful smile.

Silence swallowed my words. Not a leaf rustled. Not a bird sang. It was the stillness of death.

Leaving my trunk in the middle of the road where I had dragged it, I made my way to the neglected strip of lawn and crossed the bridge, which I noted was in need of minor repairs and fresh white paint. The heels of my travel boots on the planks thudded in the grey quiet, but no nesting bird was frightened from the black waters of the tarn. Only a few bubbles arose and broke on its surface, emitting a foul stench.

As I came near the house, I noticed a crack in the stonework that ran up from the tarn all the way to the eve of the roof in a jagged line, like the path followed by a bolt of lightning, but a path of shadow rather than a path of light. It was barely wide enough to have slid in the tips of my fingers—but it seemed out of keeping with the general state of the house, which overall was in good repair, although it had evidently been neglected during the past ten years or so.

I grasped the verdigris-covered brass knocker on the massive front door and let it fall twice against its sounding plate. After half a minute, footfalls echoed within and the door swung wide. A dignified and elderly servant in a black suit, his grey hair carefully brushed to one side of his head and his thin grey moustache waxed on the ends, regarded me through watery brown eyes with the complete lack of emotion of all good butlers. I handed him my card.

"Randolph Carter. Mr. Usher is expecting me."

The elderly servant bowed without a word and admitted me into the front hall. He withdrew through a set of double doors of age-blackened walnut, closing them behind him and leaving me to admire the sweeping marble staircase with its massive and ornately carved banister, and the enormous crystal chandelier that hung above my head. The black marble tiles of the floor were polished to such a high lustre that they reflected, as in a mirror, the portraits hanging on the panelled walls.

I approached beneath a painting that appeared from its ebony frame to be the oldest, and studied the unforgiving visage captured in oils. He was dressed in the costume of the early eighteenth century, with a powdered wig on his head. The family resemblance to Roderick Usher was unmistakable. His dark eyes glittered with life force, so that I found it disconcerting to gaze long upon them.

Here sits the patriarch of the Usher clan, looking like some Oriental potentate surveying his lands and slaves, I thought. It must have been an unpleasant experience to fall under the power of so pitiless a countenance. Yet here he was today, no more than a few daubs of paint on canvas. Such is the transient mortality of all living things.

3

The walnut doors parted with more authority than they had closed, and between them stood Roderick Usher, dressed in a blue velvet smoking jacket and matching Turkish smoking cap with a tassel that hung down to his broad shoulder. A slender black Russian cigarette glowed between his fingers.

I recognised his familiar features at once, but found myself regarding them with more alarm than affection. It was the same high brow, the same grey, heavy-lidded eyes and hooked nose, the same strong jaw and sardonically curled lips, so familiar in my memory, but how changed they were! His eyes in their hollow sockets looked haunted, and the skin across his prominent cheekbones seems stretched like dry parchment. His hair, once a glossy black, had turned to grey and hung in ragged disorder where it escaped his cap, so fine in texture that it seemed to float around his countenance like the smoke that rose from his cigarette.

He hesitated only a moment, then swept across the tiles and took my hand between his.

"It was good of you to come, Randolph."

His tone held genuine warmth. At such closeness the signs of dissolute living were plain in the lines indelibly graven across his face—lines that only a youth wasted in vice can cut on living flesh. I detected a slight tremble in his hands before he released me. Moved by some impulse of remembered youth, I clapped him on the shoulder in a familiar way and squeezed his upper arm before dropping my hand.

"There's nowhere else I'd rather be," I said, and at that moment I truly meant the words.

He glanced up at the portrait in the ebony frame.

"I see you've made the acquaintance of Uriah Usher, the builder of this house. He laid many of these stones with his own hands, did you know."

"We were having a staring contest, but I lost."

He laughed lightly, in the way I remembered from our university days.

"Well, well, come into the drawing room where we can talk. Where are your bags?"

I described the uncouth behaviour of my driver. It raised no surprise in Usher's grey eyes. He ordered his man, whose name was Simmons, to have the trunk carried into the house and up to my room.

The cavernous drawing room boasted a dizzyingly high panelled ceiling and a great stone fireplace. A grand piano occupied a corner of the floor. Beside it, near the wall, stood a harp, and across the cushion of a chair rested a guitar.

Usher guided me to a padded French settee covered in pink silk, and we sat together on it. Behind us, the weak light from the clouded sky came through three mullioned windows framed by long drapes of a deep burgundy. It illuminated with a kind of pallid glow the smoke that hung in the air and softened the edges of things, rendering the shadowed furnishings of the room vague. Opposite the settee, an open arch led into what I presumed to be the library, as I could see tall cases of books lining its walls.

"If only you'd informed me in advance of the day of your arrival, I might have arranged for your transportation from the village."

"I didn't know myself when I could get away from Boston. It's a matter of no importance."

He studied me with a smile on his lips, but in his eye lurked a calculating assessment that he failed to conceal, or perhaps did not attempt to conceal. It was hardly to be expected that his manner could be other than worldly, I told myself, given his globe-spanning travels and his varied experiences.

"I almost feel we've never been apart, I see your name so often in the literary magazines. You've gained a sizeable reputation as an artist."

I shrugged and made a deprecating gesture with my hand.

"The critics need something to write about. Next year it will be somebody else."

"You are too modest. I have all your books, in there." He nodded toward the library.

For the better part of an hour we talked of Miskatonic and Arkham, each contributing scraps of information overheard during the intervening years about boys we had known there, since grown to men and making their way in the world with varying degrees of success. The expressionless butler, Simmons, brought in a silver tray with brandy glasses and a crystal decanter filled with an amber liquid. The drink warmed my blood and made me more animated in my story telling, but I declined the offer of the Russian cigarettes that Usher continued to smoke as he listened, all the while watching me with his keen gaze.

A bit of white moving at the corner of my eye drew my

Curse of the House of Usher

attention through the arch to the library, where a woman stood before a set of shelves studying the polished leather spines of books. She drew down a slender volume and opened it, seemingly oblivious to my regard.

"Sister, our guest has arrived," Usher said without raising his voice. So silent was the house, it was scarce necessary to speak above a whisper.

She closed the book and turned with a bemused smile. Her grey eyes wandered for a moment before settling on my face.

"Come and join us, Sister."

She seemed to float rather than walk across the marble floor. The long and full white skirts of her dress concealed her shoes, adding to the illusion. The upper part covered her arms with white lace but left her hands and shoulders bare, creating a charming effect. She was even thinner than her brother, except for a portliness about the waist that her lacings could not entirely conceal. Her eyes seemed almost shining, they were so filled with vital spirits, but her lips though fuller than her brother's were pale as wax, and her cheekbones stood out sharply on the oval of her face, which was framed by her long curling hair, as black as the wing of a raven.

We stood as she entered, and Usher made the introductions.

"Madeline has been looking forward to having someone other than me to talk to," Usher said. His voice had a slight edge, and she glanced sharply at him.

"It is a pleasure to meet you at last, Randolph. My brother has told me so many of your adventures at Arkham."

Her fingers felt chill against mine, as though no blood flowed through them.

"Adventures?" I looked at Usher. "Did we have adventures, Roderick?"

Her laughter sounded hollow, as though it echoed in an empty room.

"The time you and my brother used an old book you found in the university library to summon a demon? Don't you remember?"

I forced laughter and cast a glance at Usher, surprised that he had spoken of the event, which I had uttered to no living human being.

"Our minds were filled with the spirit of inquiry, my dear. We were so young." Usher laid his hand on her arm. "Shall we play for our guest?"

She smiled and nodded. He went to the chair and took up the guitar from its seat. I expected her to sit at the grand piano, but instead she sat before the harp and tilted it back against her shoulder.

Usher noticed my gaze upon the piano.

"I suffer from a rare affliction that causes any harsh sounds to be physically painful. I can no longer bear to hear the piano—a pity, for it is a fine instrument. The softer music of strings does not torment my ears."

I realised that since entering the house I had not heard a clock chime the quarter hours.

"Have you always suffered so?"

"In my youth the condition was much less severe, but as I grow long in years, it worsens."

They played several German folk songs while I listened and watched Madeline. Her beauty was ethereal, almost fairy-like. She seemed to inhabit another realm and this one at the same moment. I could see that she was Usher's twin. It was evident in the line of her shoulder, the length of her neck, the noble height of her brow, but all that was angular and harsh in his features was softened and beautified in hers.

"Wonderful," I said, applauding effusively when they indicated the performance was at an end. "I've never heard such beautiful playing."

Usher acknowledged the compliment with a slight bow of his head.

"My family has always been gifted in music, among other things."

"Brother, I grow tired. I must go to my room and lie down."

"Of course, Madeline. How thoughtless of me. Let me help you to your feet." He called for his butler. "Simmons will help you up the stairs."

We watched the little grey man walk with her into the entrance hall and ascend the marble staircase.

"She is dying," Usher said to me without preamble.

I stared at him, uncertain if I had heard him correctly.

"It is a wasting illness, hereditary in nature. Nothing can be done in a medical way to cure it. The doctor was here in the morning. He told me in confidence that she may have as much as three months remaining, or she could take a seizure and die tomorrow."

I went to him and took his hand into mine.

"Roderick, I am saddened beyond words. If there is anything I may do, you have only to ask."

"One thing you may do for me, old friend. Remain in this house and help me to find the source of the curse that has blighted my family for untold generations, and that now kills my dear sister."

4

Taking a step back from him, I studied his face for signs of madness.

"Curse?"

"You heard me rightly, Randolph. Do not look at me so. My reason remains sound, though for how much longer, I cannot predict. Come with me into the library."

We passed through the arch, and he closed its pocket doors, sealing us away from the rest of the house. A single window let in a pale greyness, for the days are short in October and the hour had grown late.

"It is unfortunate you did not arrive sooner, but we may still have enough time. I told you there was nothing that could be done medically, but there may be another way to save her."

"Why did you not mention this curse in your letter?"

He looked at me with a bitter smile on the corners of his lips.

"Would you have come?"

I hesitated only for an instant.

"To help your sister? I would have come immediately."

"I believe you," he said, nodding so that the cloud of fine grey hair around his brow rippled like seaweed in an invisible current. "But I could not take that chance, old friend. I've grown cynical over the years, and my faith in men has often been disappointed."

He went to a sideboard and used a Lucifer match to light the wick of a glass oil lamp. The greyness from the window was replaced by a wavering golden glow, and the acrid tang of sulphur mingled with the smell of tobacco smoke.

"Come to the reading table and seat yourself," he told me.

Setting the lamp on the table, he went to a shelf behind me and drew down a leather-bound journal that was closed by means of a tied red ribbon. He tugged one end of the ribbon loose from its bow and opened the journal before me.

"This is our family record. My great-great-grandfather, Ezekiel Usher, began it, and various members of my family have added bits of lore to it over the generations."

I leafed through the journal without enthusiasm. The antique writing was in several different hands. It would take hours to read through the record from beginning to end, even if I were able to decipher all its pages.

"Tell me about this family curse."

His eyes widened with enthusiasm. There was a disturbing fanaticism in their depths. He shuffled the pages of the journal and pointed to a place near the beginning.

"The first mention of it occurs in this record, but I believe it to be as old as the house itself. Ezekiel wrote of a servant girl found drowned in the waters of the tarn. The explanation was that she had slipped off the bridge and hit her head on its edge, but my forbear never believed it. He writes here of various members of the household seeing movement in the water."

"Movement?"

"As though something were sliding beneath the surface. You may have noticed that the water is as black as ink. Nothing can be seen within it beyond a depth of a few inches, but sometimes I myself have observed ripples and heard splashes."

"Fish, perhaps? Frogs?"

"The water is poisonous. Nothing of the animal kind lives in it."

"What has this to do with your family curse?"

He straightened up and paced to the other end of the reading table.

Curse of the House of Usher

"I don't know. Perhaps nothing."

I gazed at the pages of the open journal in perplexity. "How does this curse express itself?"

Usher sat abruptly in the chair at the opposite end of the table and leaned forward, staring into my eyes with disturbing intensity.

"It has been a peculiarity of my family line that it flourishes only in direct paternal descent, and only within the walls of this house."

"I'm not quite sure I understand you, old fellow."

He clenched his fist and brought it down on the table with a thud.

"The women of my family who marry and move away to live with their husbands are invariably childless. Either they are sterile, or the fruits of their wombs abort themselves."

"Always?" I was unable to keep a sceptical tone from my voice.

He nodded.

"That is most strange, I agree," I said at length. "Still, I hardly see how it affects the health of your sister."

"There is more, Randolph. Those of my family line who remain within these walls suffer a strange wasting of their vitality and are afflicted with all manner of uncommon infirmities. In my own case, it takes the form of my preternatural sensitivity to harsh noises. Suffice it to say that the Ushers do not live into old age, but shrivel and die in their prime of life, as though the very life-force of their souls were being drained away."

"You believe that Madeline's complaint is the result of this hereditary wasting of vital force?"

"I do indeed," he said with emphasis.

Spreading my hands in apology, I shook my head.

"If the Usher family line suffers from some form of hereditary wasting disease, I fail to see how I can be of any use to you, Roderick. I am not a physician."

He ignored my attempt to placate him.

"As I said before, I do not believe my sister's complaint to be medical."

"Then what is it?" I asked bluntly.

He looked from side to side as though expecting to see something in the shadows, but what that might have been I could not imagine, as we were quite alone in the library. Leaning still further forward, he lowered his voice.

"I believe there is something in this house that feeds on the lives of my family. It has sapped my dearly beloved sister of her strength and largely of her sanity; and unless we stop it, I am convinced that it will soon deprive her of life, as it has so many of my ancestors."

In the stillness my uneasy chuckle sounded ghoulish.

"Then the solution is simple enough. You and your sister must move out of this house and return to it no more."

He closed his eyelids and sighed like a man whose heart is about to break from sorrow.

"Do you think I haven't thought of that? If only it were so easy." He opened his eyes and studied me with a solemn gaze. "I cannot expect you to understand our situation. I am the last of my line. All the Ushers are dead other than my dear sister. Were we to leave the house, it would pass into other hands, and that is unthinkable. This has been the seat of the Ushers for more than two centuries. How can you comprehend, you whose ancestry means so little to you? For the Ushers, family is everything. This house is our world. We cannot and will not abandon it."

His words made little sense. With the very life of his sister in the balance, what other considerations where there? Yet it was obvious from his sincerity that he believed what he told me, so I made no attempt to argue.

"Have you formed any conjecture as to the origin of this family curse?"

"Indeed I have. My forbearer Ezekiel mentions in the journal a family legend that old Uriah Usher, who sailed from Ireland to America in 1747 and built this house, erected it on the site of a circle of stones."

"A stone circle? Do you mean a ritual circle erected by the natives of this land?"

"A stone circle, yes, but as to who erected it—" He paused as though hesitant to finish the thought. "It was a circle of large stones. Uriah surveyed the surrounding hills and concluded that it was the best location to build upon. The legend says that he incorporated the stones of the circle into the foundations of the house itself. As for the rest of the blocks, he quarried them from nearby to save the cost of transport, which would have been considerable."

"Do you mean to say that the tarn is not a natural body of water, but a stone quarry?"

His eyes flashed with enthusiasm.

"So I believe, although it is not written anywhere in the journal or in any other family account."

Usher's ancestor was a practical man, I thought. When building of stone, the greatest cost is often that of transporting the stones from the quarry to the construction site. Yet to deliberately create such a dismal pool of poisonous black water at the very foundation of the house itself seemed folly.

Usher read my thoughts.

"We would drain the tarn were it possible to do so, but the terrain of the valley is against us. There is simply no lower-lying hollow into which to drain the water. My grandfather tried pumping it out with a stationary steam engine, but he could never lower the level by more than six or seven inches, and within a night it was back to its usual elevation, from which it never varies by more than an inch."

"Where do you suppose the water comes from?"

"When the quarry was excavated, the workers must have tapped into some concealed spring. The mass of the water above pressing down upon it keeps more water from issuing from its vent, but when the water level drops, the spring replenishes the tarn. At any rate, that is my surmise."

He fell into a brooding silence. I waited for him to speak at greater length, but he seemed lost in his interior ruminations.

"Is it your belief that this family curse is due to the desecration of the stone circle?"

"It must be," he snapped. "What else could it be?"

"If you are correct, then I suggest you consult the local Indian tribe. It may be that their medicine man—"

His harsh bark of laughter cut off my words.

"Don't you think I've tried? I spent the better part of last summer talking to Indians, and do you know what I learned? They're dead, Randolph. The tribe that built that stone circle ceased to exist centuries ago, probably before the house was erected."

The silence lengthened between us. I found myself unable to think of any words that might comfort him. That his mind was unbalanced by worry over Madeline's condition, there could be no doubt.

"You know the studies of our university days?" he said.

It took a few moments reflection before I understood his meaning.

"Do you mean our occult experiments?"

"Precisely those. It may be that they will serve us best when at last we are confronted by the source of my family curse."

"Is such a confrontation imminent?"

He looked at me across the table with dispassion, as though from some great eminence, and there was nothing of human emotion in his voice.

"I feel it must be. My sister and I are the last of our line, and when she dies I cannot imagine how I shall go on alone."

"What is it you expect me to do?" I asked, ignoring the implication of his words.

"I want you to enquire about the curse in the dreamlands, which I understand you have the power to enter at will. Seek there for an antidote, or at least an anodyne."

My expression caused him to fall silent. In a few words I told him of my inability to enter the dreamlands for the past several years, and my despair of ever regaining my former ability. Usher gave no outward sign, but I sensed the frustration within him.

"You must make the attempt. Everything I have—this house, its lands, my very life and that of my sister—depend on it. Tell me that you will try."

To humour his mania, I assured him that I would attempt to inquire in the dreamworlds about his family curse.

5

My bedroom was spacious and well appointed, but it still retained an odour of dust and mildew when I entered it to sleep. Not enough time had passed since my unexpected arrival to air it properly.

Curse of the House of Usher

By way of compensation, the staff of the house had done their best to make me welcome. One of the servants had lit a glass oil lamp similar to the one in the library and placed it on the stand beside the bed, which was a massive edifice of carved mahogany with four tall spiral posts as thick through their middles as the leg of an elephant. My trunk rested in a corner out of the way. I discovered by inspection that my clothing had been taken from it and put into the drawers in the cedar-lined armoire, or hung from the hangers on its rod. My change of shoes was set neatly beside the door.

It had been my intention to read some of the Usher family journal before sleep, and for this purpose I had carried it up the stairs from the library; but I soon found that the train journey from Boston and the ride in the delivery truck had left me so fatigued that my thoughts kept wandering. After ten minutes of effort, I closed the leather cover of the journal with a sigh of frustration and went to bed. The sheets and pillowcase had been changed and were newly laundered. For this small grace I gave silent thanks and turned down the wick of the lamp until the flame died within its glass shade.

The perversity of human nature is consistent and predictable. Now that I lay in bed, in total darkness, my fatigue lifted from my mind and the need for sleep abated. I found myself listening to the tiny sounds of the old house: the creak of a beam, the squeak of a mouse, the ticking of a beetle in the wall. Each small noise was like thunder in the silence. The clouds that all afternoon had blocked the rays of the sun at last unrolled from the darkened heavens and allowed silvery moonlight to paint itself across the foot of the bed quilt as I lay beneath it, staring upward at the dark ceiling, wide awake.

As a rule, my control over my ability to fall asleep is greater than that of the average person. Indeed, it might almost be called preternatural. This is a gift I was born with, and that I have honed through years of intense dream working. This night some inner governor refused to allow my awareness to relax into the arms of Morpheus. I even found myself holding my breath during long intervals of complete silence, when the only sound was my own heartbeat.

Tyson

The crack of a twig came faintly to my ears from outside my window. For a time I continued to lie in bed, resolved to ignore it. Finally, curiosity got the better of me. I threw off the quilt and the sheet and went to the narrow mullioned window, which looked better suited to a Gothic church than a private dwelling. My room was on the second level, and the ceilings of the ground level were uncommonly high. This gave me an elevation from which to overlook the grounds.

My bedroom was located on the side of the house against which the main body of the tarn pressed. The black mirror of the water refleted the starry sky, for the clouds of the afternoon had completely vanished. A moon nearing its fullness rode high above, painting the ragged grass of the lawn at the water's edge, and the leaves of the shade trees beyond it, with a whiteness like frost. It was a convincing illusion, but the night was too mild for frost.

A figure moved with slow steps around the far edge of the tarn. It was a woman wrapped in a green cloak, her head bowed as she watched the path before her feet, which appeared to be naked. I recognised Usher's sister, Madeline.

The elevation of the nearly full moon told me that the hour must be close to midnight. It occurred to me that Madeline might be walking in her sleep and might be in danger of tumbling into the tarn and drowning. Then she turned her head to look behind, and I saw that her eyes were wide open. Another more insidious possibility forced its way into my thoughts: that she might have come to the decision to end her own life before it was terminated against her will by her illness. If so, was it my place to intervene?

In the end, I did not descend to the lawn but continued to watch from my window. At times she seemed to look directly at me, as though she could see me standing in the darkened room, but this must have been impossible. I kept my face out of the moonlight that shone through the glass.

She continued along the edge of the tarn until she came to a stone that jutted up from the grass at a crooked angle. Here she stopped and seemed to caress the stone with her hand before turning to face the star-shot black pool. An owl sounded its night call from the trees, but she did not turn her head. All her attention was directed at the tarn. She seemed entranced, as though mesmerised, and had her eyes not been wide open I would have judged her to sleepwalk.

She raised her slender white arms in a gesture of invocation and began to speak, but in so low a voice that I could not distinguish any words. Only a faint murmur reached my straining ears. When she had done, she stood and waited.

The stars in the tarn rippled and parted, and the very water itself rose and moved toward her. For the first time the thought occurred to me that I was the dreamer, and that I lay asleep in the bed, only imagining that I stood at my window. But when I glanced back to the bed, I found it empty. My years of experience as a traveller through the dreamlands gave me assurance that I was wide awake, and even though I could no longer dream-walk at will, I trusted the old instincts.

She did not cry out or try to flee. Instead, she took a step forward so that her bare feet entered the black water. Her long cloak fell open, and I saw that she stood naked beneath it. The moonlight caught the dome of her belly and her white thighs, but shadows preserved the modesty of her sex. They cloaked her skin like a garment, save for the parts I have mentioned and the tips of her breasts, which stood forth in vivid contrast to the darkness inside her open cloak.

Something from the tarn extended itself toward her. At first I thought it was a serpent raising its head from the bulge of black water that shivered and gleamed at her feet, but it was too long and thin to have supported its own weight as it touched and seemed to caress her belly. I felt the blood flush in my face as this snake-like tentacle moved lower and passed between her thighs. The sense that I was witnessing a union forbidden by all the laws of God and nature surged within me. A mingling of outrage and shamefulness warred in my heart, but I could not turn my eyes away as she let her head fall back on her neck in a posture of ecstasy. The loose cloak slipped from her shoulders and fell behind her to the grass.

Her body shuddered and a soft moaning sounded through the night, like the cry of some forest creature mating in mingled pain and delight. In moments the serpentine extension of the water withdrew itself and the rounded bulge moved back to the centre of the tarn and descended, leaving its surface again a starry mirror as the ripples settled.

For more than a minute Madeline stood motionless. Then she shook her head, as though to clear it, and turned to pick up and put back on her cloak. Without a backward glance she returned along the margin of the black pool the way she had come, making toward the bridge and the front door—but before she reached the bridge she passed around the corner of the house and was lost to my sight.

I stepped away from the window, badly shaken. When I drew my hand across my face, I discovered that it was covered in a chill sweat. Did Usher know about his sister's nocturnal visits to the tarn? I had no illusions that this was the first time: she had conducted herself with too much self-assurance. Had I seen what I thought I had seen or was it some trick of the moonlight?

When I returned to my bed, I anticipated a sleepless night, but it could not have been more than a few minutes before I drifted into unconsciousness, my fatigue at last overpowering the heated workings of my imagination.

6

My next awareness was that of a housemaid, gently shaking me awake by the shoulder to inform me that Mr. Usher wished to see me in the drawing room at my earliest convenience. I washed in the basin of fresh water provided and quickly dressed myself before descending the stairs.

A short and rather corpulent man wearing gold-framed eyeglasses and a faded brown travel suit was in conversation with Usher in the hall. Both men turned at my approach, and Usher introduced me. The little fellow was William Hoffman, Usher's family physician. His round face bore an expression of watchful slyness, and there was an impudent smirk on the thick lips beneath his bristling salt-and-pepper moustache. With reluctance I accepted his hand and found it moist. I guessed his presence in the house so early in the morning could not bode any good thing, but held my silence as Usher finished his words of parting and allowed the physician to make his way out the door.

"It's bad, Randolph. It's very bad, I'm afraid."

Curse of the House of Usher

His face was haggard. All the lines and hollows across it were accentuated by a new sorrow that left him like a damned soul, staring back at the fading shore from the boat of Charon.

"Madeline?"

"She's dead. Her maid found her this morning. We called Doctor Hoffman immediately, but it was quite pointless. Her body was already cold when she was discovered."

I put my hand on his shoulder but he did not seem to notice the touch. He seemed dazed, like a man not yet recovered from the stunning effect of some blow to the head.

"I am terribly sorry, Roderick. Did Hoffman venture an immediate cause for her sudden death?"

"A fit in the night, he called it, but I believe he was only guessing." His face hardened. "He wanted to take her body back to Benton for an autopsy, but I absolutely forbade it. I will not have my sister cut open for the puerile study of fools."

"What will you do?"

He blinked and seemed to see me for the first time. He attempted to force a smile, but the effect was ghastly and I was glad when he ceased the effort.

"Her death was hardly unexpected, although it came sooner rather than later. I have her resting place prepared in the family crypt beneath this house. I even have her coffin. It arrived from the maker last week. If I might prevail on your good graces . . ."

"Of course, old friend, anything you need. You have but to ask."

"Will you help me to prepare her corpse and carry the coffin into the crypt? I could have the servants do it, but somehow that seems too remote and heartless. She deserves better than to be handed off to servants, don't you think?"

To me it seemed that the tasks he mentioned were best left to the trained staff of a mortuary, but I held my tongue and nodded.

"You mean to inter her without embalming?"

"It was her wish. She had a morbid horror of being embalmed, and I shall respect it, as irrational as it may have been."

"Of course, as you should."

The corpse of Madeline lay in her bed. Her cheeks were pale, but still so filled with life that I expected her breast beneath the cotton sheet to rise and fall. She was quite cold to the touch. I noted that after returning from her visit to the tarn, she had put on a nightdress of white silk.

We prepared the corpse as best we could. I withdrew to allow Usher to clothe his sister in her funeral dress, then returned to help him place her in the coffin. His cheeks were still wet with tears, but he seemed unaware of it. He informed me that Madeline had chosen the dress herself—an elegant garment of grey silk trimmed with black. Usher spent an inordinate amount of time brushing her hair with a silver hairbrush, and I received the impression that it was not the first time he had performed this function. At last he closed the lid of the coffin and latched it

"Help me to carry it to the crypt."

"Is there to be no funeral service?" I asked in surprise.

He looked at me. It was like gazing at a skull with two dark eyes set deep in its sockets, and a mask of skin stretched across its bony ridges.

"What would be the point? I am the only family she had in the world, the only one left to mourn her. When I die, there will be no one at all."

It was not the time to discuss the matter. Usher's mind was less than wholly rational. I reasoned that it would do no harm should the corpse rest in the crypt for a few days, until he regained some of his composure. Then he might reconsider a more conventional funeral arrangement for her. But it would be folly to try to bring it up this day.

The coffin was well made and consequently quite heavy. Even so, Usher would not ask his servants for their help. They watched in silence as we wrestled the box down the main staircase and into the entrance to the cellars. It was fortunate for us that the silver handles at each end of the coffin had been fashioned for more than mere display.

By the time we got it to the crypt, I was covered in sweat and had to resist the impulse to curse in frustration. Usher seemed unperturbed. Despite his thinness, he retained the strength of limb that had distinguished him at Miskatonic. He bore up under the work much better than I, at least in a physical sense.

We set the sealed coffin upon a stone table that to my fanciful mind resembled an altar. There were other similar long boxes in recesses in the walls, presumably occupied by dead members of the family. Some of them showed signs of great age. The air in the crypt had a smell that was impossible to define, but in some way cloyingly repulsive. It was not the smell of decay. It may have been the lingering scent of long-dead flowers that had worked its way into the very stones of the place. It made my stomach roll.

"Usher, I must get out of this cellar. The smell . . ."

For the first time that morning, he looked at me with something resembling human feeling.

"Of course, old man. Thank you for your help. I couldn't have managed it without you."

He gripped my arm in his hands with sudden enthusiasm and drew me close, staring into my face. The light from the oil lamp gave it a ghoulish strangeness.

"You do see that I couldn't let that oily little fool, Hoffman, touch her? You don't know what vile creatures like him do with the dead. I'm a man of the world, and I've heard stories and seen things in Europe that would freeze your blood. He would have defiled her, Randolph. At least here she is safe from his touch."

What could I say in response to this? I pressed my lips into a smile and waited for him to release my arm.

"You go," he said, waving me out of the crypt with a flick of his pale fingers. "I will stay for a time and talk with my sister."

I left him standing over the coffin, staring down at it as though he could see through the polished rosewood planks of its lid. His lips moved silently, but whether in prayer or in speaking her name, I know not.

7

In the late afternoon, while Usher lay asleep in his room from the effects of the laudanum given to him by Hoffman, I went outside and slowly traced a semicircle around the margin of the tarn, moving from the bridge at the front door around to the side overlooked by the window of my bedroom. There was a kind of path worn in the long grass, indicating light but regular traffic.

Tyson

As I walked along, I was conscious of the water at my left side, like black oil. The sunlight penetrated it no more than a few inches. From the rotting vegetation that floated on its surface there arose a faint but loathsome odour of decay. It was the scent of funeral flowers left too long untended. I suddenly realised that it was the same scent I had detected in the crypt, only stronger. Occasional clusters of bubbles burst upward, as though from the exhalation of some submarine creature, but they may have been caused by expanding methane gas.

So I told myself, as I tried not to let my imagination get the bit between its teeth and run away with me. How a woman could follow this path in the depths of night was beyond my comprehension. It tried my nerves to the limit in broad daylight, having seen what I saw from my window. Nothing in the universe would have induced me to walk here after dark.

I came to the tilted stone and stopped to study it. In the soft mud at the edge of the water I saw the imprint of her naked feet, still quite clear. The stone was a kind of menhir or standing stone. It projected some four feet above the sod, though how much of it extended below the ground I have no way to know. On the side fronting the house I found markings that looked like writing of some sort, but the characters resembled no alphabet with which I was familiar, either in this world or the dreamlands. They were greatly worn by the action of the elements, and I judged them at least several centuries old.

I straightened my back and looked slowly around, with the distinct crawling sensation between my shoulder blades of being watched. There was no movement in the line of shade trees at the edge of the lawn other than a slight trembling of the golden and orange leaves in the mild breeze. I turned to study the black windows of the house. No face confronted me in their blind eyes, which seemed to gaze blankly down with an expression of startled surprise from under the Gothic arches of their stone brows.

Movement drew my attention to the water at my feet. There was something in the water, just far enough below the surface that I could discern none of its details, other than that it was round and about the size of a dinner plate. It appeared and disappeared with regularity. A kind of yellowish-grey border surrounded a coal-black centre the size of my clenched fist. Drawn by an irresistible curiosity, I leaned my face down toward the inky surface of the tarn, standing as far out over the water as I could manage without slipping into the wet mud.

The object rose nearer to the surface. I regarded it in silence for a minute or so, unable to place its vague outline with any object or water beast in my memory. It was then that it *blinked* at me, its broad lid descending slowly and then opening again with more quickness as the black circle in its centre expanded in size.

I very nearly tumbled into the tarn when I jerked my head away. I did fall over backwards into the grass and struck the back of my head against the corner of the standing stone. There was a flash of light inside my skull. When I opened my eyes on the cloudless blue sky, it was to the sound of my name being called. I sat up slowly, and my head began to pound with a vengeance. When I felt the back of it, there was a lump but fortunately no blood. I pushed myself to my feet, leaning on the stone for aid, and saw that the elderly butler, Simmons, was hailing me from the open front door, asking if I wished to take afternoon tea with Usher.

I waved my hand to show him that I was unhurt and shouted that I would return to the house momentarily. He stood as though uncertain for several seconds, then withdrew and closed the door.

My vision was double. Blinking, I pressed my thumb and index finger to the corners of my closed eyelids, then focused my eyes on the surface of the water. The eye, if such a thing it was, had withdrawn. Was it possible that I had merely imagined it? Could a frog or a fish have caused such a bizarre fancy? The mind sees what it expects to see. I remembered in the past how often I had caught a glimpse of my cat from the corner of my vision, or seen her shape curled in the semi-darkness among the rumpled blankets at the foot of my bed, only to realise later that she was in another part of the house, and that I could not possibly have seen her. Such is the power of expectation. But why would I expect to see a gigantic eye in the tarn?

I looked again for the footprints of Madeline Usher, and to my surprise found that they had been obliterated. I must have scraped them out with my heels when I fell. Yet I saw that my shoes were not covered in wet mud. Leaving this riddle for later consideration, I returned to the house to take tea with my sorrowing host.

8

Hoffman returned with his little black leather bag the next day to examine Usher. As he was leaving, he motioned me aside with a discreet wave of his chubby hand and indicated with a jerk of his head that he wanted to speak with me outside the house. I told Usher that I would see the doctor off and went with him to his automobile, which was parked on the lawn at the far end of the footbridge.

"It is most fortunate that Roderick has a friend visiting with him at this trying moment in his life," the little man began by way of preamble.

"I would rather my visit had taken place under more agreeable circumstances."

The sly face of the portly little man did not inspire me with confide ce. I could well see why Usher distrusted him. He stared up at me with a sidelong tilt of his head, like a bird eyeing a worm.

"Roderick's mental state is most precarious. It stands balanced on a precipice above a fathomless abyss. He was never what one would call strong of mind, and his obsessive affection for his sister has only aggravated the shock of her loss."

"Obsessive affection?"

He smiled and licked his thick lips beneath his bristling moustache, which resembled a shaving brush.

"Roderick and his sister have been cut off in this house from the society of others of their social standing for many years. Her brother tells me that she has received no male admirers for a very long time, yet her physical condition at the time of her death speaks otherwise."

"What physical condition?" I asked with some heat. "See here, Doctor, what are you driving at?"

He shrugged and raised his thick eyebrows.

"But surely you noticed when you saw her? Madeline Usher was with child."

I stared at him, shocked beyond words.

"She was pregnant?"

"About six months, I should say. Perhaps seven months."

I remembered noting the rounded dome of her lower abdomen, but nothing so outrageous as pregnancy had even entered my thoughts. I could not find words.

"The servants have told me that Madeline received no male callers for over a year. The butler and the two other male servants are well advanced in years. I suppose it is possible that one or the other of them could be the father, but it seems unlikely."

Outrage built slowly within me as I stared at his toad-like, smiling face, so knowing in its slyness. What he suggested was unthinkable. The effort to hold myself back from striking him down made my entire body shake.

"Leave this estate immediately," I said in a low tone. "If you delay, I will not be responsible for my actions."

He blinked in owlish surprise.

"What do you mean?"

"If you don't leave at once I shall throw you into the tarn."

A look of sudden fear passed over his features. It was oddly intense and seemed more extreme than was justified by my very real threat. Without uttering another word, he rounded the rear bumper of his Nash and almost leapt into the driver's seat. The rear tires spun on the gravel, casting several stones into the black water, and he vanished in a cloud of dust over the crest of the hill and in among the trees.

9

By this time I wanted nothing more fervently than to leave this ghastly house of sorrows, with its black tarn and looming evergreens, behind me forever. I stayed on as Usher's guest; I could not desert him at so tragic a passage in his life. He had no one except the servants, and after two days not even them, because all of them—even the silent, silver-haired Simmons—turned in their resignations and left the Usher estate.

Tyson

I found myself cooking for both Usher and myself. He was in no fit state to do anything. The death of his sister almost unhinged his finely balanced brain. He wandered through the rooms of the empty house like a ghost, seldom speaking to me. I feared that the slightest disturbance in his life might cast him into complete madness. He did not say why the servants had left the house. Perhaps he did not know the reason himself. I wondered if it had anything to do with the creature in the tarn. Had they known about the creature? Did Usher himself know about it? On the day of my arrival he had alluded to seeing something stir beneath the black waters. I dared not mention the matter lest I sever his last link with reality.

I think it was four days after the death of Madeline, or it may have been five, that I was awakened in the night by a crash of thunder that shook the stone walls of the house to their foundations. I blinked the colours from my eyes and sat up in bed. A lightning flash while I lay asleep had impressed itself through my closed eyelids. For several minutes I sat in the darkness, listening to the wind throw the raindrops against my window like sheets of hailstones.

It came to me that the lightning might have struck some portion of the house and that it would be prudent to investigate, since there was no one within its walls but Usher and myself, and Usher was in no mental condition to do any kind of practical work. I put on my dressing gown and slippers and made my way by touch along the walls out the door of my room. My night vision began to return, and I was able to distinguish the hallway and the banister at its middle section that marked the upper landing of the main stairs.

I walked the length of the hall, sniffing for smoke. This may seem an insufficien precaution, but my sense of smell is uncommonly keen. I felt confident that if anything were burning above, I would detect the odour. There was no scent of smoke. I made my way toward the stairs, meaning to descend and go outside to examine the roofs and chimney pots of the house for damage. The lightning flashed periodically, giving me confidence that I would get brief but clear views of the roofs.

The door to Usher's bedroom was shut. I paused outside it and listened for the sound of movement, but heard nothing above the intermittent thunder aside from the gusts of wind

Curse of the House of Usher

against the walls and the rattle of rain against the windows. There seemed no reason to disturb the sleep of my troubled friend.

When I reached the hall, a noise drew my attention to the rear of the house, where the kitchen and storeroom were located. I stood listening at the foot of the stairs, but it did not come again, and I could not imagine what might have caused it. I wondered if Usher had been awakened by a crash of thunder and had himself descended to investigate before I left my room.

I walked toward the kitchen, moving cautiously through the darkness, which was infrequently broken by flashes from the windows. To my surprise, the door to the cellar stood open. Usher often descended to the crypt to mourn over the coffin of his sister, but so far as I knew, he had never done so in the middle of the night, even though it was perfectly possible that he went to her while I slept. It was not a topic I dared raise with him in his present unbalanced state.

For a time I hesitated, unsure which course to follow. I had no wish to intrude on my friend's mourning, but neither did I dare leave him alone in the cellars at night given his fragile condition. At last I descended the stones of the cellar stair and made my way along the damp lower corridor toward the crypt. A thin band of lamplight shone from under its iron-bound door.

While I was still a dozen paces from the door, strange noises from within the crypt made me stop and advance more slowly. The windowless door stood shut, but the gap beneath it was wide enough to permit the transmission of sounds. I laid my fingers on the chill iron of the latch, but hesitated. The noises continued. There was the rhythmic creak of wood, as though something were rocking back and forth. An image came to me of Usher, kneeling on the stone floor, rocking back and forth in the extremity of his mourning. Then I heard his grunt. It was a bestial sound, like that of a boar rooting in the mud with its snout. Without pausing to think, I pressed down on the latch and opened the door.

You may know the common expression, one's heart grew cold. It is more than mere words. As I stood before the door with my hand on the latch, the blood drained from my chest, and I felt a tangible chillness under my ribs, as though cool well water were being poured over my heart. My head began to spin, and it was only my grip on the latch that prevented me from falling. I swallowed and licked my lips, which had suddenly grown numb. With greater care than I had used to approach, I withdrew from the door, walking backward, as though from the very gateway of hell.

10

I was in the library when Usher found me. I needed time to think. He entered through the hall door and stopped when he saw me sitting at the reading table, my head in my hands, my fingers laced through my hair, the flame of the lamp fluttering wildly within its glass shade because in my confusion I had neglected to set the height of the wick after lighting it.

We stared at each other through the dancing shadows. Neither of us spoke. I could find no words, and Usher's tongue seemed frozen to the roof of his mouth. But his dark eyes spoke volumes in those voiceless minutes. I saw there shame, regret, self-loathing, remorse, frustration, anger, and defiance.

"You cannot understand," he said at last, his clear voice ringing out like rifle shots above the howl of the wind, for the storm was increasing in its fury.

"Usher, how could you—"

"I am the last of my line, Randolph. For the Ushers, family is everything. This house is everything. Its walls are our skin, its windows our eyes. It has endured for more than two centuries; but when I die, as I shall soon enough, there is no other of my blood to receive it or care for it."

My glare of revulsion softened with compassion.

"But surely there are other women."

"There have been many other women. But I loved none of them. All my life I have loved only one."

"Such an abomination cannot be called love."

His laughter horrified me. It had in it the ring of madness.

"You are like a child, Randolph. You have explored the strange land of dreams, but you have never seen the things I have seen or done what I have done. What I have with my sister is pure compared to those things. Vile, disgusting things."

"Your sister is dead, Roderick."

Curse of the House of Usher

He stared at me, wild-eyed, as though unable to comprehend my words.

"Madeline is dead," I repeated more slowly, emphasising each word.

"Yes," he said, nodding vigorously. A bit of spittle gleamed at the corner of his mouth. "But we came so close, Randolph, so very close, she and I."

A crash of thunder outside the front windows of the house made us both turn at the same instant toward the sitting room. She stood framed in the dividing archway. Her white limbs were naked save for a few scraps of her burial dress which she had torn away with her fingernails. Her belly, rounded no longer, was rent by a ragged gash that streamed blood and other effluvia over her thighs and shins. The severed umbilical cord hung down between her legs. In the hooked claws of her blood-soaked hands she held something small and red that wriggled feebly and waved its tiny arms in the air. A kind of mewing sound came from its lips, weak but already demanding attention.

In an instantaneous flash of lightning I saw more clearly that the premature fruit of her womb had other moving appendages beside its wriggling arms and legs. The motions of these false limbs were insect-like, too quick and skittering to be human. For some reason I cannot conceive I was reminded of the waving legs of a live lobster when it is dropped into a pot of boiling water. From its sloped forehead something projected that was like a single great blood-stained horn, and I know how Madeline's belly had been opened.

Thunder crashed with deafening force, shaking the entire house under our feet. In the wildly fluttering shadows from the lamp Usher took a step forward and reached out his hands.

"What miracle is this?" he asked with bursting joy. "Madeline, my dear love, you live!"

Her eyes stood open so wide their whites were visible all around their edges, and she smiled horribly, showing her teeth. A growling noise began deep in her throat and became progressively louder. As Usher took another step, she raised the writhing horror in her hands and brought it to her face as though to kiss it. A keening screech burst from its tiny mouth. With a violent jerk of her head, Madeline tore away its throat and began to chew its flesh, its blood glistening on her grinning lips and running down her chin.

Usher screamed like a damned soul and rushed toward her. She threw the monstrous infant at his face, and when he paused to brush it aside, she darted at him with inhuman quickness and fastened her long fingers around his neck. The two struggled. Usher seemed dazed, but Madeline was possessed of an unnatural strength. She pulled her brother's face toward hers and bit him on the cheek while his arms flailed impotently over her hunched naked shoulders.

It was the snapping of Usher's neck that roused me from my trance. I made no effort to speak to this mad thing that was no longer human but ran past her through the drawing room and into the hall, where I tore open the front door and dashed into the rain and the wind. So great was the fury of the storm that I could not hear my slippered feet as they pounded across the bridge. I did not pause or look behind until I had reached the crest of the hill at the edge of the forest. Only then did I collapse to the road and turn to view the house.

The flashes of lighting and crashing of thunder were almost continuous. By this hellish illumination I watched the main roof of the house of the Ushers fall slowly in upon itself, and after it the walls collapse inward. I blinked the rain from my eyes and squinted against the electric glare. It seemed to me that something extended itself up from the boiling waters of the tarn, which were whipped by the gusts of wind. Whatever it may have been, it was long and black, so that it was almost invisible to my sight save where the lightning was reflected from its gleaming curves. It wrapped around a chimney that still remained and, with a wrench that I heard from the hill, hurled it down into the tarn with the other building rubble.

It is long to write of this destruction, which took only a few heartbeats to accomplish. I sat for a while in the rain, staring at the low pile of jumbled stones that had once been the ancient home of a proud family, but was now returned forever to its primal chaos. The curse of Usher was fulfilled, and the house of Usher stood no more.

The Rolling of Old Thunder

After R. L. Stevenson's "The Body Snatcher"

Mark Howard Jones

That late summer Edinburgh had been plagued with thunderstorms, yet very little rain. It seemed to the inhabitants of the city as if the clouds were reluctant to release their balm, to ease the pressure and freshen the air. Instead the storms insisted on oppressing them, doing nothing to relieve the heat. The mornings were cool, on the other hand—cold enough for the mist to cling to the streets until mid-morning, lending them a near-spectral glow.

The sun was many hours from burning away the mist one morning when a tightly bundled figure hurried across Surgeon's Square. Pausing briefly, the man checked one of his pockets before disappearing down a flight of stone steps leading to an almost hidden door. Once inside, Macfarlane spent a few moments trying to brush the stink of the cramped, mist-wreathed streets from his clothes. He shook the thin layer of water droplets from his coat and hung it up. "Filthy weather again," he complained. "You're here early, Fettes."

The other man looked up from a small desk, where he was writing in a large ledger. "We had a delivery last night. I thought I'd best get things 'tidied away.'"

"Very diligent of you. It does you credit," said Macfarlane. He walked over to the examination slab and pulled back the grubby sheet. The skin of the corpse was an unsettling blue. The doctor put his hand over his nose to block out the smell. "Uuugh! Hardly fresh, is it?"

"He was hanged yesterday, according to the orderly who delivered the poor unfortunate fellow," said Fettes. His companion snorted in obvious disbelief.

Fettes looked down with distaste at the black tongue and swollen face so typical of a victim of hanging. He'd seen so many hanged criminals come through this place over the years that he'd almost forgotten what the face of someone who'd died peacefully looked like.

"The head goes to Richardson again, I suppose?" he asked.

Macfarlane nodded. "I hesitate to speculate why he has such a liking for the human cranium. I have no idea what he expects to find in there."

"The soul maybe." Fettes saw himself as a rational man, who looked down on those holding religious beliefs as being worthy of nothing but pity. "Well, after all, his father was a preacher, wasn't he?"

Richardson sat in Mr. Killian's class later that day, gazing glumly down as the surgeon explained the intricacies of the blood vessels running through the arm.

Though the topic did not excite him much, Richardson knew that the mechanics of medicine had to be mastered if he was to become anything more than a merely competent doctor. Competence was anathema to him; he demanded far more of himself.

The stink of the cadaver laid before the students as they clustered around the dissection table was nearly overpowering. One, a young Englishman called Purcell, had already succumbed to the lethal combination of summer heat and the stench. Richardson wasn't about to follow him.

He watched as the surgeon parted a delicate blue vein from its shiny, fragile moorings, all the while explaining the function of the circulatory system in the anatomy of the arm.

Poking about in rotting flesh seemed an odd path to take to become a doctor, he thought. Indeed, it was an uncomfortable and vaguely obscene route into medicine, it seemed to him. Yet what other method was open to them? They had to have material to work on. There was no other way to learn.

There were even dark rumours of two detestable Irishmen, low types who weren't beyond the practice of rudely "resurrecting" those recently laid to rest. It caused him acute discomfort to think that the heights of science might be built on a foundation of filthy business conducted in graveyards and cellars. Yet like his fellow students, Richardson put whatever qualms he had to one side in the name of medicine and advancement, both scientific and personal.

When he was being honest with himself, Richardson admitted that, like his father before him, he hoped for resurrection. Not the feeble promises of his Christian counterparts, nor yet the unholy desecrations meted out by the so-called Resurrection Men, but something that spoke of true glory and a return to man's original form.

And now, finally, he was certain he'd found the means to achieve his goal.

"All right gentlemen, you may resume your seats." Killian's words broke the spell, and the students all drifted listlessly back to their seats in the hot stench of freshly gained knowledge.

⁂

As they all filed out of the lecture room, Richardson glanced around at his fellow students. They seemed so small—both their bodies and their ambitions. They might as well be animated wax simulacra for all the good they'll ever do, he thought.

In his mind, he turned the book of miracles over and over in his hands, just as he'd done in his room last evening, relishing the uncommon texture of its strange binding. Its contents were a map to a hidden domain of strange and wonderful learning.

Why spend his time labouring with the other worker bees when he could be brilliant, celebrated? He might know in mere moments what it would take them years to discover— and then go on to learn far, far more than they would ever know.

He had the two keys that could open these unimagined new avenues of knowledge—the book and his serum, which alone allowed him to decipher it.

⁂

Outside the sky was heavy and threatening yet still, reminding Richardson of a hastily painted backdrop to a lacklustre play.

Although he was a Highlander and not a native of Auld Reekie, Richardson had grown to feel at home in the place. He'd even been known to seek out some of the more disreputable taverns, where he'd find a secluded corner if possible, there to nurse a glass of ale and watch the behaviour of the inhabitants. He'd sit and watch their pleasures and their torments pass by like a spectator at the circus or, perhaps more accurately he often thought, a visitor to the zoo. The pastimes, half bestial and half angelic, of the tavern's habitues fascinated him.

He often pondered on what kept mankind in this semi-animal state. Surely it couldn't be natural? He returned to his studies with renewed vigour following a visit to the dirty, rowdy taverns. Then he was more determined than ever to release the secrets that lay locked within each person's head.

In his anatomy classes, he handled the cadavers with a degree of dismay at how life could be reduced to these cold, dead remnants. He'd asked Mr. Killian for the opportunity to study the brain as his area of specialism. The head of each corpse was duly delivered to his table, though he was always glad to extract the cold, white orbs and pass them to another student to study. His area of interest lay behind the eyes.

The more he'd studied the pine cone—shaped structure buried deep within the brain, the more he'd become convinced that the overlooked pineal gland, as small as it was, held the key to opening new horizons for mankind.

Like the Frenchman Descartes before him, he was fascinated by the strange little structure. But he'd gone far further than the illustrious philosopher ever had in probing its secrets. With only the simplest of scientific instruments available to him in his humble lodgings, Richardson had made the best of his situation. Fortunately all the hard work could be done at the anatomy class.

It took the secretions of the pineal glands of two average-sized adults to prepare the formula he needed. There was, of course, no other method open to him than to experiment upon himself. He knew it was a great risk, but in his mind the potential rewards more than outweighed any danger.

One remarkable piece of equipment was available to him. Less than a decade ago, Dr. Alexander Wood had created the device not so far from the poor lodgings in which Richardson now sat. The hypodermic syringe that he'd "borrowed" from the dissection room allowed him to administer the formula himself. Without it he would almost certainly have needed assistance, and that would not do. This was a road he knew he had to travel alone.

He'd quickly learned that once his heartbeat began to elevate, he was able to read clearly the pages of the volume left to him by his late father. The language was certainly antique and, he thought, overly reverential. Clearly some of the beings referred to as "gods" could be no such thing.

Once the solution had taken hold of him, his mind became illuminated from within. He supposed that this was because the preparation was enhancing his pineal gland's natural secretions. He ran his eyes over the pages of the book. Some of the strange glyphs now became jumbles of letters that were either indecipherable or simply unpronounceable. They made little sense to him as words, but somehow he was able to divine their meaning.

Yet, despite his enhanced abilities, some symbols still retained their mystery. And there was an insistence upon a type of geometry that was entirely unfamiliar to him from his schooling. He did his best, but a true understanding of it still eluded him.

He knew some were words of death, but others were invocations and imprecations of great power. He could sense that the book was the key to an undreamt-of realm of hidden abilities and powerful allies, concealed just beyond the veil of the reality he saw about him. He knew his own world was partly illusion—any fool could see that—but how to tear away its mask and reveal its true face was a secret that he dearly wished to learn.

If he'd had that knowledge some years earlier, he might have been able to save his father from the wasting disease that had taken him. Instead, he and his mother and sisters had been forced to watch helplessly while the filthy thing had hollowed his father out while he still lived, dying a little more each day.

Richardson had become sickened by the two years his family spent praying to a God who didn't hear them, or didn't care.

The doctors were stuck for a diagnosis, and the spectacle of his severely ailing father had strengthened Richardson's resolve to study medicine. For he was determined to do better than those men of medicine who had failed his father so badly.

Even the odd deformity of the middle finger of his right hand had not deterred him. When Mr. Killian, the surgeon and principal anatomy teacher, had told him he'd never be able to wield a scalpel properly, he'd learned to do so with his left hand instead.

He'd determined that nothing, and no one, was going to stand in his way.

The strange summer of lingering mists and unseasonal thunder almost passed Richardson by unnoticed as his fascination with the arcane book grew.

An odd, unhealthy smell clung to the volume, and its cover had a decidedly clammy feel to it. Richardson speculated that the binding might actually be some sort of skin, though what sort of animal it came from was uncertain.

How it had come to be in his father's library was unknown, and it struck him from time to time that it was an odd thing for a churchman to own.

At first, it had seemed like any other book to Richardson. Then, some months after his father's death, a former colleague of the old man had called to pay his respects to Richardson's mother. His father's books lay scattered around, in the process of being sorted through. One particular book had caught the visitor's eye. The man, a Norwegian pastor named Saknussemm, commented on the volume and drew Richardson to one side, advising the boy to destroy it without delay.

Richardson had protested, naturally feeling proprietorial toward his late father's possessions. But the pastor had persisted, hinting that the book was a seventeenth-century transliteration of a scroll from ancient Damascus. He went on to say that all copies of the book had been ordered to be destroyed by Pope Urban VIII. Richardson thought this an odd comment coming from a Protestant clergyman and decided to ignore the man's advice.

The Rolling of Old Thunder

The following year when Richardson, convinced of the book's value, had tried to sell the volume to an Edinburgh book dealer, he was shown the door with a glare that could not have been any more icy if he'd threatened to kill the man's entire family in front of him.

His curiosity piqued still further, Richardson had found references to the mysterious indecipherable text in libraries in Edinburgh and Oxford. These references, scant as they were, convinced him that he possessed something that could be a great asset to him, if not also a tool of great power.

It was not until he took up the study of medicine that the key to unlocking the book's mysteries had accidentally presented itself.

On the first occasion that Richardson had administered the solution to himself, he had expected a certain amount of sensory disorientation. But he was dismayed at how little about his surroundings had actually changed. Perhaps he'd got the quantities wrong while preparing the solution, he thought. But then his eyes happened to fall upon a pile of books that lay on his rickety shelf.

Most of his small collection of books had maintained their mundane appearance while he was under the influence of the solution. But one, tucked at the bottom of a tottering pile of texts, seemed to glow and writhe oddly within his vision. Richardson reached down and carefully drew out the strange old book that he'd inherited from his father.

He was astonished to see that the ruined cover had been restored to a soft fine-grained brown leather. He'd been right on that count, at least, but what animal it had come from was still not apparent. Near the top, picked out in gold leaf, sat the words "Al Azif." Whoever had translated the work had obviously kept the original title; maybe because it was beyond their skills to render it accurately into another language. Yet, though he spoke not a single phrase of Arabic, Richardson sensed that the title meant "The Voice of the Tempest," or something very like it.

Richardson reached out and, as he had done several times before, opened the volume at random. Astonished, he realised that the words were drawing him in as bold new ideas took shape in his mind.

It was as if a secret eye had been opened within his brain—one that saw through the surface of mundane reality to the truth behind it. His experiments had proved him right! He ran his hands over the book with a barely suppressed sense of ecstasy, as if electricity were transferring itself from his fingertips directly to the centre of his mind.

He had no idea what this book had to do with his father's pallid religion or how or why his father came to possess it, but he knew instinctively that, just like a scalpel, if it could be wielded skilfully it could do much good.

Richardson's dreams that night were half-formed things, vague yet insistent, as if struggling to see a reflection in a mirror covered in cobwebs. The sense that something was coming from a vast distance away clung to his sleep. There was an ocean to cross, vast mountains to overcome, but whatever it was wouldn't give up. It was on a peculiar quest to find him and him alone. And when it arrived, it would come with a tremendous gift, he felt.

Yet, as relatively benevolent as the dream had been, there was something appalling about it that clung to Richardson all the next day.

Once when under the influence of the solution, Richardson had been disturbed by his landlady, Mrs. Mackenzie. The woman was a widow and, while not unattractive, had clearly grown old before her time. She seemed fond of Richardson and treated him very like a son.

She had come into his room and begun talking about some mundane subject when suddenly she stopped. Something about Richardson's manner had alerted her to the fact that he was somehow different. "Not himself," she had put it. This had made Richardson laugh—for he'd never felt *more* like himself.

He remembered going right up to the woman and

staring at her, causing her to draw cautiously back a step or two as he continued to peer at her closely. Her skin seemed to be alive with tiny crawling creatures, normally invisible. The concentrated pineal secretions had transformed her from a mere person into a fascinating collection of fauna. Rather than a single person, she appeared to him like a walking menagerie, and he wondered if his own skin was similarly infested.

The woman had soon left, declaring Richardson to be ill and claiming that she would call a doctor to him. She must soon after have realised the absurdity of her words as no doctor had shown up. If he had, thought Richardson later, I could have told him a thing or two.

The next morning Richardson had woken late. Distractedly grabbing a number of books, he had rushed out to his class, not stopping for breakfast or to wash.

In the corridor he had collided with Macfarlane, who cursed him for a clumsy clod before stooping to help him retrieve his books. By chance Macfarlane's hand alighted on the strange old volume. Richardson's heart climbed up to block his throat when he realised that he must have picked it up in error.

Macfarlane turned it over in his hands. On his face was a look of disgusted fascination. "What's this?" he demanded.

Richardson reached out to retrieve the volume, only for Macfarlane to hold it out of his reach. "It's a religious volume," Richardson offered.

Macfarlane looked down his nose at the book, which now fell open in his broad palm. "Indeed. And what language is this?" he quizzed, scanning the unfamiliar glyphs that filled the pages.

"It's Greek," replied the student.

Macfarlane smiled cruelly. "I know Greek, my boy. This is not Greek."

Macfarlane was only a few years Richardson's senior, and the younger man detested being called "boy." "It's a very old form of Greek," protested Richardson. "You must understand, Macfarl—*Mister* Macfarlane, my father was a churchman and a scholar. He owned many obscure volumes of old lore and religious thought."

"If you say so, Richardson." Macfarlane equally disliked any attempt to put him in his place. "And you claim to understand this scrawl, do you?"

Richardson looked sheepish. It took him several seconds to answer, "Yes. . . after a fashion."

"You are an extraordinary fellow," said Macfarlane, handing back the book. "It looks and smells as though you've literally dug this thing up." Then he dusted off his hands and walked away.

In his darker moments Richardson dearly wished that one day he'd see Macfarlane's head sitting on the dissecting table before him. He even speculated on how hard he'd have to press the scalpel blade into the soft spongy mass before all that had been Macfarlane, all the arrogance and cruelty and worldliness, began to seep out, ready to be collected and analysed. Not very hard, he wagered.

The cold corpse eye of the west moon looked down on Richardson as he left his lodgings that late summer night. His landlady had taken to her bed long ago and the cold, narrow streets were empty at this late hour.

With the pineal solution flowing through his veins, the grey city about him was transformed. Colours formed and flowed in peculiar pools, streaming down the walls to gather and swirl along the gutters.

The paving beneath his feet throbbed with a previously unnoticed vitality, as if the city were a living thing. If he stared down for long enough he sensed a great dark river flowing beneath everything, connecting each thing to every other thing. But he also sensed that it was filled with corruption and that to know it too well would lead to despair and emptiness. He must not get dragged under. So instead he raised his eyes to the blazing sky above, filled with its glittering supernal lanterns. He was almost sure he could see the dark star-winds, blowing life like a spore from shore to cold celestial shore.

He felt as though the thin veil of reality had been

saturated with an acid that was now dissolving it, revealing the more beautiful truth behind it. Yet he also knew that the night's task that lay ahead would be grisly and require strong nerves.

Though he was no longer a religious man, something deep within Richardson balked at what was required of him. Dissecting a cadaver in the cold light of medical knowledge was one thing; to do it under the moon's icy glare was quite another.

The book had quite clearly stated several times that the ritual needed to be performed in a burial ground and that certain materials would be required. As he headed toward the city's largest cemetery, Richardson pushed his doubts aside, musing that tonight he would find the secrets that he'd been longing to know for so long. Tonight or not at all.

As he approached a crossroads, something caught his eye in an alleyway off to his left. He was taken aback to see a naked figure moving toward him out of the gloom. At first he put the remarkable sight down to a restless sleepwalker, venturing abroad from the safety of his bed. Yet as the figure stepped into a pool of moonlight, he saw that he'd been mistaken.

The man took several more steps toward him before Richardson allowed the truth to dawn on him. The figure was that of his dead father.

Richardson began to walk away, uncertain whether his mind was not now unhinged. The strange figure began to walk beside him. Yet the man he saw before him was no animated corpse, come back to claim an unspecified revenge like some spectre from a penny dreadful. For his father had undergone a transformation.

He had clearly been dissected. Yet although he had been reduced to sections or collops of meat, still he hung together and walked like a man, keeping pace with Richardson.

From the top of his father's head grew a strange extrusion like a young sapling. Richardson recognised at once that this was the true form of the pineal gland, though he was slightly disconcerted to note its grey fungous nature.

He pondered what role the gland might play after death. Was it the true seat of the soul? he wondered.

Richardson noted his own calmness with a small pang of pleasure. He put this down to the very pineal preparation that now coursed through his veins. If he had seen the awful sight of his dead father walking abroad at any other time, he was convinced he would have dropped down dead from shock.

What had been his father put its hand on his arm and turned him around. Richardson sensed that the creature had something important to say to him.

He could clearly see the partly bisected tongue working in the gap left by several extracted teeth. But no sound came forth. "I-I'm sorry, Father. I cannot hear you," apologised Richardson to the phantasm.

In his left hand Richardson carried a small sack containing a short-handled spade, the book, and a small lantern that he would need to read it by. His father pointed to the sack, mouthing wordlessly, as if he sensed the presence of the book. Richardson peered at him for a moment, but there were no words for him to hear and no expression was discernible on what was left of the man's face.

He shook his head and, turning, resumed his path. The paternal phantom fell into step again beside him. It seems he will be accompanying me on my night's deeds, mused Richardson.

Against his will, Richardson shuddered as the moonlit shadow of a church steeple fell on him, imparting a feeling of cold and immense distance. On the horizon, heavy clouds massed, moving toward him against the night wind.

Soon the moon was blotted out by swift-moving dark clouds and, within minutes, the first peal of thunder filled the air. Richardson knew deep within him that this was a particular kind of thunder, one that had rolled around the earth since life had begun.

Once more his father detained him by placing the remains of his hand on Richardson's sleeve. The phantom seemed more agitated this time, gesturing in an odd manner in an attempt to win his son over. The uncanny semaphore meant nothing to Richardson and eventually he was forced to snatch his sleeve away. His father seemed more resigned to his failure this time.

As the thunder rolled overhead, it suddenly struck

Richardson that perhaps his intuition of the title of the ancient book had been wrong after all. Maybe "The Voice IN the Tempest" was closer to the original meaning. For he was almost certain there was something in the crashing sound that called to him, urging him onwards.

The cemetery now lay directly ahead, and Richardson reached into his sack to retrieve the lantern in readiness.

At this, the figure of his father fell back, trailing a step or two behind him. When Richardson noticed and looked round, it was clear he was unwilling to follow and began walking away. Richardson called after him once but, eliciting no response, turned his mind instead to the task ahead.

He walked the last few yards slowly, resting for a moment as he reached the huge gateposts.

As Richardson pushed open the gate to the cemetery he saw he would not need his lantern after all. He was met by the sight of several corpses standing above their graves, burning like spectral candles set ablaze to aid his task.

Illuminated by the benevolent light of his curious guardian angels, Richardson selected a relatively recent grave and began to dig. The work went easily, as if he had been granted added strength. The harsh sound of the spade scraping against the gravestone, striking off a shower of sparks, sounded like a symphony of dark desire to him. He felt on the verge of an extraordinary new life, with the path ahead filled with towering achievements.

Once the coffin was above ground, he dragged its contents free and opened the book. Its instructions were clear if unpleasant. He spent some minutes rearranging parts of the coffin's grisly contents, then began intoning the challenging and prolonged ritual.

Barely twenty minutes had passed when the noctilucent glow of the corpse candles flickered, faded, and then was gone. They had disappeared completely, as if blown away on the thin night breeze.

With the moon masked by clouds, Richardson was left in almost total darkness. He fumbled in his sack, managing at last to light the small lantern. By its glow, he saw that the marvellous tome had become a mouldering codex of unreadable antiquity once more. The syllabary of secrets had leaked away, draining out of his blood along with the false miracle of his serum; it had run its course and been purged from his system too quickly this time. But he hadn't finished the ritual . . .

Looking down at the destruction he'd wrought on the disinterred corpse, he was seized by a feeling of sickness. The decaying, dismembered limbs were twisted at unnatural angles, while a constellation of bone splinters stuck upright from the ground, spelling out the name of a black, unholy thing.

Despite the warmth of the summer night, Richardson began to shiver. The chill brought with it a sense of fear—what was he doing in this filthiest of all places alone at night? He must get out before he was discovered.

The cold creeping into him also brought an awful realisation. As he scrabbled for his coat and bag, he knew that the book, the blazing cadavers—perhaps even his vision of his father—had all been illusions born of his fevered mind.

Could it be that the pineal gland did not open a window onto a world of greater mysteries, but merely held up a mirror reflecting illusions? It sickened him to think he had merely been gazing at his own distorted features all along.

The book was no beginning. Instead it spelled the end of everything he'd hoped for. All he'd done was to uncover a path leading to nowhere but a fool's paradise. In disgust he held up the book, its pages crumbling at the rough treatment, ready to fling it into the open grave, but something prevented him from moving.

Even if the words he'd spoken earlier had been incoherent, even incorrect, something had heard him. . . or, at least, felt his yearning. Thick dark clouds had gathered over the burying ground, slow thunder rumbling deep in their throat. Richardson raised his eyes as far as possible. He waited one heartbeat. Two.

Then something impossible—all angles and no body—dropped from the cloud like a stone falling from a high cliff. He struggled to make his eyes see it, for there was almost nothing there. Almost. But it was in his head.

The thing pivoted around the odd angles at the summit of an obelisk-topped tomb. If it had eyes, then Richardson felt them on him. He'd been trapped by dreams, his own delusions, and now he was going to die. He wanted to yell out in protest but was still frozen like a stone.

The dark messenger reached out to him, too swift to see. When it gripped him, the worst thing wasn't the pain—though it burned like a branding iron; it was the secrets it told him, in a voice like a thousand buzzing insects crowding into his head.

Then, just for one moment, it allowed him to scream.

Fettes and Macfarlane met as they came into Surgeon's Square at mid-afternoon the next day. Fettes tipped the brim of his hat to the older man. "A wild night! Did you hear the thunder, eh?"

"I'd have had to be already in my grave not to," replied Macfarlane.

"And an odd storm at that. My sister has a view of Warriston Cemetery from her home. She will swear to you that not only was the storm centred upon the cemetery but that the lightning was going up into the sky from among the graves."

"Eh? Impossible! A trick of the light perhaps . . ." offered Macfarlane.

Fettes shook his head. "Perhaps so, Macfarlane, perhaps so. Her neighbour said that something was seen flying, or falling, from the sky.

"Mmmm. A large bird struck by the lightning perhaps."

Fettes fished the large key from his pocket as they descended the steps, then slipped it quickly into the lock, eager to be inside. As soon as he was through the door, he almost slipped on the topmost of the stone steps. "Damn it!" Then, as he examined the steps more closely: "There's some sort of filth all over the steps. Mind your footing, Macfarlane."

Macfarlane followed him down carefully, steadying himself on the iron railing. "Ah, you've had a delivery, I see. Excellent. Mr. Killian will be pleased."

Fettes stared in disbelief at the slab. A body lay under the sheet. "There was no delivery today. It's far too early for those foul rogues to deliver anything; you know that."

A look of slight alarm crossed Macfarlane's face. "Then what. . . ?"

"Th-there's no head on this one!" stammered Fettes, realising that the shape beneath the sheet ended just above the shoulders.

Now Macfarlane became angry. "If Richardson has taken it already, I'll strip the hide from the whelp! What impertinence!"

Fettes drew back the sheet covering the body. Both drew in their breath sharply at the sight that met them. The head had not been removed surgically, but instead had been gnawed and twisted free by some sort of beast, the exact nature of which they dared not speculate upon.

Their nerves were further unsettled when the corpse's right hand fell from below the covering sheet, revealing the disfigured middle finger of the student Richardson. And clutched between the fingers, soaked in gore and filth, was a single crumpled page from an antique volume.

Always a Castle?

Nancy Kilpatrick

"We've always lived in the castle," Martin told me.

I glanced at him, a handsome if aloof man, late thirties maybe, who looked as if he rarely smiled. I turned back to face the enormous Tudor-Jacobean edifice that I would not have called a castle, more a small estate, although it did sport turrets.

Reddish brickwork had never appealed to me—this building material reminded me too much of PS 46 in the Bronx where I'd gone to grade school—but I did like the bay windows, and especially the little windows framing the front door. The wavy glass looked Tudor—I could tell by the green color—and I was amazed the panes had lasted over 500 years. "Since the castle was built, Dana," Martin assured me, as if reading my mind.

He insisted on a tour. I was pretty sure he'd be a good guide, but I was exhausted after such a long trip to Yorkshire. First there had been the six-hour flight from New York, an overnight near noisy Kings Cross tube station in London, then the early train to Leeds, where I was met at the station by a driver in one of those enormous old black Austins that used to dominate the streets of London. The ride to Whaterley House took close to an hour, and I curled up against the car's lush upholstery and stared out the window. Enchanting as I found the increasingly rural scenery, I still managed a couple of catnaps.

At the entrance to the stately home I'd been greeted by Martin Whaterley, the nephew of Alexandra Whaterley, an aged widow in need of a companion who had selected me from "six hundred and sixty-six applicants," Martin's email quoted her as saying. I didn't know whether to believe that number, and I vacillated between feeling flattered and frightened by such a picky employer.

This was not my dream job. My recently acquired BA in history did not open doors to exciting work. To go for an

MA with its promises of employment, well, I needed money. I definitely felt I had a grander purpose in life than taking care of a sick old woman in a remote location, but still, they'd paid for the trip to England, and the contract was short term.

Martin took my coat down the hall and left my suitcases inside the door. The entrance area was large, with a grand staircase, overhead chandelier, black and white tiles beneath my feet, and a Marketry Regency table under an oil painting of goats grazing in a field.

Martin was back quickly, and I followed him on the enforced tour: the private parlor with what I judged to be a George II breakfront full of no doubt expensive knick-knacks and several damask-upholstered sofas with carved arms and legs; the library crammed floor to ceiling with leather-bound volumes that sheltered comfy-looking chairs; the "drawing room" where presumably men used to smoke after dinner; the elegant dining room, set for a dozen dinner guests with ornate silver cutlery, crystal glassware, and fine-bone china rimmed in gold; the industrial kitchen—the only modern room I saw—all gleaming copper-bottomed pots hanging over the granite counter nestled in the middle of the latest stainless steel appliances; and finally the great hall that extended at the far end into a glassed-in atrium, this long and wide space crammed with walnut and ebony Queen Anne furniture, arranged to comprise seven living room groupings. I wondered if this vast room was ever used. "We don't hold parties, because of Auntie's advanced age. Just once a year, in the spring," Martin said, with that uncanny ability to guess my thoughts, or at least read my face, since clearly I was impressed by sideboards and silver tea services ready to accommodate a multitude of visitors.

Four large tapestries depicting medieval forest scenes hung from the walls, but most of the space was devoted to at least fifty gilded-framed portraits going back to what Martin assured me was "six generations, including the current generation, of course." These ancestors had been painted with downturned lips, beady eyes, and severe expressions on their goat-like faces as they stood aggressively before pillars and thrones, or were presented in woodsy scenes with weapons and hunting dogs. I leaned in to the closest one to read the name on the brass plate: *Wilber Whaterley*. "My great-great-uncle, an American," Martin informed me.

I stared at Martin and blurted out, "You don't resemble your ancestors."

"Traits are often refined through natural selection," he said, with what I took to be a minuscule smile. Clearly the man knew his Darwin!

All the portraits were of men, and I wondered where the wives' images were stashed, but felt it a little too early to say anything controversial other than, "Interesting features, your male ancestors." I left it to Martin to say more, but he didn't.

Instead, he led me up the massive oak staircase, the same polished wood used throughout the first floor, the steps lined with a faded Oriental runner, almost threadbare, and Martin nodded downward, saying, "This has been here since the nineteenth century. The wood is original, but furniture, drapes, carpeting have been added with each generation. Nothing has ever been removed, only added."

As we ascended, I noticed traces of a nasty odor, the smell getting sharper as we rose. We turned right and entered a door at the end of the hallway. My bags had been brought to this room by someone. The large space contained a Chinese Red lacquered dresser, a Louis XIV writing desk and accompanying walnut chair upholstered in red, an enormous gilded mirror above the desk, a black wrought-iron fireplace I could walk into if I felt like it, and a high narrow bed the length of which pressed against a wall. A gold filigreed *ciel de lit* attached above the bed, the red and rose gauzy curtain draped at the head and foot. A small wooden footstool had been placed beside the bed in order to climb up. Every wall was covered with flocked wallpaper—scarlet!—but for the wainscoting. The British would have said I was nonplussed; I would have called that an understatement. At least the smell wasn't so bad in here, but I wanted to open a window.

"I understand you've a degree in antique decor," Martin said. That wasn't quite right—my major had been English history, and antique furnishings had been a minor, not much more than a serious hobby. I decided on a smile instead of words because, again, I was feeling both overwhelmed and tired, and that smell was getting to me. Later, with the door shut and the old leaded casement open, I hoped I could air out the room.

"I've put you here, in what we call the Hell-Fire Chamber. A bit of family humor."

"Interesting," I said, not sure how to respond to that. "Come, I'll show you Auntie Alexandra's rooms and you can meet her," Martin offered as, grim-faced, he led me back into the hallway, gesturing in a dismissive way as we passed a half-dozen closed doors, saying, "There's nothing worth seeing in these."

I'd have *loved* to see what was inside. Among other favorites, I'm a huge fan of *petit point* and mahogany Chippendale—I spotted an ornate Chippy tilt-table in the great hall! I'd also seen a gorgeous embroidered three-person *indiscret* settee there, obviously not dating back to the house's inception, but who cares!

As we walked down the long hallway toward the other end, I noticed the rank odor growing stronger. It was so foul that I found a tissue in my dress pocket and dabbed it at my nose, pretending I had the sniffles, an obvious and vapid attempt to disguise my revulsion. Martin didn't seem to notice my reaction or even the smell for that matter, so I gave up discretion in favor of crudeness and just held the tissue to my nostrils. Still, as we walked along the hallway, the odor became overpowering; I felt an urge to gag but had the sense to control myself. *Nice reaction, Dana, your irst day on the job!*

We reached the other end of the hallway, turned left, then went up six steps to a massive door. This area was so dark—no windows or lighting—that I couldn't make out the carvings in the wood. A horizontal crystal door handle was positioned in the dead center of the door; I'd only seen door handles—mostly knobs—in the centers of the enormous doors of eighteenth-century cathedrals. I leaned in and squinted. When I realized that the handle was shaped like an arm bone, I jerked back.

Martin knocked three times with one knuckle, so quietly I wondered if Mrs. Whaterley would hear him. He didn't wait for a response but pushed the bone handle down and the door creaked inward.

I found the source of the stink! It was so bad in there that I did gag, and clamped the tissue over my mouth too.

Martin still didn't seem to notice as he led me further in.

We'd entered an almost lightless room. As my eyes adjusted, I figured this to be a kind of sitting room, the curtains drawn tight against the early afternoon sunlight, and I couldn't make out anything but vague outlines of furnishings. We quickly passed through the open double doors into the large bedroom where the drapes were also closed. One fat pillar candle in a tall iron holder next to the double bed made a valiant attempt to pierce the darkness of this suite, but faced a losing battle. If it hadn't been for the stark white face, I probably wouldn't have noticed the small form lying on the bed, covers pulled to above the chin. And despite knowing I was being rude, I held the tissue firmly over my nose and tried to breathe through my mouth with small breaths.

"Auntie, this is Ms. Dana Keenan, your new companion."

I expected a feeble response, or none at all, but a booming voice with a register low enough to be a baritone burst from the bed. "I know who in hell she is!"

I waited a respectful second, but when Mrs. W did not acknowledge my presence, I suppressed my surging "fuck you, lady!" attitude, removed the tissue from my nose, and said, "Hello, Mrs. Whaterley. It's a pleasure to meet you."

"Is it?" the voice snapped. "We'll see what pleasure you feel in my presence."

This shocked me. Martin, whom I could not see, said in a soft voice, "Auntie tires easily these days. We'd best keep this first meeting short.

To her he added in a louder and vaguely cheerful voice, as if the old lady was deaf and dumb—and I doubted she was either—"We'll go now, Auntie, so that Ms. Keenan can get settled. Perhaps you can come down this evening and—"

"I'll come down if I feel like it and not if I don't!"

Martin reached out of the shadows and took my arm, turning me from the cranky old woman and leading me back through the sitting room. I'd brought the tissue up to my nose again, aware that the vile odor was now trapped in my sinuses. I *really* wanted to get outside for some fresh air.

Just as we reached the door, that voice reverberated

through the two rooms and surrounded us. "I'll want attending to this night!"

My heart sank. I realized I could not do this job. I needed the work, and this was England after all—a real opportunity—and in such a bad economy I was lucky to even find a decent-paying job; but no matter how much I tried to dissuade myself, this was too much. The woman was nasty, and the rancid odor that clogged the air. . . No, I wouldn't be staying at Whaterley House!

I followed Martin to the first floor and as we reached the bottom of the stairs, I was about to tell him of my decision and did manage to say, "Martin, I'd—"

That was as far as I got. He interrupted me with, "Come, Ms. Keenan—may I call you Dana?"

"Uh, yes, of course," I said, thinking, *You already have!*

"Let's walk through the grounds and I'll show you the gardens—we've prize-winning antique roses. It's crisp today. I'll get your coat."

Before I could respond, he vanished, leaving me standing at the entrance. I thought about how I could phrase my quick resignation without being either obnoxious or obtuse, because I had no intention of staying in this house even one night, let alone fulfilling a contract that spanned the better part of a year. That wasn't going to happen!

Martin returned with my coat and scarf and led me out the door to the flagstone walk where we turned right. This paved path wound away from the house and even from here I could see massive gardens ahead. All the while Martin chatted about the construction of the garden by Capability Brown in the eighteenth century, the maze at its epicenter, expanded over the centuries, and the variety of flowers and shrubs. I've never been able to identify flowers, unless they appeared on upholstery, but I knew what I found visually beautiful and pleasant scented, and this garden was that.

We stopped at the heirloom roses, only one miraculously still in bloom. "The weather turned a fortnight ago," Martin said, again exhibiting his uncanny skill of mind-reading. "Flowers, unfortunately, die from the cold. But the bushes are perennials, you know. Each spring they bring forth new life."

He bent and snapped the stem of the single white rose still in bloom, and for some reason that aggressive act seemed violent to me, destroying the last living thing in this bed of decay.

He turned and handed it to me, his ashen eyes still expressionless, his lips an even straight line, as if they were incapable of turning either up or down. I found his benign face mesmerizing and absently reached out to take the rose.

And cried out as pain shot through my fingertip. I jerked my hand away from the thorn, and blood flecks splattered the flower's pristine petals.

"Be careful!" Martin snapped, his voice a sudden imitation of Mrs. Whaterley's in tone, depth, and annoyance, and I glanced at his face. "We don't want you infected!" His eyes had turned steely, his look so intense I had to turn away.

I glanced toward the house and saw movement at the corner of an upstairs window and suspected it was Mrs. Whaterley, watching.

All this so unnerved me that I blurted out, "Martin, I'm really sorry, but I can't take the job. I'm not the right person to be your aunt's companion."

His eyes settled into the flat grey and he said in an even voice, "But, Dana, you've come all this way. Surely you might give the position a chance."

He sounded so reasonable, and I realized I'd had a tinge of hysteria in my voice. I tried to calm my tone. "You have hundreds of résumés. You'll find someone else, I'm sure." Why was I trying to reassure *him?*

As if on cue, thunder rumbled overhead and the sky darkened quickly. "I think we'd best retreat to the house," he said, firmly grasping my upper arm and leading me back quickly.

We had to run the last hundred yards when a cloudburst soaked us.

"Here," he said when the door closed, "let's get that wet coat off." As he did this, I felt his body behind mine, too close, his cool breath on my damp neck, and I shivered with an unknown fear.

Suddenly he moved a step back. "I'll bring a towel."

When I turned, he handed me the rose, saying, "Between the thorns should prove less painful."

Like a child, I took the rose and stood inside the entrance with hair dripping and shoes squishing water, staring at the white petals tainted with small dots of my very red blood. Suddenly a deeper chill swept over me. This house was dangerous! I don't know how I knew this, and I refused to analyze the thought: *I want out!*

Instead of waiting for Martin to return, I placed the rose on the hallway table and, shivering, ran up the stairs to my room. My bags were still packed and I picked them up, moving out the door and into the hall toward the stairs.

And stopped dead at the sight before me. Out of the gloom from the opposite end of the corridor a diminutive form, pale as a ghost, swaddled in white like a mummy, floated quickly toward me. Bringing with it the noxious odor!

I took two steps back and instinctively my eyes squeezed tightly closed to block out this rank apparition.

You're imagining this! I told myself. I opened my eyes slowly to find inches from my chin a long, goat-like face with hairs sticking out here and there, the features twisted in fury, the skin puckered and pale as a corpse, the glassy black eyes staring malevolently at me. The odor was beyond impossible and I gagged and jerked back, banging the heaviest suitcase into my shin.

The downturned lips parted, and it was as if an impossibly black, fetid cavity opened, one that would go on forever. The odor was the same as I'd smelled in her room, something from the other side of death, and the word *Evil!* popped into my head. Horrified and frozen to the spot, because she was so close, I was forced to breathe in that odor, and sensed I was inhaling poison.

I stared, nearly mesmerized as her lips formed the words: "I will come below tonight and you will join me. Below." Her voice was as deep as before, and suddenly I wasn't sure if this was a woman or a man.

Stunned, I could only nod, half paralyzed by terror.

"Prepare yourself!" she snapped, the tone beyond harsh and demanding.

Too frightened to speak, I backed up several steps, then turned and ran into my room, slamming and locking the door behind me. I leaned against the door gasping for air, shaking with fear, confused, doubting what had just happened.

Always a Castle?

This is ridiculous! I told myself. *What did you see? An old woman with the voice of a man, eccentric, smelly, that's all. She acts like a queen, this matriarch, clearly used to being obeyed.*

But I had no intention of obeying. I decided to wait for a few minutes, crack the door to make sure the coast was clear, then get away from this house. Even if I had to *walk* back to the station in the downpour, I was leaving Whaterley Hall with its repulsive smells and creepy people. Let them hire applicant 665!

Suddenly, a rush of heat filled my body from my toes to my head and sweat gushed from every pore. My head felt light and empty, and I had to sit down. I dropped the one suitcase I was still holding and staggered to the bed, stepping on the little stool to sit. The dizziness increased, and with it I went from hot to cold as a chill stabbed my body. I shivered, at first mildly, then uncontrollably, and crawled under the covers, wishing I had more blankets, wishing there was a fire in the fireplace, shaking so much my teeth chattered.

I'm sick, I thought. *How can I be sick?* And then I lost awareness, slipping in and out of sleep, of dreams and hallucinations. Between freezing and burning, I drifted through time. Someone must have entered the room and built a fire in the fireplace: yellow-orange-red flames licked the black screen as if trying to reach me, wood crackled, too loud, a tree felled by lightning. Heat raged, scorching the room, making the air wavy to my vision, barely touching my icy, trembling flesh. Then, suddenly, I was engulfed, kicking off the blankets, my body on the verge of igniting.

The flocked wallpaper's raised velvet became blood-red figures, alive, squiggling like maggots, swarming all around me! I felt so depleted I couldn't move to escape. All I seemed capable of doing was emitting low, wretched sounds, cries of dread. My world had turned into a nightmare. But the worst was yet to come.

At my weakest, most vulnerable point, Mrs. Whaterley appeared. This... creature stared down at me, crinkly animal-face severe, black-hole eyes glinting, downturned lips shifting into something like a wicked smile that parted into a black expanding abyss. I trembled and sobbed, wishing I could sleep to ward off the sight of this abomination. I did close my eyes. That was a mistake. When I opened them she was still there, but the shroud no longer encased her. The naked body was a shock, forcing a gasp and then a scream from me, one that reverberated inside my head. What loomed above me reached out for me, not an old woman, or even an old man. This was no human being! The bony torso protruding against death-white flesh, skin wrinkled and layered like centuries of erosion, this . . . thing . . . I can only call it a *thing* . . . had a dozen arms! But they *weren't* arms, they were appendages without hands, extending from her back, weaving and swaying like the maggots in the wallpaper. And now all those arms came at me!

The shock of this abhorrent touch left me screaming, vomiting, choking, gasping for air, suffocating, incoherent.

Suddenly Martin was there, behind her, then in front of her, and then she was gone. He lifted me up, pounding my back so I could breathe, holding me upright, telling me to relax, and I realized I was naked. "Where . . . is it?" I stuttered. "The arms . . ."

"There, there," Martin said, in an attempt to be comforting in his distant way. "Drink this," he said, and turned to reach for a cup of tea. In that moment I glanced down at my naked body and saw blood between my legs. And screamed, "Help me! Help me escape!"

"You're not a prisoner, Dana. You can leave, if you're strong enough. Right now you're weak. You'll need to rebuild your strength for the coming months."

"What do you mean? What are you talking about?" I shrieked. I sounded incoherent and had no idea if he understood me, because he didn't answer. I only knew that as much as I longed to leave Whaterley House, I could not move.

My fever lasted days, weeks. I don't know, I lost track of time. When it was most intense, the thing called Mrs. Whaterley visited me. While I struggled to stay conscious, all I could remember was the tentacle-arms, reaching for me, touching my bare skin with an otherworldly iciness. And the blood afterwards. Always the blood.

When the fever finally broke and I came back to myself, I wrapped up in the comforter stinking of sweat and

Always a Castle?

other things and managed to get out of bed, dizzy as I stood, my head empty, but I was determined. I needed to get out of here!

I staggered to the window and saw fields covered with snow. How much time had passed? My legs were weak and I had to sit. On the small table beside the chair sat a plate of fruit, some bread and butter, a teapot, cup, and saucer. Also on the table was the white rose flecked with my blood, now withered, dried, in a vase with no water, the thorns in death still sharp.

A soft knock at my door made me cringe and pull the cover tighter around me. Without my answering, Martin came in.

"I'm delighted to see you're feeling better," he said, his tone even, his face showing no signs of delight. "I'll help you dress and you can come down for sustenance."

"I don't want to go downstairs and I don't want dinner," I said. "I want to leave."

Martin ignored me. He went to the armoire and selected one of my flower-print dresses—apparently someone had unpacked my bags.

He walked to me and said, "Stand, please."

"No! Leave me alone."

"You're very weak, Dana. Please don't struggle. You need to come down."

But I did struggle, pointlessly. Despite his slim frame, he was incredibly strong and quickly had me unwrapped from the comforter and the dress over my naked body.

Rebelliously I whined, "I need underwear!"

"You don't," he said, like a parent to a child.

He pushed my feet into the shoes I'd worn on my arrival and then lifted me from the chair, half carrying me out the door, along the hallway and down the steps of the main staircase. Instantly, I was keenly aware of the foul smell—it was gone!

As if reading my thoughts, Martin said, "My aunt has had a turn for the better. Things have normalized."

"Normalized?!" I muttered as we reached the ground floor.

Instead of turning toward the dining room, we entered the great hall with the paintings of the severe ancestors. The room was so vast that at first I didn't notice Mrs. Whaterley, or who or whatever she was, seated in the middle of the red-velvet three-person *indiscret* settee.

Now she looked almost normal to my eyes, an old lady, her thin, pointed face resembling that of her progenitors. She was wrapped in a large velvet cloak of a robe, her diminutive figure nearly swallowed by the settee on which she sat.

"Sit there," Martin said, and, exhausted, I dropped onto the seat on her right. Martin took the one to her left. The snake-like settee meant we could all look at one another easily, and around the room. Despite the pretense of dinner, we sat silently, me dozing now and then, all through the dark hours until dawn, at which point Martin stood and helped his aunt up and they left the room.

This is your chance! I told myself. *You might only get one!* I moved as quickly as my depleted frame could to the front door, flung it open, and stared at the snow blowing wildly across the walks and garden. The wind sweeping through the skeletons of shrubs, trees, and hedges howled. How could I escape? The station was an hour away by car, half a day by foot. I was trapped here!

From behind me came the cold, even voice I'd grown to loathe. "Only trapped for nine months," Martin said.

What was he talking about? A sudden awareness descended and I realized that inside me life was growing. How had that happened? Martin must have raped me when I was unconscious with fever. I hated him in that moment and spun to face him.

His face seemed to shift, taking on the features of his ancestors, and in an instant I knew what had *really* happened to me. To preserve my sanity, I quickly blocked it out, the reality too horrifying to comprehend fully. All I let myself know was this: I was pregnant. I was not ready to face the rest of the horror.

Martin said I would be trapped for nine months, but he also said nothing ever leaves here, nothing is taken away, the roses die but the bush brings forth new life in the spring. Nine months from now it would be spring. At that moment, I realized that the moment I had set foot in Whaterley House, my fate was sealed.

Knowing that Martin could read me too well, I

turned away and blocked thoughts of revenge. But this. . . creature . . . within me, if I could help it, would never be born. I would not add to this dynasty of grotesques!

My days are spent alone in the Hell-Fire Room. I sleep, write this journal which I hide under the mattress, sleep more, stare out the window at the endless winter. Martin brings meals to me before sunset and after sunrise. Each night I am forced to join the Whaterley's on the *indiscrete*.

I bide my time, planning two things: my escape, and the murder of these alien creatures. I must escape soon—the longer I wait, the harder it will be. My body is growing large and heavy, and the storms outside rage. I *must* escape because I know once the thing draws breath, they will bury me in the rose garden with the other dead roses who came before me, the human women used to evolve the line of this hideous "family" of non-humans so that they *appear* human. But they are not. These are cold, alien beings, without sympathy, without empathy, without human kindness. Their cold kills.

There are monsters in our world, and I have come to understand my higher calling. I have amassed a small arsenal of tools, spending my hours alone sharpening pieces of wood, honing dinner knives, collecting shards of pottery I shatter until the edges are as sharp as scalpels.

I may or may not succeed in killing all three of them. I may or may not escape. If you're reading this, know that I will try.

One thing I have learned and what humanity needs to understand: there is an ancient, savage line, one not from earth. I've figured out that they've existed all over the world, throughout time, even before the first *Homo sapiens* evolved. These . . . *things* . . . are bent on propagating, populating the planet with their kind in the guise of our kind. I don't know their final goal, but what I'm absolutely certain of is this: their end will lead to our end!

As Red as Red

Caitlín R. Kiernan

1

"So, you believe in vampires?" she asks, then takes another sip of her coffee and looks out at the rain pelting Thames Street beyond the café window. It's been pissing rain for almost an hour, a cold, stinging shower on an overcast afternoon near the end of March, a bitter Newport afternoon that would have been equally at home in January or February. But at least it's not pissing snow.

I put my own cup down—tea, not coffee—and stare across the booth at her for a moment or two before answering. "No," I tell Abby Gladding. "But, quite clearly, those people in Exeter who saw to it that Mercy Brown's body was exhumed, the ones who cut out her heart and burned it, clearly *they* believed in vampires. And that's what I'm studying, the psychology behind that hysteria, behind the superstitions."

"It was so long ago," she replies and smiles. There's no foreshadowing in that smile, not even in hindsight. It surely isn't a predatory smile. There's nothing malevolent, or hungry, or feral in the expression. She just watches the rain and smiles, as though something I've said amuses her.

"Not really," I say, glancing down at my steaming cup. "Not so long ago as people might *like* to think. The Mercy Brown incident, that was in 1892, and the most recent case of purported vampirism in the northeast I've been able to pin down dates from sometime in 1898, a mere hundred and eleven years ago."

Her smile lingers, and she traces a circle in the condensation on the plate-glass window, then traces another circle inside it.

"We're not so far removed from the villagers with their torches and pitchforks, from old Cotton Mather and his bunch. That's what you're saying."

"Well, not exactly, but . . ." and when I trail off, she

turns her head towards me, and her blue-grey eyes seem as cold as the low-slung sky above Newport. You could almost freeze to death in eyes like those, I think, and I take another sip of my lukewarm Earl Grey with lemon. Her eyes seem somehow brighter than they should in the dim light of the coffeehouse, so there's your foreshadowing, I suppose, if you're the sort who needs it.

"You're pretty far from Exeter, Ms. Howard," she says, and takes another sip of her coffee. And me, I'm sitting here wishing we were talking about almost anything but Rhode Island vampires and the madness of crowds, tuberculosis and the master's thesis I'd be defending at the end of May. It had been months since I'd had anything even resembling a date, and I didn't want to squander the next half hour or so talking shop.

"I think I've turned up something interesting," I tell her, because I can't think of any subtle way to steer the conversation in another direction. A case no one's documented before, right here in Newport."

She smiles that smile again.

"I got a tip from a folklorist up at Brown," I say. "Seems like maybe there was an incident here in 1785 or thereabouts. If it checks out, I might be onto the oldest case of suspected vampirism resulting in an exhumation anywhere in New England. So, now I'm trying to verify the rumors. But there's precious little to go on. Chasing vampires, it's not like studying the Salem witch trials, where you have all those court records, the indictments and depositions and what have you. Instead, it's necessary to spend a lot of time sifting and sorting fact from fiction, and, usually, there's not much of either to work with."

She nods, then glances back towards the big window and the rain. "Be a feather in your cap, though. If it's not just a rumor, I mean."

"Yes," I reply. "Yes, it certainly would."

And here, there's an unsettling wave of not-quite déjà vu, something closer to dissociation, perhaps, and for a few dizzying seconds I feel as if I'm watching this conversation, a voyeur listening in, or I'm only remembering it, but in no way actually, presently, taking part in it. And, too, the coffeehouse and our talk and the rain outside seem no more concrete—no more *here and now*—than does the morning before. One day that might as well be the next, and it's raining, either way.

I'm standing alone on Bowen's Warf, staring out past the masts crowded into the marina at sleek white sailboats skimming over the glittering water, and there's the silhouette of Goat Island, half hidden in the fog. I'm about to turn and walk back up the hill to Washington Square and the library, about to leave the gaudy Disney World concessions catering to the tastes of tourists and return to the comforting maze of ancient gabled houses lining winding, narrow streets. And that's when I see her for the first time. She's standing alone near the "seal safari" kiosk, staring at a faded sign, at black-and-white photographs of harbor seals with eyes like the puppies and little girls from those hideous Margaret Keane paintings. She's wearing an old pea coat and shiny green galoshes that look new, but there's nothing on her head, and she doesn't have an umbrella. Her long black hair hangs wet and limp, and when she looks at me, it frames her pale face.

Then it passes, the blip or glitch in my psyche, and I've snapped back, into myself, into *this* present. I'm sitting across the booth from her once more, and the air smells almost oppressively of freshly roasted and freshly ground coffee beans.

"I'm sure it has a lot of secrets, this town," she says, fixing me again with those blue-grey eyes and smiling that irreproachable smile of hers.

"Can't swing a dead cat," I say, and she laughs.

"Well, did it ever work?" Abby asks. "I mean, digging up the dead, desecrating their mortal remains to appease the living. Did it tend to do the trick?"

"No," I reply. "Of course not. But that's beside the point. People do strange things when they're scared."

And there's more, mostly more questions from her about Colonial-Era vampirism, Newport's urban legends, and my research as a folklorist. I'm grateful that she's kind or polite enough not to ask the usual "you mean people get paid to do this sort of thing" questions. Instead, she tells me a werewolf story dating back to the 1800s, a local priest supposedly locked away in the Portsmouth Poor Asylum after he committed a particularly gruesome murder, how he was spared the gallows because people believed he was a werewolf and so not in control of his actions. She even tells me about seeing his nameless grave in a cemetery up in Middletown, his tombstone bearing the head of a wolf. And I'm polite enough not to tell her that I've heard this one before.

Finally, I notice that it's stopped raining.

"I really ought to get back to work," I say, and she nods and suggests that we should have dinner sometime soon. I agree, but we don't set a date. She has my number, after all, so we can figure that out later. She also mentions a movie playing at Jane Pickens that she hasn't seen and thinks I might enjoy. I leave her sitting there in the booth, in her pea coat and green galoshes, and she orders another cup of coffee as I'm exiting the café. On the way back to the library, I see a tree filled with noisy, cawing crows, and for some reason it reminds me of Abby Gladding.

2

That was Monday, and there's nothing the least bit remarkable about Tuesday. I make the commute from Providence to Newport, crossing the West Passage of Narragansett Bay to Conanicut Island, and then the East Passage to Aquidneck Island and Newport. Most of the day is spent at the Redwood Library and Athenaeum on Bellevue, shut away with my newspaper clippings and microfiche, with frail yellowed books that were printed before the Revolutionary War. I wear the white cotton gloves they give me for handling archival materials and make several pages of handwritten notes, pertaining primarily to the treatment of cases of consumption in Newport during the first two decades of the eighteenth century.

The library is open late on Tuesdays, and I don't leave until sometime after seven P.M. But nothing I find gets me any nearer to confirming that a corpse believed to have belonged to a vampire was exhumed from the Common Burying Ground in 1785. On the long drive home, I try not to think about the fact that she hasn't called, or my growing suspicion that she likely never will. I have a can of ravioli and a beer for dinner. I half watch something forgettable on television. I take a hot shower and brush my teeth. If there are any dreams—good, bad, or otherwise—they're nothing I recall upon waking. The day is sunny, and not quite as cold, and I do my best to summon a few shoddy scraps of optimism, enough to get me out the door and into the car.

But by the time I reach the library in Newport, I've got a headache, what feels like the beginnings of a migraine, railroad spikes in both my eyes, and I'm wishing I'd stayed in bed. I find a comfortable seat in the Roderick Terry Reading Room, one of the armchairs upholstered with dark green leather, and leave my sunglasses on while I flip through books pulled randomly from the shelf on my right. Novels by William Kennedy and Elia Kazan, familiar, friendly books, but trying to focus on the words only makes my head hurt worse. I return *The Arrangement* to its slot on the shelf, and pick up something called *Thousand Cranes* by a Japanese author, Yasunari Kawbata. I've never heard of him, but the blurb on the back of the dust jacket assures me he was awarded the Nobel Prize for Literature in 1968, and that he was the first Japanese author to receive it.

I don't open the book, but I don't reshelve it, either. It rests there in my lap, and I sit beneath the octagonal skylight with my eyes closed for a while. Five minutes maybe, maybe more, and the only sounds are muffled footsteps, the turning of pages, an old man clearing his throat, a passing police siren, one of the librarians at the front desk whispering a little more loudly than usual. Or maybe the migraine magnifies her voice and only makes it seem that way. In fact, all these small, unremarkable sounds seem magnified, if only by the quiet of the library.

When I open my eyes, I have to blink a few times to bring the room back into focus. So I don't immediately notice the woman standing outside the window, looking in at me. Or only looking *in*, and I just happen to be in her line of sight. Maybe she's looking at nothing in particular, or at the bronze statue of Pheidippides perched on its wooden pedestal. Perhaps she's looking for someone else, someone who isn't me. The window is on the opposite side of the library from where I'm sitting, forty feet or so away. But even at that distance, I'm almost certain that the pale face and lank black hair belong to Abby Gladding. I raise a hand, half-waving to her, but if she sees me, she doesn't acknowledge having seen me. She just stands there, perfectly still, staring in.

I get to my feet, and the copy of *Thousand Cranes* slides off my lap; the noise the book makes when it hits the floor is enough that a couple of people look up from their magazines and glare at me. I offer them an apologetic gesture—part shrug and part sheepish frown—and they shake their heads, almost in unison, and go back to reading. When I glance at the window again, the black-haired woman is no longer there. Suddenly, my headache is much worse (probably from standing so quickly, I think), and I feel a sudden, dizzying rush of adrenalin. No, it's more than that. I feel afraid. My heart races, and my mouth has gone very dry. Any plans I might have harbored of going outside to see if the woman looking in actually was Abby vanish immediately, and I sit down again. If it was her, I reason, then she'll come inside.

So I wait, and, very slowly, my pulse returns to its normal rhythm, but the adrenaline leaves me feeling jittery, and the pain behind my eyes doesn't get any better. I pick the novel by Yasunari Kawbata up off the floor and place it back upon the shelf. Leaning over makes my head pound even worse, and I'm starting to feel nauseous. I consider going to the restrooms, near the circulation desk, but part of me is still afraid, for whatever reason, and it seems to be the part of me that controls my legs. I stay in the seat and wait for the woman from the window to walk into the Roderick Terry Reading Room. I wait for her to be Abby, and I expect to hear her green galoshes squeaking against the lacquered hardwood. She'll say that she thought about calling, but then figured that I'd be in the library, so of course my phone would be switched off. She'll say something about the weather, and she'll want to know if I'm still up for dinner and the movie. I'll tell her about the migraine, and maybe she'll offer me Excedrin or Tylenol. Our hushed conversation will annoy someone, and he or she will shush us. We'll laugh about it later on.

But Abby doesn't appear, and so I sit for a while, gazing across the wide room at the window, a tree *outside* the window, at the houses lined up neat and tidy along Redwood Street. On Wednesday, the library is open until eight, but I leave as soon as I feel well enough to drive back to Providence.

3

It's Thursday, and I'm sitting in that same green armchair in the Terry Roderick Reading Room. It's only 11:26 A.M., and already I understand that I've lost the day. I have no days to spare, but already I know that the research that I should get done today isn't going to happen. Last night was too filled with uneasy dreaming, and this morning I can't concentrate. It's hard to think about anything but the nightmares, and the face of Abby Gladding at the window, her blue eyes, her black hair. And yes, I have grown quite certain that it *was* her face I saw peering in, and that she was peering in *at* me.

She hasn't called (and I didn't get her number, assuming she has one). An hour ago, I walked along the Newport waterfront looking for her, but to no avail. I stood a while beside the "seal safari" kiosk, hoping, irrationally I suppose, that she might turn up. I smoked a cigarette and stood there in the cold, watching the sunlight on the bay, listening to traffic and the wind and a giggling flock of grey sea gulls. Just before I gave up and made my way back to the library, I noticed dog tracks in a muddy patch of ground near the kiosk. I thought that they seemed unusually large, and I couldn't help but recall the café on Monday and Abby relating the story of the werewolf priest buried in Middletown. But lots of people in Newport have big dogs, and they walk them along the wharf.

I'm sitting in the green leather chair, and there's a manila folder of photocopies and computer printouts in my lap. I've been picking through them, pretending this is work. It isn't. There's nothing in the folder I haven't read five or ten times over, nothing that hasn't been cited by other academics chasing stories of New England vampires. On top of the stack is "The 'Vampires' of Rhode Island," from *Yankee* magazine, October 1970. Beneath that, "They Burned Her Heart... Was Mercy Brown a Vampire?" from the *Narragansett Times,* October 25th 1979, and from the *Providence Sunday Journal,* also October 1979, "Did They Hear the Vampire Whisper?" So many of these popular pieces have October dates, a testament to journalism's attitude towards the subject, which it clearly views as nothing more than a convenient skeleton to pull from the closet every Halloween, something to dust off and trot out for laughs.

Salem has its witches. Sleepy Hollow its headless Hessian mercenary. And Rhode Island has its consumptive, consuming phantoms—Mercy Brown, Sarah Tillinghast, Nellie Vaughn, Ruth Ellen Rose, and all the rest. Beneath the *Providence Sunday Journal* piece is a black-and-white photograph I took a couple of years ago, Nellie Vaughn's vandalized headstone with its infamous inscription: "I am waiting and watching for you." I stare at the photograph for a moment or two and set it aside. Beneath it there's a copy of another October article, "When the Wind Howls and the Trees Moan," also from the *Providence Sunday Journal*. I close the manila folder and try not to stare at the window across the room.

It is only a window, and it only looks out on trees and houses and sunlight.

I open the folder again and read from a much older article, "The Animistic Vampire in New England" from *American Anthropologist*, published in 1896, only four years after the Mercy Brown incident. I read it silently, to myself, but catch my lips moving:

In New England the vampire superstition is unknown by its proper name. It is believed that consumption is not a physical but spiritual disease, obsession, or visitation; that as long as the body of a dead consumptive relative has blood in its heart it is proof that an occult influence steals from it for death and is at work draining the blood of the living into the heart of the dead and causing his rapid decline.

I close the folder again and return it to its place in my book bag. And then I stand and cross the wide reading room to the window and the alcove where I saw, or only thought I saw, Abby looking in at me. There's a marble bust of Cicero on the window ledge, and I've been staring out at the leafless trees and the brown grass, the sidewalk and the street, for several minutes before I notice the smudges on the pane of glass, only inches from my face. Sometime recently, when the window was wet, a finger traced a circle there, and then traced a circle within that first circle. When the glass dried, these smudges were left behind. And I remember Monday afternoon at the coffeehouse, Abby tracing an identical symbol (if "symbol" is the appropriate word here) in the condensation on the window while we talked and watched the rain.

I press my palm to the glass, which is much colder than I'd expected.

In my dream, I stood at another window, at the end of a long hallway, and looked down at the North Burial Ground. With some difficulty, I opened the window, hoping the air outside would be fresher than the stale air in the hallway. It was, and I thought it smelled faintly of clover and strawberries. And there was music. I saw, then, Abby standing beneath a tree, playing a violin. The music was very beautiful, though very sad, and completely unfamiliar. She drew the bow slowly across the strings, and I realized that somehow the music was shaping the night. There were clouds sailing past above the cemetery, and the chords she drew from the violin changed the shapes of those clouds and also seemed to dictate the speed at which they moved. The moon was bloated and shone an unhealthy shade of ivory, and the whole sky writhed like a Van Gogh painting. I wondered why she didn't tell me that she plays the violin.

Behind me, something clattered to the floor, and I looked over my shoulder. But there was only the long hallway, leading off into perfect darkness, leading back the way I'd apparently come. When I turned again to the open window and the cemetery, the music had ceased, and Abby was gone. There was only the tree and row after row of tilted headstones, charcoal-colored slate, white marble, a few cut from slabs of reddish sandstone mined from Massachusetts or Connecticut. I was reminded of a platoon of drunken soldiers, lined up for a battle they knew they were going to lose.

I have never liked writing my dreams down.

It is late Thursday morning, almost noon, and I pull my hand back from the cold, smudged windowpane. I have to be in Providence for an evening lecture, and I gather my things and leave the Redwood Library and Athenaeum. On the drive back to the city, I do my best to stop thinking about the nightmare, my best not to dwell on what I saw sitting beneath the tree, after the music stopped and Abby Gladding disappeared. My best isn't good enough.

As Red as Red

4

The lecture goes well, quite a bit better than I'd expected it would, better, probably, than it had a right to, all things considered. "Mercy Brown as Inspiration for Bram Stoker's *Dracula*," presented to the Rhode Island Historical Society, and, somehow, I even manage not to make a fool of myself answering questions afterwards. It helps that I've answered these same questions so many times in the past. For example:

"I'm assuming you've also drawn connections between the Mercy Brown incident and Sheridan Le Fanu's 'Carmilla'?"

"There are similarities, certainly, but so far as I know, no one has been able to demonstrate conclusively that Le Fanu knew of the New England phenomena. And, more importantly, the publication of 'Carmilla' predates the exhumation of Mercy Brown's body by twenty years."

"Still, he might have known of the earlier cases."

"Certainly. He may well have. However, I have no evidence that he did."

But, the entire time, my mind is elsewhere, back across the water in Newport, in that coffeehouse on Thames, and the Redwood Library, and standing in a dream hallway, looking down on my subconscious rendering of the Common Burying Ground. A woman playing a violin beneath a tree. A woman with whom I have only actually spoken once, but about whom I cannot stop thinking.

It is believed that consumption is not a physical but spiritual disease, obsession, or visitation . . .

After the lecture, and the questions, after introductions are made and notable, influential hands are shaken, when I can finally slip away without seeming either rude or unprofessional, I spend an hour or so walking alone on College Hill. It's a cold, clear night, and I follow Benevolent Street west to Benefit and turn north. There's comfort in the uneven, buckled bricks of the sidewalk, in the bare limbs of the trees, in all the softly glowing windows. I pause at the granite steps leading up to the front door of what historians call the Stephen Harris House, built in 1764. One hundred and sixty years later, H. P. Lovecraft called this the

"Babbitt House" and used it as the setting for an odd tale of lycanthropy and vampirism. I know this huge yellow house well. And I know, too, the four hand-painted signs nailed up on the gatepost, all of them in French. From the sidewalk, by the electric glow of a nearby street lamp, I can only make out the top half of the third sign in the series; the rest are lost in the gloom—*Oubliez le Chien.* Forget the Dog.

    I start walking again, heading home to my tiny, cluttered apartment, only a couple of blocks east on Prospect. The side streets are notoriously steep, and I've been in better shape. I haven't gone twenty-five yards before I'm winded and have a nasty stitch in my side. I lean against a stone wall, cursing the cigarettes and the exercise I can't be bothered with, trying to catch my breath. The freezing air makes my sinuses and teeth ache. It burns my throat like whiskey.

    And this is when I glimpse a sudden blur from out the corner of my right eye, hardly *more* than a blur. An impression or the shadow of something large and black, moving quickly across the street. It's no more than ten feet away from me, but downhill, back towards Benefit. By the time I turn to get a better look, it's gone, and I'm already beginning to doubt I saw anything, except, possibly, a stray dog.

    I linger here a moment, squinting into the darkness and the yellow-orange sodium-vapor pool of streetlight that the blur seemed to cross before it disappeared. I want to laugh at myself, because I can actually feel the prick of goose bumps along my forearms, and the short, fine hairs at the nape of my neck standing on end. I've blundered into a horror-movie cliché, and I can't help but be reminded of Val Lewton's *Cat People,* the scene where Jane Rudolph walks quickly past Central Park, stalked by a vengeful Simone Simon, only to be rescued at the last possible moment by the fortuitous arrival of a city bus. But I know there's no helpful bus coming to intervene on my behalf, and, more importantly, I understand full fucking well that this night holds in store nothing more menacing than what my over-stimulated imagination has put there. I turn away from the street light and continue up the hill towards home. And I do not have to *pretend* that I don't hear footsteps following me, or the clack of claws on concrete, because I *don't*. The quick shadow, the peripheral blur, it was only a moment's misapprehension, no more than a trick of my exhausted, preoccupied mind, filled with the evening's morbid banter.

Oubliez le Chien.

Fifteen minutes later, I'm locking the front door of my apartment behind me. I make a hot cup of chamomile tea, which I drink standing at the kitchen counter. I'm in bed shortly after ten o'clock. By then, I've managed to completely dismiss whatever I only thought I saw crossing Jenckes Street.

5

"Open your eyes, Ms. Howard," Abby Gladding says, and I do. Her voice does not in any way command me to open my eyes, and it is perfectly clear that I have a choice in the matter. But there's a certain *je-ne-sais-quoi* in the delivery, the inflection and intonation, in the measured conveyance of these seven syllables, that makes it impossible for me to keep my eyes closed. It's not yet dawn, but sunrise cannot be very far away, and I am lying in my bed. I cannot say whether I am awake or dreaming or if possibly I am stranded in some liminal state that is neither one nor the other. I am immediately conscious of an unseen weight bearing down painfully upon my chest, and I am having difficulty breathing.

"I promised that I'd call on you," she says, and, with great effort, I turn my head towards the sound of her voice, my cheek pressing deeply into my pillow. I am aware now that I am all but paralyzed, perhaps by the same force pushing down on my chest, and I strain for any glimpse of her. But there's only the bedside table, the clock radio and reading lamp and ashtray, an overcrowded bookcase with sagging shelves, and the floral calico wallpaper that came with the apartment. If I could move my arms, I would switch on the lamp. If I could move, I'd sit up, and maybe I would be able to breathe again.

And then I think that she must surely be singing, though her song has no words. There is no need for mere lyrics, not when texture and timbre, harmony and melody, are sufficient to unmake the mundane artifacts that comprise my bedroom, wiping aside the here and now that belie what I am meant to see in this fleeting moment. And even as the wall and the bookshelf and the table beside my bed dissolve and fall away, I understand that her music is drawing me deeper into sleep again, though I must have been very nearly awake when she told me to open my eyes. I have no time to worry over apparent contradictions, and I can't move my head to look away from what she means for me to see.

There's nothing to be afraid of, I think. *No more here than in any bad dream.* But I find the thought carries no conviction whatsoever. It's even less substantial than the dissolving wallpaper and bookcase.

Now I'm looking at the weed-choked shore of a misty pond or swamp, a bog or tidal marsh. The light is so dim it might be dusk, or it might be dawn, or merely an overcast day. There are huge trees bending low near the water, water which seems almost perfectly smooth and the green of polished malachite. I hear frogs, hidden among the moss and reeds, the ferns and skunk cabbages, and now the calls of birds form a counterpoint to Abby's voice. Except, seeing her standing ankle deep in that stagnant green pool, I also see that she isn't singing. The music is coming from the violin braced against her shoulder, from the bow and strings and the movement of her left hand along the fingerboard of the instrument. She has her back to me, but I don't need to see her face to know it's her. Her black hair hangs down almost to her hips. And only now do I realize that she's naked.

Abruptly, she stops playing, and her arms fall to her sides, the violin in her left hand, the bow in her right. The tip of the bow breaks the surface of the pool, and ripples in concentric rings race away from it.

"I wear this rough garment to deceive," she says, and, at that, all the birds and frogs fall silent. "Aren't you the clever girl? Aren't you canny? I would not think appearances would so easily lead you astray. Not for long as this."

No words escape my rigid, sleeping jaws, but she hears me all the same, my answer that needs no voice, and she turns to face me. Her eyes are golden, not blue. And in the low light, they briefly flash a bright, iridescent yellow. She smiles, showing me teeth as sharp as razors, and then she quotes from the Gospel of Matthew.

"Inwardly, they were ravening wolves," she says to me. "You've seen all that you need to see, and probably more,

I'd wager." With this, she turns away again, turning to face the fog shrouding the wide green pool. As I watch, helpless to divert my gaze or even shut my eyes, she lets the violin and bow slip from her hands; they fall into the water with quiet splashes. The bow sinks, though the violin floats. And then she goes down on all fours. She laps at the pool, and her hair has begun to writhe like a nest of serpents.

And now I'm awake, disoriented and my chest aching, gasping for air as if a moment before I was drowning and have only just been pulled to the safety of dry land. The wallpaper is only dingy calico again, and the bookcase is only a bookcase. The clock radio and the lamp and the ashtray sit in their appointed places upon the bedside table.

The sheets are soaked through with sweat, and I'm shivering. I sit up, my back braced against the headboard, and my eyes go to the second-story window on the other side of the small room. The sun is still down, but it's a little lighter out there than it is in the bedroom. And for a fraction of a moment, clearly silhouetted against that false dawn, I see the head and shoulders of a young woman. I also see the muzzle and alert ears of a wolf, and that golden eyeshine watching me. Then it's gone, she or it, whichever pronoun might best apply. It doesn't seem to matter. Because now I do know exactly what I'm looking for, and I know that I've seen it before, years before I first caught sight of Abby Gladding standing in the rain without an umbrella.

6

Friday morning I drive back to Newport, and it doesn't take me long at all to find the grave. It's just a little ways south of the chain-link fence dividing the North Burial Ground from the older Common Burying Ground and Island Cemetery. I turn off Warner Street onto the rutted, unpaved road winding between the indistinct rows of monuments. I find a place that's wide enough to pull over and park. The trees have only just begun to bud, and their bare limbs are stark against a sky so blue-white it hurts my eyes to look directly into it. The grass is mostly still brown from long months of snow and frost, though there are small clumps of new green showing here and there.

The cemetery has been in use since 1640 or so. There are three Colonial-era governors buried here (one a delegate to the Continental Congress), along with the founder of Freemasonry in Rhode Island, a signatory to the Declaration of Independence, various Civil War generals, lighthouse keepers, and hundreds of African slaves stolen from Gambia and Sierra Leone, the Gold and Ivory coasts, and brought to Newport in the heyday of whaling and the Rhode Island rum trade. The grave of Abby Gladding is marked by a weathered slate headstone, badly scabbed over with lichen. But, despite the centuries, the shallow inscription is still easy enough to read:

HERE LYETH INTERED Y^e BODY
OF ABBY MARY GLADDING
DAUGHTER OF SOLOMON GLADDING ^{esq}
& MARY HIS WYFE WHO
DEPARTED THIS LIFE Y^e 2^d DAY OF
SEPT 1785 AGED 22 YEARS
SHE WAS DROWN'D & DEPARTED & SLEEPS
^{ZECH 4:1} NEITHER SHALL THEY WEAR
A HAIRY GARMENT TO DECEIVE

Above the inscription, in place of the usual death's head, is a crude carving of a violin. I sit down in the dry, dead grass in front of the marker, and I don't know how long I've been sitting there when I hear crows cawing. I look over my shoulder, and there's a tree back towards Farewell Street filled with the big black birds. They watch me, and I take that as my cue to leave. I know now that I have to go back to the library, that whatever remains of this mystery is waiting for me there. I might find it tucked away in an old journal, a newspaper clipping, or in crumbling church records. I only know I'll find it, because now I have the missing pieces. But there is an odd reluctance to leave the grave of Abby Gladding. There's no fear in me, no shock or stubborn disbelief at what I've discovered or at its impossible ramifications. And some part of me notes the oddness of this, that I am not afraid. I leave her alone in that narrow house, watched over by the wary crows, and go back to my car. Less than fifteen minutes later I'm in the Redwood Library, asking for anything they can find on a Solomon Gladding and his daughter, Abby.

"Are you okay?" the librarian asks, and I wonder what she sees in my face, in my eyes, to elicit such a question. "Are you feeling well?"

"I'm fine," I assure her. "I was up a little too late last night, that's all. A little too much to drink, most likely."

She nods, and I smile.

"Well, then. I'll see what we might have," she says, and, cutting to the chase, it ends with a short article that appeared in the *Newport Mercury* early in November 1785, hardly more than two months after Abby Gladding's death. It begins, "We hear a ſtrange account from laſt Thursday evening, the Night of the 3rd of November, of a body diſinterred from its Grave and coffin This most peculiar occurrence was undertaken at the beheſt of the father of the deceaſed young woman therein buried, a circumſtance making the affair even ſtranger ſtill." What follows is a description of a ritual which will be familiar to anyone who has read of the 1892 Mercy Brown case from Exeter, or the much earlier exhumation of Nancy Young (summer of 1827), or other purported New England "vampires."

In September, Abby Gladding's body was discovered in Newport Harbor by a local fisherman, and it was determined that she had drowned. The body was in an advanced state of decay, leading me to wonder if the date on the headstone is meant to be the date the body was found, not the date of her death. There were persistent rumors that the daughter of Solomon Gladding, a local merchant, had taken her own life. She is said to have been a "child of ſingular and morbid temperament," who had recently refused a marriage proposal by the eldest son of another Newport merchant, Ebenezer Burrill. There was also back-fence talk that Abby had practiced witchcraft in the woods bordering the town, and that she would play her violin (a gift from her mother) to summon "voraciouſ wolveſ and other ſuch dæmonſ to do her bidding."

Very shortly after her death, her youngest sister, Susan, suddenly fell ill. This was in October, and the girl was dead before the end of the month. Her symptoms, like those of Mercy Brown's stricken family members, can readily be identified as late-stage tuberculosis. What is peculiar here is that Abby doesn't appear to have suffered any such wasting disease herself, and the speed with which Susan became ill and died is also atypical of consumption. Even as Susan fought for her life, Abby's mother, Mary, fell ill, and it was in hope of saving his wife that Solomon Gladding agreed to the exhumation of his daughter's body. The article in the *Newport Mercury* speculates that he'd learned of this ritual and folk remedy from a Jamaican slave woman.

At sunrise, with the aid of several other men, some apparently family members, the grave was opened, and all present were horrified to see "the body freſh as the day it waſ conſigned to God," her cheeks "fluſhed with colour and lufterous." The liver and heart were duly cut out, and both were discovered to contain clotted blood, which Solomon had been told would prove that Abby was rising from her grave each night to steal the blood of her mother and sister. The heart was burned in a fire kindled in the cemetery, the ashes mixed with water, and the mother drank the mixture. The body of Abby was turned facedown in her casket, and an iron stake was driven through her chest, to insure that the restless spirit would be unable to find its way out of the grave. Nonetheless, according to parish records from Trinity Church, Mary Gladding died before Christmas. Her father fell ill a few months later and died in August of 1786.

And I find one more thing that I will put down here. Scribbled in sepia ink in the left-hand margin of the newspaper page containing the account of the exhumation of Abby Gladding is the phrase *Jé-rouge,* or "red eyes," which I've learned is a Haitian term denoting werewolfery and cannibalism. Below that word, in the same spidery hand, is written "As white as snow, as red as red, as green as briers, as black as coal." There is no date or signature accompanying these notations.

Now it is almost Friday night, and I sit alone on a wooden bench at Bowen's Wharf, not too far from the kiosk advertising daily boat tours to view fat, doe-eyed seals sunning themselves on the rocky beaches ringing Narragansett Bay. I sit here and watch the sun going down, shivering because I left home this morning without my coat. I do not expect to see Abby Gladding, tonight or ever again. But I've come here, anyway, and I may come again tomorrow evening.

I will not include the 1785 disinterment in my thesis, no matter how many feathers it might earn for my cap. I mean never to speak of it again. What I have written here, I suspect I'll destroy it later on. It has only been written for me, and for me alone. If Abby was trying to speak *through* me, to find a larger audience, she'll have to find another mouthpiece. I watch a lobster boat heading out for the night. I light a cigarette and eye the herring gulls wheeling above the marina.

Four Arches

Robert S. Wilson

"Okay, class. Does anybody know how Michelangelo recreated the human body with so much anatomical detail?"

The room of seventh graders stared dumbly at Mrs. Kemp.

"Anybody? . . . Billy?"

Billy Johnson shrugged, nearly dunking his gangly head into his collarbone.

"Josh?"

Josh Baker was whispering in a silly, high-pitched voice to Jeff Dower from behind sandy blond bangs. He sat up straight and in the normal voice he barely used, a tone of forced seriousness, he said, "No, Mrs. Kemp," then turned back to Jeff and giggled.

"Well, since none of you bothered to read the chapter I assigned last week, I suppose I'll have to tell you the *entire* story."

The class moaned in protest.
"Michelangelo was so obsessed with painting the human body accurately that he went out and . . . dug up bodies . . . to study the way the muscles and bones and flesh worked together." The class stared back in awe as she explained, in vivid detail, the Renaissance painter's preferred techniques of dissection until, glory of all glories, the bell rang out its monotonous tone.

"Now, kids, please don't go around telling everyone 'Michelangelo was a grave robber,' okay?" Some of the students laughed as they picked up their books and made their way out of the art room.

In the hallway, Josh Baker yelled above the buzzing roar of crowding students, "MICHELANGELO WAS A GRAVE ROBBER, MICHELANGELO WAS A GRAVE ROBBER." Billy and Jeff walked beside him, laughing along the way.

When Josh was finally done chanting about Michelangelo, Jeff turned to them. "Hey, you guys, we should go out to Four Arches tonight."

Billy pushed up his thick gray plastic glasses, his face covered in pimples and framed in long straight brown hair, and asked, "What's the deal with that place, anyway?"

Josh perked up. "Nanny? You've never been to Four Arches?" *Nanny* was Josh and Jeff's pet name for Billy. It made entirely no sense and only Josh and Jeff seemed to think it was funny, but the way they laughed when they said it, Billy was sure there was some big joke he wasn't getting.

"Well . . . no—I mean, I've heard about it. But not enough to really—"

A deranged smile grew across Jeff's face, and his voice took on that same high-pitched derisive tone that he and Josh always used. "What's-a-matter, Nanny, you hear about the Goat Man?"

"What the hell is a *Goat Man?*" Billy asked.

Jeff's face straightened and, in his normal voice, he explained. "Four Arches is a bridge, man. It's these big concrete arches outside town that train tracks cross over. They're covered in graffiti, and everyone says people go out there and worship the devil and shit. And just under the top of the main arch, there's these tunnels in the concrete that—if you're in them when the train is on the bridge—vibrate and shake the inside like crazy. It's awesome!"

"And they say if you're in there at night when the train comes, the Goat Man—a man with a human body and the *head* of a *goat*—will come out and kill you, Nanny!" Josh raised his hands and reached out for him.

Billy pushed the boy's arms aside, and they slid away. "All right, let's go. I wanna see this place. It sounds cool." Josh and Jeff looked at each other, brows furrowed in mocking contemplation.

"All right, let's go tonight then." Josh peered with one eye open back and forth at Billy and Jeff until they both nodded in agreement.

That night they met at Josh's house, since it was closest to the Arches. They rode their bikes into the dusk, tires tossing up gravelly dirt from the blacktop of County

Road 500 West. The sun dove deeper in the sky the further from town they pedaled. By the time they sped around the curve and the giant aged structure of the bridge came into full view, it was lit only by the blue glow of the moon. Staring intently, Billy nearly rode his bike off the road.

The dull gray-green concrete seemed to grow out of the side of the hill and then arch over the road and down into the grass where the next several arches hovered over the creek beyond the trees. Near the top of each arch, wrapped around the curve of them, tubular cavern-like open spandrels stretched all the way across, growing from the middle outward with the thickness of the bridge. Billy counted eight of them in all, staring back at him like black wide open eyes shining in the moonlight.

Jeff set his bike down and held his arms out in a display of showmanship. "*This* is Four Arches, Nanny." Billy was too mesmerized by the sheer coolness of the thing even to care what Jeff called him at the moment. He dropped his bike and started walking toward the bridge like some flesh-hungry zombie. He could barely make out brightly colored graffiti on the side facing them:

Jason and April forever.
Satan loves you.
The Goat Man is coming.
For the best blowjob you ever had call Cindy—653-1129.

Billy had just begun to realize how quiet it was when he felt cold stiff hands grip his shoulders and turn him around. Standing just below his line of sight, Billy stared into two huge, black, glassy eyes. The hoarse beginnings of a scream crept from his lungs as he staggered backward to get away.

The muffled, high-pitched screech of Josh's giggling snapped Billy back into reality as he realized it was just a goat's head on a stick, gore oozing down from its neck. "You asshole! You scared the shit out of me."

Josh and Jeff replied by diving and nearly drowning in a sea of laughter. Josh's shrill voice crept above the surface saying, "Oh my God, Nanny—you should've seen your face!" Billy was anything but amused. He stood there tall with anger in his tight blue jean jacket, all gangly posture and big goofy glasses, trembling.

"That was *not* fucking funny." His voice echoed back at him from the bridge towering behind him, reminding him of the fascinating place surrounding them. He turned then, trying to ignore his two *friends*. The darkness in those open caverns called to him. But the terror he'd felt seeing those cold, dead, animal eyes was a sure sign that even these two idiots couldn't piss him off enough to go in one of them alone.

"All right, guys, you had your fun. Let's go up there. I wanna see inside." Josh and Jeff's laughter died down to a light cackle. They nodded at each other and back at Billy, then made their way alongside him, Josh still brandishing the goat-head stick. The three boys began slowly climbing their way up the hill where the bridge melded into the earth. Twigs snapped and owls hooted occasionally as they rustled up the mound through trees and a thick layer of wet dead leaves on the ground. All the while Billy had to fight to look in front of himself; he couldn't take his eyes off the huge structure above them.

As they neared the bridge, Josh led the way like some morbid Gandalf with baggy clothes and goat-head staff. He stopped next to the first open spandrel and gestured for Billy to go ahead. "Ladies first, Nanny." Billy didn't hesitate. He stepped up onto the concrete, making sure to grab hold of the arch as he went inside. It was pitch black. A moment later the inside was lit up with a flickering yellow light. Billy turned to find Josh and Jeff standing there, Jeff holding a Zippo lighter and lighting a cigarette.

The place was littered with rusted empty beer cans and remnants of food and trash. Over in the far corner a few small sticks were piled half-ashened from the makings of a poorly made fire. And the walls in here were covered with more graffiti—all colors, shapes, and styles. Billy leaned over and motioned to Jeff. "Hey give me one of those." Jeff produced a thin, half-empty pack of Kools and pulled one out.

"Yeah, yeah. Here."

Billy took the cigarette and lit it off of Jeff's still open Zippo. Josh stood there making weird shadows against the opposite wall with the goat-head stick and laughing.

"This is just too fucking cool," Billy said.

Jeff made a fake-menacing gaze, holding the lighter

under his face. "Yeah, just wait till the train comes."

"Yeah, that's when the Goat Man appears, Nanny —a boogety boo, hoo, hoo!" Josh's attempt at a deep tone ricocheted off the curved walls of the tunnel in an explosion of echoes.

They sat against the cold concrete and waited around for what seemed like hours, no sign or sound of a train. When the moon had set and it was getting late, they decided it was a lost cause. Jeff and Josh were up on their feet, making their way for the opening, when the far off sound of a train whistle pierced the air. Billy was still trying to get up when he looked at Josh, who stared back at him, goat-stick in hand, his usual humor betrayed by the nervous look in his eyes.

Jeff was just about to jump down when he turned around and made eye contact with Josh as the bridge began to shudder. Both of them glanced back at Billy and stared past him—eyes wide and breath caught in their throats. The train rumbled closer and the ground beneath Billy's feet shook, his teeth buzzing in his mouth. Following the boys' staring eyes, he turned slowly, expecting to see some scary homeless guy with a hook, or worse yet . . . the Goat Man himself. When he faced completely away, staring into the darkness outside the other opening, the sounds of fast rustling leaves and jumbled laughter came from the hill behind him. *Those bastards.*

By the time Billy turned around and made his way to the opening, the boys were gone and the train was getting closer. Practical jokes aside, he couldn't get the look of those empty goat eyes out of his mind. And as the train roared overhead, the feeling of someone—something —behind him grew with a tingling at the back of his neck.

This time, as he turned to look out the other end of the spandrel, his eyes were flooded with a dark yellow glow filling up the opening. He stood there frozen, staring at the light, the concrete bridge shaking with the weight and movement as train car after train car pummeled over the railroad tracks above. The light grew closer, enveloping the inside of the tunnel and surrounding Billy with its unsettling presence.

A faint buzzing whispery voice rose in the air chanting over and over, "The Lord of the Woods . . ."

Billy woke to the sound of chirping birds and the dim blue light of the morning sky, lying on the most uncomfortable surface he had ever slept on. He sat up, his head dizzy and pounding. He was still in the same open tunnel inside Four Arches. The place looked completely different in the wee-hour twilight. Cool moist air blew on his face as he stared out the opening where he now suddenly remembered the glowing light.

Trees and the road below had replaced it. But that voice. . . "Jesus," he said, turning back to face the way he'd come in. He didn't want to think about it anymore. Carefully, he made his way down from the bridge and onto the hill below. He let gravity dictate his speed as he stumbled his way toward the road. He was almost to the bottom when an unwelcome familiar face caught his attention.

"Goddamnit, Josh!" Standing upright before him, the goat-head stick was plunged into the ground, head purposely facing up the hill at him. Billy kicked the stick over, knocking the head to the ground, and raced down to his bike. If he didn't hurry, he wouldn't have enough time to get ready for school by the looks of the rising sun. He wasn't sure he should call it luck, but unlike the other two boys, Billy didn't have to worry about coming home to pissed-off waiting parents. His dad probably didn't even realize he was gone. Kenny—his father—hadn't given much of a shit about anything the boy did for going on a decade now. And his mom had been out of the picture since before he could remember.

Billy straddled his bike and took off for home.

In third period English, Jeff grinned like an idiot, stifling a laugh as Billy entered the classroom. He gave Jeff the evil eye, but that only seemed to make the kid let loose with laughter. When the bell rang and the classroom conversation died down and Jeff was still laughing, Mr. Koby sent him out into the hall. It wasn't long before Jeff peeked into the rectangular window from time to time to point and laugh at Billy. By then it really didn't matter. Billy's head hurt too much to do more than barely notice.

Four Arches

As Billy made his way to fifth-period Art, a nervous growl called from his stomach at the thought of facing both Jeff *and* Josh. Especially Josh. Jeff was far more intimidating in a physical stature kind of way, but Josh's sharp, witty sense of humor was more destructive than any fist could be. Deep down Billy knew it was because he actually liked the little prick and had only ever wanted his respect, but never got so much as a scrap.

He shuffled into class, heading straight to his desk, eyes facing front so as not to notice the two boys giggling loudly at him. Then he waited for Mrs. Kemp to start her lesson for the day. But ignoring them wouldn't last long. They had ways to get his attention, to make him burn with humiliation too much to keep looking away. It was something about the two of them when they were together. As if they could have embarrassed God and still wouldn't be sated.

When class was over and Billy made it to the hallway, Jeff and Josh trailed behind him. His dizziness and headache seemed to intermingle with his rising anger. A tug on Billy's sleeve told him they weren't going to give up that easily. He shook his hand violently to get whichever bastard was pulling on him to release their grip.

Josh's sarcastic, whiny voice cracked, "Well, Nanny, did you see him?" Laughter.

"Yeah, Nanny, did you piss your pants or . . . even worse, did you fill them up with shit?" Jeff said. More laughter.

"Oh, come on, Nanny, we were just kidding." Josh somehow made his mocking tone even more annoying. "Nanny?"

"Oh, just fuck off, okay?" Billy picked up speed and left the two cackling brats behind.

Sunlight gleamed off the rearview mirror as Harley pulled up to the Big Four. He parked off the side of the road just in front of the bridge, got out of the white *Town of Greencastle* truck carrying a long black trash bag, and crossed the street. "Oh, Goddamnit. Not another goat head."

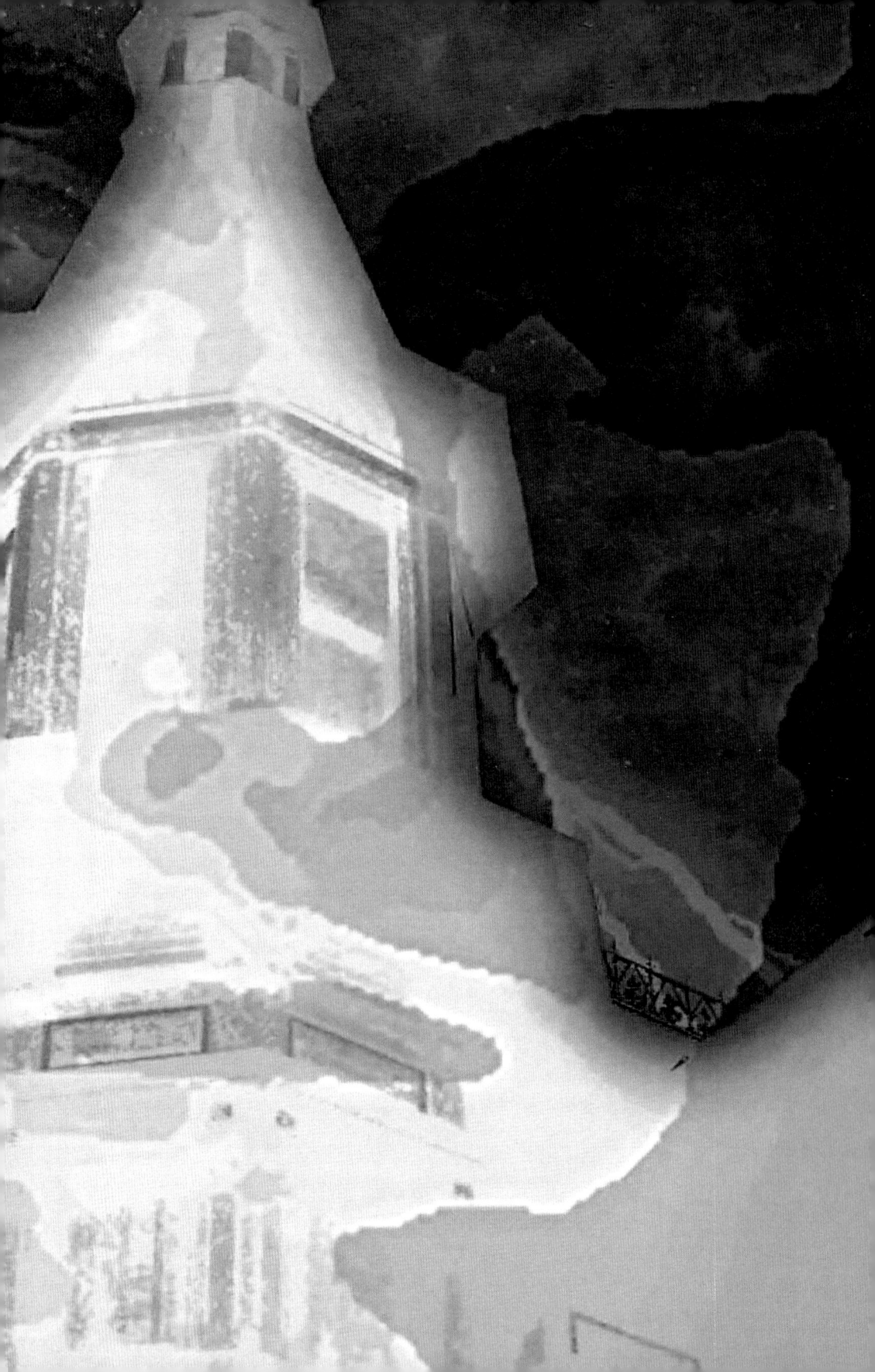

He leaned down and picked up the long, gray, bark-covered stick with the severed head stuck at the end. "Fucking kids."

It was Harley's job, at least once a week, sometimes more if needed, to pick up around Four Arches and various other locations around town. He'd gathered up more beer cans in and around the bridge than anywhere else. Including DePauw campus. He sighed and grabbed the head by one of its horns and carefully put it in the bag, trying but failing to keep from dripping blood on his pants. "Mother—fucker."

Once the head made its way securely to the bottom of the bag, he twisted the top of the black plastic to hold it temporarily shut and climbed uphill toward the bridge. From halfway up he could already tell he'd be stuck here at least a couple of hours from the bits of trash and debris he could see within the spandrels. When he came to the top, he stepped up into the first tunnel, pulled the dust bin from his waist, and started scooping up cigarette butts and scraping gum from the ground level of the tubular concrete.

When he was done, he picked up a pile of sticks covered in ash and tossed them into the bag. He was just about to scoop up the ashes when something shiny in the distance caught his eye. Something small but gleaming, just beyond the other end of the open tunnel on the ground below. Harley set his bag down and climbed out of the back end of the bridge and carefully walked down at an angle through the trees and leaves and sticker bushes. Whatever had been shining, the light was no longer hitting just right, so he went in the general direction where he'd seen it.

As Harley came closer to where he thought he'd seen the shiny object, the hair on the back of his neck began to prickle and his chest grew heavy. He didn't know why, but he sensed that someone was there. Someone. . . or *something*. He'd heard all the Goat Man rumors—who hadn't? Besides, he'd seen so many goat heads around there that if he hadn't, he would have gotten curious and heard the story anyway. But he didn't believe small-town horseshit and he wasn't about to start now. The devil was another story. He'd scrubbed down more than his share of satanic symbols from the old brittle concrete.

His tension was only confirmed when he nearly slipped in a thick congealing puddle of blood. From there a trail of spots and splatters led onward and he followed, heart racing behind his ribs. He kept turning around to look back, sure that at any moment some red scaly beast with solid black eyes and a flaming pitchfork would puff into being and tear him limb from limb. The same limbs that were trembling now, shaking.

  He wanted to go back to the truck so bad he could taste it. It was the sensible thing to do. Go back to the truck and head into town and get the sheriff. It's not as if he worked for the law or anything. He didn't need to be out here if someone had been murdered. A stick snapped somewhere by the bridge and Harley turned to look, but kept on walking, in case he needed to run. Another twig snapped and Harley picked up his pace just a little bit. When the third twig snapped, Harley turned to haul ass, and his foot knocked into something solid and sent his body forward, head first, right at the ground. But ground wasn't what he hit.

  A high-pitched scream gargled its way from Harley's mouth as he realized he was lying face to face with the pale sunken eyes of a dead man. Leaves rustled all around him as he scrambled to get to his feet. His hands pressed against what quickly became obvious wasn't a human body, but the body of a goat. He tried to block out this notion as he turned and walked several meters away and leaned down to vomit next to an old thick hickory tree.

  Heart still beating like a motorboat, Harley looked up between heaves, chunks of red hanging from a long line of saliva dripping from his mouth. When he could retch no more, he wiped his mouth on his sleeve and circled around looking for whatever had snapped those sticks. Only the typical woodsy sounds surrounded by far-off traffic from town could be heard. And no animal, person, or red devil was waiting for him as far as he could see.

  He glanced back over at the body on the ground remembering what he'd felt between his fingers. Fur. . . and lots of it. Sure enough, the wet body of a goat lay on the ground where he had just been. But when Harley's eyes made their way up the black furry neckline, his body curdled and he began to heave again, nothing but air making its way up his esophagus. He would never get that image out of his mind.

Those same sunken human eyes stared back at him from a man's bruise-purple face attached to the neck of the black goat.

Billy stepped off the school bus, backpack dragging from his left hand, and walked across the street to the small rundown blue house nearly hidden behind a lawn of waist-high grass. Loose boards moaned in protest as he walked up to the front door, kicking crushed beer cans and makeshift paper-plate ashtrays off the side of the porch. The quiet, empty living room greeted him inside, and he set his backpack on the couch and went straight for the fridge.

An odd smell of chemicals permeated the kitchen, coming up from the basement—Dad's "laboratory." Billy didn't know what his father did down there, but he knew whatever it was wasn't legal, had something to do with drugs, and he was better off not ever finding out. It was the only rule he had to live by in his old man's house. Don't go in the basement. The last time he'd broken it, his father had beaten any chance he'd ever want to return out of him for good.

Billy put his dishes in the sink, got a beer from the fridge, and went to his room to get his electric guitar. A night jamming out on the porch smoking and drinking was just what he needed to relieve the tension that had built up in him ever since he came back from Four Arches. He sat down holding his black generic Les Paul copy with pearl-like square inlays in between certain frets; *three, five, seven, nine, and twelve,* he remembered to himself. They always made it easier to remember where on the fretboard he was playing.

He put his lit cigarette, butt first, between the strings where they were attached to the tuning gears on the headstock at the end of the neck. When he was sure it would stay there, poking an end lit with fire out from his guitar, he strummed out some power chords and started to sing the song he had written a few nights before. Across the street, the empty field lay listening, a gentle breeze coursing through the bits of weeds and sticks beyond its rusty barbwire fence.

From the corner of Billy's eye, the cigarette was just

about to burn up its last drag of tobacco and he stopped, setting his pick on the porch and reaching for the long trunk of ash hanging from the glowing butt. A sharp sting bit his fingers when he grabbed it, not realizing he'd grabbed it by the cherry, and he cried out, "Shit!" The sting sent a chill up his arm as he tossed aside the cigarette, and when its cold fingers brushed up his neck a flash of memory hit him like an ice pick stabbing into his eye—in intensity and pain.

He grabbed for his eyes, dropping the guitar on the ground in a loud dissonant chord that was cut off as quickly as it was played. Bright yellow light filled his vision and was interrupted with flashes of different scenes in between one moment of glowing from the next. In one flash, he saw a man with a frightened dirty face and pale blue eyes running through some woods in the dark. In another he saw the stars through the branches of some trees from a vantage point that had to be on the ground. The next flash was different—alien in a way he couldn't place. What he saw was vivid and grotesque, but his mind could barely fathom it, let alone process it into shapes and colors. It was vast as the universe and just as cold. Evil in every way—he knew it was so.

The last flash showed him something he recognized, something he'd seen somewhere recently but couldn't remember where. Dark red liquid dripped down from the hieroglyphic-like symbols crudely written on white flesh. The symbols moved in his vision as the yellow light flashed in and out. In between, the movement was rhythmic as moonlight glinted off the streaming red now dripping further.

Her hands pressed against his chest as her body undulated, blood dripping off her right breast, sweat gleaming from her face and neck, long black and flowing hair behind her as she rode him, staring into his eyes with a hunger that turned his insides apart. Then the flash came again and she was different. Monstrous. In place of her head a black furry horned head much like the gray one Josh and Jeff had scared him with stared down at him, tongue lolling at the side of its mouth, eyes open and staring blankly. That same droning voice whispered in his ear: "The Lord of the Woods . . ."

Its whispery voice grew in intensity: "Shub-Niggurath!"

Billy woke up lying in the thick grass in front of

his house, a queasy feeling in his stomach and an erection throbbing in his pants. He rolled over and sat up, listening to the crickets and looking up at the stars with a sense of deep, chilling unease. What the hell was he doing having nightmares in the middle of being awake? And those fucking bastards must have really freaked him out to make him see the kind of shit he'd just seen. *That fucking goat head . . .*

Billy got up and grabbed his guitar, dusting off the grass and dirt, and went in to go to bed, crushing his empty beer can under his shoe on the porch along the way.

The next day at school Jeff and Josh were at it again. Billy was able to avoid them his first few classes, but when Art II came along, there was no hiding from kids whose desks sat directly next to yours. As Mrs. Kemp droned further on about Michelangelo's late-night digging habits, Josh passed a folded note back to Jeff and Jeff almost immediately reddened with laughter. He whispered over to Billy.

"Nanny, you gotta see this. It's so great." He kept his girlish nasal laughter low and under his breath, his face near to bursting. Jeff stared at Mrs. Kemp, his arms crossed stiff across his chest, and in a flitting movement he tossed the note over to Billy's desk so fast he hardly seemed to move.

Billy's face went red with something other than humor as he opened the unevenly folded paper. A crude caricature of a boy with long hair and glasses and a face full of acne wearing a T-shirt with the word "NANNY" scribbled across its front stood with his arms out, lines coming away from the hands and a cloud of text over his head. "The Goat Man made me shit my pants!"

The two boys were laughing at an audible level now that the butt of their joke had taken the bait. Billy was tired of always getting the hook. He liked Josh and Jeff, but they were starting to get under his skin and he wasn't sure how much longer he could take their shit.

"Ahem. . . Mr. Baker and Mr. Dower, just what's got you two in such an uproar?"

Jeff pressed his lips together in silence, but Josh's laughter instead grew to a near-howling madness.

"You two, out in the hall."

"But I stopped laugh—"

"I don't care, Mr. Dower, you shouldn't have started. Go right now, this instant." Jeff's eyes were dark as he shoved his way up from his desk and grabbed his books. A scowl twisted his face as he turned and walked out, slamming the door behind him. Meanwhile Josh was still laughing like a hyena as he gathered up his things and headed toward the door. When Josh left the room and Mrs. Kemp went back to her lecture, Billy let out a quiet sigh and crumbled up the paper note.

The last bell rang and Billy found himself again unable to ward off the blond wonder twins. Instead, he tried to ignore them as they walked alongside him, spouting off gibberish and giggling incessantly. They talked him into ditching the bus and walking with them, something he wouldn't usually consider given recent events, but he couldn't get out of his mind the night they went to Four Arches: the yellow light, the goat's head, and that woman...

On the road, Jeff stopped and lit a cigarette as Josh and Billy kept walking. "That fucking bitch. I hate her."

Josh waved away smoke from his face. "Who?"

"Mrs. Kemp, that's who, the fucking cunt. I should go find her car in the parking lot and key it or pop one of her tires."

Josh stared at Jeff in a rare moment of quiet. Billy took his opening.

"You guys, I think I wanna go back to Four Arches."

Josh laughed and launched into baby-talk mode: "How come, Nanny? You wanna shit your pants again?" Jeff laughed blowing out a huge cloud of smoke, his laughter ending in a long rasping cough.

"Okay, don't call me crazy, but I saw something weird when you guys left me there the other night."

"Oh, maybe Nanny did see the Goat Man," Josh said, his eyes wide with exaggerated fear.

"I didn't see no fucking *Goat Man*." Billy was trembling, the three of them standing there in the middle of the street, frozen.

Jeff threw out his cigarette, looking at Billy quietly. "Shut up, Josh, I think he's serious."

Four Arches

After Billy calmed down, the three of them continued walking and Billy told them about the light in the spandrel. He kept the visions to himself, though, not wanting to sound completely nuts. By the time he was done talking, Josh and Jeff were excited—not that they believed him; it was obvious they didn't. But the coming Friday was Halloween and Josh had the bright idea of telling some other kids and getting a whole big group together to go that night and check it out. Billy was sure Josh and Jeff would be planning some kind of underhanded prank to pull off when they got there, but he didn't care. He wanted to go back and he was too goddamn scared to go on his own.

Friday came quickly, the anticipation of going to the Big Four eaten up by the worm in Billy's stomach that squirmed around every time Josh and Jeff invited another kid to come along with them. It wasn't that they were inviting more kids; it was the fact that each and every time they told the story they made Billy sound more and more out of his skull.

By the time the final bell rang, they'd talked nearly thirty kids into meeting out by the bridge around 11:30 that night and then heading up into the arches together as one big crowded group.

When Billy arrived at the hill by the bridge, Josh and Jeff at each side, he was the only one in the whole group not wearing a costume. Josh was dressed as Frankenstein's monster; Jeff pedaled along as Elliot from *E.T.*, complete with a basket mounted on the front of his handle bars and a big stuffed brown ALF doll sitting wrapped in a blanket inside. There was an Axel Rose lookalike, a kid with a werewolf mask wearing a thick gray hoodie with *Teen Wolf* written with a Sharpie across the front, and several ghosts in long white sheets with eyeholes cut in them.

The buzz going around was that the *Banner Graphic* had reported a body had been found out by the bridge. Justin Collier said the place had been swarming with cops when he arrived, so he turned around and came back later.

They waited around for about ten minutes for any

last-minute arrivals. About half the kids didn't show, but a few more straggled in just as they were about to leave.

The night was still as the group walked up the inclined road toward the bridge. The sounds of chatter, footsteps on pavement kicking loose gravel, and costume plastic rubbing against costume plastic surrounded Billy. Otherwise, even the crickets were silent. A rare side-hanging orange crescent moon hung in the sky like a fiery sickle raised to strike in battle. And yet, Billy barely noticed, his eyes fixated only on the bridge and the watching spandrels, empty holes of darkness waiting to be filled with something else.

Josh and Jeff led the way, climbing up the hill, pulling themselves along with low-hanging branches. The rest of the kids followed, Billy somewhere in the middle, having fallen behind in his slow awkward stumble. Sweat dripped down his back as he climbed the hill.

The anticipation was aching in his chest, the hair on the back of his neck standing on end. Deep in the far corners of his mind there was a voice screaming for him to run, to grab anyone who would listen and get the hell out of Dodge. But that voice was drowned out in a pool of growing terrifying fascination inside him. It was as if some magnetic force was pulling him from inside those concrete arches and would drag Billy kicking and screaming if need be to get him back there.

"Look at Billy—look. I think Nanny's shitting his pants again." Josh pointed to Billy as Billy tripped his way in between the crowd of kids, who were all now laughing at him. But Billy wasn't angry; he didn't take the bait this time. He knew something none of the other kids knew. This place was dangerous. Something was definitely here. Something malign and hungry. And it waited.

On top of the hill, the crowd parted and Josh and Jeff took Billy by the arm and herded him over in front of the first spandrel.

"Is this the one, Nanny?" Jeff asked. Billy nodded.

"Okay, Nanny, it's time to go in there and show the Goat Man who's boss," Josh said, pulling on Billy's arm weakly.

"Yeah, Nanny, go inside. We didn't see anything here— you did." Jeff plopped his head upward, sending his long blond bangs to the other side of his scalp and out of his eyes, then grabbed Billy's other hand.

Four Arches

Josh turned and, in between short fast giggles, called into the dark shadowy opening, "Here he is, we brought him back." He smiled at Billy with a snide sense of pleasure, then started to chant, lifting his arm up and hammering at the air with his fist along with each syllable. "Sac-ri-fice. Sac-ri-fice. Sac-ri-fice."

The crowd of teens took up the mantra and started to scoot Billy forward. The initially silent night began to whip and holler with wind. An icy cold gust blasted through the spandrels and out at the kids as Billy had no choice but to step up onto the concrete lip entering madness.

A distant spark in the darkness beyond mesmerized Billy like a cobra trapping its prey in a chill blast of paralysis. The same unseen force pulled him against his will, sweating and trembling. The wind called out in long howls, swirling into one another in the night.

The ground below began to shake as if the gods were threatening to tear open the earth, and Billy realized it was the train. The long blast of its whistle caught everyone's attention but Billy's. He couldn't stop staring at the small yellow glowing dot growing and getting closer.

"Look at Nanny—I think he really is going to shit his pants. It's just a train, Nanny," Josh said, the nervous look on his face saying otherwise.

The ground rumbled as the train grew closer, bits of dust falling at random from the concrete above. And all the while Billy stared out at the yellow light, now grown to about the size of a Frisbee and speeding toward the open spandrel. Toward them all. Billy tried to push away, to turn around, even to scream, but his body was pinned, frozen, and not by the kids. The vibration of train wheels on the tracks and the noisy teenagers chattering exclamations grew to a fevered pitch, and in the blink of an eye the yellow light burst open like a huge explosion and everything was bathed in golden light.

Josh and Jeff each put a hand up to shield their eyes from the bright intensity of it. The train crossed overhead, shaking the inside of the arch like an earthquake. But all the children stood still, staring into the light.

The woman from Billy's visions stepped out of the glow, naked, as if gracefully coming up from a river or an ocean, hair tangling about her, the light dripping off her body like beads and streaming lines of water. Her eyes were filled with the same yellow glow. Someone from the crowd screamed in a long carrying pitch, yet still none of them moved.

She reached out her hand and Billy took it in his. Her touch was cold but soft and gentle, just as he remembered it now. She smiled and what must have been a thousand hooves clattered against the concrete as dozens and dozens of small goats came out of the light behind her bleating with hunger in their goat voices as they made their way toward the teenagers.

All around Billy the children screamed as the small goats bit into their flesh and bone and chewed and chewed and chewed, blood dripping from their furry chins and splattering everywhere. One minute they were goats; the next Billy saw them as something else. Tall black grotesque things of mostly rope-like tentacles, each one standing on two tiny hoofed legs. Billy grinned in unison with Her and she gripped his hand tightly. Even Jeff and Josh's screams, as they were torn apart, didn't cause his gaze to waver. The power within her was creeping through their touch and entering Billy. The faint outline where the hieroglyphic symbols had been on Her chest caught his attention and he could read them now.

Shub-Niggurath! The Black Goat.

And just as soon as the words went into place Her hand locked down on his like a vice and Her flesh trembled as it flowed into something else. The smile remained but the head was now horned and covered in black fur, the eyes still emitting that eerie yellow glow. The thick furry neckline slid down to meet charcoal-colored human-like muscular flesh. The huge, now-masculine body was covered in only a loincloth of dry dirty leaves.

Hooves clattered in droves as the horrid black creatures shrank back down into little goats and scurried back into the light from where they came, slipping here and there in puddles of blood. The Black Goat grabbed Billy by the throat and pulled his limp, scrawny body into the light, glasses, blue jean jacket, and all.

Then the light faded until only the stars and the orange crescent moon remained.

The Old Schoolhouse

Gwyneth Jones

Ten days after Eliud's plane vanished I drove to Norfolk, with my cello and Fenris in the back of the car. It was a warm, dull August day; the sky over Eastern England the colour of dust. Driving in silence (no music, no news or chat I wanted to hear), I felt strongly that I had company. Over and over I'd glance at my rearview mirror, wondering who was in the back seat. My black cello case and the little black dog gazed solemnly back, puzzled by my unease. Of course I thought I had company: I'd probably never been alone on this journey before. At least one of us, usually Renton, would always have been with me.

The garden looked tended, and was just as I remembered. The wildflower beds had gone to seed, in a mad tangle of baked stalks and tottering poppy-heads, but the swathes of grass between them were neatly shorn. I'd collected the keys from Eliud's house-agent. I let myself in, dumped my bag and the cello beside a stack of flat-packed storage boxes, and walked around in the cool gloom. Nothing seemed to have changed. The Victorian Board School's single classroom, long and high, was all the living space. At one end, French doors opened onto the brick terrace. At the other, between his study and the kitchen, rose the white-painted, crooked stairs to Eliud's bedroom suite. I would sleep up there. The house agent hadn't been keen on making a bed in the studio for me. The outdoor buildings, our summer camp, had probably been allowed to go to seed, like the flowers.

The floors shone, the rugs were brushed. The kitchen, and that inconvenient little lower-orders bathroom next to it, sparkled. The piano was in tune: which startled me, though I knew Eliud had been here. He'd called me from the schoolhouse three weeks ago.

The great man had finally agreed to let his official biographer get to work. He'd wanted someone to help him sort his old papers: pack everything up and send it to his new

house outside London. I'd agreed to meet him here, after his trip to Sydney. But Eliud Tince had vanished, along with his current entourage and a planeload of other passengers and crew, over the Southern Ocean (where the plane shouldn't have been at all). In the end, failing all news, I'd decided to come alone, and tackle the job myself. Probably, mainly, because I couldn't face cancelling his arrangements—

I didn't know who the biographer was. Before their break-up it would obviously have been Michael Renton, Eliud Tince's amanuensis, his *éminence grise;* the "torturer" who got the best out of him, as Eliud used to say. But Renton was gone, Renton could no longer be mentioned, so who? I'd been wondering, picking over the eminent specialists who might be in line, and thinking it had better not be *me* the master had in mind. I'm an instrumentalist, not a biographer. I wouldn't know how to begin. But you never knew with Eliud. He had strange ideas. I unlocked his study; I checked his desk; I climbed the crooked stairs and poked around in his suite. There weren't many places to hide a mountain of paper in the schoolhouse: the task looked manageable.

I wandered, studying framed photographs, mostly black and white; so much better-looking than colour. I found myself in a dark smock under an apple tree, long thin arms and a shock of short dark hair; legs like two white, tilted sticks propped against my cello's flanks. And here was Maria Wenger, Eliud's stepdaughter by his second marriage: not yet the wonderful, the unique soprano, but already my best friend; in a summery dress all over roses. Yellow roses; I remembered it. . . It was usually Maria who took the pictures. She was a good photographer. The rest of us were rubbish: Maria was lucky she'd kept her head. Here was Rikard Glode, the pianist, throwing Frisbee with Renton and Julia while Julia's daughter, Perseis, aged about two, sat by on a rug. My ex-boyfriend in that shapeless green polo shirt and the baggy shorts with the frog-pattern. . . I recognised my friends by their clothes, the way people recognise relatives after a disaster. Only Eliud, grinning in a deck chair, those famous plaid trousers secured around his scrawny waist by an enormous leather belt, hadn't changed at all. I wondered how old he'd been then, more than two decades ago, when I was nineteen. He'd started admitting to "the mid-eighties" nowadays, but he was notoriously hard to pin down. He wanted us to believe he was immortal, the vain old turtlehead.

We'd been like family, like courtiers, with Eliud as our ruler and Renton his grand vizier; reigning here in deepest Norfolk, and all the luminaries of the *avant-garde* music world came to us. . . But nothing lasts forever. After the big fight Eliud returned to the U.S. to take up a prestigious post in California, not his native New England, and we all went our separate ways. I'd had my successes since then, but never again known such a magic circle. And here I was, drawn back to the source: staring at a black and white photo of my ex-boyfriend at thirty, his merman eyes reduced to punctured grey. His tarnished-gold hair, already receding even then, flew around his head in thick metallic scales; so soft to the touch.

I set the photograph down, making a mental note to find the digital copies of all these pictures: save them off and put them with the biographical material.

Later, in dusty twilight, I whistled Fenris from wherever he'd been roaming. We walked up the lane to the Flint Barn—like the schoolhouse, a relic of the former agricultural community of Hindey—where I knew I'd get a signal. Connectivity at the old schoolhouse was as dire as ever. There was no news: just the same figures, diagrams, and graphs; the same rumours that went nowhere. I knew that Maria, an Australian herself, was at the airport, keeping vigil with the horde of dignified, tearful, terrified relatives, lovers, and friends. I was glad Eliud had someone on the spot. His third wife, Lucia Ventto, had been on the flight with him, along with her son, Martin, and Martin's newly pregnant girlfriend Annemarie; Maria's sister, the choreographer Judit Saed; and Maria's dear friend, ex-husband, Mel Colman the operatic conductor. . . Almost a clean sweep. It was eerie. I thought of trying to send Eliud a text, *hope you're okay,* but that would be ghoulish. I texted Maria instead.

The harvest was over. The old barn stood foursquare, a monument to the days when farm labour was plentiful and poor, facing the remains of sunset on a vast, stubbled, prairie horizon. It was still empty, just as it had been in our day: unconverted, un-reclaimed. I sat with my back to a flint wall that held the heat of the day, waiting for Maria to respond and reading an article that listed all the vessels, air and sea, that had crashed, been turned back by extreme turbulence, or plain vanished over the Southern Ocean recently. The phenomenon was blamed on climate change. Or sunspots. Or both.

No reply from Maria. It would be early in Sydney. Maybe she was asleep.

As I headed back a figure approached me on the lonely track, strangely stooped and blurred in the gloom. I was almost frightened until I recognised our neighbour: the artist who had a studio and showroom at the dandy, urban end of our lane, where there was a strip of actual grey asphalt instead of ruts and grass.

"It's Aiode, isn't it?" he said, when we came face to face.

"A-ee-the," I corrected him uneasily. I couldn't remember his real name. He hadn't been friendly, as far as I recalled, and nor had we. We called him "Mr. Raven," after a large, ugly black metal raven that stood at his gate. It was still there; I'd noticed it as I drove by.

"I knew you must be back. I saw Mike Renton walking down the lane yesterday."

He was never Mike. Always just *Renton* with us. "I don't think so!"

Mr. Raven looked at me oddly, head on one side. "I'm sure I'd know Mike Renton."

I shook my head. "I don't believe he's even in the country."

"Well, my mistake. I hear old Eliud's finally selling off the ancestral home?"

"Ancestral—?"

Mr. Raven gave me the sideways look again. "Lord, yes! He had family here going back to the old Hindey times, and beyond. They only left when the village got razed, before the war. That's why he bought that little old place you're in. Didn't you know?"

Thankfully Fenris was exploring and didn't reappear, scrambling from under the hedge, until our nosy neighbour had walked on—saving me the embarrassment of explaining the presence of Renton's dog: my inheritance from a foundered relationship.

It was an unsettling conversation. I hadn't known Eliud was selling up. But why would Mr. Raven say that if it wasn't true? I was sure he couldn't have seen Renton, anyway. The last I'd heard my ex-boyfriend was living in Japan. He'd become a bit of a recluse, just firi g off the occasional brilliant article or paper to let the *avant-garde* world know he was still alive.

In the morning, I set up my work camp. I moved most of the furniture back against one wall, clearing a wide space on the schoolroom floor. I assembled several of the flat packed storage boxes and stacked everything that could be described as "papers" on the long table where we used to eat. The digital stuff—the contents of a desktop PC's hard drive; a jumble of data sticks, memory cards, and discs— could wait. The vintage electronic instruments, vials of Eliud's alchemy, might hold buried treasure in their "computer memories," but I'd leave them alone. . . Biographical material, catalogue material, discography. Original scores, household accounts. Personal letters, business letters, autographed concert programmes . . . All I could do was make a start.

I broke out a new, lined A4 pad. Hopefully a system would take shape as I worked.

The flatpacks puzzled me, when I came to think about it. It wasn't like Eliud to be so organised. Had he got himself a new Renton, and I didn't know? The idea jarred. Renton could be so overbearing, so possessive. . . Of course Eliud didn't want me for a biographer, but he'd definitely hinted at *something*. Maybe a new piece—a renewal of our partnership? It wasn't so far-fetched. He hadn't produced a major new work for years. It was about time, if it was ever going to happen. So I'd let my mind run on (why else had I brought the cello? and now I felt ashamed of myself, but still threatened by this imaginary new power-broker—

I chose the *Shock and Awe Fantasia* (for prepared piano, cello, and white noise) on the schoolroom's sound system and set to work, to the raw, sonorous background of Eliud's elegy for the soul of the U.S. He'd fallen out with *Shock and Awe,* it was "too emotional," but I still loved the sound of my own bowing: the inhuman, incredible *precision* Eliud demanded. I'd left the crazy little world of the *avant garde* behind, I'd been a pretty-good classical soloist for nearly twenty years, but I missed the master's intensity so much—

The first sheet of odd, childish drawings triggered a new category: a heap all on its own. When I'd run into four or five of them I looked more closely.

The figures were drawn in coloured pencil, scattered at random over different-sized sheets of plain paper. The most common was a triangle, like a child's first approximation of the human form: two strong lines jutting from the base, one each from the diagonals, and a small circle balanced at the apex. Ovoids and squares, less frequent, followed the same pattern. The circular "heads" had no features. Softer, wavy lines often emanated from the "heads" and "bodies," like tentacles; or sine waves. Nearly all the figures were carelessly coloured: blue, red, yellow, or dark green. Size and configu ation varied. Some figures were isolated, some in rows, some clustered: some were *very* small, some much larger.

At first glance I'd thought they really were a child's drawings. There had always been children in Eliud's life. But each sheet was annotated and dated, in the master's own handwriting. The dates were years apart, and the drawings seemed less childish, the more I looked. There was decision and purpose in them, sharp as the knife-edge arpeggios of *Shock and Awe*. They seemed faintly familiar, too. Had I *known* about these odd geometric fish? Clearly they were part of something, something important gestating over decades, but what did they mean? I pondered over one of Eliud's annotations. *Other dimensions are not spatial but exist at right angles to our own...* Was there was some kind of optical illusion involved? Obedient, from long training, to my composer's weird demands, I held up one of the sheets, edge-on to my nose, and tried to look along it sideways; *at right angles.*

I caught a glimpse of something whipping out of sight; or opening and swiftly closing—

But Fenris was barking and barking. I dropped the paper and rushed around the house: I couldn't find him. I ran outdoors in a panic, calling "Fenris, Fenris!" I raced around, charging over the swathes of turf, crashing through flower beds to the ancient orchard, but he just went on barking madly, somewhere out of sight. Our summer camp lay derelict under twisted boughs, around the shady lawn where Rikard had pitched his tent. The studio that Renton and I had shared; the cabin; the tenements, the treehouse; the sauna (not a sauna, but another spare bedroom in our day). I didn't have the keys with me, I couldn't get in. I could only rub at cobwebs and peer through dusty glass, feeling like a ghost.

I shouted "Fenris, Fenris!" But the little black dog had stopped barking—

Then he started up again, much further away. I realised he must have chased something, probably a rabbit, into Eliud's parcel of trees—a narrow slip of woodland attached to the property, but jutting into the emptiness of the prairies. I stepped over the polished root that made a doorsill, in a gap in the orchard's hedge, and followed.

Nothing had changed in here, either. There was the same brooding atmosphere; the same narrow path, straight down the middle, leading the eye to a distant lozenge of colourless daylight. I followed it, still calling "Fenris!" but more calmly. The trees were a mass of shadow. Straggling young oaks competed for light with big old twisted chestnuts, above a dense understorey of holly, bracken, and bramble. Insects buzzed; birds scolded unseen. Once I saw the wings of a big hunting hawk flash between branches. . . I didn't like the wood. None of us had ever liked it; but I thought I knew it. About two-thirds of the way through I came across something I'd never seen before.

Long ago one of the massive chestnuts had fallen. The timber must have been dragged out and taken away. Only the stump remained, tipped on its side, grey starfish roots reaching for the sky; guarding a hollow, open space. We'd tried to enjoy this secret glade in the old days, bringing picnics, rugs, and wine; building midnight bonfires. But not often. The parcel of trees repelled us, literally. It drove us away. It was dark, ugly; everything prickled and there were biting insects.

I was tired and hot, and Fenris was still barking, but now he was behind me. I realised the stupidity of chasing a little dog who was just running round in circles. I saw pale

The Old Schoolhouse

patches in the leaf litter, like splashes of sunlight where there was no sunlight. I stepped onto one of them: and it was a stone. There was a ring of pale stones, set in a circle as wide as the glade. They must have been buried in our day, carried to the surface maybe by last winter's spectacular rains. There were markings on them—patterns. I hunkered down for a closer look: I saw traces of colour and seemed to hear a kind of chiming, a kind of chattering—

But Fenris was barking and barking.

In a panic I ran through the trees and the tearing brambles; I followed his terrified cries to the parking space by the brick terrace, where I'd left my car. Beyond that point, greenery had completely overwhelmed the old drive. I fought my way through the tangle, ambushed by sticky burrs, savaged by nettle stings, and found the little dog. He was crouching on the doorsill of the caravan, which still stood in its old place; immovable now, white flanks devoured by choking weeds. I sighed, picked up the little black dog, and hugged him tight.

"It's no use, Fenny, everybody's gone. Nobody lives there anymore."

He stopped barking and lay quiet in my arms. I carried him back to the schoolroom; his warm, compact, muscular little body snuggled close. As we walked in, I saw something—something I could not describe, could not imagine. An awful terror shook me, a sick abyss deeper than the worst nightmare I'd ever had... And then I was kneeling on the floor, a sheet of coloured doodles in my hand. *Shock and Awe* was on the sound system; and there was Fenris, curled up on an armchair, nose to tail, where he'd been since breakfast.

It was the strangest feeling. I touched my cheeks; my bare arms. Not a scratch, and I was perfectly cool. I even looked at the soles of my shoes. Not a trace of dark leaf litter. It was almost dark. I hadn't eaten since morning. A dizzy spell... I decided it was time to quit.

The weather stayed dull and warm. I ate my meals outdoors, at our old breakfast table outside the kitchen.

Yogurt and honey, oatcakes and coffee in the morning; a bowl of soup and maybe some fruit in the evening. In the calm stillness of the fading light, Fenris laid a small furry animal at my feet and looked up at me hopefully, ears cocked. I could see that he'd broken its back. Its front legs moved; little paws groping. Blood trickled from its mouth.

I sipped coffee. "You want me to mend your toy? Sorry, no can do. You should have been more careful."

I would have liked to put the creature out of its misery, but I knew it's not that simple to kill anything cleanly, so I didn't try. When it had breathed its last and its eyes dimmed, I thought of burying it, wrapped in soft leaves. But a dead animal wants no covering but time; no shroud but the air. So I just tossed it into the long grass.

There had been no recent papers in Eliud's desk. I found no evidence that he was "selling up," but I soon found the "Hindey" folder. I shook out the contents of the battered foolscap envelope and studied Eliud's treasured photographs. The old church, St. Iaad's, with a squat, square tower, at one end of a straggle of hovels, bordering what was now our lane; a familiar bulk at the other end. The schoolhouse itself in close-up, with its last generation of pupils. Girls in pinafores, boys in breeches, some barefoot, some in enormous boots; their shrunken little faces pinched with malice or hunger, or maybe just boredom. A page from St. Iaad's parish register, photographed a little more recently: the entry for the birth of a boy circled in red. Another "Eliud Tince": I couldn't remember if that was supposed to be Eliud's grandfather or great-grandfather. The date was too faded to be made out. A plan of the schoolhouse property. The parcel of trees was labelled, in spidery copperplate: *Hindey Playground. . .* We used to say we betted it had been a miserable "playground" even then, and Eliud would get insulted: he was proud of his tiny wood—

The ancient, crackle-surfaced sepia photographs made my skin creep. Why had I been so astonished when Mr. Raven called the schoolhouse Eliud's "ancestral home"? I'd always known this history. How could I have forgotten?

The Old Schoolhouse

In a different folder I found a modern studio colour print: Eliud and his children. It seemed to be his birthday, but the cake (of course!) had no revealing forest of candles. They'd signed their names in the margin: Bich, the Vietnamese baby he'd adopted with his first wife, already in her sixties in this picture; Gogo and Siaka, daughter and son of the dancer Djènèba Khady, the great love of Eliud's life; Maria and Judit; Martin Ventto, and of course Perseis, the baby of the gang... How happy Eliud looked! How proud he'd been of them all. And yet none of them was his biological child.

Renton, who could be cruel, used to say the master had "a touch of the tar brush" and was afraid of passing the taint on. It was true the old man had strange ideas and could get himself into trouble. He'd once startled a famous musician by congratulating him on his "pure Mandingo bloodline"... Yet how could anyone call him a racist, looking at that United Nations of happy smiles? Really (it came back to me...) the problem was a horrible cancer that ran in his family. He'd escaped, but he was afraid his biological offspring wouldn't—

Everyone forgets. Of course I had forgotten things. But the lapses in my memory, Eliud's ancestral past, the name of that dark little wood, even that "touch of the tarbush" jibe, started to bother me, like a fog in my skull that could be hiding monsters. What else had I forgotten? What bitter words, what angry scenes I would never want to recall—?

Later than time lag demanded, because I didn't want to meet Mr. Raven, I walked up to the Flint Barn and talked to Maria. "It's a good atmosphere," she said gallantly. "We're looking out for each other." She was no longer at the airport. She was back at her gorgeous waterfront house with a couple from Singapore, whose son and little granddaughter had been on the flight, and a young New Zealand woman who had lost her mother. There was still no news. Nothing had been found, not a clue, not a scrap of debris.

"It's so hot," said Maria. "More like Christmas than August... They're saying weird atmospheric pressure might have screwed up the plane's instruments. Might be screwing up the search data... There are empty islands, far south. The pilot could have made a safe ocean landing. Some of them could be safe, at least: but unable to make contact—?"

I hesitated too long. "I saw that story. Yeah, it sounded hopeful."

Maria sighed. "How are you doing? Have you found a will?"

"It'll be with his lawyers," I said. "It's not like that. Eliud had kept the house up, but he hasn't lived here for years. What I'm sorting is archive stuff, nothing vital."

"Oh. I see. I didn't realise—"

I heard her unspoken question: *So why are you doing this?*

Maria had her imaginary island, I had Eliud's papers. I could tell from her voice that she'd accepted the loss of the old man; but irrationally, she was trying to hang onto the others, her family and friends. I was the other way round. I just couldn't let go of Eliud.

In the jumble of documents and souvenirs from the desk drawers, I ran into a CD of NASA's *Music of the Planets:* radio emissions from space probe flybys, converted into sound. I put it on. I hadn't forgotten *this.* Eliud had called NASA's confection "poppycock" and "fake," but he'd been fascinated. He'd quoted from this CD shamelessly in the *Dark Matter Suite...* The sighs of Jupiter did nothing much for me. Mercury's eerie crackles conjured pictures in my mind, evil little crustaceans that crept over blood-red rocks. I suddenly wondered if there was a connection with the drawings. Weren't Eliud's annotations littered with references to "aliens" and "other worlds"? I looked back over my notes.

Alien intelligence can be perceived in certain conditions without resorting to data from so-called outer space, AND THEY ARE LISTENING!

Our universe is an illusion. Worlds on worlds interpenetrate ours.

There is no "out there"... Everything is in reach; time is not an object. Auditory and Visual Alternatives occupy "space" in superposition. . . precisely interleaved layers. . .

But I felt no curiosity this time, just an immense nostalgia for the days when I used to take Eliud's bizarre, semi-scientific pronouncements absolutely seriously. And a great sadness: the knowledge sinking in at last that I would never see the old man again.

I worked all night, forgetting to eat but finishing a bottle of wine. At dawn I woke from a catnap, curled on the rug in the midst of my boxes. I took a quick shower and whistled for Fenris, and we walked out into the cool bright day: up the lane, over a stile and around the outer margin of Eliud's parcel of trees. The little black dog scampered ahead, burrowing under the fence and popping out again joyously at my feet. I watched a pair of goshawks, hunting the trees' high margin: scissoring the pale sky with their razor cuts until it seemed as if Eliud's other worlds might come falling through. A roebuck leapt from a hollow in the stubble and rocketed away. . . When we reached the far end of the path through the wood, Fenris naturally vanished into the thickets. I was left behind, struggling with a gate that had been (for some stupid reason) lashed shut with sheaves of barbed wire.

I caught up with him, having lost a little fabric and gained some painful scratches, in the bonfire glade. I saw the ring of pale stones at once and stared at them, bewildered. So my dizzy spell didn't happen? So that sinister *Alice through the Looking-Glass* moment: when I came in from the wood and saw myself *inside out* was real?

I picked up the little dog and hugged him. "*Why* were you barking like that?" I asked him. "Why did you drag me out here? They're only stones." Fenris licked my nose.

This time I noticed that the circle had a centre. I put Fenris down and kicked at the leaf litter until I'd uncovered the whole of a larger plaque. What did it all mean? A radiating star, a sun surrounded by planets? A playground game. . . The sky above the glade was bright today; the markings were much easier to make out. I saw the faded figures and knew I'd found the originals of Eliud's drawings. Suddenly I had the glimmering of an *amazing* idea.

I took photographs. I sketched the marks on the individual stones in my pocket notebook, carefully as I could, and hurried back to the house.

My sketches matched the drawings. Eliud's ovoids, triangles, and squares, with their little heads and stick limbs, *had* to be derived from the markings in the wood. But they weren't copies. Eliud's figures were more formal and very differently organised, on scaffolds, in long rows, in layered chords; in tiny clusters of grace notes. Intensely excited, I saw that my insight was correct. It had to be. This was a form of musical notation.

I spread the drawings on the floor and stared at them. I took out my cello; the first time I'd touched it since I arrived here. My old playing chair was by the piano, where it had been waiting for me all these years. I pulled it out and sat for a while with the instrument between my knees, the bow in my hand. It was a kind of meditation, a reverence; a commitment to the new work (which I couldn't begin to study yet!). I tuned my strings. I played a few scales, and then the challenging arpeggio passage from *Shock and Awe:* without a slip, which seemed a good omen. I looked down at the drawings. Notation, definitely, but how the hell was it supposed to be played? Eliud hadn't left me a single clue.

Sideways, I thought; and I had another miraculous insight. In what I thought was the most significant annotation, Eliud had referred to *superposition:* many alternatives occupying the same auditory space. *A superposition of alternate worlds, collapsed by sound*. . . He must have made a multilayered recording! And it must be here in the schoolhouse!

I abandoned my meditation and searched the digital material, which I hadn't yet touched: the PC's hard drive, the memory cards, the datasticks, CDs, and discs. I checked the "computer memories" of the vintage electronic orchestra. I found nothing that was unknown to me, nothing that I could recognise as new. I was in despair. Even if the drawings could be deciphered, translated into nuanced sound, by some fantastic process I couldn't imagine, they were scraps and sketches. It would be impossible to reconstruct the new work. Finally, my head spinning and ringing, I took the house agent's keys and went outdoors.

I'd have looked in the studio first, just to cross it off my list: except that I didn't want to see what I knew I'd see. The key turned easily, but the door was laced with ivy tendrils, and knee-deep in leaf litter. I had to wrestle my way in, and it was as I'd expected: mouldering relics in a cobwebbed tomb. My bed, my nest among the recording desks, was gone. So was all the equipment, of course. Soundproofing baffles hung festering from the ceiling and the walls. I backed out again, sick at heart. As I struggled to drag the door shut, I heard something fall down inside. I opened the door again and saw a dusty cardboard tube, about fifty centimetres long, lying on the floor. It was labelled *Aiode*. It rattled. I unwound withered tape and pulled off the cap at one end. I peered inside and saw enough to make my heart beat like thunder—

But Fenris was barking and barking.

He'd gone back to the caravan. He was on the step again: on his back legs, pawing at the door, yapping and yapping. I grabbed him, shouting. I was so keyed up, and the little dog was so infuriating. I hauled him, fighting me all the way, through the tangles, thorns ripping my arms, nettles stinging. He tried to bolt for the caravan again as soon as I slackened my grip. "Oh no you don't!" I yelled. I twisted his collar. I shook him, I *slapped* him—

"What's he done then, poor little dog?"

Mr. Raven was there, stooping by my car. "The gate was open," he said. "I thought I'd drop by. See how you're getting on. Sorry if it's inconvenient."

Like hell had the gate been open. One fist locked round Fenris's collar, embarrassed that I'd been caught beating the little dog, I glared at him, trying to shove the hair out of my eyes.

"Getting on with *what*?"

"With the cleaning work," said Mr. Raven, unperturbed. "I saw those storage boxes delivered. You're clearing the old place out. Isn't that what Eliud sent you for?"

"The work's going well. Close the gate on your way out."

I carried Fenris indoors. He was quiet now, and trembling, and I was so ashamed. I told him I was sorry. I hugged him, I kissed his rough head, I combed the burrs from his coat and shut him in the kitchen, giving him tinned tuna for a treat—

It would drive me crazy if he ran away again.

The cardboard roll was on top of the piano, where I'd left it. I eased the scroll out, gently, and unfurled it. Not only a recording, but a *score*. An amazing, marvellously detailed pictogram score, several metres long; and a datastick, firmly labelled *Hindey Playground.*

Take that, Mr. Raven. I am not some *skivvy,* whistled up to do the house-clearing.

Eliud trusted me. I am *important.*

It was very late when I went up to the barn. I found I had a text from Maria, sounding more resigned, more hopeless, very tired. I sent a reply, without mentioning the new work. I ran my own news checks on the lost flight (for form's sake: there was no change) and headed back, still thinking, fast and furiously, about Eliud's notation—

The moon, which had been getting brighter and brighter since I'd arrived in Norfolk, was full tonight, and the sky was clear as the dust would let it be. Impelled by an idea that wouldn't wait for morning, I took to the prairie and climbed that barbed-wire gate again. It was dark in the trees, but the bonfire glade was full of moonlight. Eliud had copied the marks on these stones—probably the traces of an old children's game; probably more than a hundred years old— and used them for his pictogram notation. I had photographs and sketches of the individual stones, but no image of the whole configuration; *and the configuration must be crucial.* I'd brought my good camera. I looked for a vantage point and found footholds in the grey squirming grooves of the chestnut stump. . . so convenient I had the weird idea I might have carved them myself and forgotten doing it; except that they were weathered and old. Maybe Eliud had carved them; or the children.

I climbed as high as they would take me, and the radiating star was directly below . . .

What all this business had meant to *Eliud* was important, obviously; but not to me. I didn't have to understand Eluid's strange ideas about the cosmos, or how those ideas meshed with his childhood memories of Hindey, (or memories of his grandfather's stories?). All I need to know was how to play. I was still lost without him, but I thought

I'd gathered all the pieces of the puzzle now. My rendition would be drastically imperfect, but I could make an attempt.

I uploaded the moonlit pictures; I printed them on photo paper and compared them minutely with some tiny pictogram annotations on the score. I prepared the vintage instruments, following Eliud's instructions. (I'm probably the only cello soloist in the world who also knows how to tamper with antique sound channel cards.) I unrolled the first part of the score and laid it at my feet, with the radiating star images set above and below. I played along with Eliud's recorded scaffold for the cello part, over and over, until I could match the exacting directions—not accurately, but at least note by note, term by term.

This preparation took a long time. But I felt alert, when I was finally, roughly satisfied—though hazy about when I'd last slept or eaten—and I didn't feel like waiting. It would take months to perfect my performance, but I was ready to try the notes.

I corrected the recording levels, set the timings for the electronics, and sat down to play, the pictogram at my feet and Eliud's machines around me.

When I set my bow to the strings I almost started to cry, because the old man wasn't here. He wasn't here and he would never know. . . It passed. Soon I was calm; engrossed. I can't say I *liked* the music. Actually I didn't like it at all at first pass; but it was compelling, and outrageously, technically challenging in a way I'd never been able to resist. The difficulties demanded a trance-like, flow-state concentration. As my body played and my mind worked; as I stopped, unrolled the score to the next passage, and returned to my chair, over and over: some part of my sleep-starved self fell into a dream. A mighty city took shape, rising impossibly from the schoolroom floor; extending for miles, in height, in depth. . . I knew this vision; or so it seemed. Unless my mind was now inventing memories instead of destroying them, this city had haunted my nights since the flight vanished, or even longer: triggered by something I'd read about how Antarctica might rise, released from the immense pressure of the ice sheets. But tonight it seemed created directly by the music. At first it was a toy, a coloured game; then it filled the room, and then it was huge, unutterably vast. I left my mind and body playing and walked in its streets.

The walls were tall and black as basalt, or the black-green of very deep water. They glistened like polished ice. The streets were wide and grooved; they had decorated, raised sidewalks. I had no clue how tall I was, whether I was an ant or a giant, until I reached a wide stone ramp leading in a spiral to the doors of a huge building. The doors were the same dark red as the rocks of Mercury. The crustaceans that crept on those rocks were carved there, glinting and chittering. They were much larger than I had imagined. I watched them, feeling that I was being watched myself; but with indifference. I could do no harm.

I walked into a gallery on the outside of the huge building—a kind of conservatory, full of opulent plants. A figure moved among them. It turned and looked at me, with a knowing smirk that reminded me of Mr. Raven. The shock was staggering. *It looked at me,* I looked at it; and I was no longer dreaming. I was awake, and my body was turned inside out. In the schoolroom someone played the cello. In the city I, the same I, was looking at the red-grey, pulsing, twining inside of my own skull. I saw myself the way I was, in *its* dimensions. I was like a string twisted the wrong way in every fibre. And *it* was one of Eliud's figures, actually one of them; but at home, a giant in its own world's conditions.

It came closer, in some sense. It was curious. The sinewave emanations engulfed me, an indescribably horrible feeling. I was inside it. No more than gut bacteria, but still I *was* the alien, walking in the massive, convoluted city; seeing others of my kind, and others of my race, the ovoids and the squares, but *ovoid and square* was nonsense now. I unrolled the score again, I played again, I heard the chiming, the chattering of children's voices, their chorus distorting and rising. Revulsion and terror gripped me again, as once in the wood, a *horrible* revulsion, an otherworldly disgust that took images from slime and vomit, from suffocation and strangling, from eyes put out and a mouth full of earth—

I dropped the bow. My cello fell with a crash. I stumbled to the sound desk and stared at Christmas trees of vibration, propagating across the screens. I had dropped my bow, thrown down the instrument, but my part continued, sampled and repeated. I could see it, twining there in the mix, and I couldn't remove myself, I couldn't stop this. I ran out of the room and through the kitchen; Fenris's claws came clattering after me. I swooped down and grabbed him as I fled the house.

    I kept running, the little dog silent and terrified in my arms, all the way up the track. When we reached the Flint Barn I was breathless. I set Fenris down and looked back. The moon had vanished; the air felt thick and electric. From that slight elevation, under the roiling clouds that covered the sky, charcoal veined with silver, I saw hidden concavities in the prairie fields: the ghosts of old Hindey. In the hollow where St. Iaad's church had stood, shadowy things struggled, like huge new-born animals in their birth-caul. I heard a friend's voice muttering long ago: *He might knock down a few hovels, but what kind of landowner razes a church, Aiode?* The little dog pressed himself against my ankles, shivering. I could still hear *Hindey Playground,* unfolding its horrible music; in the distance, and inside my skull. The city was rising, in all its immensity, filling me with awful, sickening terror—

    I woke up in Eliud's bed, missing Fenris's warm small weight at my feet. My head ached. I couldn't even remember whether I'd finished playing the piece. Thank God Eliud wasn't here. Whatever he meant by his new work, he'd surely be disgusted if I confessed to hippy-dippy hallucinations. In the kitchen I found an empty red wine bottle, a glass, and no sign that a meal had been eaten: which explained the throbbing head and the memory lapse! In the schoolroom there was confusion. The score was intact, but my photos were gone, and somebody had been burning treated paper in the fireplace. I set the old hardware to rights (thankfully nothing was broken. I put my cello back in its case. I ate breakfast, drank strong coffee, and resumed my task.

    Deflated, hollowed out, I didn't check the playback. I didn't try, then or later, to resume my performance of *Hindey*

Playground. I felt as if I'd woken from a long, exhausting dream about working with Eliud again; and now I would let somebody else decide what the new work was worth. When I was packing up the material—the drawings; the pictogram score; Eliud's recording; the settings for the vintage electronics—I noticed that the dusty label on the score tube was in Renton's handwriting, not Eliud's; which seemed strange, but I didn't let myself dwell on the puzzle. It didn't matter. Everything went into the box labelled "Unfinished Works"—which was by no means empty.

I didn't go back into the wood. I felt no desire to say goodbye to that dark parcel of trees. I made my nightly trek up to the Barn, but didn't get through to Maria again. I wasn't terribly concerned. Good news or bad, or (most likely) no news, it would wait until I'd returned to civilised connectivity. I taped the boxes. I called the removal firm's number and left a voicemail, telling them everything was ready to pick up, and drove away.

I drove away, heading for the local market town, to leave the keys with Eliud's house agent. It was another dull, dusty end of summer day; just like the day I'd arrived. A few miles down the road, I glanced in my rearview mirror and saw the cello case, all alone. My God! I had left Fenris behind! How the hell did that happen? Horrified, I slammed on the brakes: thank God the country road was empty behind me. I pulled over, my heart hammering. *Calm down,* I told myself. *When did you last see him?* When *had* I last seen Fenris? Why did that question make my hands shake—why did it sicken me? Think, think. All I could remember was talking to Eliud on the phone, that conversation when he asked me to come to Norfolk. He was whispering, his voice sounding hoarse and strange. I remembered wondering whether there was somebody with him, wondering if it was Renton of all people; and then nothing. Then I was driving to Norfolk. . . But when had I last seen Fenris? I couldn't think, I just started to shake.

Thankfully I still had the keys.

I sped back to the old schoolhouse. I called him. He wasn't in the house. I ran around searching, calling for him, getting frantic, and at last I heard him bark.

Beyond my parking place, greenery had overwhelmed

the drive. I fought my way to the end, vaguely puzzled by signs that someone had burst through the tangles before me, and there was the white caravan: where it must have been standing derelict since the big fight; since Renton walked out. Fenris was barking right in front of me, but he was invisible. He must be inside. How could he be *inside?* I dragged at bindweed, scalded my hands on nettles and thorns, an icy sweat running down my spine. I forced the door open and saw what Fenris had been trying to show me ever since I arrived—

I fell to my knees, staring at Renton's partly skeletal remains. I heard Eliud's voice again: obviously his own voice this time, a grimly desperate Eliud, whispering that though he was my lover, *there were parts of Mike Renton that I had never seen.* I believed it now. His merman's eyes, his tarnished-gold hair, were gone. All gone, the human flesh that had masked these strange bones, these sinuous declivities; cusps and protuberances—

"Now you see how it was," said Mr. Raven, behind me. "Your boyfriend, he was Hindey bred from a long time back, same as the old man; same as me. Anyone could see by looking at them, if they knew the signs. But Eliud was too human to *want* to be Hindey bred. Mike Renton, he was just a little bit better endowed, if you take my meaning. He was a feller with a mission. Only he didn't have the power to carry it out; and the other lad, the one that didn't want—he did. So Mike, he got his hooks into Eliud, called him a genius, and convinced him to write the music. For the pure strangeness of it, as Eliud believed. Then afterwards, when he figured out what Renton was really after, that's when Eliud told you your boyfriend had to go. And you didn't take too much persuading, did you, Aiode? You don't remember? Righto, I suppose you wouldn't. You'd bury a deed like that—"

So I had helped to kill Renton. I could believe it. I knew the memories were there, the hideous memories trying to crawl out of that fog in my head: what a brutal thing it was, the two of us hacking away. But there was another heap of bones, much smaller bones, and maybe Renton was a monster, maybe I hated him—but the little dog, oh, the little dog too! Poor little Fenris! How could I have done that, how *could* I?

"He wouldn't stop barking."

"Didn't do any good, though," Mr. Raven continued, with satisfaction. "You didn't change a thing, and Mike Renton, *he* didn't care. He's not gone far. An' he knew you'd be back here, when the time was right. You'd do what was needed, thinking you were following your master's orders, you silly bitch. So you've opened the way. Eliud's gone, along with a whole parcel of other lower forms, and it's becoming *their* world again. Don't you feel it?"

I didn't turn my head. I didn't want to find out if Mr. Raven was real or if he'd never existed. I stared at the dog's poor little bones, and at the other remains; and Renton's skeleton *did* look strange, but how could I tell what was real, how could I explain to myself, how had this happened, why had it happened, even as my lover's mummified corpse began to stir and fatten; even if it was true that the terrible city had risen and world was ending—?

I didn't know, I didn't know.

Dream House

Orrin Grey

It was the last night of the festival, and we were all sitting around one of the long tables out behind The Moon and Sixpence. It was cold enough that my feet were freezing and my hands were shoved into the pockets of my jacket when not gesturing or picking up a drink. Above us, a suitably gibbous moon dipped in and out behind clouds that would otherwise have been invisible.

There were still a couple of movies playing, so the back patio wasn't too crowded yet, but I'd talked Simon out of watching *Curse of the Crimson Altar* on account of it being five minutes of awesome and an hour-and-change of people walking around in dark houses, so we were staking out the table till the festival ended and the last movies let out. Simon was telling me about some French movie he'd seen this year that came off as a poor man's John Carpenter, one that seemed to get worse every time he mentioned it.

As the table gradually filled up, the conversation twisted and turned—as conversations like that, in places like those, always do—and somehow or other we got on the subject of Lovecraft in old TV shows. Maybe there was a panel on it, or someone was suggesting one for next year. They'd shown the Stuart Gordon "Dreams in the Witch House" that year, and Nick mentioned the "Pickman's Model" episode of *Night Gallery,* which I'd always loved. I told him it was my favorite adaptation of the story, and someone else—probably Ross—agreed. Sooner or later, of course, somebody brought up *Dream House.*

There wasn't anyone at the table who hadn't seen at least a few episodes—some back when it was still on the air, most of us on reruns on Saturday afternoon when we were kids, or on those two-episode VHS packs that floated around video stores for a while—and nobody had much that was nice to say about it, beyond the fact that it had "potential," the faint praise with which we damn things that we want to like but can't quite. Mostly, we all agreed that it barely counted as Lovecraftian, for all its swinging and missing in that direction, but then a voice brought up the lost episodes.

I didn't recognize the woman doing the talking, but by then that was true of about half the people around the table. She was sitting on the other side of Jesse, and I thought I remembered her coming back with him from one of his trips to the bar for drinks. The corner she was sitting in was the darkest on the patio, her back against the bulbous tree that broke up the back fence line. Her features were mostly lost to shadow, but she was smoking a cigarette, and when she took a pull the glow from the cherry would flare up enough to illuminate the edges of her face, which seemed a little worn and creased—not that any of us were looking our best in the dim patio lights at the dregs of the festival. I asked around afterward, but nobody seemed to know her name or remember seeing her anyplace else during the weekend.

When she mentioned the lost episodes, someone at the other end of the table laughed and said something like, "Yeah, they're probably great, since nobody's ever seen them." She let out a sigh, the cherry on her cigarette bobbing like the bouncing ball in an old sing-along. "They're around," she said. "They were on YouTube for a while, but they got pulled down."

"The story goes," Cody said—because of course, if anybody knew the story, it was going to be Cody—"that they used to circulate them on recorded tapes, back in the pre-Internet days. Some kid supposedly watched them and then cut up his family and asphyxiated himself with a garbage bag taped around his head. That got more press than the show ever did, even if it's probably not true."

"Early days Marilyn-Manson-made-me-do-it stuff," someone else said, nodding, remembering the legend now. "Wonder if anyone ever got sued over that."

The initial speaker shook her head, grounding out her cigarette on the tabletop so that the shadows swallowed her face again. "Naw," she said, "nobody ever got sued, because there wasn't anybody left."

The next morning, most everybody besides the locals flew out, and I drove up with Simon to spend a couple of days in Seattle before heading home. We stayed up late watching *The Lurking Fear* and *Virgin Witch* in his apartment, but I couldn't get the conversation about *Dream House* out of my head. I'd seen maybe seven or eight episodes over the years: it used to play late at night on one of the channels that we got when I was growing up, after *Renegade* and *Kung Fu* but before *Beauty and the Beast* with Ron Perlman, so I usually didn't stay up late enough to catch it.

Now, though, my curiosity was piqued, so I looked it up on Wikipedia and skimmed through episode synopses and cast lists until I came to a headline that simply said "Tragedy" in big black letters.

It seemed that a fire had broken out on set during principal photography. All told, ten people died as a result of the blaze. Investigators expected arson, but according to Wikipedia no arrests were ever made in connection with the disaster, which was partially responsible for the show folding after shooting less than a season's worth of episodes. A couple of the main actors died in the fire or at the hospital later as a result of smoke inhalation, including Judy Becker, the woman who played Jennifer Cristain/Lady Jenny, the show's main star.

Digging a little deeper, I found that our nameless *Dream House* fan hadn't been wrong. Nobody involved in the show was still alive. A few people who had played bit parts in individual episodes were still around; some of them had even gone on to have real acting careers, and the actress who played a little girl in the third episode was going to be in a movie opposite Ryan Gosling next year. But anyone who had played a recurring character or been involved in writing, directing, or shooting the show was dead. Not one had survived the show's cancellation by more than five years.

The reasons for those that I could find reasons for spanned the range of typical Hollywood causes of death—from cancers to car accidents, drug overdoses and suicides, and at least one disquieting mass-homicide about which I could find almost no detailed information online. I was reminded of the rumors about the various fates of the people involved in making *Manos*—famously the "worst" movie ever shown on

MST3k, though for that particular plum my pick might have to go to *Hobgoblins*. This, though, seemed a little more real, the tragedies and mysteries a little easier to verify.

Before I closed my laptop and turned in for the night, I sent an email to Shawn, asking him about the so-called lost episodes. He'd helped me track down hard-to-find flicks for my Vault of Secrets column before, so I figured if I knew anyone who could find the *Dream House* episodes, it would be him.

I didn't hear back from Shawn until after I'd gotten back to Kansas, but the email he finally sent me had links to two of the "lost episodes" in it. "The most innocuous ones, I'm told," he said. "There's supposed to be one more, the really bad one, but I couldn't find hide nor hair of it. Not even a plot synopsis. Seems like it disappeared into the wild blue yonder."

It took a few days of post-trip recovery and catching up on work before I managed to queue up the episodes. I watched them downstairs in my office, on my laptop, with all the lights out and my headphones on. They looked like shit and sounded worse, and had obviously been recorded by hooking two VCRs together. The picture swam and shifted, as when we used to try to pirate pay channels on my friend's cable when we were kids. One minute the dialogue was so muted that I couldn't make it out; the next I was snatching my headphones off to keep from being deafened.

The first episode seemed like a pretty standard series entry. It focused on the Jennifer/Lady Jenny character, one actress playing both the young woman who came to open Dream House back up and turn it into a bed-and-breakfast, and the young wife of the slave owner who ran it back when it was still a plantation. It was the main thing I remembered from late nights watching the series as a kid: lots of flashing back and forth between the past and the present. It got a lot of mileage out of that portrait-in-the-entryway-looks-exactly-like-me trope that Gothic movies love so much.

In this episode, Jennifer was having nightmares about Lady Jenny's life, and when she woke in the mornings the sheets were all mussed alluringly, and her bare feet and the hem of her nightdress were dirty. As the episode progressed, she found damp, shapeless footprints on the stairs of the house and saw bulbous shadows moving along the wall. In my notes I wrote down, "Fungus people?" and circled it. Eventually, the episode culminated in what was perhaps supposed to be another dream sequence. A door opened in the corner of Jennifer's bedroom, spilling out a weird greenish light. She rose from the bed and crossed the room, though a close-up shot of her face made it very clear that her eyes were staring, vacant, and asleep.

On the other side of the secret door she descended a spiraling hidden staircase until she came to a basement. There, half-glimpsed figures awaited her, surrounding something that I couldn't make out in the murky darkness of the terrible video transfer. A shape that might have been a man knelt on the ground before her, and she was suddenly holding a knife. The scene cut to darkness, like a commercial break, and when it came back up it was daylight, birds were singing in the trees outside, and Jennifer was lying safe in her bed, but with those same telltale dirty feet.

The second episode introduced a new character, a reporter named Wayland whose grandfather had been a slave on the plantation. Wayland was planning to write a book about the strange things that went on at Dream House back in the day, and to that end he convinced modern-day Jennifer to rent him a room, even though the bed-and-breakfast didn't seem to be technically up and running yet. He snuck around the place a bit, saw some ominous stuff, and found a secret graveyard out behind the main house, but then the episode got really weird.

A door opened into Wayland's room while he was sleeping, spilling that same green light as in the previous episode. A woman came out of the door. It looked as if she might have been played by the same actress who played Jennifer/Lady Jenny, but there was something wrong with her face, and the picture was too low-res for me to tell for sure. Whoever she was, she was pale as death, and she had what looked like a man with her, albeit on the end of a leash and walking on all fours. It was either wearing some kind of suit—a bondage suit, on TV in the '60s?—or was supposed to be an ape or something, because it was so dark that it blended into the shadows.

Wayland got up and followed the woman down the stairs, and in the middle of the same dirt-floored basement that Jennifer had ended up in during the other episode, he found an idol of green stone. It stood roughly the height of a man and was carved in the shape of a crouching figure, its head spreading out into, well, tentacles, I guess, though their angles were sharper than that word usually calls to mind. There was a noise on the soundtrack like clanking chains, and then Wayland started to scream and the episode cut to black.

That would probably have been the end of it if I hadn't hit a dry spell. I finished catching up on the work that I'd missed while I was in Portland, and there was nothing waiting on the other side. Just doldrums and streaming movies on Netflix. I knew that I should take advantage of the slow days to chip into my to-read pile or work on some of my own projects, but I just found myself feeling listless, rewatching old episodes of *The Simpsons* and drifting.

I don't know what would have happened if I hadn't gotten the second email from Shawn. I guess he hadn't been able to leave well enough alone either, and sometime in the midst of my fallow period I got a message from him saying that he'd tracked down the place where they had shot the exteriors for *Dream House* on one of those websites that show you the shooting locations of movies and TV shows.

The website showed a screen grab from the show and, below it, a photograph of the actual house from the same angle. It said that some fans of the show had bought the house back in the late '90s and actually turned it into a bed-and-breakfast for real. They even kept the sign from the show: DREAM HOUSE, Est. 18—. Of course, those of us who had seen even a few episodes knew that while the house itself may have been built in 18—, the basement was much older. Hewn from the earth, not by the hands of white settlers, nor by the native tribes who once lived on the land, but by some older race. Knowing Lovecraft, probably serpent men or something.

At the bottom was the address, and a link to the website of the bed-and-breakfast. Before the end of the day, I had called and booked a room.

I told Grace it was a research trip, figuring I could get something substantial out of this whole "lost episodes," visit-to-the-actual-house thing. Something I could maybe sell to *Rue Morgue* or some website that paid more than $50 an article. Maybe I even believed it at the time, or maybe I knew better, even then. "If nothing else," Grace said, "it'll be a tax deduction."

She almost went with me, but then her office signed on a big new client and that meant long weeks that she couldn't skip, so I ended up going alone. That's maybe the only good thing that came out of any of this—that she wasn't able to come with me. That she, at least, was spared.

Driving to the place took a couple of days, and I spent the night in a nice suite at a Holiday Inn watching old episodes of *Night Gallery* and *Alfred Hitchcock Presents*. In a story, there would have been a rerun of *Dream House* on, or at least the "Pickman's Model" episode of *Night Gallery*, but in real life nobody shows *Dream House* anymore, and the *Night Gallery* episode maybe had something to do with a lady vampire on a house boat. I was mostly asleep already by the time it came on.

That night I had a dream where I stood outside the front of the bed-and-breakfast. Someone had spray-painted over the sign, adding the letters "s in the witch" between the words "dream" and "house." My eye was a camera lens taking a time-lapse photo, and I watched the clouds scud across the sky too quickly, the light changing in jerky, stop-motion switches.

In the dream there was a blink, and I was looking at the house from behind and above. It looked strangely innocuous, like a dollhouse, and between me and it there was a field where cars were parked, car after car, from different ages. Old Packard's and '50s convertibles with big fins. Nature was gradually erasing their distinguishing features,

sun and time scouring the paint from their hoods as kudzu grew up around them, devouring them as it would one day devour everything else.

I woke up feeling unrested and almost turned the car around then and there, but the website for Dream House had said there was a fee for last-minute cancellations, and I was already so close.

By the time I pulled up in front of the house it was the middle of the afternoon. The sunlight was golden and soft, and everything looked almost exactly like the opening titles of the show—the golden light, the old plantation house with its white paint and columns. I could almost hear that tinkling theme song playing somewhere off in the distance.

When I walked in through the front doors, I expected to find a big painting of Lady Jenny looking down at me. But of course, that had been filmed on a set, and instead I walked in to find the front desk with a painting hanging above it showing some kind of hunting scene, something brought over from the Old World.

The woman behind the counter looked like the mother from a TV show about a pioneer family, her black hair just beginning to go iron-gray at the roots. She wore a blue dress with white flowers—magnolias, perhaps, which would seem appropriate.

She introduced herself as Irene and had me sign in. I asked her a few questions about the inn and about the show. It turned out that she and her husband had bought it from the fans who'd originally converted it after they'd gone under, and she wasn't a fan of the show, though she knew a little. "Some of it was shot right here," she told me—"at least that's what they say. I can give you her room, if you want."

I didn't have to ask to which "her" she was referring, and said that yes, I'd love to have Lady Jenny's room if it was available. She asked if I needed any help with my bags, but I declined. Years of attending conventions had taught me how to pack light.

My room was, in fact, Lady Jenny's, down to most of the furniture, though the knick-knacks on the shelf were different. There was the dressing mirror where Lady Jenny combed her long brown hair. Irene told me that some of the scenes of the bedroom were shot at the house, while others were shot on a sound stage somewhere else. I had the disorienting feeling that comes with walking into a place you know intimately but have never visited—a feeling, I imagine, that is unique to the generations who have grown up with TV and movies.

    The room had a window that faced the back of the house, and when Irene left I peered out beyond the lacy curtains, holding my breath in case I was presented with a field of rusting cars. Instead, I saw only picturesque trees strung with Spanish moss. I resolved to go exploring tomorrow and spent the night setting up my laptop, typing up notes from the road, and responding to emails and Facebook messages. I called Grace and told her goodnight before falling asleep to black-and-white *Dragnet* episodes on the little TV that they'd anachronistically stuck in the corner of the room.

    In my dream it was as if I were a camera again, mounted on a tripod in the corner, watching myself sleep. I saw a door open in the wall, the wainscoting and Victorian wallpaper sliding apart to reveal a gap, first of darkness, then filling with a familiar green light. I watched as I rose from my bed and followed the light through the door and down the stairs, my dream-camera coming unmoored and drifting over my shoulder.

    The basement was clearer in the dream than it had ever been in the show, the shadows sharp and in high definition, the blackness crisp and hard-edged. Shapes waited for me in those shadows, figures hooded and cowled, shambling things and squirming things that made me think of the rubber-suited ghoul from that *Night Gallery* episode, or the Toho mushroom people in *Matango*. I wanted to look closer, to peer into the shadows and pick out the comforting fakeness of their suits, the seams and zippers; but I was a camera and I had no free will, so I saw them only peripherally, my gaze fixed ahead.

    What I *could* see were the manacles and chains affixed to the stone columns that held up the ceiling. Generations of blood had seeped into the earthen floor and changed its color forever, and I thought of Jennifer's dirty feet in the lost episode, the rusty red that hadn't translated well to the color palette of '60s TV.

In the center of the basement was a statue that I had seen before, its bulk almost human but hunched like a toad up on its haunches, its face a mass of angular tentacles. It was limned in the same sickly green illumination that engulfed me, a light that seemed to sweat from the statue's surface. Next to it stood a figure draped in a black robe, a figure that I recognized as Lady Jenny, though her features were askew, like a mask poorly fitted over some shifting form beneath. Beside her crouched a darker shape that she held on the end of a chain, and when she spoke it wasn't with the voice of Judy Becker; it was the voice of an old drunk, dying from tuberculosis. The voice of a thousand worms, suddenly given the power of speech.

I woke with her words on my tongue, though I couldn't fit them to human vocalization, couldn't make any sense of them, even to write them down. I'll spare you any Lovecraftian attempt at approximating the sounds, which began to die in my memory even as I scrambled for pen and paper.

Irene confirmed my suspicions that many of the rooms in Dream House—my own included—had once had servants' entrances that let onto back stairways winding down to the kitchens and, of course, even the larder in the basement. The doors themselves had been lost to one of the building's renovations, but some of the stairs remained buried behind the walls, and she confirmed, when I pointed to the spot where my dream door had been, that it was about where the servants' entrance appeared in old photographs of the room.

I asked her about the basement, but she said that most of it had been filled up and bricked over since before her time there. "If there's any way into it," she said, smiling, "I've never seen it."

So here's the lightning-round bonus question: When you're dealing with things that exist outside of our normal conception of either space or time, is a dream sequence really any less real than anything else? I think we both know the answer to that one.

Dream House

That morning, I went out to walk the grounds. I picked my way along a trampled-down path that led around the side of the house, past the trees with their almost staged moss and across a footbridge that spanned a small stream. The sun was shining, but there was no birdsong, and the farther I walked the more I began to notice kudzu creeping up the trunks of the trees, crowding in on the sides of the path.

I was almost unsurprised when I rounded the corner and saw the rusted shell of the first car. It wasn't a field, as it had been in my dream. Trees grew up among them, hiding them from view from the air or the windows of the house, but here they were, car after car, when you could find them among the foliage run riot. What's more, I'd paid attention on the walk, and I knew that I'd taken more or less the same path that Wayland had in the lost episode, when he'd stumbled upon the secret cemetery.

I didn't get immediately back into my car and drive away, leaving all my stuff up in the room, as I would have encouraged a character to do had I been watching a movie. It wasn't stupidity that drove me back inside—remember that, the next time you're watching a scary movie and someone goes down into the basement—it was curiosity, maybe the only emotion in our repertoire that is capable of overpowering our fear.

Inside the house, I scrutinized the painting on the wall behind the front desk, looking for subtle changes. I asked Irene casually about her husband, and she said that he was around there someplace, that he usually tended the grounds while she kept up the house itself. She looked straight at me as she spoke, her eyes brown and deep as wells, and I thought of the scene in *In the Mouth of Madness,* the kindly old lady behind the counter with her husband shackled to her leg, the bloody ax waiting out in the greenhouse.

I went upstairs, packed my bags, and checked out of my room a day early. I drove home without stopping except to fuel up and buy sodas, deleted the lost *Dream House* episodes from my computer, kissed my wife, and lived happily ever after. But of course you and I both know, dear reader, that's not how these stories end. I called yesterday to make my second reservation

Grey

at Dream House. Irene didn't sound at all surprised to hear from me.

I'll kiss Grace goodbye one last time. I wonder if she'll know, if she'll try to stop me, but I'm beyond stopping now. I'll return to the Dream House, and when I get there I'll drive around the side, along the road I've never taken, to the parking lot that I shouldn't know about, and pull my rental car up alongside the other rusting hulks that lie beneath the kudzu. I'll collect my key from the front desk, and I'll go up to my room—the same room as before—and I'll lie down on the bed and go to sleep, perchance to dream.

The Unknown Chambers

Lynda E. Rucker

In the lightless places he waits, in the dark that is darker than the dark of the day and the dark of the night and the dark of the soul, he waits he waits for his father he says "father I am waiting for you" and the sun is falling in a blistered sky and the night is roaring in and still he waits.

—From *Asmodeus,*
by Garland William Stevens, 1936

"Is Asmodeus seeking this?"

Catherine jumped. "What?"

"I asked if anyone was reading this."

Reality righted itself. A stoop-shouldered man of indeterminate age with a craggy face and a wad of tobacco in his cheek was pointing at the newspaper on the edge of the plastic orange table where she sat. "No," she said, "no, go ahead and take it." The spell was broken. Outside the window was not the weird world of Garland William Stevens's ruined plantations and degenerate Southern families but a drab four-lane highway and a gas station across the street. Around her, the Bojangles fast food restaurant was rapidly filling up with the post-church crowd: hefty middle-aged ladies and their balding husbands, small children in Sunday finery, grandmas and great-grandmas with walkers, and shiny-faced teenagers. What Garland William Stevens would have called the filthy mess of humanity. Small wonder really that the town of Eudora did nothing to honor the man, given the contempt with which he chronicled its perceived shortcomings. In fact, most likely no one around her had ever even heard of him.

Catherine gobbled down the rest of her ham and cheese biscuit, shoved her tablet into her bag, and headed back out to her car. Back on the road, she soon turned off the four-lane onto a poorly maintained two-lane, bumping over railway tracks. She passed two abandoned granite sheds, long metal buildings, the stonecutting shops where local families had made their fortune carving monuments—tombstones, that is—out of the granite unearthed from quarries throughout the county until China proved able to do it more cheaply and the industry died, leaving the town with nothing. She supposed that at one time the four-lane must have brought visitors to Eudora as well, back in the day when people used to travel by state highways instead of the Interstate. Now it was just another tiny Southern town closing in on itself and clinging to its outmoded ways as a confusing and frightening twenty-first century unfolded before it

But commerce was not her concern, and she drove on as the road grew rough with potholes and narrowed even more, and then pavement gave way to Georgia red clay. She slowed, as the recent heavy summer rains had turned the clay to mud, and more than once her car skidded gently toward the wide ditches on either side. She wondered what she would do if she met another vehicle on the narrow lane, but then she rounded a corner and there it was. The old Stevens homeplace.

Catherine left her car on what must have once been a grand circular drive outside and approached the place. It was in less disrepair than she expected, given that the man had no heirs and the place seemed to be owned by an out-of-state company from whom she had been unable to get a response. The house was more modest than she had imagined as well. Stevens had loathed the place, of course, as he loathed everything. Despising his slave-owning forefathers as evidence of the essential evil that poisoned humanity, he was equally contemptuous toward abolitionists and their civil-rights activist descendants—"do-gooders," he called them—finding their efforts exercises in futility against a backdrop of cruelty and indifference. In Stevens's worldview, savagery toward one another was the natural state of humanity; any efforts on the part of the species to rehabilitate itself were at best pointless and at worst roads to hell paved with good intentions.

Or *was* this his belief system? That the man had been virtually hypergraphic was both a blessing and a curse for an

The Unknown Chambers

ambitious young graduate student. During his short life he had not only produced a not insubstantial volume of published fiction and nonfiction but reams of letters, notes, and diaries. So difficult and contentious a figure was Stevens that he was little studied and thus largely unknown, and much of his archive remained unsorted decades after his death. As repulsed as the man was by people, he carried on a prodigious correspondence with dozens of them, and from the one side of the exchange she was able to read, those correspondents praised his unfailing generosity and sensible advice. It was as though having established for himself that humanity as a whole was a disgusting, bestial, evolutionary dead-end, he set out to contradict that assessment with his own behavior at every turn. These paradoxes, and the fact that she didn't yet really know what shape her dissertation would take, were part of what made the research so intriguing.

"They're waiting at the edge."

She jumped and whirled round. The speaker looked to be in his twenties, lanky and blond, wearing a black T-shirt, jeans, and a trucker hat. He was also startlingly homely, with features overlarge in an otherwise too-small face. She snapped, "What did you say?"

"I said, are you the lady from the college? They sent me your letter. The owners. They said you would be coming by."

She frowned. "Nobody ever replied to me."

The man shrugged. "They wouldn't. They don't never answer nobody about nothing." She couldn't place his accent; it was thick, Southern but not local.

She said, "Who are you?"

"I'm the caretaker." The man extended his hand and pulled back his lips in what she assumed must be a smile; she wished he hadn't. There seemed to be too many teeth in his mouth. She felt off-kilter; she had not expected anyone to be here, and here he was, and he knew who she was and why she was here and so far she still didn't know anything about him.

She was being silly. This was a terrific opportunity, particularly since she'd never imagined she might be able to go inside.

"But I'm afraid I can't help you with your research,"

he said. "I don't know nothing about this guy. My family's not from around here. I just look after the place."

"I promise, just being shown around the place is a huge help," she said. "Where are you from?"

"Down South Georgia. My people come from the swamp," he said, in a way that let her know no further questioning would be welcome. Well, she didn't care who he was or where he came from anyway. If he didn't want to engage in small talk, all the better; she could get on with the business of exploring the house.

"We can go inside, can't we?" she said, but he already had keys in his hands and she followed him up onto the wide front porch.

When the door swung open, she took a step back in surprise. Whatever she had expected, it was not this. Based on the interior of the house, anyone would be forgiven for thinking that Stevens had not only not been dead for decades but had only stepped out to run an errand that morning and would be back if she just waited around long enough. The place was minimally furnished, but beyond that it *felt* lived in.

But of course. "*You* live here," she said to the caretaker, and he shrugged. "I'm sorry," she said. "I didn't know anyone was out here. I couldn't get any information from anyone about it and I just assumed it was abandoned. I didn't mean to disturb you." She almost added *I can come back at a better time if you want,* but bit back the words before they were out. There would never be a better time: she might never have another chance like this one.

"It's left the same as when *he* lived here," the caretaker said.

"Oh. So you live here, or. . . ?" She left the question dangling so he could pick it up and answer it, but he remained silent. "Oh, God," she said. "Sorry for my rudeness." She held out her hand. "I'm Catherine, and what was your name. . . ?"

"Don't matter none. You can just call me the caretaker."

"That's fine, but it would really help if I could get your name. For my research."

"Let me show you the downstairs first," he said, heading off any further questions. She followed him round the spartan rooms. What seemed to be the living room contained only a single wooden chair and a small rickety table that appeared to function as a desk, stacked high as it was with papers and open books. The caretaker hustled her through too quickly to get a closer look at them. The remainder of the tour was equally rushed: a kitchen with old but modern appliances, an upstairs bedroom that was as bare as the living room save for a single bed and another wooden chair, and a whole host of rooms behind closed doors that she was not invited to look behind.

She tried one last question. "Just to be clear... those books and papers in the living room are yours, right? They aren't unarchived papers from Mr. Stevens, are they?"

"That's all I can show you of the place," the man said. "I hope it helped you out. You ought not to come back here."

"I'm sorry for being so nosy," she said. "It's just, you know, there's been almost no work done on Mr. Stevens, and so primary sources are mostly all I have to go on. Which is kind of simultaneously a scholar's dream and nightmare. Would it be possible for me to contact you again at some point?"

"I got to get to work now. We ain't set up for tourists here, you know."

The protest that she was not a tourist—and what tourist could possibly be interested in this anyway?—died on her lips. "I'm sorry I disturbed you," she said. Driving back into town and heading toward home, something niggled at the back of her mind, something she felt she had missed, but she could not put her finger on what it was.

Degeneracy is the disease of the human race. For every lie told by biblical sources there are truths as well, and none so true as that tale of the Fall of Man. From the time man drew his first breath, this disease seized him, and whatever gifts might have been innate were quickly subsumed by his lust: for power, for violence, for sex. The Garden of Eden withered and died with the exhale of that first breath. Human beings tell tales about monsters to hide their own monstrosity.

—From the unpublished papers
of Garland William Stevens, c. 1925

"The natural explanation is that Garland William Stevens himself is still alive, having achieved some sort of unnatural longevity just like a character in one of his stories." The bar around her and her best friend Marisol was starting to fill up with students, even though it was a Sunday night, and she had to shout it in order to be heard. Three beers in, her theory did not seem so unlikely.

"Or," Marisol said, "the so-called caretaker is his inhuman progeny, the result of some kind of weird mixing with an ancient inhuman race of beings." Marisol had sensibly dropped out of their PhD program, abandoning her own dissertation on women in cannibal films two years earlier to start a catering business, a shift in focus that spawned its share of jokes both in and out of the department about just what the menu would consist of. She still worked the same insane hours she had as a graduate student, but she actually got paid well for doing so and still had time to read for pleasure, unlike Catherine. And she'd devoted some of that spare time to remaining Catherine's first reader, even before her adviser, helping her start to shape years' worth of writing and notes into something resembling a critical analysis and a book-length dissertation.

"Both, probably," Catherine said. "Why couldn't I have picked someone normal and easy to study like. . . well, pretty much anyone else?"

"Because your parents never told you, but you were actually adopted, and are also the unnatural progeny of Garland William Stevens, drawn back to your birthplace and destiny by some inexorable force . . ."

"Oh god. All these scenarios just write themselves, don't they? I've been mired in reading this stuff for so long I've pretty much lost touch with reality, but what's your excuse?"

"Listening to you for the last few years."

"I'm not that single-minded, am I?" She saw her friend's face. "I am, aren't I? Jesus. Sorry. But seriously, everything about it was weird, and there was more weird stuff about it I can't put my finger on.

Marisol was looking at her more seriously now. "Like he was a creep or something? You probably shouldn't have gone out there on your own."

"No, not weird like that. Anyway, who would've ever imagined someone would be out there in the first place? No, it was like something I saw that didn't register consciously. Or something I heard, or smelled, or even just a feeling."

Marisol grinned. "I have the feeling you need more beer."

"I have the feeling I have to be on campus before eight tomorrow morning to proctor an exam so, no, I'm gonna take a raincheck on that one. But seriously, can you do me a favor?"

"Depends on what it is." They had been friends for more than a decade; it was how they always answered the question, and neither had ever refused the other.

"If you're not working tomorrow afternoon, I want to drive back out there. It's going to piss off Mr. Caretaker, but if he's that mad about it, he can just accuse me of trespassing and tell me to leave and I will."

Marisol frowned. "Are you sure? What if he's one of those shoot-first-ask-questions-later assholes?

Catherine shook her head. "No, if there's one thing we don't have to worry about, it's that. He's not the type."

"How can you *know*?"

"Look, I'm not asking you to go back out there with me because I'm scared to go by myself. I'm asking you because I need a second set of eyes and ears and another brain to give me impressions. There's something weird and very much *not dangerous* going on out there, and you know how I've been spinning my wheels on this dissertation lately. Please, Marisol. You *know* what an impossible dream it is to get a tenure-track job in the humanities these days. If I could come up with something truly ground-breaking and something that had both academic *and* popular appeal I'd be—well, I wouldn't be set, but it would help me out a lot, and it could be life-changing for me. And if there's more stuff out there, or if this caretaker guy could give me information. . ."

Marisol said, "How could you need more information? Especially from some random guy who just lives out there? Or even use it? You've still got mountains of material in the archives you haven't gotten to yet." But Catherine could see it in her face as her resolve wavered, and she almost felt bad about giving her the hard sell—almost.

"Remember the time you took off on a road trip with

that French guy you'd just met and then you called me at two in the morning from Mobile, Alabama, and said he'd taken off in the middle of the night and stuck you with the motel bill and anyway he wasn't French? And I drove all night to come and get you?"

"All right," Marisol said. "I'll go, but if we end up abducted as part of a master plan to breed their nightmare progeny, I'm totally blaming you."

Catherine grinned. "Deal. And this time tomorrow we'll be back here talking about what a weird freaking place that town is."

"Okay." Marisol pushed herself up from the bar stool. "I'm off tomorrow, and I'm not going home yet. There are too many cute boys in here to go home. Like that one over there. I'll see you tomorrow."

"I'll just head back to my nun cell," Catherine said, but Marisol was already striding across the bar.

Catherine liked knowing what awaited her at home: stacks of books and papers, what the writer Fritz Leiber had called the scholar's mistress. She lay down at night with Garland William Stevens and woke beside him in the morning, but the metaphor failed there; she thought of her subject not as a lover but a mentor, a guide even. Sometimes even, she thought, *psychopomp*, but those were only in the darkest times, and she did not tell anyone about those.

> *As the human race embraces degeneracy, it also fears and despises it. This is not the degeneracy of everyday standards of behavior and morality the small-minded among us fret over, for man is in truth without morality beyond an ever-changing social construct. This is a terror of literal physical and mental degeneracy of the species, and it explains our repulsion toward invertebrate forms of life, toward the types of creatures scientists find existing on the bottom of the ocean, toward snakes and insects and all the other beings that remind us what we were before we were human and what we will be again when our nature asserts itself over our intelligence and draws us back into darkness.*
>
> —From the unpublished writings
> of Garland William Stevens, date unknown

The Unknown Chambers

The following morning, Catherine headed over to the rare book room once she'd discharged her duties supervising freshmen exams. She reflected as she let herself in on what a sheer stroke of luck her course of study had been—whether good or bad luck remained to be seen. She'd arrived at the University of Georgia primed to study advertising and make her fortune cynically hawking products at those too well off to care that they were being lied to. Her friends gave her shit about taking her writing and design skills and selling out, but she didn't care; she'd been raised in near-poverty, with parents who always had a scheme to hand that was going to turn things around for the family and never did. She'd grown up in clothes from the Salvation Army, nourished on crappy fast food and cheap supermarket staples, and steeped in the knowledge that one inconvenient illness or untimely car breakdown could mean an eviction. She was determined to lead a different life.

So it was sheer luck that had landed her a work-study position in the rare book room of the library, and luck that within her first weeks there she'd stumbled across the archives of an obscure Southern writer known as Garland William Stevens. She'd never heard of him, and neither had anyone else she spoke to; apparently even in his lifetime he had been little known, composing stories and books that veered from grim little horror vignettes to a couple of bizarre experimental novels to book-length philosophical musings on the ultimate meaninglessness of life and the degradation of being trapped in a human skin. The last of his line, his short and unhappy life had ended in 1940 when he was but thirty-five years of age. The possible causes of his death ranged from tetanus to tick fever to tuberculosis—various claims he made in the final delirious lines he penned to an ill-advised effort to kick his alcoholism cold turkey (her theory, particularly given the delusions and hallucinations he appeared to suffer in the final weeks of his life).

What she had pieced together about his own life story had been bizarre and grim. Both of his parents had been born during the Civil War. Stevens's family had been among the most prominent in Eudora but appeared to have lost their wealth well before the war for reasons that were unclear. Both parents grew up steeped in a sense of bitter entitlement and loss. Garland had been born when they were both in their forties, having long since abandoned the idea of having any children. His father had been a virulent racist, penning regular send-them-back-to-Africa op-eds for the local paper and articles about the inherent superiority of the white race—and the town indeed had a reputation for being particularly inhospitable to non-whites even by the standards of the time and place. Garland had despised both of his parents, his father in particular, but lived with and cared for them his entire life until their deaths. In the final decade of both their lives, they suffered multiple strokes and dementia, and the already isolated, angry man fell deeper into an abyss. They had all died the same year, several months apart, first the father, then the mother, then Garland himself.

The university had no record of who was responsible for the donation of Stevens's archives decades earlier or who had originally accepted them, and no one really knew who was responsible for them or what was to be done with them. Because in a library there is always more to be done than there is time to do, they had mostly sat there, largely undisturbed, until she had come across them. And began reading. And reading, and reading. And before she knew it, she had changed her major to literature and set off on the very path of hard work and penury she had sworn to avoid, struggling through graduate school and unsure whether she was onto something groundbreaking and revolutionary that would make her a scholarly superstar or something obscure and irrelevant that was gradually turning her into a crank. She told herself the first; she suspected the second.

Over the past decade, since her first discovery of the archives, she had done a great deal to organize them and even made efforts to bring Stevens wider attention. She genuinely did believe that at his best he was truly a talented stylist, easily on the same level as any of the other great regional writers like Faulkner and O'Connor. She had managed to interest a couple of small presses enough to allow her to edit one book of short fiction and a reprint of one of his "philosophical musings," as he dubbed his nonfiction work; but even the obsessive-minded customers of specialty presses had shown little interest in her discovery. Around her, friends finished their schooling and began real careers and had disposable incomes and partners and spouses, and some even were starting on homes and children, while she felt herself growing smaller and dustier and more desperate deep in the bowels of the same rare book collection where she'd been hiding out since the first quarter of her freshman year of college. She constantly questioned herself, but she could not deny that in the end she still believed it was worthwhile. For one, it wasn't just the scholarly pleasure of discovering an unknown writer—she actually *appreciated* the work of Garland William Stevens, thought it the work of a twisted, misanthropic genius, rife with metaphor about the ugliest side of the human condition. And for another, she knew she was ever on the verge of a great discovery. She could not say why; she had no evidence to show that had led her to this conclusion. Instead, it was a growing certainty that rose from the deep waters of intuition. She knew that it was not wishful thinking. She knew that her work on Garland William Stevens was the most important thing she could possibly do with her life.

They gathered in their churches day and night, worshipping every hour of every day, churches that might have been churches of the damned had they souls to damn or a god to damn them, but by then they understood what must one day be understood by all: that there is nothing, nothing but the depths, the deep ones, and an unfortunate evolutionary error that calls itself the inheritor of the earth for the few milliseconds that it believed in its own dominion, not just of the planet, but throughout the universe.

—From *Asmodeus,*
by Garland William Stevens, 1936

Eudora was about an hour's drive and a world away. As they entered the city limits the following day, Marisol commented, "They sure do love Jesus here, don't they?"

"Was it the multiple signs about repenting, or the dozen churches you see just after crossing the county line?"

"It's kind of disturbing. I mean, it's not the usual sort of bland Bible-belty stuff. The signs were creepy, like children of the corn stuff or something."

"Luckily we're not in the Midwest. No need to worry about demon kids coming out of a cornfield after us."

"Oh, pull over," Marisol said. "This might be Creepytown but they also have a Bojangles. I want a biscuit. I had a late night."

"So many cute boys, so little time?"

"Something like that."

Back inside the same fast food restaurant, Catherine said, "Do you notice anything odd?"

Marisol looked around. "Well, everyone looks a tad overdressed. I mean, I realize there's not a lot to do around here, but surely a trip to Bojangles doesn't require suiting up in your Sunday best."

"They all looked like this yesterday too, only I didn't think it was a big deal because, well, it was Sunday. I thought they were all coming from church."

As she spoke, one man detached himself from the line in front of them and went over to a small man in an ill-fitting suit alone at a table and bellowed, "Great sermon today, reverend! Praise the Lord! What are you doing sitting over here all by your lonesome?"

"Oh. Well then, I guess they go to church all the time here," Marisol murmured. "Definitely children of the corn. We'll turn around and leave now if we know what's good for us."

"Probably they really don't have anything better to do than go to church. Nobody has jobs any more since the granite industry died," Catherine replied.

"They look—kind of messed up?" Marisol observed, and Catherine saw what she had missed the previous day. All around them most people had unhealthy complexions shading to a kind of waxy greyness that Catherine identified with her grandfather's face in the final days of his life. They moved oddly as well, and she thought it was as though they weren't accustomed to using their limbs in quite this manner or were concealing deformities under their clothes. But then she came from a small town, too, not terribly unlike Eudora, and everyone there seemed to be everyone's cousin. Catherine herself had a sprawling batch of relatives back home. Maybe in Eudora they were all just a little bit too closely related to one another.

"Also," and now Marisol was whispering, "um, what did they do with all the black people here? Or Mexicans? I'm feeling a little unwelcome, truth be told."

"It's not a historically tolerant community," Catherine whispered back.

"Fuck that," Marisol said. "I'm getting my biscuit to go. You didn't tell me it was some kind of KKK enclave."

"It's not really that. It's—they don't like any outsiders. The town's always been that way, if you go back and look at census records. Nobody really moves here. It's just the same families have been here since the nineteenth century."

"I can't imagine why—it has so much to offer. I'm already thinking of relocating myself."

Back in the car, Catherine commented, "I know this town's been in dire economic straits over the last ten years or so, but I didn't think it meant they just spent all their time in church."

"It was probably a big funeral or something," Marisol said.

"Yeah, you're probably right." Catherine started the car but felt unconvinced. "It didn't seem like a funeral," she said after a few minutes.

"Look, you're the one who insisted on bringing me out here on the grounds that there was nothing creepy to worry about. You can't go making things creepy now."

"Garland William Stevens *is* creepy. There's no getting around that."

"I can't argue with that," Marisol said. "Also, this biscuit is gross. What the fuck do they put in it?" She dropped it back into its bag and tossed the entire thing out the window.

"Marisol!"

"Sorry. You can make a citizen's arrest on me for littering if you want, but it smelled awful too. I was going to puke if I kept it in the car with us. So what's with all the old granite sheds? You were saying. . ."

"Just that it was the industry here, and now it's mostly closed down. Now there's abandoned granite sheds and quarries all over the county. Actually, do you mind if we make a stop before we head out there?" Catherine didn't wait to hear an answer; she was already doing a U-turn on the four-lane.

"Got a sudden hankering to go to church yourself now?" Marisol said.

"The local museum," Catherine said. She drove a few blocks, turned off the main road, and parked in front of a nondescript two-story granite building with a huge glass front. "Let's go in," she said.

"Are you going to tell me what's up?"

"Not until I'm sure." Inside, she thrust a few dollars for their admissions at the bland-faced man working the front desk. The man said to her, "He waits, changed."

"What?"

"The rates changed." The man tapped the sign beside the register. Catherine sighed and gave him two more dollars.

She had been here so many times that she knew exactly what she was looking for, and went to the enormous stone figure of a man in the middle of the place. It was lying on its side, legless and broken at the torso, about twenty feet long and several feet across, surrounded by a set of worn velvet ropes.

"What *is* this thing?" Marisol asked. "It's hideous."

"This," said Catherine, "was meant to be a statue commemorating the Civil War, from around the turn of the last century—1905, to be exact. He's supposed to be a Confederate soldier, only the statue was carved by an Italian artist, and he—well, let's just say he wasn't quite in tune with what people wanted. The thing was torn down by angry townspeople on the day of its dedication, and nobody cared enough to right it. Eventually it was buried. They just unearthed it about ten years ago, when they opened the museum."

"Fascinating," Marisol said, in a tone that said she found it exactly the opposite. "And you just have to come back and visit it from time to time?"

Catherine said, "It's the face on the statue. I had to be sure."

"Sure about what?"

She took a deep breath, because she knew how she was going to sound. Marisol was going to say that the research had finally gotten to her, that she was going to start imagining things just as Garland William Stevens had done in the final weeks of his life.

She said, "The statue. Its face. It's the caretaker."

The horrors birthed themselves from the quarries. Those who first dug deep into the earth and stone found them sleeping there and woke them, and were driven mad by their hideousness, and then mated with them, and if they did not then die from the shame, brought others back with them. These orgiastic frenzies of worship and lust and annihilation might go on for days or even weeks. It was said by some that their cities were so vast and so unspeakable that they broke the human mind..."

—"A Tale of a Hollow Earth,"
by Garland William Stevens,
originally published in *Weird Tales,* 1934,
reprinted 2013 in *Lost Worlds: The Weird Tales of Garland William Stevens,*
edited by Catherine J. Framer,
published by Gloaming Press

Back in the car, Marisol was still laughing and shaking her head. Of all the reactions Catherine expected—shock, horror, concern—this was not one of them. "You *have* been working too hard," she said. "I bet when you shut your eyes at night all you see is Stevens's manuscripts, and now you're seeing hundred-year-old statues in living men's faces. Maybe what you need *is* a live dude for a night or two..."

"I'm serious," Catherine said for the third time. "Look, you'll see when we get out there."

"I'm sorry," Marisol said. "I'm not making fun of you, I swear. It just sounds crazy. You know what? I bet this dude totally looks like that statue back there. I don't even know why it cracked me up so much; it just did. You know how those things happen. It's like when I was a kid, we noticed my brother looked just like the boy on that one commercial—Hey, are you okay to drive?"

Catherine's hands were shaking. She lay them flat on the steering wheel to still them. "I'm okay," she said. "I'm just a little freaked out. You know, I've been here so many times. I've got sketches of that thing—Stevens was intrigued with stories of it even though he never saw it himself because it was destroyed the same year of his birth, and they didn't find it till decades after he was dead. That was the thing that was in the back of my mind yesterday, the thing that was bothering me. The caretaker's—his resemblance. That's all."

"Yep," Marisol said. "Look, I seriously doubt the caretaker is a golem. Or a homunculus. Or whatever it is he would be. I think we can clear that up right here and now."

"You know what?" Catherine said suddenly. "I don't think it's such a good idea after all, us going out there. You were right."

She could feel Marisol's incredulous gaze on her without even turning her head.

"I was *what?* When have you *ever* admitted somebody else was right? Look, I know what this is about."

"I do so say people are right sometimes. Don't I?"

Marisol said, "You've just now decided that there's something dangerous out there and, like a heroine in a poorly constructed horror movie that *we would yell our damn heads off at all the way through,* you're going to go out there on your own and investigate it."

Catherine sat for a moment before she replied. "Okay, fine. Is there anything you can't figure out about me?"

"Why you want to devote yourself to Garland William Stevens."

"Anyway," Catherine said. "You'll see what I mean about the statue when you meet the caretaker."

We have come to the end of everything that is or ever shall be.

> —"In the Quarters of the Lost,"
> by Garland William Stevens,
> originally published in *Unknown,* 1939,
> reprinted 2013 in *Lost Worlds: The Weird Tales of Garland William Stevens,*
> edited by Catherine J. Framer,
> published by Gloaming Press

She would not have been surprised if, on her return, the house had fallen into disrepair, its state of the previous day the result of some glamour, but it was as sturdy and well-kept as the day before. Marisol sat beside her, gripping her phone like an emergency was imminent. "What are we going to do?"

"I just want to talk to him again."

"Didn't he tell you to leave and not come back?"

"Well, but I won't take up that much of his time. And I just want you to tell me what you think about him."

Catherine got out of the car. She had to press on because she knew Marisol was right. She shouldn't have come back here at all. She turned around to tell Marisol that if something happened, if she disappeared, if anything, she should just drive away, she shouldn't feel bad, she shouldn't think about it at all, but that sounded crazy. And that would only panic Marisol and she would make them leave.

Catherine went up on the porch and peered in all the windows, but she couldn't see what was inside. There was no sign of the caretaker. She had always been able to explain anything to Marisol except this, the compulsion she had toward Stevens and his work. Marisol said she was just driven, and that it was a good thing, an admirable thing, but it was a drive that scared her. Because it was a drive without any sense to it. Who really did care about Garland William Stevens besides her? The world didn't need Stevens and his bottomless nihilistic despair. She was unsure what she found more appalling: the knowledge that her years of painstaking study would probably in the end leave her qualified for little more than a minimum-wage service job, or the sheer scope of Stevens's loathsome worldview, expanding as it did to encompass every living being save for the savage, primordial beasts at the heart of his fiction. As much as she tried to assume a disinterested scholarly attitude toward his work, in fact she found herself alternately repelled and consumed by the man's madness.

Almost without thinking, she tried the door, and the doorknob turned in her hand.

She pushed it open and called out, "Hello? Is anyone there? It's Catherine Framer, from the university. I just wanted to ask you a few more questions."

In the silence that followed, she turned back and gave a thumbs-up sign in Marisol's direction accompanied by a big smile she did not feel. Marisol looked so worried and vulnerable sitting in the passenger seat, and Catherine felt a rush of emotions toward her—affection, concern, but most of all a sorrow so profound that she gasped as it flooded her even as she was unable to make any sense of it. Then the sorrow passed and left her feeling empty, hollowed-out, and there was a small space where she knew she would turn back after all, and then she did not.

I returned last night to that place, to their place, to that monstrous city on the edge of the world in the bowels of the earth. The city has teeth; the city shrieks, but not at me, because it no more notices me than I notice microscopic beings on my own flesh. Time and space turn inside out there, and reason ceases to be. I stood for a moment and for a thousand years on the edge of what I could only think of as hell. My flesh cracked and my bones turned to powder and the city devoured itself and spat itself back up again. It was planet-sized; no, larger; it was an entire galaxy, its own universe: suns, worlds flared and died within its immense gates.

—From the unpublished writings
of Garland William Stevens, 1940

"Hello," she said again, but only from habit, because she was certain she would not be answered. The interior of the house was just as she had seen it the previous day, but now she could explore at her leisure. She went over to the desk with the stacks of books and papers and pawed through them. The books all appeared to be very old, and none of them were in English; several did not use an alphabet she recognized. Two were handwritten, one in something similar to but not quite Arabic script. She could not read most of the papers either, which were not old and definitely not part of the Stevens archive. Some of them were covered not in words at all but in symbols and drawings of ancient creatures with no eyes or limbs, with notations such as "cephalopod, Paleozoic era." There were tracing of fossils with latitudinal and longitudinal locations scribbled next to them and notations regarding dates of discovery.

She took out her phone and began photographing

The Unknown Chambers

the papers, but she quickly found them so distressing that she shoved them all aside. They overwhelmed her with that same revulsion that Stevens had written about, and perhaps he was right. Perhaps such sights wakened an instinctive, atavistic terror—one of the few things that could remind humans what late arrivals they were to this earth, and how fragile was their tenure.

    How his parents must have resented what they imagined to be the decay of their own society around them; how they must have loathed the sense that their way of life was passing into irrelevance. As different as they were, both father and son attempted to stem the despairing realization of their own insignificance with fortresses of words. Not for the first time, Catherine wondered about the parents' deaths; two mad, helpless old people trapped in this house and their failing bodies with an increasingly demented son. It wouldn't have taken much, just a palm placed over a sleeping nose and mouth. First one, then the other. Afterwards the guilt would have driven him to an alcoholic despair followed by a final, fatal bid to sober up, at which point his lifelong imaginings seemed to him to become reality: in those final weeks, his writings had become frenzied, surreal, barely coherent descriptions of a nightmare subterranean dwelling beneath the house that opened onto another, horrific dimension where the creatures from his stories tormented him without mercy.

    She heard a noise then from upstairs, that of someone treading on floorboards, and a thump and a sound like something heavy being dragged, and it brought her to her senses. What had she been thinking, letting herself into someone's house, poking through their private papers? She scrambled for the front door, suddenly in a panic, and raced across the porch and threw herself into the driver's seat.

    "What the hell happened in there?" Marisol said.

    "Nothing," Catherine said, "nothing happened. There's nothing in there," and she tried to catch her breath, which was too fast and too shallow. She shut her eyes and saw all the closed doors inside the house that she had not been allowed to open, and she wondered what lay behind them. "You know," she said, "all this was ocean once. First it was ocean and then it was swamp and everywhere creatures like things you'd see in nightmares, only worse. And someday it's going to be ocean again. Maybe even in our lifetimes if they don't fix the climate, what do you think?

Marisol said, "I want to go home."

Catherine started the car and forced herself to guide it deliberately back onto the road, and they didn't speak at all on the journey back into town. Passing through Eudora, Catherine noticed just how shabby and depleted the town truly was: deserted shopping centers with weeds sprouting through the asphalt, shuttered gas stations, and a main road that was almost empty of other vehicles. She stopped at a red light and wondered why it was there, because surely there was never enough traffic to require it. The only signs of life were at the museum, the churches, and the single fast food restaurant. How was it possible for a town to isolate itself so thoroughly in this day and age? By ensuring that nobody cared enough to give it any thought, let alone visit it or move there.

Soon, she thought, it would vanish from maps altogether, just as Garland William Stevens's archives had been lost for so many decades. Maybe the roads that ought to bring people here would start to lead in different directions; satellites passing overhead would record endless days of cloud cover. Then perhaps someone might slip through, stumble upon it just as she had found Stevens's writings; perhaps that someone would find himself or herself unduly obsessed with a town that did not by any reckoning exist. But how long could you stay real yourself when you were devoted to something that only existed in liminal spaces? She wanted to ask Marisol if she was still real; she wanted to reach across the space between them and grasp her hand, but the gap between them was too great. The light went to green and then back to red, and if Marisol was speaking to her, she could not hear her any longer; but she could hear their hymns, strange melodies with stranger words, calling to her, and she did not know how she came to be out of the car and walking up the middle of the abandoned state highway, but she knew at last where she belonged.

She had driven out to a few of the Eudora quarries, once or twice a long time ago. Bored country kids from nearby counties used to go swimming there. They told her it was such a long jump that you had to point your feet downward so you jackknifed into the water below, otherwise you could hurt yourself; but then they were all warned off going there in the first place because it was said there were dangerous things below the surface, abandoned equipment that could injure or kill you as you plunged deep underwater. She never swam there herself; she was too afraid of the depths, and you did hear stories from time to time about kids disappearing. The drop from the edge had always looked endless to her, and surely the water and whatever else lay below was endless as well.

  She had always been afraid of the depths, along with so many other things, but now the fear was gone, replaced by something for which she had no name, because the depths were singing to her, and the sky yawned above, a black expanse trembling with stars. She walked down an abandoned highway, down a muddy red clay lane, down corridors lined by locked doors, down deep; she would walk as long as she had to, until they came for her, or until she came to them, for it was only a matter of time now, and she knew they would be waiting for her, in the depths, under the surface of things, and in all the places where it was dark.

Notes on Contributors

The Editors

Lynne Jamneck is a fiction writer and editor. She has been nominated for the Sir Julius Vogel and Lambda Awards for fiction and editing, and holds an MA in English Literature from Auckland University, New Zealand. Her fiction has appeared in *Unconventional Fantasy: A Celebration of Forty Years of the World Fantasy Convention, Fantastique Unfettered, H. P. Lovecraft's Magazine of Horror, Jabberwocky, Weird Fiction Review, Tales from the Bell Club, Something Wicked,* and the SJV award-winning anthology *Tales for Canterbury.* She edited the Lambda Award shortlisted SF anthology *Periphery* and has published nonfiction for, among others, *Weird Tales, Strange Horizons,* the *Lovecraft Annual,* and *Fantasy Magazine.* For Dark Regions Press, she has edited *Dreams from the Witch House: Female Voices of Lovecraftian Horror,* which debuted in 2016.

S. T. Joshi is the author of *The Weird Tale* (1990), *H. P. Lovecraft: The Decline of the West* (1990), and *Unutterable Horror: A History of Supernatural Fiction* (2012). He has prepared corrected editions of H. P. Lovecraft's work for Arkham House and annotated editions of Lovecraft's stories for Penguin Classics. He has also prepared editions of Lovecraft's collected essays and poetry. His exhaustive biography, *H. P. Lovecraft: A Life* (1996), was expanded as *I Am Providence: The Life and Times of H. P. Lovecraft* (2010). He is the editor of the anthologies *American Supernatural Tales* (Penguin, 2007), *Black Wings I–IV* (PS Publishing, 2010–15), *A Mountain Walked: Great Tales of the Cthulhu Mythos* (Centipede Press, 2014), *The Madness of Cthulhu* (Titan Books, 2014–15), and *Searchers After Horror: New Tales of the Weird and Fantastic* (Fedogan & Bremer, 2014). He is the editor of the *Lovecraft Annual* (Hippocampus Press), the *Weird Fiction Review* (Centipede Press), and the *American Rationalist* (Center for Inquiry). His Lovecraftian novel *The Assaults of Chaos* appeared in 2013.

The Authors

Donald R. Burleson is the author of twenty-two books, including the short story collections *Lemon Drops and Other Horrors, Four Shadowings, Beyond the Lamplight,* and *Wait for the Thunder,* as well as four novels. His fiction has appeared in *Twilight Zone,* the *Magazine of Fantasy and Science Fiction, Lore, Cemetery Dance, Inhuman, Deathrealm, Terminal Fright, Weird Fiction Review,* and many other magazines, as well as in dozens of anthologies, most recently *Black Wings I & III, Dead But Dreaming 2,* and *Horror for the Holidays.* He lives in Roswell, New Mexico, with his writer wife Mollie and numerous cats.

Mollie L. Burleson's fiction and poetry has appeared in such magazines as *Lore, Crypt of Cthulhu,* and *Midnight Echo,* and numerous anthologies, including *100 Vicious Little Vampire Stories, 100 Wicked Little Witch Stories, 100 Creepy Little Creature Stories, Horror for the Holidays, Black Wings I & III,* and *Horrors! 365 Scary Stories.* Her literary criticism has appeared in *Lovecraft Studies* and *Studies in Weird Fiction.* She lives in Roswell, New Mexico, with her writer husband Don and numerous cats.

Lois H. Gresh is the six-time *New York Times* and *USA Today* bestselling author of over thirty books and more than sixty short stories. Her books have been published in twenty-two languages. Look for *Sherlock Holmes versus Cthulhu: The Adventure of the Deadly Dimensions* (Titan Books, 2017), the first in a new trilogy of thrillers. Recent titles include *Cult of the Dead and Other Weird and Lovecraftian Tales* (Hippocampus Press, 2015), and *Innsmouth Nightmares* (as editor; PS Publishing, 2015). She has received many Bram Stoker, Theodore Sturgeon, and International Horror Guild Award nominations for her work.

Orrin Grey is a writer, editor, amateur film scholar, and monster expert who was born on the night before Halloween. He is the author of *Never Bet the Devil and Other Warnings* and *Painted Monsters and Other Strange Beasts,* as well as the co-editor of *Fungi,* an anthology of weird fungus-themed stories. You can find him online at OrrinGrey.com.

Gothic Lovecraft

Gwyneth Jones is the author of many fantasy, horror novels, and ghost stories for teenagers using the name Ann Halam, and several well-regarded SF and fantasy novels and stories for adults. She has won a few awards, but never lets it worry her. She lives in Brighton, England, with her husband, three intelligent goldfish, and two cats called Ginger and Milo; she likes old movies, practicing yoga, and staring out of the window.

Mark Howard Jones was born on the twenty-sixth anniversary of H. P. Lovecraft's death. He is the author of the collections *Songs from Spider Street* (SD Publishing, 2010) and *Brightest Black* (SD Publishing, 2013), and the editor of *Cthulhu Cymraeg: Lovecraftian Tales from Wales* (SD Publishing, 2014). His Lovecraftian fiction appears in the anthologies *Black Wings III* (PS Publishing, 2014) and *The Madness of Cthulhu 2* (Titan Books, 2015). He lives in Cardiff, the capital of Wales.

Caitlín R. Kiernan is the author of nine novels, including, most recently, *The Red Tree* and *The Drowning Girl: A Memoir*. Her copious short fiction has been collected in several volumes, including *Tales of Pain and Wonder; To Charles Fort, with Love; Alabaster; The Ammonite Violin and Others; A Is for Alien;* and *Confessions of a Five-Chambered Heart*. She is a two-time winner of the World Fantasy Award, a winner of the Bram Stoker Award, a three-time nominee for the Shirley Jackson Award, and has also been honored by the James Tiptree, Jr. Award. She lives in Providence, R.I.

Award-winning author **Nancy Kilpatrick** has published eighteen novels, more than two hundred short stories, six collections, and one nonfiction book, and has edited thirteen anthologies. Her recent award-winning titles are the anthology *Danse Macabre: Close Encounters with the Reaper* and the short fiction collection *Vampyric Variations*. Current work appears in *Searchers After Horror, A Darke Phantastique, Zombie Apocalypse: Endgame!,* and the forthcoming *Blood Sisters: Vampire Stories by Women, The Madness of Cthulhu 2,* and *Stone Skin Bestiary*. Recent anthologies include *Expiration Date* and *nEvermore! Tales of Murder, Mystery and the Macabre*. Join her on Facebook.

Lynda E. Rucker is an American writer born and raised in the South and currently living in Dublin, Ireland. She has sold more than two dozen short stories to such places as *F&SF, The Mammoth Book of Best New Horror, The Year's Best Dark Fantasy and Horror, The Best Horror of the Year, Black Static, Shadows and Tall Trees,* and *Nightmare Magazine*. She is a regular columnist for *Black Static,* and her first collection, *The Moon Will Look Strange,* was released in 2013 from Karōshi Books.

John Shirley is a novelist, screenwriter, television writer, songwriter, and author of numerous story collections. He is a past Guest of Honor at the World Horror Convention and won the Bram Stoker Award for his story collection *Black Butterflies* (Ziesing, 1998). His screenplays include *The Crow*. He has written teleplays for *Poltergeist: The Legacy, Deep Space Nine,* and other shows. His novels include *Demons* (Del Rey, 2002), the *A Song Called Youth* trilogy (1985–90), *Wetbones* (Ziesing, 1992), *Bleak History* (Simon & Schuster, 2009), and *Everything Is Broken* (Prime Books, 2012). His newest books are *New Taboos* (PM Press, 2013) and *Doyle After Death* (HarperCollins, 2013). His latest story collections are *In Extremis: The Most Extreme Stories of John Shirley* (Underland Press, 2012), and *Lovecraft Alive!* (Hippocampus Press, 2016).

Some of **Jonathan Thomas**'s forebears dwelt in Salem and somehow evaded arrest during 1692's general hysteria. Others include New Englanders who identified as German and reviled Yankees as "the damned English" before World War I. Later, a spinster great-aunt related heroic, most probably apocryphal, accounts of Welsh ancestors. Until such time as he springs for genetic testing, Thomas designates himself a Swamp Yankee, which is how his parents referred to each other when out of the other's earshot. His most recent collection is *Dreams of Ys and Other Invisible Worlds* (Hippocampus Press, 2015).

Donald Tyson was born in Halifax, Nova Scotia. He began to write professionally after finishing university and has pursued this career single-mindedly for the past forty years. His short stories have appeared in the anthologies *Black Wings II & III, Searchers After Horror, Weird Fiction Review 4* and *5, The Madness of Cthulhu 1 & 2,* and *A Mountain Walked.* A collection of his John Dee and Edward Kelley occult-mystery stories, titled *The Ravener and Others,* is available from Avalonia. Presently he lives in Cape Breton with his wife, Jenny, their American bulldog, Ares, and their Siamese cat, Hermes.

Don Webb has attended ArmadilloCon since 1986, taught SF writing for UCLA since 2002, and read Lovecraft since 1970. In high school he was once described as the "person most likely to be waiting in a dark corner." He has shot fireworks professionally, owns two tuxedo cats, and is married to the most beautiful woman in Texas. His Lovecraftian fiction was gathered in *Through Dark Angles* (Hippocampus Press, 2014).

Robert S. Wilson is the author of *Shining in Crimson* and *Fading in Darkness,* books one and two of his dystopian vampire series Empire of Blood. He is the Bram Stoker Award–nominated editor of *Blood Type: An Anthology of Vampire SF on the Cutting Edge,* a co-editor of *Horror for Good: A Charitable Anthology* and *Nightscapes, Volume 1,* and lives in Middle Tennessee with his family and a silly obnoxious dog. His stories have appeared in numerous anthologies, online, and paper publication, and his cyberpunk horror novella *Exit Reality* was chosen as one of *E-thriller.com*'s Thrillers of the Month in July 2013. His debut fiction collection *Where All Light Is Left to Die* was released in September 2014.